from G Visconti

# The Joint Venture

*Gilbert D. Visconti*

Voyageur Publishing Co., Inc.
NASHVILLE / TENNESSEE

THE JOINT VENTURE

*Copyright © 2002 Voyageur Publishing Co., Inc.*

All rights reserved. No part of this book may be reproduced or transmitted in any form or by any means, electronic or mechanical, including photocopying, recording, or by any information storage and retrieval system, without the written permission of the Publisher, except to the extent permitted by law. For information, address Voyageur Publishing Co., Inc. P. O. Box 121001, Nashville, TN 37212-1001

ISBN: 0-929146-04-2

*Book and Cover design by John R. Robinson*

Printed in the United States of America
First Trade Edition

Library of Congress Control Number: 2002108598

## DEDICATION

*The Joint Venture* is dedicated to the Italian Alpine Corps, whose traditions of courage and self-sacrifice have made the Alpini a legendary military unit and fraternity, and particularily to the memory of the many thousands of gallant Alpini who perished or were captured on the Russian Front during World War II.

## AUTHOR'S NOTE

All of the characters and events in *The Joint Venture* are fictional or, if real, are used fictitiously. No similarity between characters and events in the story and actual characters or events is intended or should be inferred. Events during World War II involving Italian Alpine divisions on the Russian Front and OSS assistance to Italian partisans are based on historical research.

I used Italian expressions only where I felt they were appropriate for emphasis and translated them unless I felt that their meaning would be apparent from the context. The reader should assume that, unless otherwise indicated, conversations in Italy take place in Italian if one of the speakers lives there.

To assist those readers who may not be familiar with northern Italy, I included maps – actually, only rough sketches – to help them locate the places that are central to the events in my story.

# PREFACE

### Brigadier General Claudio Graziano (Alpine Corps)
### Military Attache, Embassy of Italy, Washington, D.C.

It was quite a pleasant surprise to turn the pages of *The Joint Venture* written by Gilbert D. Visconti. It is a volume that recounts the lives of characters who, at one point or other in their lives, have each donned the Alpine Hat. But it is also a story that, when it moves to Italy, takes place in my homeland, in the area between Piedmont and Val d'Aosta.

These are places that belong to me, in which I spent my youth and later where I commanded Alpine units from platoons to regiments. This is why I felt particularly honored to accept the invitation extended to me to write this preface, also because, for one to fully understand the spirit of the "Alpini" (Alpine Troops) and the mountain men of the Italian Alps, one really needs to have lived among them for some time. For how else could one come to understand their sense of comradeship and their *esprit de corps?* Theirs is a sense of brotherhood which transcends the limits of space and time, arising from a difficult and enchanting mountain life.

Beginning many, many years ago, once a year in May as many as 300,000 Alpine troops can be found gathering together in an Italian city. Not all of these men are still in service. On the contrary, very few of them still are. Many are old men who served in an Alpine battalion some fifty or more years ago; many cursed when they received the orders calling them to arms and complained bitterly during the grueling marches in the mountains. Almost all of them cursed their months of military service, which the Alpini referred to as *naia* (military service). When they retired, they set their alpine hats to rest on a shelf in their homes . . . and then came the memories.

They would remember the snow in the woods, the freezing nights and the tents in the nearby valley of refuge - even the wine they drank and the Alpine sun reflecting off the mountains, the hardship and the joy. In their minds they would begin to compare their lives back then, when they were young men and Alpini, with their lives today, when they have perhaps some money, but few friendships. And they would return their hats to their heads, with a silent but urgent prayer in their hearts that some day somehow they might be recalled into the Alpini.

And this is precisely what happens to the main characters in the book; although they are often separated even for long periods of time, they are never apart. This they always know: in a moment of need, they may be sure they can count on one another.

The book has considerably more adventure, mystery and suspense than one would expect, considering that the story takes place against the backdrop of a particularly unfortunate period in the history of Italy, that of terrorism and the Red Brigade. Now, fortunately, this period has passed with the victory of democracy and freedom.

At the time the book takes place I was in Piedmont, a young lieutenant in command of an Alpine platoon. It was a strange period in history, following the youth protest of 1968.

I was young then, but so much of what is described in the book easily brings to mind what my eyes saw back then, beginning from the crime while descending the hills of Turin - a place that perhaps not even the author knows - is the site of an atavistic aura of mystery.

The pages of the book unfold a not-so-distant past, the memory of alpine battles and tragedies of a corps, clearly tracing the ties that form a profound bond that unite a people, the Italian people.

It is a book one reads in one sitting, in which the characters begin to take shape little by little as you read, and then becoming so real, it seems you have known them forever. Then the plot thickens; the memories intertwine; and the paths of the protagonists cross, turning towards an ending that is unexpected up till the very end. Looking back, however, one sees it was the only ending possible.

*The Joint Venture* is all this and more. I'm not familiar with the American places in the book, but I do, as I said, know the Italian ones very well. I remember them all, even the restaurant near Orbassano, a place so familiar it's as if I've known it forever, even when really I haven't. It doesn't even matter whether it's a real place, because there are many other town centers just like it. And then there are my mountains - the path halfway up near Courmayeur when the snow is falling...

I am certain that those who read this book, besides enjoying the passionate story, will have an opportunity to come to know a truly unexpected slice of Italian reality. This is a world few people know and a world not for beginners but for initiates - the Alpini.

# ACKNOWLEDGMENTS

The author wishes to thank the following persons and organizations for their generous and valuable assistance: The Chicago Medical Examiner's office; The Chicago Public Library; friends at Fiat, S.p.A.; the Headquarters of the Italian Alpine Corps at Bolzano, Italy; The Federal Bureau of Investigation and the Rome office of the Legal Attache; The Boston Police Department; Torino Nuoto; Dr. Luigi Monga, professor of Italian at Vanderbilt University; karate expert T.J. DeMartino; friends and family members who have willingly read his manuscript and shared their comments; and most of all his sweet wife, without whose unfailing encouragement and patience he could not have completed this novel.

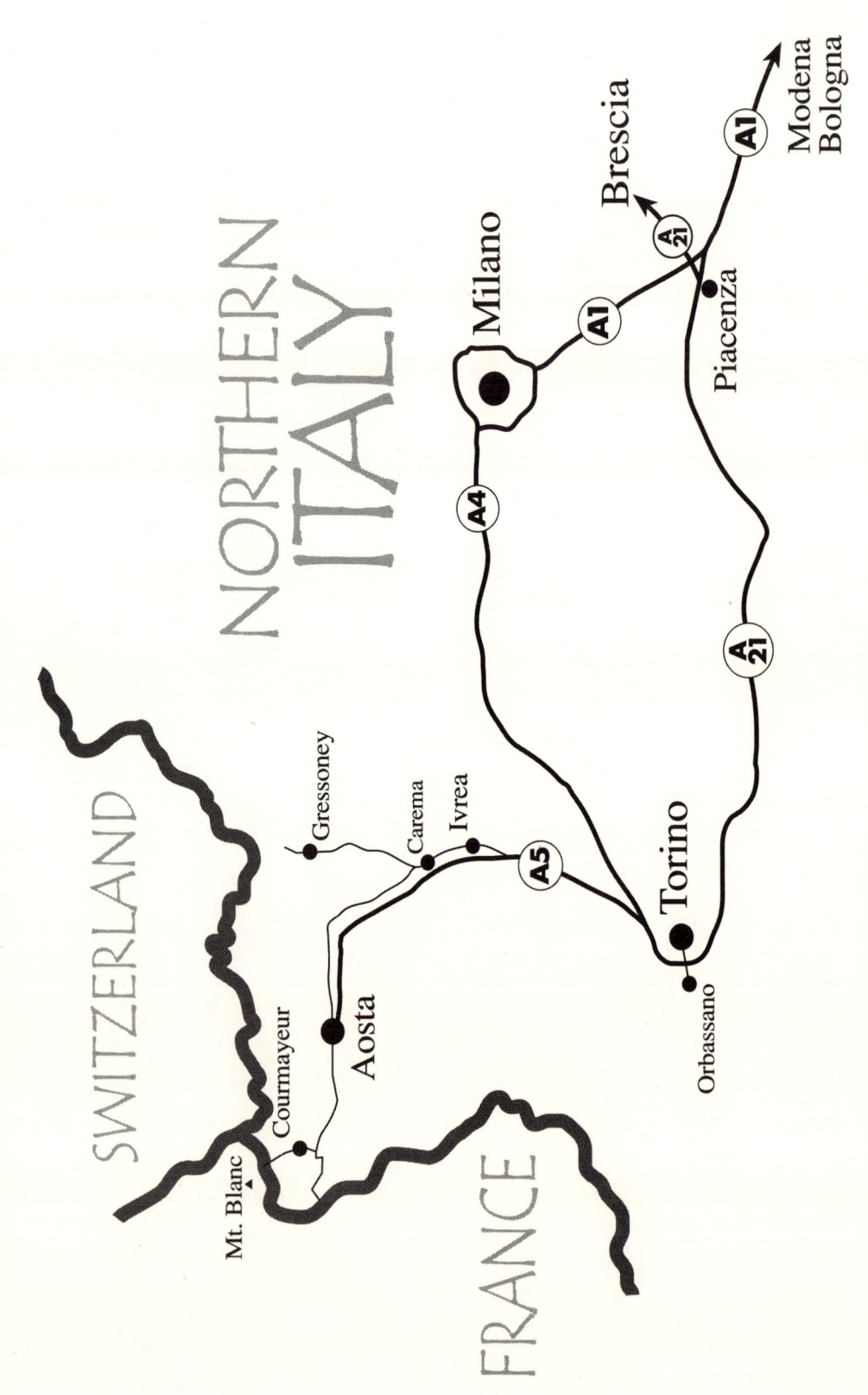

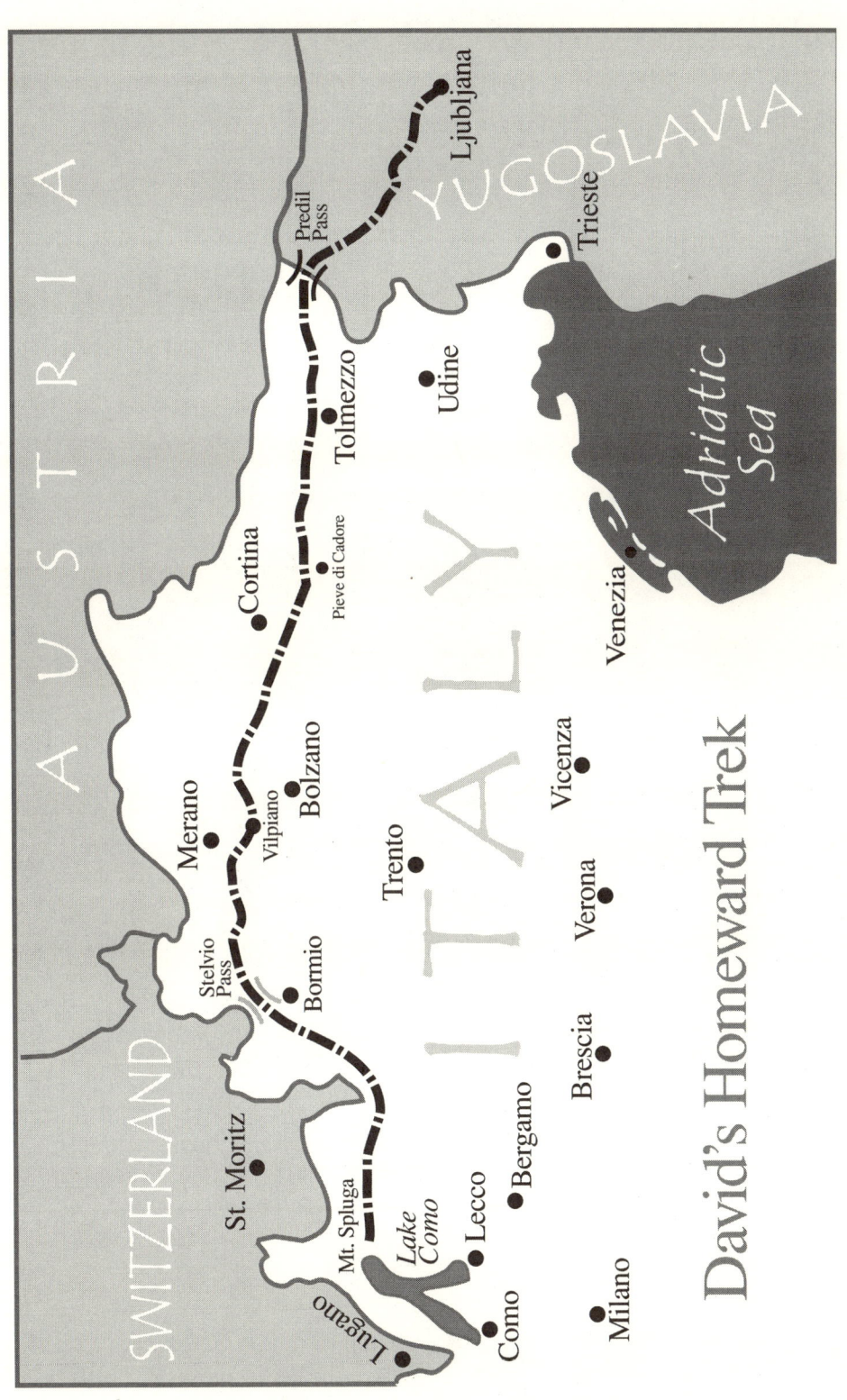

*"And character, after all, is everything."*

CHAPTER ONE

# *The Plot Begins*

### X minus 24 Days

*Torino, Italy*
*Tuesday, November 4, 1980*

All the cars were in place, waiting.

Inside a sunlit courtyard, behind tall wrought iron gates bearing the Bassino coat of arms, stood Vittorio Bassino's sleek black Fiat 130, its powerful engine idling. His uniformed Alfindustria chauffeur picked up the morning edition of *La Stampa* from the seat, ignored the headline from the USA about Ronald Reagan's challenge to President Carter's re-election and turned to the latest soccer scores. Following corporate directives, he had arrived fifteen minutes earlier than the day before, varying his daily pickup schedule.

Three hundred meters down the winding road from Bassino's estate a blue Renault waited. To avoid arousing suspicion in this exclusive residential suburb nestled in the wooded hills fifteen miles north of Torino, the two young men inside had waited at a different place each day. Three other cars were waiting at key intersections on different routes to the city. All four had been stolen in other cities: Genoa, Milano, Bologna and Vicenza. They had been repainted and given false license plates bearing the 'TO' prefix for Torino.

The chauffeur glanced at his watch: *2:13. Two minutes to go.* This was his last day driving for Bassino. He had nothing against the man, but he was glad that his four-week assignment was almost over and he would be rotated again. The other executives, even the old *pezzonovanti*, would at least chat with him about sports, politics or even the Company, but not Bassino. With him everything was business: *Good morning, Good evening, Thank you,* and sometimes not even that.

Vittorio was just finishing lunch. He, too, checked his watch. None of the executives at Alfindustria followed security rules as scrupulously as he did. Each day he carefully scheduled his departure and arrival so that he followed no set pattern, and he insisted that his driver follow different routes to and from the office on a random basis. Some routes took him several miles out of his way. He refused to accept any driver who had not completed an evasive driving test within the past six months.

Vittorio was reluctant to leave for the office. These midday hours with his wife were precious to him—a peaceful time, when they could talk quietly about their children, hopes, plans, problems, whatever. He could go back to his office refreshed and rested. Today, however, had not been restful; he had been preoccupied about his meeting with the Chairman. As he adjusted his tie in the hall mirror, his wife came and stood beside him. She had noticed how his frown lines had deepened and she was concerned. "Do you have to leave right away?" she asked, straightening his collar. "You really should rest more. You're so tense."

"I'm meeting the Chairman in an hour . . . and I couldn't even tell him why I had to see him."

She brushed her hand lightly across his furrowed brow. "Dario himself?" Her voice took on a worried tone. "Is something wrong?"

His face was grim. "Everything . . . I think."

Checking his watch again, Vittorio's chauffeur got out of the car and stood looking up at the massive front door of the residence. Vittorio had salvaged it from the gatehouse of his grandfather's country home near San Nicola. Made of dark, burnished walnut and studded with large hand-wrought rivets, it contrasted sharply with the crisp white stucco of the new house, yet seemed to belong there.

Precisely at 2:15 the door opened and Vittorio strode briskly toward the car. A man of medium height, he had a lean build that was shown to advantage by his tailored charcoal silk suit. He was only in his mid-thirties, but impressed people as being older because of the gray that already streaked his temples.

The chauffeur held the rear door open. *"Prego, dottore,"* he said, giving a half salute. Vittorio gave a slight nod in response. As the chauffeur settled into his soft leather seat, he caught a glimpse of the young executive in the rear-view mirror. Vittorio was already busy sorting through papers, getting ready for the urgent appointment he had requested with Dario Alfieri, Chairman of the giant conglomerate Alfindustria. One of its subsidiaries, a joint venture with an American company, had been plagued by unexplained problems recently, and Vittorio had been assigned to investigate. A financial genius, and one of the rising young stars of the Alfieri empire, he was expected to find the answers. He usually did. But this time he had come up with disturbing suspicions. Bypassing the chain of command—a cardinal sin at Alfindustria unless one had a very good reason—he had gone straight to the Chairman, calling Alfieri at the Zurich office. He asked to meet privately as soon as Dario returned to Italy later that afternoon, and had refused even to discuss the matter on the telephone.

Before the chauffeur closed the car doors, the gardener pushed the gates open, swinging them clear to let the Fiat pass. He looked in both directions and, seeing no traffic, signaled 'all clear' to the driver.

As Vittorio's car passed by, tension gripped the men inside the blue Renault. The days of waiting were over. The passenger spoke into a walkie-talkie. "He's on his way. Acknowledge. Over."

All three other drivers reported that they were ready.

The blue Renault pulled away from the curb smoothly, following the Fiat at a discreet distance. The passenger spoke into the set when they passed the first main intersection. "One out. Get ready, two. You're next."

Vittorio's car slowed down and turned onto Viale Giulio, a narrow, winding road skirting the hills on its way down to the northern suburbs of Torino.

The passenger switched on his walkie-talkie again. "He's yours, Two. Pick him up! Over."

The set crackled with static. "Two here. All set. Out."

Vittorio's chauffeur looked in his rear view mirror and saw the Renault closing on him. Normally, there was hardly any traffic on this narrow road, and he was somewhat surprised to see another car. He accelerated slightly and was satisfied when he saw the Renault drop back. Coming to the intersection with Corso Venaria, he slowed down to look for cross traffic. Seeing only a red Volvo that was turning onto his route ahead of him, he ran the stop sign and came up behind the Volvo, preparing to pass. The driver of the Volvo speeded up to stay ahead of the Fiat as the two cars went around several tight curves. When they came to a long narrow stretch in the road, the Volvo shot forward and stopped, spinning so that it was broadside and blocking the road.

The chauffeur reacted immediately. On his right, a stone retaining wall came almost to the edge of the road; on the other side, the shoulder was narrow, dropping off sharply onto a steep hillside that ended in a grove of trees and tangled undergrowth. Realizing that he could not get around the Volvo, he put the Fiat into a spin, reversing direction. When he saw the Renault bearing down on him, he knew that he was in trouble. Swearing under his breath, he shifted into low and headed for the shoulder, wheels spitting gravel and grass as he fought desperately to pass the Renault and stay on the shoulder.

Vittorio's first reaction was annoyance as he was jarred rudely from his reading and thrown roughly from side to side. His papers scattered wildly. He saw only a blur of cars, a wall, and then dust as the car spun sharply around. He heard the chauffeur turning the wheel ferociously and cursing, and felt himself thrown against the side of the car as it leaned far over. The Fiat hung for a moment with two wheels off the ground and then heeled over and began rolling down the hillside. Instinctively, Vittorio covered his head with his arms, conscious only of tumbling and finally the sound of crunching metal as the car smashed heavily against a tree.

For an instant, all was silence. The car had ended upright. Vittorio was lying on the floor with his face pressed against the carpet, looking under the front seat. Raising himself, he could see nothing to his right except underbrush and the massive trunk of a plane tree. He crawled from the floor onto the seat. The bulletproof windows were still intact. The impact had sprung the lock on the right rear door and it hung ajar. Vittorio groaned involuntarily. His elbow hurt, but otherwise he was not injured. He could hear the chauffeur still cursing in the front seat and fumbling for his gun.

The peaceful, sunlit hillside echoed with the blasts of an automatic rifle, and armor-piercing bullets ripped through the front door of the Fiat, reinforced steel and all, cutting the chauffeur apart and hurling his shattered body against the other side of the car. Vittorio could not believe what was happening. He looked toward his left window. In the final split second of his life, he saw shapes of people outside; then he felt himself being pushed backward violently, surrounded by a deafening haze, and his last image was a burst of white flashes that seemed to erupt from within his skull.

§ § §

A white and robin's egg blue corporate jet cleared the snow-covered peaks of the Alps, descended slightly over Valle d'Aosta and began its long approach to the Torino airport at Caselle. His seat reclined, Dario Alfieri dozed. A folder of memoranda and financial reports lay unopened in his lap. He was the only passenger. The co-pilot opened the cockpit door, came back and touched Dario's shoulder.

"Dr. Alfieri. You have an emergency call. It's the captain of the *carabinieri* unit at Torino."

Dario picked up the telephone on the panel next to his seat and listened grimly as the captain explained what had happened to Bassino. He said nothing for several seconds, his eyes closed as if in pain. Then, in a weary voice, he thanked the captain and asked what the press knew.

"They know someone from Alfindustria's been shot, but no names yet."

"Good. Please try to keep it that way as long as you can. I'll have to notify the families."

As the co-pilot returned to the cockpit, Dario slumped back in his seat and looked out the window, deep in thought. Vittorio had been one of his brightest hopes. The only son of an Alpini officer who had served with him on the Russian front, Vittorio had come to his attention early. He had made the young man his protégé, grooming him for eventual leadership in the company. Vittorio had become almost like his own son.

Dario thought about Vittorio's urgent call that morning and was puzzled. *What had he found that was so important? And why had he been so secretive?*

A gaggle of reporters, flanked by aides with video cameras and microphones, trailing yards of cords and equipment, jostled noisily for position in the terminal, lying in wait for Dario. Two airport security cars leading his private limousine moved slowly onto the tarmac as the Gulfstream approached. The cars roared out to the end of the runway to meet the plane where the pilot had stopped. Within a minute they had whisked Dario out of the airport grounds and the limousine was speeding toward Torino. The reporters were thrown into confusion by his quick escape. Some dashed for their vans; others commandeered telephones to alert their colleagues in the city that Dario was on his way.

As soon as he arrived at his office, Dario asked his secretary to call Boston. He had to speak to his old friend and counsel. *David will know what to do.* He and David Della Croce were more than friends; in a sense they were closer than brothers. They had known each other from childhood, and their relationship had been forged during World War II. They had served in the same Alpini unit on the Russian front, where they had faced death together.

*Boston*

David was just crossing the office lobby on his way to the elevator when he heard the receptionist take a call for him. He started to signal to her to take a message, but stopped and came back when she whispered that the call was from Dr. Alfieri. Very few things were more important for David than talking with his old and dear friend.

The years had dealt kindly with David. He was now managing partner of Barnett, Daly & Della Croce, a leading Boston law firm, with offices in London and Torino. There was a spring in his step, a strength and suppleness that came from regular exercise and many winters of cross-country skiing. Just under six feet tall, thicker through the chest than in his youth, he still had a trim, military bearing; other men unconsciously straightened up and pulled in their stomachs when they were near him. He had a face that was easy to like; the sort that always seemed on the verge of smiling. When he did smile, which was often, deep creases appeared in his cheeks and his eyes sparkled.

Dario greeted David in dialect. His voice broke slightly. *"Brute notissie, amis* (bad news, my friend): Vittorio's been killed. Terrorists."

They talked quietly, and David sensed that Dario was reluctant to speak on the telephone. "How can I help, Dario?"

His friend's voice was heavy. "I need you here. Something's wrong with the joint venture," referring to the company he had started in the U.S. "Can you come over...right away?"

David looked at his watch: *I can still catch an afternoon flight.* "I'll be there tomorrow if I can."

"Let us know when you're coming and I'll have Guido meet you at the airport. *Bon viagi.*" Then Dario hung up.

In his usual calm and unhurried way, David moved into action. First, he asked for the complete files on the Alfindustria joint venture, and had the receptionist make his flight reservation. Then, pacing slowly back and forth in his office, he methodically dictated a vacation memo, listing every case he was handling, its present status, what needed to be done on it, day by day, and which of the partners or senior associates would be responsible for it during his absence. He also dictated short letters to his clients explaining that he had to be out of the country for an indefinite period and who would be substituting for him. Then he asked his secretary to make a file of recent news clippings about the company. Finally he called his son, Mark.

David was just untying one of the several brown expandable folders crammed with documents when Mark, a junior partner in the firm, knocked and entered. Mark noticed the title on two of the unopened files. "What's up with the joint venture?"

David did not look up. His voice was barely audible. "Dario just called. Bassino's been killed. Terrorists."

Mark murmured condolences and waited. After a pause, David continued. "Dario asked me to come over there—right away. He's really worried. I can feel it."

"But why the joint venture? Bassino have anything to do with that?"

"I don't know. But I do know Dario, and he's sure that something important's going on." He pushed his chair back, picked up the folders and went to hand them to his son, who was almost two inches taller than he. "Please take this stuff and work me up a quick summary of the joint venture. You know: how it was set up with the U.S. company, that sort of thing. I need it ASAP, so just give me the bare bones."

"Get right on it," Mark said, putting the papers back in the open envelope and taking all three envelopes with him.

David smiled slightly to himself as he watched Mark leave. He was so proud of this young giant, his first-born—what Italian father wouldn't be? *If only Elena could see him now; he's so much like her, bless her soul. But still we're so alike, the two of us: so much drive, so damned serious.*

David left that evening from Logan Airport. After the Lufthansa 747 reached cruising altitude, he opened his briefcase and began reviewing the notes about the joint venture that Mark had dictated for him. Though the company was small, it was Dario's first direct entry into the United States market, and he wanted it to succeed. If Dario was worried, David knew that there had to be a good reason.

## X minus 23 Days

*Wednesday, November 5*

David was roused from a fitful slumber. A stewardess was telling him to fasten his seatbelt. His plane would be landing soon at Malpensa, Milano's international airport.

Before his baggage arrived, David went directly to the customs exit, spotted the dark blue uniform of the Alfindustria driver waiting in the lobby and waved to let the driver know that he had arrived. When David walked through customs, the driver gave him a token salute and handed him a small envelope before taking his bags. David recognized immediately Dario's personal stationery and his flowing, yet regular handwriting. He read as they walked to the car:

> *Welcome back to Torino, old friend. Please join me for dinner. Guido will call for you at 1930.*
> *Dario*

As David settled back in the soft leather seat of his car for the drive to Torino he was tempted to sleep, but knew that he would not. He had made this trip between Malpensa and Torino three or more times each year during the last twenty years, and never slept, no matter how exhausted he was. Coming back to Piemonte was always a special delight for him. But it had become a bittersweet delight, because this was also a time when he was painfully reminded of Elena's absence. For years they had shared the pleasure of returning to Italy. She would be as excited as a young girl, pointing out familiar sights: farms, trees, flowers, and birds. Finally, after her initial burst of enthusiasm, she would invariably wrap her arms around one of his, snuggle close to his side and say something like, "Isn't it just wonderful to be back again!"

Every time he thought about Elena he was also dragged back to that day five years ago. He would experience again the sinking feeling in his stomach when he answered the phone in his office and heard, "There's been an accident, Mr. Della Croce. I'm sorry, but your wife...." The rest of the words were a blur. In that instant, his future—at least the future that he and Elena had talked about so much—was blown away. He was completely unprepared for the loss, and the grieving process was slow and seemingly unending.

Still, he was always happy to be back. He drank in the landscape as the car sped smoothly along the *autostrada*. The day was unusually clear, and gradually he was able to see the outline of the Alps ahead.

Guido, looking in the rear-view mirror, noticed David's expression as David looked out at the countryside. "Good to be back home again. Right, *consigliere?*"

"Certainly is," David said with feeling. "Back home."

By the time the car reached Torino, the majestic peaks of the Alps were in full view to the north and west of the city.

Guido stopped in front of the Principi, or Excelsior Grand Hotel Principi di Piemonte, a luxury hotel where visitors to Alfindustria always stayed. In his room, David checked his watch, adjusting it to local time. *Only 1:30. Still time for four, five hours sleep.* He left a wake-up call, then took a hot shower and shaved. After closing the outside shutters and drawing the curtains, he flipped the switch over his bed to turn on the 'Do not disturb' sign outside his door, then collapsed on the bed and was asleep in seconds. When the hotel operator called, David awoke rested and alert. Since he still had more than an hour before Guido was due, he dressed quickly and left the hotel to stroll around the city.

The evening air was crisp and dry, and David moved briskly along the esplanade, past the elegant stores along Via Roma, and headed toward the spacious *piazze* that gave downtown Torino its uniquely open character. The rush hour traffic was heavy, with buses and streetcars full of homeward-bound office workers. He caught the pulse of the city, the current of activity, familiar sights and sounds. Going through the archway by the rococo church of Santa Cristina, he entered Piazza San Carlo, and then turned down one of the busy side streets. Some of the shops were already closed, their heavy metal grates rolled down and locked.

David slowed down as he approached two older men standing on the sidewalk. They were arguing heatedly about the season's prospects for the local soccer teams. Pretending to look in a nearby shop window, he stopped to listen. The waves of *Piemontese* dialect swept over him; even without looking, he could picture their emphatic gestures, their body language.

"Hey," one of them called out to two other men, evidently friends of his, who were standing near David, "Wanna know what Gino here says? Milano Inter's gonna whip Juventus next time. Whatta joke, right?"

The others chimed in:

"Fat chance. Inter's a bunch of old farts. No speed. Zero."

"Yeah. You know why they can't run? It's their beards. They trip on 'em."

General laughter.

The beleaguered Milano partisan stood his ground. "Yeah, Juventus wins, but it's only 'cause of all the dough they get from Fiat, that's why."

David smiled to himself and moved on. *Some things never change.*

He knew that people were watching him. Even though Torino is a cosmopolitan city and foreigners are a common sight, Italians are naturally curious about people, especially strangers. Passersby and local shopkeepers, seemingly oblivious to David's presence, instantly classified him as an American from the cut of his clothing. Assuming from his behavior that he could not understand the local dialect, some of them were not at all reticent about making comments about him. He was highly amused by their frank and often unflattering observations about his suit (foreign, therefore ill-fitting), his appearance (rich American) and his reason for wandering on one of the side streets (he was probably lost).

David resisted the temptation to react, to let them know that he was not an outsider, but one of them.

Beside the open door of a family *trattoria*, he stopped to read the evening menu. He could hear the sounds of dinner preparation, tables being set, discussions about seasoning for the meat sauce, orders to the youngsters to grate more *formaggio*. From the small bar near the entrance he caught the rich aroma of freshly brewed espresso. He walked on, feeling an emotional surge. *This is me. I'm an American, and I talk like one, but these are really my people, down deep.* He walked down Corso Vittorio Emanuele to the bridge dedicated to King Umberto I, the main span over the Po River, and took a deep breath, savoring the many smells of the city. For several minutes, he stood looking down at the slow-moving current of the river, fascinated by the lights of Castello del Valentino reflected in the black waters. In recent years, particularly after losing Elena, he had felt more and more the call of his heritage. *This is where my roots are.*

He hailed a cab back to the hotel. Guido was already waiting for him, parked across the street by the newsstand. He waved and Guido swung by to pick him up. They started down Via Roma toward Porta Nuova, Torino's main railway station, and then turned left, passing in front of the station. When Guido turned again by the station and headed down Via Nizza, David was puzzled at first. Instead of going out of town, they were headed toward Edificio Alfindustria, company headquarters. Then he remembered Dario's latest security measures.

As Guido approached the rear of the undistinguished

ten-story building that housed Alfindustria's corporate offices, he flicked his lights. The guard on duty opened the heavy metal gates leading to the outdoor parking lot, saluting as the car moved toward the ramp for the underground garage. A large door opened ahead of them. Guido did not stop in the usual parking area, but drove along a wall toward a darkened corner of the basement, where he stopped by a wall panel. Taking out a card, he inserted it into a slot, causing the panel to slide to one side, revealing a lighted keyboard. He pressed several keys in rapid succession, and then removed the card. As the panel closed, a portion of the wall in front of them moved noiselessly aside, leaving room for the car to pass into a tunnel dimly lit on both sides by tiny fluorescent lights. David could see that the tunnel curved sharply to the right about twenty meters ahead. The wall closed behind them and they drove briskly through the firefly-like gauntlet of lights for what seemed more than one hundred meters to David, then Guido opened a second door identical to the first. Leaving the tunnel, they entered what appeared to be a small room, but was actually an elevator. It took them up to ground level, where Guido turned off his lights and opened the outer door.

David saw that they were now facing a small, dead-end street more than a block away from Alfindustria headquarters. *Only Dario could've managed permission for that tunnel. Probably had to buy all the buildings on the surface. He can afford it.*

Dario Alfieri and his family controlled one of the country's largest corporations, with factories or offices in every major city and more than 300,000 employees. Started as a steel mill in 1910 by Dario's father, the company grew very rapidly during World War I, when it became a major supplier of armament and heavy military equipment. It diversified later into other fields such as mining and pharmaceuticals, through companies that it acquired at distress prices after World War II. As soon as Dario took over control of the company in 1961, he began broadening its base further, through an aggressive export program and foreign investment. He foresaw the disastrous effect that the government's socialist policies would have on new investment and began channeling his company's expansion into overseas markets. Pressing the company's board of directors into an ambitious diversification program, he acquired or built factories in the Middle East and South America and intensified the company's traditional ties with the Eastern bloc. Primarily as a result of his efforts, Alfindustria now boasted annual sales of more than $8 billion.

Dario was waiting for David in his small private dining room above the restaurant Da Alfredo, tucked away in the hills north of Torino. The owner (Dario was a silent partner) had served with him in the Alpini, and they had fought together in the Resistance.

The table was set for two, with an antique linen tablecloth. The linen napkins under the sterling silverware were folded to show a small embroidered crest of the Alfieri family, which was repeated on the delicate, almost translucent china. The light from a single candle shone through a cut crystal carafe next to it, creating a pattern of rich red from the Barbera that Dario had brought from his own wine cellar.

The walls of the room were bare except for a single framed photograph from World War II showing a group of men from Dario's Alpini battalion lined up by the train that was supposed to take them to the Caucasus. He looked up at the photograph, then stood and walked over to study it. Faces looked out at him from the past. More than half of his unit had died in the war, their lives squandered on the snow-covered wastes of Russia. He and David and a few others had survived. Many of Dario's closest friends were former Alpini; at their annual reunions, he would drink prodigiously and join in singing the Alpini songs, his rich baritone leading the rousing choruses.

Guido waited at the opening facing the dead-end street for at least a minute, looking in both directions for signs of movement. He started the engine, put the car in gear and moved forward slightly, then shifted into neutral and allowed the Fiat to roll out of its 'garage' onto the short driveway. The door closed automatically behind them. Traffic was heavy on Corso Marconi, a half-block away to their left. Still keeping his lights off, Guido moved slowly toward the Corso. Instead of entering the main road, he turned into the parking or access lane alongside, which was separated from the main traffic by a ten-foot-wide island where cars were parked diagonally between the sycamore trees. Moving deliberately down the lane until he came to an opening between two cars, he mounted the curb and stopped on the island as if to park. Again he waited.

After a minute or so, he grunted: "Here we go."

Waiting for an opening in the traffic, Guido moved forward off the island, descending the curb smoothly and accelerating to catch up with the last of a passing group of cars. He turned on his lights and was soon in the midst of traffic moving north out of Torino, across the Po and into the countryside.

Several times, Guido stopped on narrow streets after turning corners, turned out his lights and waited to make certain that their car was not being followed. In twenty-five minutes they passed through Cirie and reached the small town of Roccianero. Just off the main square they turned down a long lane, eventually arriving at a small restaurant perched on a hillside overlooking the valley. A dimly lit sign above the entrance said DA ALFREDO. Cars were crowded into the restaurant parking lot and along the street, and David noticed several Ferraris and Porsches, and two Maseratis. As Guido drove by the entrance, two well-dressed couples were just going inside. Both women were wearing long mink coats.

Guido chuckled as they drove by. "Reservations two months in advance, but it helps if you own the place."

He drove into an alleyway by the house next to the restaurant and parked the car in a space behind the house, very close to the rear entrance of the restaurant. They got out and moved slowly in the darkness toward the building. A security guard posted at the side door came to attention as they approached, then relaxed when he recognized Guido. He opened the door for them and reached in to turn on a light at the head of a flight of stairs.

Guido led the way up and stopped. "First door on the left. I'll wait here."

David knocked on the door and entered. The sight of David made Dario's face light up, and he strode forward to greet David, clasping him roughly by the shoulders. David was one of a handful of people outside of Dario's immediate family with whom he could be completely himself, free of the facade that he had to wear in public. Their families had been close for many years, they had known the same teachers, and they had grown up with the same friends. They shared many years of memories, so that a simple phrase, a gesture, a name would be sufficient to conjure up people, places and situations they had both known, and would carry instant meaning.

He motioned David toward a chair. Beside the table stood a waiter in tails, in the midst of preparing a meat sauce. David nodded to him, and the waiter, Alfredo's son, bowed slightly and smiled. As David and Dario ate, they talked quietly about the political situation in Italy and the United States, family affairs and the weather. When they had concluded the social conversation, David leaned back. "So tell me, old friend... what's wrong?"

"So many things... and it's always the joint venture. You've probably heard about some of them."

David nodded and mentioned that he had read about a scandal involving the general manager of the U.S. branch of the joint venture, and the recent death of its chief engineer, Renato Bertaccini.

Dario raised his hand slightly and shook it as if in dissent. "Those are only a few of the problems, and I don't think they're all coincidences. Just hear me out."

David prepared himself for an exhaustive, well-organized review and analysis. This was the way of educated people in Italy; none of the back and forth exchanges he was used to in the U.S., where an explanation often consisted of a series of partial questions and partial answers, with gaps filled in by assumed common knowledge. In Italy, if one asks a serious question he will rarely receive a short or simple answer; generally, the response will be fully organized and complete, covering every aspect of the matter.

David listened intently while Dario listed, one by one, the things that had happened recently at AB Industries. The two that David had already read about were difficult to explain. The general manager's scandal was not news; it had happened twelve years ago. Dario questioned why someone had chosen this time to give it to the press. The engineer who had died had been the company's chief designer; his loss was a serious blow. He had been in perfect health, according to company records, and Dario could not help being suspicious.

What only Dario and a few of his key executives knew, however, was that the joint venture had been struck by a series of other setbacks recently, none of them fully explained. Taken singly, they could be accepted as unfortunate accidents, but they had begun to assume an ominous pattern. A fire had destroyed part of the company's components plant at Modena, halting production at the main plant for almost two months. That was followed by a rash of transmission failures in the test models of the company's new 300 hp tractors. Because the company had built a heavy promotional campaign around the introduction of the new tractor, emergency measures were needed to correct what appeared to be a metallurgical defect in the drive gear. The senior engineer who analyzed the defective gears, which had come from a new supplier, was convinced that someone had tampered with them. What really hurt the joint venture, Dario pointed out, was that, despite the strictest security, news of the transmission problem was leaked to the trade, even before the company's research team had completed its analysis. As a consequence, the company's marketing program for the new tractors was set back several months.

The joint venture had lost three huge sales in the Middle East recently, even though its bids should have been clearly the lowest. Dario was told afterward that someone—as yet unidentified—had substituted key figures just before the bid packets were assembled, and as a result one of the bids came in high and the other two were unresponsive to the bid specifications and were rejected.

"The official line on these is that they were bureaucratic mix-ups, but I have my doubts."

Two months ago, the joint venture had had problems with its financial reports. At the time, Dario had dismissed them, but now they appeared to be part of the same problem. Just as the team of outside auditors began consolidating the joint venture's year-end financials that the U.S. parent, Burlingame, had to file with the Securities and Exchange Commission, one of the accountants noticed that some sales and profit numbers from the European branches had been changed. He had worked on the data himself in Torino, and was puzzled when he saw some figures that appeared unfamiliar. Checking the rest of the report carefully, he found that several other key figures had been altered, and he called Torino to have the data re-computed. The accountants there were dismayed: the disk on which they had stored most of the data had been erased—'accidentally' was the term used. The accounting staff had to work overtime and all weekend as well, using their original worksheets, to redo the report. By the time it was completed and checked, the filing deadline had passed. Mr. Burlingame,

CEO of Dario's joint venture partner, had to request an extension from the SEC. Sarcastic telexes flew back and forth between the US and Torino. As before, news leaked out, and the rumor mill began again. The parent companies had gotten calls from the trade asking what was wrong, and the press had even begun to speculate on the possibility of a 'divorce' between them.

"The whole situation was most embarrassing," said Dario.

David nodded, waiting for Dario to continue.

Dario then told David about the disappearance of two senior managers at AB Industries. At first it appeared as if they had been taken prisoner by a left-wing terrorist group, but he found out differently. The day after the two men were kidnapped, Dario received a call from one of his friends from Resistance days. The friend refused to talk on the telephone, but at lunch the next day he said he had heard that the two managers had been taken by a 'button man' from a Calabrese family operating in Torino and Milano. The friend offered to help arrange the men's release 'for old time's sake.' That very day, AB Industries received a ransom note signed by a group that called itself 'Workers Arise.'

A few days later Dario's friend called again and apologized. His contacts had located the kidnapper, but too late. He was already dead. Just a week before the two men were seized, the kidnapper had made a large deposit in a Swiss numbered account, and the day after the kidnapping he had made a second deposit. He must have sensed that he was not safe, however, because he had tried to leave the country. He called his wife and told her to pack immediately and drive to Geneva. They were going to meet there after he picked up airline tickets for Argentina. He was killed before he even reached the travel office. The bodies of the two men from AB Industries were never found, but Dario's friend was sure that they were dead even before the ransom note was delivered. So Dario knew that whoever kidnapped them were not really interested in ransom, but they wanted others to think they were.

"If you're right, and all these things are connected," David interjected, assuming the role of investigator, "someone's willing to spend a lot of money, and kill if necessary. Do you have any idea what they might be after?"

Dario shook his head. "None at all. But it must be something important." He paused. "And now Vittorio."

David's eyebrows rose slightly. He was surprised. "Vittorio? He didn't have anything to do with AB Industries, did he? Wasn't he on corporate staff, working with Giambetta?"

"Until last week. That's when I asked him to see if he could perhaps find a connection in these things. You know how bright Vittorio was. Never stopped until he found an answer. Well, I think he was onto something."

Seeing David's questioning look, Dario continued. "Early morning on Tuesday—the day he was killed—he called me at Zurich, on my private line. *No one* does that unless it's really important. He said he needed to see me privately as soon as possible. I couldn't even get him to tell me why."

"What exactly did he say?"

"Just...'I can't tell you now.'"

"And where was he calling from?"

"His office, I assume."

"Mmm." David tried a new tack. "How about workpapers, notes, things he was working with? Can we look at them?"

Dario shook his head. "Vittorio carried everything in his briefcase, and that wasn't in the car when they found him. But stuck under the front seat there were some papers that look like parts of shareholder lists." Then Dario leaned forward slightly. "So, *consigliere*, what do you think?"

David did not reply immediately. He had no instant answer. While he pondered what Dario had told him, David lifted his wineglass and held it in front of the candle, watching the flame through the deep red of the wine. After several moments of thoughtful consideration he lowered the glass. His voice was businesslike. He was thinking aloud. "Let's see what we *can* do. First, there's Vittorio. Not much we can do there. You've got the police working on it already. The real question is AB Industries. Why on earth would anyone be after that small company? And what would they gain by hurting it? Embarrassment for you, of course, but one doesn't kill for that."

"Exactly," said Dario. "I know something's wrong—terribly wrong. I can feel it. But you have to help me, my friend. Find out what's going on. I need you."

"*Certo, amis,*" said David. Then, after a pause, he asked, "Who else will be working on this with us?"

Dario lowered his voice. "We can't use outsiders. This whole affair has to be kept confidential, and you and Mark can do it. We don't want everyone suspicious and starting rumors." He paused and clenched his fist, his knuckles turning white. "If someone's after one of my companies—I don't care how small it is—I want to know who, and I want to put a stop to it. No one pushes the Alpini around ... Right?"

David clenched his own fist and nodded grimly. Even while Dario was talking, David had begun mapping out a plan of action. He would start with the engineer's death and ask Mark to look into some of the other things.

After they finished the last of the Barbera, Dario looked at his watch and prepared to leave. He was sorry they could not leave together. With terrorism rampant in Italy, his security people wouldn't like it, he said with a sigh. He felt almost like a prisoner. "Remember what it was like ten, fifteen years ago? Some mornings I'd walk by myself all the way over to the market at Piazza della Repubblica to get some fresh fruit. A little old lady there always saved her best peaches for me. Can't do that any more, can we?"

Dario pushed his chair back and the waiter sprang forward to take it. Dario shook hands with David and then he left.

David sat deep in thought, barely touching his dessert, sipping his cup of espresso as the waiter began clearing the table. He mulled over what Dario had told him about the joint venture's problems, trying to find a hint of some common objective. The more he thought about the different incidents, the more random and unrelated they appeared.

His thoughts were interrupted by Guido, who came to announce that it was time to leave.

At the car, David was about to open his door when Guido put out a hand to stop him. "*Un attimo, dottore,*" he said as he studied both sides of the car with a tiny flashlight. Then he knelt beside the car, feeling gingerly with his hand by the rocker panels under the doors. Apparently satisfied, he moved forward and felt under the fenders. Finally he straightened up and came to open the rear door for David. As he was driving away, he explained ,"These days, what with terrorists and all, we gotta be careful as hell. They give us drivers a whole list of things we gotta check whenever one of the cars has been parked. If something don't check out, we don't even touch the car."

After he returned to the hotel, David called his local partner at home. David kept a small office in Torino, primarily to handle minor everyday matters for Alfindustria and serve as a point of contact with the Boston office. David had to let his partner know that he was in town, but he did not want to visit the office because he knew that that would lead to more questions. He simply told his partner that he and Mark were doing some preliminary work for Alfindustria on a small acquisition in the US. He asked the partner not to tell others that he was in town because he had no free time at all and was leaving right away. The partner was curious, but David gave him no opening to probe further. He didn't evade questions, however, because that in itself would have convinced the partner that something was amiss, and David wanted to forestall any rumors. He explained he would be back soon and promised to stop by when he was finished.

Back in his hotel room, David lay awake, thinking, evaluating, trying to analyze and interpret everything that Dario had told him. The possibility of personal danger did not cause him any real concern. Danger had never affected him as it did most people. In a crisis situation, David never panicked, but actually became calmer and more in control.

# CHAPTER TWO

## X minus 22 Days

*Boston*
*Thursday, November 6*

As soon as David cleared customs at Logan Airport, he took a cab directly to his office, where he knew Mark would be waiting for him. On the way, he debated with himself—for the tenth time at least—whether it was wise to have Mark work with him in Italy. A sixth sense told him that Dario was right: there was an unknown something working against the joint venture, and that that something could be deadly. He trusted his son's good judgment, he knew that Mark could take care of himself, but still he hesitated to get him involved.

Mark came to the lobby to meet David and they walked together to David's office. David went directly to his desk and sat, thinking. Mark followed and sat on the corner of the desk, waiting for his father to say something. Finally, he could not contain his curiosity. "So what happened over there? How'd your meeting go?"

After a few moments of hesitation, David answered. "Dario's positive that someone's trying to sabotage the joint venture. But all we have so far are questions, and no answers." He handed Mark a large manila folder. On the cover he had listed every problem or accident that had bedeviled AB Industries during the past twelve months, and inside were detailed reports on each of them. Their job, he said, was to find out whether the various incidents were connected in some way and, if so, who was responsible and what were they after. Only then could they decide what to do.

Mark began leafing through the papers in the folder. Eager to start, he turned to his father and waited for instructions.

David rose and went to the window and stood there for a moment, lost in thought. Looking into the dark of the evening, he could barely make out the shapes of boat traffic moving slowly through Fort Point Channel. He hated to get his son involved, but saw no alternative. He pointed to the folder that Mark was holding. "The one on top's the engineer who died in Illinois somewhere. I'm going out there first thing Monday to check on what happened. I'd like you to get over to Torino as soon as you can, and see if you can find out what went wrong with those Middle East bids and the financials, then down to Modena and see what happened with the fire. I'll join you later."

For his part, Mark was glad to help, and delighted with the notion of a secret project as well as the prospect of spending some time in Italy. He could adjust his schedule, and he could ask other partners and senior associates to fill in for him. And he was secretly relieved to get rid of the 110-page trust indenture that he was reviewing. But he was puzzled why Dario wasn't using private investigators. David explained that Dario was deeply concerned about security and did not want to arouse suspicion by having strangers asking questions.

"Dario likes you, Mark, and he knows you'll keep everything confidential. Besides, you've worked with the joint venture from the beginning, so you know the organization."

But David knew that the investigation would not be easy. They would not be able to operate very freely in a foreign country, and would have to be careful. So long as they only interviewed people in the Alfindustria group, they would have no problems. Beyond that, however, they would have to work closely with the police, or *Pubblica Sicurezza*, for their own protection if nothing else. Otherwise, the Italian authorities would take a dim view of what they were doing. Finally, David suggested that—for protection—Mark ought to have a gun while he was in Italy. Dario's office would be able to arrange that.

As they were leaving the office, a thought occurred to David and he turned to Mark. "It's been months since I've been to the range. How about going out there tomorrow early? Squeeze off a few rounds?" He enjoyed target practice, and wanted some time alone with his son.

When David offered to drive, however, Mark demurred, and said that he would come by for David. He had something he wanted his father to see.

## X minus 20 Days

*Friday, November 7*

It was early when David heard the sound of a deep-throated muffler outside. Looking out the window, he watched as Mark pulled into the driveway in a peacock blue 1956 Thunderbird hardtop convertible. He chuckled to himself. *Mark must have just gotten the car back together. I'll bet this is its first road trial.*

Mark had found the car three years before in back of a motel in Springfield, on its rims, surrounded by high weeds, a rusted derelict. The owner was happy to get rid of the wreck, and thought he had scored a coup when Mark agreed to pay $1200 for it. When Mark first looked at it, though, what he saw was not the rust, the gutted interior with mice nests in the lone cushion that rested against the steering wheel, or the hole in the quarter panel large enough to put his fist through. He saw the car that he had dreamed about for years, and he saw it fully restored, sleek and immaculate.

Mark and David drove over with a long trailer and hauled the car back to Boston, where Mark installed it in his garage. Then he began the long process of disassembly, cleaning, sanding, repairing, and finding authentic replacement parts.

Re-assembly was time-consuming. Fortunately, Mark had kept complete records, so he was able to retrieve the correct parts from the various places he had stored them: on shelves in the garage, in boxes piled in the utility room, inside the car itself, even under his bed. When the engine arrived just a week ago, David had helped him re-install it, and they had fussed together over the timing so that it was perfectly balanced. Mark placed a glass of water on it while it was running, and the water barely rippled.

After a quick breakfast, David and Mark walked out to the Thunderbird, which looked as if it had just been driven off the showroom floor. David examined it carefully. Its new trim and factory paint job gleamed. Even the tires were new. David could see that the tiny knobs left by the molding had not worn off yet. He could tell that his son had prepared the car specially for this trip.

Mark looked for his father's reaction. "How do you like it?"

"What can I say? It's gorgeous. Hard to believe it's the same wreck we hauled over here."

The compliment from his father pleased Mark, and he smiled to himself, realizing how he had worked so hard just to hear his father give his stamp of approval. Not that David was hypercritical or negative— he was never that— it was just that he was by nature reserved, as his own father had been. David did not often express his feelings verbally. For Mark, a squeeze of the hand, an arm on the shoulder, a smile; these were the compliments he learned to appreciate as a child. The spoken ones were rare, and their very scarcity made them that much more precious to him.

They started out in typical November weather: cold, damp and gray. The sky was an unbroken sheet of sodden-looking clouds that appeared to hover just above the tops of the buildings, and a light mist was blowing in from the sea. Heading south on the Interstate, they passed Dorchester and then went east onto the causeway leading toward Long Island, a finger of land sticking out into Quincy Bay. On Moon Island, they turned off into the Boston Police Department's outdoor range area, which was nestled against a sandy, scrub-covered hill. A chill sea breeze met them as they stepped from the car, and they were glad of their down jackets.

At first glance, one would not have thought of David and Mark as father and son. Mark was taller, with broad shoulders and slim hips, while his father was more compact. Mark's unruly shock of reddish-blond hair and gray eyes contrasted sharply with his father's wavy jet-black hair—just beginning to show streaks of gray—and dark brown, flashing eyes. On closer inspection, however, one could see that both father and son had the same straight, narrow nose and the same steady, unwavering gaze. They automatically fell into step with one another as they walked to the range office.

The rangemaster, a retired sergeant, was glad to see David; they had worked together many years ago. After exchanging a few 'war stories,' David explained that he wanted to show Mark the range and maybe do a little shooting. The sergeant was curious, and he tried indirectly to find out why they had come. David kept smiling and chatting, as if the visit were nothing more than he said it was: a Saturday outing with his son.

"We won't keep you long, Sarge. Just want to squeeze off a few rounds. Say, a couple targets slow fire and then a little work with the silhouettes."

The sergeant showed them the handguns that they could use and supplied them with targets, ammunition and headsets for hearing protection. Both David and Mark chose Smith & Wesson .38 caliber revolvers. Then they walked out to the range.

The smell of gunpowder brought back memories for Mark. He had been only eight the first time his father took him to the

Department's small indoor range in the basement of Division 2, on Milk Street. The sound of the first shots had hit him like a shock wave, but he had become used to it quickly. He had always envied the easy, knowing way his father handled a gun. Often, in the evening, he would watch his father practice dry-firing. David would balance a dime on the barrel, hold the revolver out and aim, fire, cock and repeat the sequence for fifteen minutes. Mark sat on the floor waiting for the dime to fall. If he caught it, he could keep it. But the dime rarely fell until near the end of the session, when David purposely tilted the barrel so that Mark would have his reward.

Mark had pestered his father continually to let him shoot. Each time, David would put his hand on Mark's shoulder and tell him: "Not yet, son. You're not really old enough. Maybe when you're twelve."

Two weeks before Mark's twelfth birthday his father set the day when Mark would go to the range and shoot. He taught Mark how to handle a revolver properly and he insisted that Mark practice at home before they went to the range. Mark already knew the three cardinal rules by heart: always treat a gun as if it's loaded and ready to fire; never play with a gun by pointing it at someone, even if you're sure it's empty; and don't point a gun unless you intend to shoot.

He learned the fourth rule later, in the Bureau: don't shoot unless you intend to kill.

When they were at the range, David lectured his son again.

"Remember, *me fij* (my son), you can't shoot straight if you don't squeeze the trigger. Never jerk it. Just a steady pressure, like you're shaking hands with the gun. You can't blast away and expect to hit anything. That only works in the movies. If you do it right, you won't even know when the gun's going to fire."

He pointed to the ceiling and walls of the range, where the insulation board had been torn by the tracks of countless stray bullets. Even police officers get careless, he said.

When David was sure that Mark understood what he was to do, he moved back so that Mark was alone at the firing line. The rangemaster gave the commands and Mark raised the revolver to fire. He tried his best to hold it steady, but the sights kept wavering across the target. Finally, his arm grew tired and he had to lower it. His father wanted to speak out and encourage him, but he kept silent, admiring the boy's determination.

Mark tried once more, but had to bring the gun down. His shoulder muscles ached. After a while, he tried again, his lips pressed tightly together. He held his breath and kept the sights aligned. They seemed to drift all over the center of the target, but he waited patiently and only squeezed when they were in position under the black. Suddenly the gun fired, and he felt as if he were surrounded by the explosion. The recoil pushed his hand up so that the revolver was pointing almost at the ceiling.

Mark's hopes fell as he looked at the target. He could not see any hole. "Aw, did I miss it?"

The rangemaster looked through his scope. "Nope. You're in the black."

When Mark finished his tenth round and the target was reeled back, he could hardly contain himself. He wanted to know his score.

The rangemaster checked two shots to see whether they had cut a ring and then added up. He was impressed. "Eighty-eight, young fellah. Not half bad." He didn't say what he was thinking: some of the police officers did a lot worse.

The memory of those early experiences frustrated Mark now. His first shots almost missed the black, and he cursed himself under his breath. Gradually, however, he brought his breathing under control and began concentrating. As he and David walked up to their second targets, he was content. *That's more like it. Finally a decent group.* He glanced over at his father's target: five shots were grouped so tightly that that they could be covered by a silver dollar. David saw Mark looking at the target and gave him a small smile, but did not say anything. Mark was not surprised. *That's just like Father,* he thought with a smile: *no bragging, no preening, just get the job done.*

After an hour, Mark and David gathered their brass, thanked the rangemaster and headed home.

## X minus 18 Days

*Monday, November 10*

Driving his rental car west from the Indianapolis airport, David soon found himself in farming country. He could have taken a later flight all the way to Terre Haute, right next to the Illinois line and only 25 miles from Fillmore, but then he would have arrived two hours later. He enjoyed driving much more than flying. *Better to be on the move. And besides, you'll get there faster this way.* He glanced at the dashboard clock. *Ten. Should be there before lunch.*

David maneuvered smoothly into traffic on Route I-465 and exited at Route 36, heading west toward Danville. The countryside flashed by: flat fields with only rows of stubble showing where luxuriant stands of corn had grown; the distant skyline dotted here and there with clusters of buildings; farmhouses dwarfed by massive silos that were connected by spider-web arrangements of pipes; here and there a rusting harrow or hay rake, almost obscured by grass and weeds during the summer but now visible amid the browned and matted vegetation; bright green fields of winter wheat; cattle milling in feedlots. He could almost sense the onset of hibernation. Now and then a small town punctuated the highway: shops along a one-block street; dirt-covered pickup trucks parked cheek by jowl with clean late-model cars; a lone traffic light that impeded, without really controlling, the traffic that reluctantly slowed to 40 mph as it droned through.

He switched on the radio, listened to the news. Soon, he crossed into Illinois. "Fillmore - 5 miles." More and more businesses appeared along the highway as he neared the county seat of Dupre County: dealers for farm equipment, with tractors, combines, harvesters and other implements scattered about their lots, gleaming new ones all in a row nearest the road, on gravel-covered spaces where the grass had been trimmed and, to the back of the lot, older machines that had been taken in trade and 'reconditioned' and rental units, weather-beaten and tired, pocked with rust, as if someone had forgotten they existed; car dealers with reflectors and plastic pennants swinging overhead, and rows of windshields with whitewashed prices to entice purchasers: "Real Beauty, Lo Mileage, Best Buy." Then a large sign:

FILLMORE - POP. 16,540 DUPRE COUNTY SEAT
*The City of Enterprise*

surrounded by a mural painted by local high school students showing factory buildings, farmworkers and schools, and below, a list of the various civic and community organizations of the town and where and when they met.

David found his way quickly to the town center, parked in front of the gray limestone courthouse and climbed the twenty worn marble steps to the entrance. There was no information desk in the unlit lobby, so he opened the door of the nearest office and asked the secretary where the Sheriff's office was.

She stopped filing her nails and waved her hand in a vague circle. "Out and around back."

He located the Sheriff's office in a two-story annex behind the courthouse. Three dirty blue and white patrol cars took up most of the parking space. The sergeant at the desk facing the door looked up as David entered. David handed him a business card and asked to speak with the Sheriff.

The sergeant flicked an intercom switch. "Jason, there's a fellow here wants to see you." He glanced at David's card. "An attorney...from Boston."

A gruff, staccato voice answered: "O.K. Send 'im over."

Following the sergeant's directions, David headed down a poorly lit corridor, the sound of his footsteps on the marble floor echoing as he walked. He could see that the cleaning crew had not visited recently; he passed a standing ashtray full of cigarette butts, with several crumpled plastic coffee cups surrounding its base. Up ahead was the Sheriff's office, and he immediately recognized the frosted glass door from countless other police stations and sheriffs' offices he had known. From the far jamb of the door, just above head height, a sign poked into the corridor: *SHERIFF*.

Painted in neat black letters across the middle of the glass:

*JASON B. TATE*, Sheriff

David knocked, and as he opened the door his eyes immediately took in the standard drab official furnishings: gray metal desk, filing cabinets, bulletin board, heavy wooden chairs. He had seen them all so many times before. A heavy man seated behind a paper-strewn desk looked up as David stood in the doorway. The smell of stale cigar smoke hovered in the air.

"Sheriff Tate?"

"That's me. Come on in."

Jason Beauregard Tate, munching on the remains of an unlit cigar, motioned to David to enter. When he leaned forward to shake hands, the edge of the desk made a deep impression in his ample paunch. The wide belt below had long since given up trying to find a waist. Jason extracted a now shapeless stub gingerly with two fingers and jabbed it at a chair. "Have a seat."

David introduced himself. His iron handclasp, steady gaze and calm air of authority generally stifled any jokes about big-city DA's or lawyers.

David registered impressions immediately. Jason was strong and he was proud of it. David had felt the extra pressure in the sheriff's grip and the way the big man had looked for his reaction. Jason was also proud of his position, even though he gave the impression of good-old-boy sloppiness. His teeth were badly stained by tobacco, but he was clean-shaven, and his expensive gabardine shirt was spotless, with sharp creases in the sleeves.

"Well," Jason said expansively, spreading his hands. "Welcome to Dupre County." He pronounced it as if it rhymed with 'super'. "I see you're a lawyer."

"Yes...but I did time in the trenches on your side, too. Boston Police Department for a few years and then the DA's office."

"Bet you don't miss it, right?" Jason asked with a wide grin.

They chatted briefly about police work, then Jason leaned forward heavily in his chair, causing it to squeak and complain. The preliminaries were over.

"So what's a Boston lawyer doing all the way out in corn country?"

David was always able to work easily with law enforcement officials, from the lowest deputy in a small town to senior staff in the FBI. He treated all of them with respect, as fellow professionals, and they looked upon him as, in a sense, joined with them in a common cause. He came right to the point.

"There was an Italian here by the name of Bertaccini. Died about ten days ago. His company asked me to find out what happened. What do you have on it?"

"Yeah, I handled that one myself. The guy was staying at the

Holiday Inn north of town, visiting the plant near here. I've got the file right here."

As Jason struggled out of his chair, David glanced around the office. He noticed some personal touches on the wall behind Jason's desk: directly behind his chair were three citations, one from the State Attorney General and two from the Fillmore Common Council; on one side, a trophy from two years ago when Jason's team had won the municipal bowling league championship; and on the other, a framed glossy publicity photo of a snarling Jason as third string tackle at the University of Illinois. Jason boasted often that he was still at his old playing weight of 245 pounds, and he was right, but it was clear that a redistribution of global proportions had taken place.

Jason was wearing black cordovan trooper boots, with a spit-polish shine that made them glow. Even the buckles had been shined. David smiled to himself. *He really loves that uniform.*

Jason took a battered wooden clipboard from one of the drawers, sat down again and began riffling through some report forms. He studied one of them briefly, then summarized it for David.

"This is what we got: your guy—I could never pronounce that name—he's having dinner at the motel. About 8:30 he complains he's got these chest pains and heartburn, and almost passes out. Doc Townley looks at him later that evening. By that time, your guy's in bed. The pain's almost gone, but he still ain't feeling so hot."

David interrupted: "What did the doctor say was wrong with him?"

"Angina attack. Doc said his heartbeat wasn't regular, or something, so he gave the guy a pill and told him to rest. Said he'd come by the next day. That was about half past nine."

"Was anyone with Bertaccini?"

"Yeah, another Dago, a guy called Pavone."

David's eyes hardened momentarily at the ethnic slur, but he could tell that Jason was not even conscious of giving offense, so he was careful not to let his voice show his displeasure. "How about when the doctor left? Was anyone in Bertaccini's room?"

"Nope," Jason said, more carefully this time. "The night manager locked the door, and Pavone went to his own room."

David could tell that Jason must have caught his slight eye movement and realized what he had just said. "When did they find the body?"

Jason consulted his clipboard again. "Next morning. Your guy's supposed to be at an early morning staff meeting at the plant but doesn't show, so they call at nine to find out where he is. When no one answers, the manager and cleaning lady open his door and find him in bed. Looked like he died in his sleep."

"Any idea what time he died?"

"The coroner—that's Adamslee—says somewhere between eleven and midnight, 'cause most of his dinner was still undigested. That checked with the rigor mortis that was left."

"Anyone lift any prints?"

"Yeah, we got a few, but no surprises. Just the people I told you about."

"Anything else?" David probed. "How about the fellow who was with Bertaccini? What do you have on him?"

Jason bit down extra hard on his cigar stub and rubbed his chin. He couldn't remember much beyond the usual passport information—nothing out of the ordinary. Since the man didn't speak English very well and since Adamslee had already decided that there had been no foul play, Jason hadn't bothered to detain him for further questions, and he had checked out that afternoon.

David was not satisfied. "Remember anything unusual about this guy Pavone? Anything at all?"

Jason bent forward and rose from his chair, put his hands on the small of his back, leaned back, stretched and grunted. Then he lumbered over to the hotplate to get some more coffee. He turned to face David, his spoon clinking against the sides of his cup as he stirred the cream in his coffee. He was frowning slightly, trying to remember.

"When you can't speak a guy's language, y'know, it's kinda hard to size him up." He paused. "Let's see . . . He was a couple inches shorter'n me, say about five-nine. Weighed like 140. A whole lot less than me." He patted his stomach, which resounded heavily. "His passport said he was fifty-seven, but I think he looked a little younger. And he wore these tinted glasses, so you couldn't hardly see his eyes. That kinda threw me off a little."

As Jason spoke, David noticed that the sheriff's voice became crisper, more professional.

"I'm an eye man myself," Jason continued. "I gotta make eye contact with a guy." He rubbed his chin, still thinking, then looked up and snapped his fingers. "Yeah, now I remember. There was this one time, when he got something on his glasses and took 'em off to clean 'em. It was kinda odd, y'know: one of his eyes—the left one, I think—didn't focus right at me. It was like he had a glass eye or something." He paused and seemed to reflect. "That's about it."

David was impressed. He could see that Jason was no buffoon at all, and could be a real professional when he wanted to be. He said thanks and started to leave. At the door, he turned and asked Jason to call ahead so he could speak with the coroner before he left for lunch.

As soon as David stepped out of the elevator into the antiseptic, white-tiled corridor by the coroner's office, he was overwhelmed by the familiar sickly sweet smell of the deodorant used to mask the smell of death. Sensitive to smells, he had always needed a moment or two to get used to it. He walked in, introduced himself to the lone secretary and was shown into Adamslee's office.

Louis Adamslee, Dupre Country Coroner, had only a limited range of vision from where he was sitting. He could see directly ahead, but in any other direction his view was blocked by stacks of folders piled here and there on his desk. Papers protruded from several of them and were in danger of falling. In his late fifties, with a long, narrow face, a light mustache and thin lips that turned down slightly at the corners, Adamslee was nursing a mug of hot coffee in both hands, his elbows resting on the desk. He peered over the folders and invited David in.

"Come on in...have a seat. Care for coffee?"

"No, thanks," David said. "Not right now." He paused and their eyes met. "I'd like to ask a couple questions about the engineer who died here last week. His name was Bertaccini."

Adamslee looked away, brushed back an unruly lock of blond-gray hair, and reached in a desk drawer for a sheet of tissue paper and began cleaning his glasses. He spoke slowly and carefully. "Do the Boston police have an interest in him?"

Signals went off for David. Adamslee, he decided, was a typical bureaucrat, not frightened of making mistakes, but frightened of having his mistakes discovered. *Probably tries to cover his incompetence with this appearance of overwork. And he's hiding something.*

David tried to reassure Adamslee. He said he had no connection with the police; Bertaccini's company had sent him. The death of their chief engineer had been a great blow, and management had asked him to find out what had happened.

"Be glad to help," Adamslee said, "but there's not a whole lot to check out. Simple heart attack."

"Could I see your report?"

Adamslee hesitated briefly, as if he were going to object. Then he said, easily: "Sure, just a second." He shuffled to one of his file cabinets, looked through some folders, and took one out.

"Ah, here it is." He handed it to David almost reluctantly.

David scanned the report quickly, noting that only a routine autopsy was performed. "Did you draw any blood samples or take any specimens for lab examination? I don't see any listed here."

Adamslee's voice stiffened slightly. "We sent stomach contents to the central lab in Chicago for routine toxicology check. Not really necessary, at least not in this case, but it's part of the routine."

His voice began to sound more official as he described what had happened. Since Doctor Townley had reported severe angina, Adamslee had concluded that the engineer had died of myocardial infarction. During the autopsy, they had found no external signs of injury and no structural alteration of any of the vital organs.

"Unless your guy ate something that really disagreed with him, I lay odds on the infarction. But Dr. Samuels did the autopsy. If you'd like to talk to him, he's down at the end of the hall."

David saw that he would not be able to get any more from Adamslee, so he said thanks and left.

As he entered through the door marked 'MORGUE', David saw that the autopsy room was separated from the rest of the area by a partition. Someone was talking, and David continued past the partition. A medium-sized man with a round face and sandy hair was standing beside an autopsy table, dictating the findings of his external examination of the nude corpse stretched out on the slab in front of him. Dressed in a light green surgical gown, he was pulling on thin rubber surgical gloves, flexing his fingers to get a good fit. When he noticed David, the man switched off the recorder. David introduced himself and said that Adamslee had sent him over.

The man smiled. "Just call me Ben. "If you'll bear with me a while, I have just a bit more on this one."

Watching Ben work, David was reminded of the countless times he had stood by marble slabs like this, seeing bodies being readied for their final indignity. As a rookie cop, he had had difficulty at first in looking at a cadaver without thinking of the living person it had once been: someone's son, husband, lover, whatever. But like all who deal regularly in death and violence, he soon became inured to the sight, and was able to view them simply as flesh and bones to be cut, sliced, probed, tested—all in the name of discovering what had put out the spark of life.

Moving carefully, Ben made the usual Y-shaped incision in the chest and down the center of the abdomen. A layer of yellow fatty tissue showed as the scalpel sliced through the flesh. Peeling back the skin of the V-flap portion, he exposed the sternum. Then he reached over to the cart for an instrument that resembled a linoleum cutter, and used it to rip through the cartilage on both sides of the sternum, severing it from the rib cage. After removing the sternum to gain access to the chest cavity, he cut carefully through the remaining muscle and tissue on the leg of the Y to expose the abdominal cavity. Then he straightened up and gathered his instruments.

"O.K." We can get started now. What is it you'd like to know?"

"Do you remember a fellow named Bertaccini? Died about ten days ago at the Holiday Inn?"

"Yeah, I did the autopsy on him."

"The report was also signed by a Dr. K. Lewis. Is he your assistant?"

Ben laughed. "No money in this county for assistants. The 'K' stands for Karen. She's a forensic pathologist, works out of Springfield. This is part of her territory and she was here with me when I cut him open."

After a few minutes, Ben had completed his internal examination and had dictated his findings in a flat, unemotional voice. "There. That oughta do it. Now all I need are a few samples to send off to the lab. Won't take a sec." After finishing, he stripped off his surgical gloves, dropped them into a plastic-lined trash can and untied his gown, rolled it up and tossed it like a basketball into a nearby laundry bag.

They walked over to Ben's office, where David came right to the point. "Y'know, Ben, when I read the report on Bertaccini, something seemed to be missing. Nothing about heart damage. Why do you think he had a heart attack?" David watched Ben closely, and saw the younger man's eyes narrow slightly.

Ben looked questioningly at David and then turned away to arrange some papers on his desk. He kept looking at the papers as he spoke. His voice was uncertain and guarded. "Lots of cases are borderline, y'know. You take anyone in his mid-fifties who has an angina attack and then dies, you can practically bet it's a heart attack. With any guy that age the heart'll show some damage. You know you're going to find some blockage in the coronary artery, some evidence of age. So you always have some basis for saying heart attack. But it's still a percentage call."

David could tell that Ben was holding back. He leaned forward in his chair. His voice was soft. "Ben, what I'm really interested in is your own professional opinion. If it were up to you, what would you say killed him?"

Ben became uneasy. He tried to look at David, but could not. Finally, he got up, shut the door to his office and lowered his voice. He was upset. "Now wait a minute. That's not fair. You know Lou's the one who makes the decisions. Go ask him that question. All I can tell you is what I saw."

It was clear to David that Ben was not going to be much help, but he had already given David something to go on. Ben did not really think Bertaccini died of a heart attack. *But then what killed him?* He thanked Ben for his help and returned to Adamslee's office, knocked on the jamb of the open door and walked in. He would not have seen Adamslee seated at the desk except that the top of the coroner's head showed above the pile of folders on the desk.

Assuming that David's visit with Ben had already produced the answers that David was seeking, Adamslee greeted him with a smile, but the smile faded when David said he still could not see how Bertaccini had died. They fenced back and forth, and Adamslee's voice took on a slight edge as he repeated his original diagnosis: Bertaccini had died of a heart attack brought on by myocardial infarction. To him the matter was closed.

David was still not satisfied. He brought out the folder containing the engineer's medical records and handed it to Adamslee. He said that the records showed that Bertaccini's heart was sound, and that a cardiologist who reviewed the file agreed completely. A heart attack for the man would be highly unusual.

Adamslee took the folder but did not look at it. His voice was defensive. "Your expert didn't see the body, and he didn't do the autopsy. You know as well as I do that medical records only take you so far. Your expert knows that, too."

"Then how would it be if I brought him here to conduct a second examination? Would you object to that?"

Adamslee was unable to meet David's eyes. "Doesn't make any difference what I want. The body's already been cremated, and we shipped the ashes to Italy."

It took all of David's self-control to keep his voice calm. "You mean to say you released the body before you even received the toxicology report?" he said, evenly. "Any reason for that?"

Adamslee was immediately on the defensive again. He spoke stiffly, his voice rising slightly. "I don't need a reason. It's my job to decide why someone died, and that's what I did. As far as I'm concerned, this case is closed. Your engineer died from natural causes and that's that."

Since it was obvious that he could get nothing more from Adamslee, David asked where he could find Dr. Lewis.

"She's at her office in Springfield," Adamslee said, "and she's not due back here until tomorrow." He rummaged through his desk drawer. "I'll give you her phone number. It's here somewhere."

He handed David a business card. David copied down the number, thanked him and left, returning to Sheriff Tate's office, where he ran through his notes with Jason just to make sure he had not missed something. After summarizing what he had learned from Adamslee and Ben, David asked for passport information on Pavone.

Jason flipped some pages on his clipboard and read from his report:

>*Ing. Cesare Pavone*
>BORN: *March 18, 1923, in Verona*
>ADDRESS: *418 Via Napoli*
>   *Piacenza*
>BUSINESS: *Engineer, Intermec, SpA.*

"Did you check that out?"

"What for?"

Sensing that Jason was fencing with him, David said: "Maybe nothing, judging from what I've seen so far." Then, in a confidential tone, he added: "Jason, you ever had a case where you got the feeling that things were just too easy? You know, that nagging in your stomach when everything you see says one thing, but it still doesn't satisfy you?"

"Who hasn't?"

"Well, this business with Bertaccini gives me that feeling. Adamslee acts like it's open and shut, but Ben's not so sure. I can tell." He paused then asked, "How about you?"

David knew that Jason had to be cautious. To be a survivor in small-town politics—and Jason was a survivor—he could not afford to create problems unless he had a good reason. He hesitated a bit before answering..

"Come to think of it, sure. There were some things I kinda wondered about. Didn't pass the old sniff test. If it'd been up to me I'd have gone after that Pavone guy." He paused. "But not after Adamslee's report, though."

"Can't stir up things, right? I know what you mean."

Jason walked David out to his car, where they said good-bye. David extended his hand. "You're a good man, Jason. Thanks" He could see how Jason sucked in his stomach a bit: the compliment meant a great deal to him.

As David pulled away from the curb, Jason waved. "You need anything more, you give me a buzz, O.K.?"

David was encouraged. *Jason and Ben are sure something's not right, and Adamslee knows it, too, but he's afraid to do anything.*

As soon as David reached his motel room, he called Dr. Lewis. A woman's voice answered, husky yet businesslike.

He introduced himself, then asked to meet with her to discuss Bertaccini's autopsy. When she asked why, he explained that the company Bertaccini worked for wanted to know what had happened. He had already spoken with Adamslee and Ben, but wasn't sure that he had the whole picture yet.

Her voice was hesitant. "What is it you'd like to know? If you've already spoken with Adamslee, then you know as much as I can tell you."

"I guess you're right," David said, trying not to pressure her. "May be just a waste of time for both of us. Still, there are some things about this case that puzzle me. I spent a few years in police work myself, so I guess that makes me see problems where there aren't any. But couldn't you spare me just a few minutes? I'd really appreciate it."

She paused and then said yes, she would try to answer his questions. They agreed to meet for breakfast at a restaurant near the courthouse.

# CHAPTER THREE

## X minus 17 Days

*Fillmore, Illinois*
*Tuesday, November 11*

Karen was already seated at the restaurant when David arrived. He went over to her table and introduced himself, and when she reached out to shake hands, he took her hand in his and kissed it lightly. When he sat down opposite her she was looking at her hand. David could see her cheeks redden slightly. As he looked at her he caught several impressions, observing her instinctively on three different levels: as an individual; as an attractive woman in her mid-thirties; and as a series of clues. *This is a woman with breeding, and she takes good care of herself.* Her fingernails were manicured; her teeth even and white; her voice well modulated. Although she did not have an athletic build, her trim, narrow waist and the strong, supple way she moved told him that she exercised regularly. This was also a woman with the kind of taste he responded to: nothing extreme, no obvious makeup except a hint of lipstick, hair softly curled, jewelry simple and understated-a single-stranded gold necklace, small pearl earrings and a dainty antique pearl ring.

They chatted, and David found that he really enjoyed being with her. She was direct and open, but without any forced assertiveness. She knew her work, she knew she was good at it, and she did not give the impression that she trying to compete in a man's world. If anything, her clothing—light gray matching cardigan and wool skirt, with a cream-colored silk blouse that framed her face—emphasized her femininity. Most of all, however, it was her buoyant enthusiasm that David found captivating. It reminded him of Elena.

Karen was captivated, too, but far more deeply than David could have imagined. She was surprised at first that he was so much older than she was. His voice had prepared her for a man nearer her own age. The moment passed quickly, though. She felt completely disarmed by him and was unable, or perhaps unwilling, to resist the direction in which he steered their conversation. It was almost as if she had surrendered to the strength that she felt in him. His eyes, warm and unthreatening, held her, but she could not look into them for long. Every time their eyes met, she felt as if she were being caressed. For the first time in over a year, she found herself blushing at small compliments. David was one of the favored few to whom people naturally gravitate for support, and Karen had fallen completely under his spell.

For his part, David was simply playing a role, doing his job. He was an investigator and he needed information, so he tried to make people want to give it. If that required a little honest flattery in exchange, he gave that. David succeeded with Karen in a way he had not expected.

She was as bright as she was attractive: Phi Beta Kappa from Penn and MD with honors from Columbia. After medical school, she had specialized in pathology. On the recommendation of one of her professors, she had found a position with the Medical Examiner's Office in New York City. Resourceful and hardworking, and brilliant on the witness stand, she was an immediate success. District attorneys would automatically raise their odds of success if she testified for them.

Her marriage began to come apart, however, after her husband lost his job. An associate with a large Wall Street law firm, he had worked long hours, supremely confident of being made partner. In the middle of his seventh year, the time-honored up-or-out period in his firm, he was not among those chosen for partnership, and that had devastated him. Instead of staying on with the firm as a senior associate until he found another position or waiting for his firm to place him as corporate counsel with one of its clients, he resigned in a pique of anger, alienating himself from the firm and all of its contacts. With four other young lawyers, he established his own partnership. Unfortunately, the small firm was short on paying clients, so that he and Karen had to live on her salary alone. Drugs came soon after, followed by more alcohol than he could handle. Counseling did no good. When he began to abuse Karen physically in his drunken anger, she left him and got a divorce. That was a little more than a year ago.

The position in Illinois had come as a welcome escape. The local officials at the Department of Health were so delighted to have her that they equipped a laboratory in the basement of her home, where she could work on the 'hunches' that so often proved stunningly correct.

David began directing the conversation toward the engineer's death. "They tell me you're from New York. This must be quite a change for you. I mean professionally. How d'you like it so far?"

"Not bad, really, but sometimes I miss the City. You know, the hectic pace and all. And the variety."

"How about the people you work with?" David asked, probing a bit. "Like Adamslee?"

She looked down at her plate. "Oh, Lou does what he can. He's not a whole lot different from the other coroners down here."

David could see that she was trying to protect Adamslee, and he smiled as he handed her a folder. "Well, to business. This is the fellow's medical history. I've got charts and x-rays, too. Our people just can't believe he had a heart attack."

She studied them for a minute, then looked up. "I'd agree, based on these."

"You were at the autopsy. What happened?"

"It was strange. We didn't find any external trauma, and the organs were all normal. The heart was typical for a healthy man in his fifties. We couldn't see any definite cause of death, but as soon as Adamslee heard what Doc Townley said about angina, he put down heart attack."

"And what would Dr. Lewis have done?" David asked softly, searching her eyes.

Karen, almost hypnotized by David's gaze, blushed slightly and fingered a stray curl. She was distracted by her reaction to his attentions. She felt drawn to this strong, yet gentle man, and was keenly aware of his physical nearness. The thought that he had seen her blush embarrassed her and made the situation worse. Finally, she could stand it no longer and excused herself. In the ladies room, she looked at herself in the mirror. Her cheeks were still flushed. *What's the matter with you? He had to see you blushing. He probably thinks you're trying to turn him on.* She splashed some cold water on her face, took several deep breaths, and when she felt composed again she returned to the table.

Torn between loyalty to Adamslee and her desire to help David, she hesitated a moment before answering David's question, and she kept her voice calm. "Frankly, I didn't think we really had enough for a death certificate. And Ben agrees with me, but he's too afraid of Lou to say anything."

David nodded, urging her on.

"You see, Ben and I were both puzzled. Here was a man, apparently in good health, who suddenly drops dead and we couldn't find out why. Take away the angina and there wasn't anything you could point to as a cause of death. It just didn't add up. That's why I thought we should've probed further."

"What about poison?"

She pondered a moment, then shook her head. "Possible, but it'd be pretty much of a long shot. There aren't more than six, seven cases a year, and that's for the whole state. Down here, years go by without even one. Still and all, I thought we had to do a toxicology check."

"And did you?"

She nodded. "It took a lot of talking, but I finally convinced Lou to send the stomach contents to the Chicago lab."

David heard what she said, but could almost hear her say, "I want to tell you more." He pressed. "Did you do anything else?"

"Well, yes," she said, reluctantly. "I had Ben take a block of each organ for me, plus a section of the brain and brain stem. I didn't dare send them to Chicago, though, because Lou would've had a fit. So... I... I took them home with me. I was planning to work on them later."

David felt like shouting. Impulsively, he reached out and covered one of her hands with his. "Ben was right. You *are* something special."

Her flesh tingled at his touch.

David leaned forward and lowered his voice. "What I need to know is how Bertaccini died. If we're talking about foul play, then other people could be in danger, so we don't have much time. Is there any chance you could work on the sections right away?"

She felt his eyes looking deep inside her, and her voice broke slightly. "I'll... do what I can."

"Where can I get in touch with you this evening?"

"I'm leaving for Springfield about four. Here's my home number." She was about to give him her card when she hesitated and, on the spur of the moment, she said, "Why not drive over there with me? It's only an hour. You can keep me company, and then you wouldn't have to wait for your answer."

David accepted the invitation gladly. He liked being with her, and wanted to save time. At Springfield, he would be close to St. Louis, and should have no trouble catching a flight back to Boston, so he arranged for the motel to turn in his rental car and left with Karen that afternoon.

They talked about many things on the way. David, whose knowledge of music, art, literature and history was encyclopedic, overwhelmed her. Such a refreshing change from the dullards she had met since coming to Springfield, whose interests were limited largely to sports and local politics. Anything that happened outside of Illinois or more than ten years ago (except for sports records, where their memories were detailed and exhaustive) might as well have taken place on a distant planet as far as they were concerned. He laughed heartily when she said that one of her dates actually believed that Botticelli played tight end for the New York Jets. She was starved for intellectual conversation, and bubbled with enthusiasm as they discussed the new Egyptian exhibit at the Metropolitan, the latest Broadway hits, classical music. Time passed quickly. Karen kept her eyes on the road and seldom looked over at David, so he was able to study her as they talked. He decided that her profile was almost perfect: forehead perhaps a trifle high, but her nose turned up just enough and her lips were full, yet finely drawn. He noticed other things as well: hands that were strong, muscular thighs that rippled against her skirt as she shifted gears, and generous breasts that swelled her light sweater and were outlined by the shoulder strap of her seatbelt.

At breakfast, he had wondered a bit why she blushed so often and why she seemed so uneasy whenever their eyes met. Had she been older he would have noted them immediately as signs of sexual interest, but because of the age difference between them, he had discounted the signals.

As they drove, he reflected on it. *Remember your age*, he reminded himself. Although he found younger women quite attractive, he automatically assumed that they regarded him as ancient—an old bull on the outskirts of the herd, far from the females who were ripe for mating—a sort of harmless eunuch who could be shown everything. Little did they realize, he thought, that the only difference that increasing age meant—at least as far as he was concerned—was that it expanded the range of women whom he found attractive. Age might have reduced the frequency of sex for him, but certainly not its richness or enjoyment. Far from it. Sex with Elena had never ceased to improve and develop during their long marriage; not necessarily more exciting than when they were first married, but fuller, like the rich overtones of a well-used string instrument.

He glanced over at her. She was a stunning woman, young enough to be his daughter and she looked even younger. *Could she really be interested?* She was talking excitedly about a W.C. Fields movie she had seen recently, and was laughing like a little girl, almost bouncing on the seat. *No*, he decided ruefully, *she's just being herself, just trying to impress an older man, a kind of father-figure. And yet....*

As soon as they arrived at Karen's house, she called the head of the toxicology laboratory in Chicago. They had not completed their tests, he said, but they had found a trace of something suspicious. They could not identify the compound yet, but he thought it could have induced chest cramps and nausea. He would have a positive identification tomorrow.

Karen relayed this to David. Then, she added, "I've got this wild hunch. I'm going to make up some slides from the brain blocks and run them over to our lab. It's a long shot, but I want them to test something for me." She called ahead and arranged for one of the assistants to set up the proper equipment. Then they drove downtown. David waited in the lobby of the lab building. After an hour, she rushed out and David could see from the expression on her face that she had important news.

"I've got it!" she said triumphantly. "I know what killed him! It wasn't heart failure. He was murdered. It was succinylcholine chloride, just like I thought."

"Wait a second," David interrupted. "Succini-what?"

"Succinylcholine chloride. It's used a lot as an anesthetic, but a large dose can cause cardiac arrest. From the brain section I checked, that engineer must've had a massive injection. I'll bet Toxicology would've missed it, though."

"Why's that?"

"'Cause it gets broken down in the blood. In a few minutes it's gone, and nothing's left except succinic acid and choline, and they're already in the blood anyway. A normal test would never pick it up."

"So what do you think happened?"

"Well, I figure that whoever killed him injected the drug directly into his brain, probably at the base of the skull, and under the hairline so you wouldn't see the puncture unless you were really looking for it. That's why Ben missed it."

"Why, that calls for champagne," David said exultantly and hugged her.

When she felt his strong arms encircle her and she touched his broad, lean back, she was swept up once again by desire, and this time she allowed her hips to press briefly against him. The brief, erotic contact surprised David; he could not imagine that it had been deliberate. The moment passed quickly, but he began to re-evaluate the situation.

Since his wife, Elena, had been killed five years ago in an auto accident, he had slept with several women. Eligible females had been thrust upon him by well-meaning friends and relatives, and several others had tried. Perhaps Elena had spoiled him for other women; they had known one another so intimately and passionately for so many years. A few of the women he had met were great in bed, but their limited range of interests made them tiresome after a while. Still, he was unprepared for Karen.

She drove them to her home, and David called to book a noon flight out of St. Louis. Karen cooked a light dinner.

Afterward, David lit a fire in the fireplace and they sat together on the sofa and talked quietly. She was delighted to have an opportunity to find out more about him, but he was reluctant to talk about himself, and kept turning the conversation back to her, asking about her family, her interests, her ambitions. She began telling him things about herself, intimate details that she had not shared even with her closest friends. When she went to the kitchen and returned with drinks, David noticed that she sat closer than before.

"I've been talking about me all the time," she said. "Now it's your turn. Tell me about Alfieri. Where did you meet him?"

"Seems like I have always known Dario. We sort of grew up together; had the same friends, same school, same Alpini uni..."

"Alpini? What's that?"

David laughed softly. "Don't get me started on that... If I had a couple days, maybe I could tell you."

Karen noticed the spark in his eyes and tried to encourage him to talk. "Oh, no, you don't," she said stubbornly and snuggled next to him. "I want to hear all about your Alpini."

David, amused by her eager interest, began to explain what made the Alpini special. "The Alpini... David said slowly. "Where to start? Well, first off, they're soldiers trained to fight in the mountains. That's where they got their name."

"Are they in the army, then?"

"Army?" David exclaimed in mock horror. "Heaven forbid! No. They've got their own organization."

"What makes them special, then?"

"It's partly tradition. It's a real honor to belong to the Alpini, so there's lots of pride involved. And you serve in the same units with your neighbors and friends. Like a big fraternity, I suppose."

"I remember studying about the war in school," she said with a small sigh. "But you... You were really *there*. Was it bad?"

David chuckled slightly. "Yeah, at least where we were, on the Russian front. It was so cold that winter that everything froze, even the oil in our trucks. We had to light fires under them just to get them started." He told her about the Russian offensive. His voice was proud. "We held the Russkis back, though. Took the best they had and didn't budge. For five weeks. But by that time we were all alone and had to pull back, and we just barely made it. But lots of our men didn't..." His voice trailed off.

"And then?"

"Then came Yugoslavia. Almost got stuck there, too." He gave a wry laugh. "Say, this must sound like ancient history to you, right?"

"Oh, no!" she said quickly, afraid he would stop. "Tell me what happened. I really want to know."

David smiled and continued. Well, in September '43, the Italian government decided to stop fighting the Allies, and announced an armistice. As soon as we heard that, we knew we'd be caught between the Germans and the partisans, so we left."

"So how did you get back to Italy?"

"Old-fashioned foot power. We traveled at night a lot, and followed ridges where the Germans couldn't see us. But I didn't make it all the way back."

She looked at him questioningly, and he explained how he had been shot and had to stay behind while his unit continued west to Piemonte.

"But it all worked out for the best," he said lightly. "Otherwise I wouldn't have met Elena."

"Your wife?"

David nodded. "Lucky for me, actually. If she hadn't taken care of me I'd have died right there."

As the sun set, the room gradually darkened and the flames from the log fire furnished the only light. They began flickering and died down to a warm glow from cherry-red coals.

Karen pressed David to continue talking about himself, and

began asking him questions that he could not evade. It was easy for him to talk with her, here in the warm half-light, and he began telling her about growing up at San Nicola, about his family and the war. He even told her about Elena: how they had met and some of the tender moments they had shared. He had never spoken about Elena like this; it was as if that part of him had been sealed shut. When he realized what he was doing, he stopped in mid-sentence.

She looked up at him. "What's wrong?"

"Nothing," he said, shaking his head. "It's just that this is the first time I've really talked about Elena—with anyone."

When he looked down at her, he decided to make a tentative move: one that would not necessarily be interpreted as romantic. He put an arm around her shoulder and drew her gently against him, as if to reflect the intimacy they were sharing. He kissed her forehead lightly. Her skin was soft, and he could smell the faint scent of the cologne she had placed on her temples. Karen responded by moving still closer, pressing her body against him.

One by one, the logs had crumbled, and the red coals had died, leaving only a dim glow that cast faint shadows against the walls and ceiling.

He raised her chin and kissed her lightly. The effect was more than he expected. She put her head back, her lips parted slightly. A long and fervent embrace followed, and he held her closely, their bodies touching. He could feel her straining toward him, and he caressed the places he knew she would enjoy.

"Touch me, touch me," she moaned weakly.

They undressed one another in the dark and clung together. The full contact of flesh to flesh was overpowering. Reality receded for Karen; she surrendered to deep passion and complete abandon. It was as if she had become two selves: one self dimly conscious of the surroundings and the surges of pleasure as their bodies entwined; the other self hovering on the edges of reality—as if she were on a giant wave that rose and rose, carrying her higher and higher until she was suddenly overwhelmed by a series of delicious, frantic bursts within her. Then gradually she felt a sense of complete release, free to soar and soar, drifting, gliding like a rose petal caught by the wind, dropping gently onto a grassy hillside.

For several minutes, they lay united, breathing heavily, their bodies suffused with warmth, reluctant to break the spell.

## X minus 16 Days

*Wednesday, November 12*

Early the next morning, Karen drove David to the airport. There were no regrets, no embarrassed silences between them. They had shared an intensely personal experience, one that had stirred powerful emotions, and they were grateful to each another.

He asked her not to change Bertaccini's autopsy record. "In fact, don't do anything until I've had a chance to look into this in Italy. There's a killer over there who thinks we don't know what happened. I'd like to keep it that way as long as possible."

She nodded. "But when will I see you again?"

He cupped her chin and brushed her lips with his. "Whenever you want to. That I promise."

On the plane, David had to put aside thoughts of Karen and force himself to concentrate on what he had learned about Bertaccini's murder. It was clear that he was faced with a serious problem and needed help. There was a killer in Italy, and he had to warn Mark. Then he had to see the Don.

# CHAPTER FOUR

## X minus 14 Days

*Boston*
*Friday, November 14*

David was in his car, heading toward the North Shore, but his mind was not on driving. He kept mulling over what had happened to Bertaccini, and could not put it out of his mind. *This was no amateur job; this was the work of a pro, sent all the way from Italy. That meant money—and connections. And now my son's over there, an obvious target. But what can I do—warn him? Against what? What can I say except 'Be careful'? And what good would that do? Being careful's already second nature to Mark.* David felt powerless. The enemy, unseen and unknown, had the initiative and the advantage. They already knew that he was working with Alfieri, and would also assume that Mark was. They could strike whenever and wherever they wanted. David could only wait. He felt exposed, defenseless.

David dealt easily with problems that he could see and grapple with, but he felt frustrated by the unknown, where he had no fixed base to work from, no place to get a purchase. The puzzle he was struggling with was like some of the cases he had handled when he was on the police force, when he had had to sift through lies, counter-lies, theories and counter-theories until he finally found the one true fact, the one relationship, that would begin to resolve everything. It was as if the facts suddenly assumed a pattern for him. That is what he needed now.

He already did have something: Bertaccini's murder had given him a starting point, a toehold. Now he knew that Dario's suspicions were correct. He also had a crucial clue: a paid killer, one who used poison, had been sent from Italy to kill the engineer. Since the enemy were unaware that he knew this, he had reduced their advantage slightly. But he had to find out who had hired the killer, and quickly. That would be impossible by himself. For the first time, he was going to ask for the help of his old and dear friend, Don Oreste Marini.

David turned off Highway 1A south of Marblehead. He passed through an upper-middle class area, with four-bedroom Georgian homes and two-car garages, set on earnestly landscaped one acre lots. As he neared the shore, the homes seemed to vanish and he found himself passing long stretches of walls and fences of various types: some made of field stone, others of stucco-covered block, and still others of wooden pilings. Driveways curved and vanished behind trees and shrubs. Now and then in the winter months one could see, through the bare trees, the shapes of large homes in the distance. Often, a common entrance onto the main road would be shared by two or three residences, with the only evidence of habitation a row of mailboxes beside a gate. No names, only numbers, as if to say, *If you don't know who lives here, you're in the wrong place.*

On his right, David recognized the familiar boundary of the Marini estate. Shrubbery and ivy almost obscured the cut granite wall—the work of a team of master masons from Aosta—but the barbed wire on top made its presence known. It was rumored that a switch in the gatehouse or in the main building could send a paralyzing jolt of electricity through the wires. Closed circuit TV cameras constantly probed the perimeter of the property.

David stopped short of the heavy anchor chain stretched across the entrance. When he waved, the gatekeeper waved back and dropped the chain so that David could drive through. David recalled vividly the first time he had come there to meet the Don. The events that had caused their paths to intersect began during World War II, on the frigid steppes of Russia.

Gilbert D. Visconti

*On the Russian Front*
*December 16, 1942*

A light snow was falling on the Italian 8th Army position. The sun itself looked cold, a dull circle that glowed white and pink behind the distant morning mist. In a covered lookout post above the icebound Don River, two haggard Alpini officers and a corporal stood stamping their boots on the frozen ground. With their hands, they were warming their ears against the fierce morning temperature that had plunged far below zero during the night. The feathers in their olive green felt hats bobbed in unison. For months now they had scanned the horizon east of the river, watching the fall colors fade, to be replaced by an endless expanse of white that was peaceful, yet lifeless. But all that was changing now. One of the officers, tall and lean, moved to his right, bending slightly to avoid the rafters. He trained his binoculars on a line of tanks and men advancing over the snowy plain, barely visible in the distance. The low rumble of artillery fire rolled up the river valley.

The other officer, shorter but well-muscled, spoke in a matter-of-fact voice. "How many tanks can you make out, Dario?"

"I've counted thirty already."

David raised his own binoculars and scanned the distant southern horizon. "Looks like smoke way down there by the river."

Almost as if on cue, an orderly burst in. He saluted hastily. "The Russians are attacking to the south! They're already near the river."

"Where's Colonel D'Adda?" David asked.

"At the command center. He wants you and Major Alfieri over there right away for a briefing. General Reverberi's here from Rossosch."

"Tell him we'll be right there," Dario said.

The two friends trudged over to the main bunker. The bitter

cold closed their nostrils as they breathed, and the hard-packed snow complained shrilly under their boots. They arrived at the command center just before General Reverberi began the briefing. David eased himself onto the low bench beside Colonel D'Adda. Ten minutes later, one of the lookouts interrupted the meeting to report that some of the Russian units were headed in their direction. Within minutes, the shelling began. David could feel the earth tremble with each explosion.

The Italian Alpini, proud bearers of a fighting tradition stretching back more than one hundred years, were ready to meet the enemy. They were an elite corps, recruited from the mountain villages in northern Italy, and like a military fraternity. Brothers and neighbors served together in the same units. In their green felt Tyrolean hats, decorated with a rakish black feather, they were a breed apart, swaggering, brave and romantic: a combination Green Beret and Ranger. Highly trained, expert marksmen and skiers, their specialty was forest and mountain combat.

A caprice by Mussolini had sent these Alpini to the Russian front. They were already on their way to the Caucasus when he abruptly changed their orders. Hitler wanted to recall some of his own troops along the Don River, and he persuaded il Duce to send Alpini to relieve them. Four Alpine divisions, from Cuneo, Giulia, Vicenza and Tridentina (which included Dario's Montenegro battalion), were diverted to the Russian steppes.

It was a monumental waste of fighting men. The Alpini and their faithful mules were superbly fitted for battle in the woods and on difficult, mountainous terrain, where maneuverability and individual skills and bravery were critical. On the vast plains of Russia, however, they were only a small link in a long chain of troops on the west bank of the Don, facing the massed might of the Russian army. The Alpini fought gallantly, but could do nothing except delay the Russian tide that began to sweep over the German lines.

In two lightning thrusts, the Russians attacked the Italian regulars, separating them from the Germans in Group Hollidt. Kharitonov's 6th Army smashed through on the right flank, to the south of the Alpine troops, penetrating more than thirty miles to the main base of Kanemirovka. Meanwhile, the Alpini to the north were under fierce attack by Lelyushenko's 3rd Guards Army. The Russian movements created a giant pincers, threatening to surround the Italian troops. The Alpini refused to give way, despite heavy losses. To the south, however, the German 24th Armored Corps was overrun, and their retreat soon became a disorderly rout. Position after position was destroyed, and troops abandoned equipment and supplies in a pell-mell rush to the west. Still the Alpini held.

For five weeks the Russians hammered the Alpini lines without success. With every passing day, however, the Italian position grew more and more desperate, because they were by themselves on the front. The Russians had already penetrated deeply above and below them. To the south, thousands of regular 8th Army troops had been encircled and captured. To the north of the Tridentina Division, the 2nd Hungarian Army had already started pulling back, exposing that flank. No word had been given to the Alpini about the withdrawal. The Russian 4th Army and 18th Armored Corps poured across the Don into the area vacated by the Hungarians. The two Russian lines were threatening to close far to the west of the Don, trapping the Alpini. The star-crossed Giulia Division found itself holding off three Russian divisions that had vastly superior arms and equipment. When their commander, General Ricagno, saw how critical the situation was, he made a comment that became part of the Alpini legend: *"Coraggio, figlioli. Ciascuno di noi ha di fronte tredici russi."* (Courage, men. For each one of you we've got thirteen Russkis out there.).

Finally, in mid-January, the Alpini received orders to pull

back. David and Dario called their unit together and broke the news. Without air support and with both flanks exposed, they were about to be cut off completely by the Russian advance.

"We don't even know where the Hungarians are," Dario explained. "They haven't been in position up there for days. The Germans and our regulars to the south have been pushed back, too, so the Russians are on both sides of us. They've already reached the main base of Kanemirovka."

He paused and went to a map on the wall of the command center. There was one possibility for them, he said, because the road was still open just south of Nikolajewka. He pointed to it on the map. That was where they were headed. They had to move out quickly and had to keep lines intact. They were the only troops left from the Montenegro now, and their only hope of survival was to stay together.

The Tridentina Division moved swiftly to the west, sweeping through minor skirmishes along the way until they reached the Waluiki - Nikolajewka railroad ten days later. They found the entire area occupied by well-equipped Russian troops. If the Alpini were unable to break through they would be trapped. Prospects looked grim: the most direct route to the west led straight into the strength of the Russian position, and the Russian line of defense followed the railway along a north-south ridge, overlooking a broad valley that the Alpini would have to cross. Mortars, field artillery and rifle fire could rake the area.

The Alpini commanders discussed alternatives and finally decided to make what would appear to be a frontal assault, hoping to draw troops away from adjacent areas. At the same time they sent a strong detachment to the north, with orders to break through and attack the Russian flank.

On command, the Alpini troops poured into the valley, taking cover wherever they could, in craters, behind fences, tree stumps or their comrades' bodies. On the left flank, the Verona battalion flung itself time and again against the deadly

Russian fire. They were supported in the center by units from Vestone, Val Chiese and Val Camonica. Only twenty-three of the two hundred forty Alpini from Verona survived. The tide of the battle turned when General Reverberi leaped on a truck and exhorted the battalion from Edolo: "Tridentina avanti!" ("Charge, men of Tridentina!").

On the right, the men from Edolo, together with Dario, David and all of the Montenegro survivors, plunged through the snow toward the shallow valley and began fighting their way forward. They were surrounded by the sounds and smells of battle: brilliant flashes of mortar explosions, whining of artillery shells, firing of their own rifles, shouting of men, cries of pain, smell of gunpowder. The earth trembled as the artillery barrage continued.

Everywhere Dario looked he saw gaping holes in the turf, men moving forward, bodies here and there. Somehow, he and his men made it across the valley, and now were nearing the breastworks. Just then, he heard a tremendous explosion and everything went blank. A mortar shell had hit so close that the force of the explosion had lifted him into the air and flung him aside like a rag doll. He lay unconscious against the stump of a tree, next to other comrades who had died in the initial attack.

In the confusion, the two friends lost sight of each other. David was behind Dario, advancing with Enzo. When he reached the tree stump, he took cover behind it and started reloading his rifle. When he heard a groan from one of the bodies nearby, he reached out and turned it over. It was Dario. He was barely conscious, and he winced in pain again when David moved him. His cheeks and nose already looked pale and possibly frostbitten, and one leg was covered with blood.

David wrapped his own scarf around Dario's face to protect it from the cold, then leaned down and spoke softly: "Dario? It's David."

Dario felt that he was being moved, and suddenly felt cold. When he heard David's voice, he opened his eyes slightly. David's words seemed to come to him out of a mist. Finally, he was able to make out his friend, who was leaning over him. When he tried to move, his legs would not respond.

David took coats from two bodies nearby and carefully worked the coats under Dario so that he was protected from the snow. "Don't worry. We'll get you out. Hang on while I get help."

Dario nodded.

"Enzo!" David called out to his burly master sergeant who had found cover nearby in a mortar crater. He motioned for Enzo to come. "Dario's hit!"

The two inspected Dario's leg more closely. Bleeding had pretty much stopped, but from the way Dario reacted, they decided that his leg probably was broken below the knee. Since it appeared that the broken bone was still aligned, all they did was immobilize the leg. Working quickly, David broke a ski pole, placed one half on either side of the leg and secured everything with strips of cloth.

"You'll be all right now, *amis*," he said, leaning over Dario.

"Don't bother with me. Go on with the men."

"Not a chance. We stick together, no matter what."

Dario smiled wanly. He knew better than to argue once David had decided something had to be done.

Suddenly, up ahead, they heard volleys of rifle fire and shouts. Alpini had penetrated to the north and were beginning a deadly flank attack on the Russian positions. Soon the Russian line wavered and began to drop back. The retreat became a general rout. After ten bloody hours, the Alpini finally dislodged the Russians, capturing much-needed materiel and equipment that the Russians had abandoned in their flight. Carrying their wounded, the weary Italian troops poured through to the west. David and Enzo carried Dario up the hillside between them and stopped when they reached the railroad. There they managed to rig a makeshift sled for Dario. For the next weeks, until Dario was able to hobble along on crutches, Enzo and the other Alpini took turns pulling his sled across the snow.

The Tridentina Division had escaped from the Russian trap but the other Alpini divisions were not so fortunate. Without radio communications, the divisions from Cuneo, Giulia and Vicenza had followed old orders and found themselves surrounded by Russian units. After heavy casualties, they were forced to surrender.

For the next two months, the Russians continued to batter the retreating army. David and what was left of his unit harassed the Russian troops along the lines, often fighting by themselves. The Alpini were the only Italian troops reasonably well prepared for the Russian winter, with skis and clothing specially designed for cold weather warfare.

The Russian campaign was tragic for the Alpini: of the more than 57,000 men sent to the Eastern Front, only 16,000 came back in 1943.

After their return to Italy, the two friends were separated. Dario remained in Italy to recover and was assigned to general staff, and David was sent to northern Yugoslavia to train Italian Army regulars in mountain combat and survival.

They did not see one another again until 1944.

*Ljubljana, Yugoslavia*
*September 8, 1943*

David and a small unit of handpicked Alpini from Valle d'Aosta had been stationed at a camp on the outskirts of Ljubljana for four months. They had established a regular routine and now their training of the regulars was proceeding tine and now their training of the regulars was proceeding smoothly. David was in his office going over reports and enjoying the cool autumn breeze. A reddish sunset lingered in the west. As he reached over to turn on his reading lamp, the outer door opened and Enzo, his top sergeant, burst in without knocking and handed him a piece of paper.

"Sorry to barge in, Sir, but we just got this on the radio."

David read the hastily written message. It was an announcement by Prime Minister Badoglio:

> *The Italian Government, having recognized the impossibility of continuing the unequal struggle against overwhelming enemy power, with the object of sparing the nation any further and graver disaster, has asked General Eisenhower, Supreme Allied Commander of the Allied Anglo-American forces, for an armistice. This request has been granted. Consequently, all acts of hostility against the Anglo-American forces on the part of the Italian forces shall cease.*

David saw immediately that he and his men would have to leave. There was no time to lose. Now the Germans as well as the partisans would be hunting them. He asked Enzo to round up the troops and get ready to move out at once, with as much equipment and food as the men and their best mules could carry.

The armistice spelled disaster for almost four million Italian soldiers in German-occupied territory. They were left with three alternatives: surrender, desert or resist. Some, such as the garrisons at Savona, Corfu and Kefallinia (Cephalonia) fought bravely against the Germans, but they were completely outnumbered and overrun. The survivors were executed. Within 48 hours, the entire Italian land forces were decimated. Over 500,000 troops were shipped to German prisons and work camps. Thousands fled to the hills. The many thousands of Italian troops in Yugoslavia, Greece and Albania were placed in an untenable position. For most of them, the armistice was their death sentence. They were caught between the Germans and the partisans. Rommel moved in extra German troops around Trieste to seal off the border with Yugoslavia.

David called in Roberto, his lieutenant, and showed him the message from the Prime Minister, almost certain what the younger man's reaction would be.

Roberto read it quickly and said, without hesitation: "Let's get the hell out of here. I'm for trying to get back home."

"Exactly what I thought," David added. He spread out the local area map on the desk and pointed to a spot just northwest of Ljubljana. Tracing a route with his finger, he said, "Here we are. We'll have to head west eventually, but first I think we ought to go north to this range of hills and regroup."

Roberto thought they ought to take the most direct route, but David was cautious. He knew that the Germans would also be retreating to the north, so low-lying areas would be dangerous. With Germans concentrated in and around Trieste, the Alpini would have to sweep around it, holding to the high ground. To avoid the risk of losing any of his men, David wanted to take an indirect route, following the ridges. But he did not force his view on Roberto. He listened carefully while the younger man explained what he would do, and only then said why he felt the route to Bretto would be safer.

Together, they studied the map, and David pointed out the route he wanted to take to reach the Predil Pass. It would take longer, he said, but it would give them a better chance of avoiding the Germans. Once they reached the Pass, the rest would be easy. Roberto nodded in agreement.

Just then, heavy footsteps announced that Enzo had returned. His broad shoulders filled the doorway. Raising his hand in a semblance of a salute, he announced that the men were gathered outside. David addressed his troops from the steps of the barracks. It was dark. Standing with the light from the windows behind him, he could make out faces in the first two rows. He spoke slowly, and his voice was grave as he announced that the Italian Government had reached an armistice with the Allies.

The men started talking, and David raised his hand for quiet. "We don't have any orders, but it's obvious we can't stay here. It's not safe. The Lieutenant and I have decided we should pull out right away and head for home."

Some of the men started to cheer, but David held up his hand again and continued. What they were going to try to do, he explained, would not be easy. They would have to stay together, which meant that they would have to leave wounded behind until they reached Italy. The next two days would be hardest, because they would have to make a forced march to their first camp. Any of the regulars who were not in good shape would have to press to keep up. Anyone who was not in the Alpini unit had to decide whether to stay or come along with him. David stressed again that once they started they would stay as a unit until they were safely over the border. Only dead men would be left behind.

"Our only real enemy now is Germany. Since we'll only be carrying enough ammunition for defense we'll only attack if we can take a small unit by surprise. We'll try our best to avoid the Yugoslav partisans." He paused. "I expect the best from you—and then some. I know I won't be disappointed."

Enzo organized the troops' withdrawal, selecting only as much food and necessary supplies as the men and mules could carry, along with skis and snow gear, ammunition and grenades. As he reported to David that the men were ready, Roberto joined them.

"I don't know about those regulars who are coming with us. They're mostly recruits. How're they going to keep up with us?"

"Not much choice," David said firmly. "If they don't, our whole outfit will be in danger. We've got to move as fast as we can to get to the grouping point." He turned to Enzo, "And you, Toro. What do you think?" David had unshakable faith in his sergeant.

"No problem," Enzo said after pondering David's question a while. "Push like hell. Get there in two days. No more."

As David and his men reached the hills north of their camp, a squadron of Stuka dive bombers passed low overhead, heading for the camp. They turned and followed its flight. Soon white clouds erupted among the buildings and some seconds later they heard the dull sounds of the explosions. In the course of a few minutes, the camp was reduced to burning rubble. All that day, they could see smoke rising and spreading behind them as they made their way through the hills.

David and Roberto led their men toward Passo di Predil, near the Austrian border, staying near the ridges and avoiding open areas. Progress was slow. Five days after they started north, they heard another broadcast from Prime Minister Badoglio, this time instructing all Italian troops to begin fighting the Germans:

> *Take to the hills, cut the German communications, blow up his supply dumps, throw yourselves against German equipment and personnel. Above all, do not give up your arms....*

Enzo snorted: "Now the old fart tells us!"

David increased their daily mileage, wanting to get back to Italy as soon as possible. Several times, because of the inexperience of the regulars, his unit was almost detected, but narrowly escaped. Working closely with the crack Alpini, however, and under Enzo's not-so-gentle prodding, the regulars quickly learned. Eventually, the unit began to function to Enzo's satisfaction. Twice they were able to surprise and destroy German patrols. When their food began to run low, they overran a small German company and replenished their supplies. Finally, they reached the Italian border.

David called the men together. "Well," he announced, "This is it. That town over there is Bretto di sopra. We're home" He stood for several moments, silent, his hands behind his back, scanning the faces before him. "I want to thank each of you for your loyalty and bravery. You can go wherever you want now, but be careful. They say that the Krauts are rounding up men and shipping them up to Germany to work in labor camps. And watch out for Fascist spies. They're all around. As for me, I'm pushing on west toward Piemonte. If you want to come along, fine. Otherwise, this is where we split up. Sergeant Santucci will divide equipment and supplies tomorrow morning."

The entire Alpini unit, and all but five of the regulars, elected to continue west with David.

The next morning was damp and cold. David and Roberto sat by the campfire, studying their map. They decided to head north along the Tagliamento River after crossing the Predil Pass, then cross the Mauria Pass to the town of Pieve de Cadora. From there, they would stay in the high country and cross the Bolzano road at Barbiano. They were headed for rugged terrain, and would have to stay just below the ridgelines to avoid being spotted. David was concerned, and he went to speak with Enzo, who was currying his mule. He reviewed the situation, and asked Enzo to remind the men to check all their own equipment. The trail ahead would be difficult for the men and the mules. Then he came to what was really on his mind. He was worried about the five regulars who were leaving, and he wanted them to have some rations and whatever equipment Enzo thought could be spared. But he had a favor to ask. He wanted Enzo to stay with them and delay their departure for a few days so that the main unit would have a head start. He didn't want the five to know what route he was taking, because they might be caught.

"Who knows what they might tell the Germans if the SS questions them."

Enzo nodded.

"So, give them a map. If they can get by the Germans around Trieste, maybe they can make it down to - where was it they're from?"

"Modena," Enzo said, rubbing the back of his neck. "I don't know how they're going to get across the Po Valley. Maybe they'll make it."

David started leaving, then turned back. "And Enzo - no mules."

Enzo gave a half salute and started to leave. As he turned away, his mule nipped at his shirt and began tugging it. He disengaged himself with a laugh and scratched behind the mule's ear *Those guys wouldn't know how to take care of a mule, anyway.*

In mountain warfare, the Alpini would be lost without their beloved mules. Sure-footed, strong and patient, and far more intelligent than horses, mules occupied a special place in Alpini history and tradition. They became pets. It was said that an Alpini spent so much time with his mule that he would tell it things that he would not even tell his wife.

It was almost noon when Enzo announced that all of the men were ready to move out. David took the point, with Roberto by the regulars. David waved to Enzo. "Take care, *amis*."

"*Ciao, Capitano.*" To Enzo, David was always Captain, whatever his rank. 'I'll catch up with you in a week."


No one was surprised when Enzo strode casually into camp on the sixth day. It was late in the evening. Without a word, he walked over to the fire and began warming his hands.

One of the Alpini came alongside him. "What took you so long, Toro? We've been waiting here three days for you."

A hint of a smile worked at the corners of Enzo's mouth. "Damn lucky for me you waited. If I'd started yesterday instead of this morning, I'd have passed you."

David came over and clapped the sergeant's massive shoulder. "Everything go all right back there?" he asked softly.

Enzo nodded. "No problem."

David and his unit struggled for more than a month to reach Barbiano. In the mountain passes, night temperatures plunged below freezing. Heavy frost coated their packs each morning. The weather was crisp and clear most of the time, with only a few days of freezing rain and snow. The unit followed old trails through the woods, and skirted the edges of high summer pastures, making painfully slow progress. What appeared on the map like a straight distance of five kilometers became fifteen or more kilometers of walking and climbing, as they traversed the steep slopes between the ridges, picking their way cautiously among the boulders in the mountain streams.

Along their way, they met several Italian partisan groups, most of which were disorganized and ineffective, without supplies or discipline. They were made up largely of left-wing dissidents and soldiers who had fled to the hills to escape being drafted for Nazi labor camps. Escaped convicts and other social detritus also found their way into the partisan movement.

Finally, the Alpini neared the Bolzano road. David, Roberto and Enzo stood on the heights looking toward Barbiano. The lights of the town twinkled in the cold night air. They decided to head west right away, avoiding the troop concentrations around the German headquarters at Bolzano. Still following the ridges, they came to the Talfer River and headed for the Adige River, near the little town of Vilpiano.

# CHAPTER FIVE

*Vilpiano*
*November 5, 1943*

A leaden sky hung over the hills. A light mist was falling. David and his men had reached a high plateau above Vilpiano, overlooking the valley of the Adige. Below them, pastures lay in patchwork patterns among the evergreens, dotted here and there with large boulders. Orchards and vineyards crawled up the lower slopes and covered the valley floor as far as they could see. In the summer, when the apple trees blossomed, the valley would turn into a sea of white.

"Which side of the valley should we take?" Roberto asked.

Enzo, who knew the area, did not hesitate. "West side's best," he pronounced. There would not be as much sunlight as on the east side, but the slope would be easier.

The three decided to go further downhill to find the best place to cross the river. As they passed along the edge of the woods, they were spotted by a Fascist agent, who reported them to the local SS commander. A patrol was sent to intercept them.

The Alpini were returning to the unit when Roberto noticed a truck ahead of them, parked by a low stone wall that ran along a hillside pasture to their right. He was suspicious. "Wait!" he said, motioning the others to stop. "See that truck up ahead? Can you see anything along the wall? It looks like..."

Enzo noticed men crouched behind the truck. Yelling 'Ambush!', he scrambled over the wall and started running up the hill. The others were close behind.

The German patrol, taken by surprise, started firing late. The three zigzagged up the field, taking advantage of boulders when they could, heading for the woods above. When the Germans started to climb over the wall to follow, Roberto stopped, turned and dropped one of them with a single shot. The others hesitated, two of them fired wildly and then all crouched back behind the wall again. By this time, the runners had reached a clump of trees in among several boulders.

"Open fire on my signal," David called out in a low voice. "Head for the other clump of trees farther up the hill - and keep moving. Ready?"

Enzo answered, but not Roberto.

"I think he was hit," Enzo said.

"Cover me." David started crawling back to where Roberto had stopped.

Enzo took careful aim, sending bullets ricocheting off the top of the wall below and keeping the Germans pinned behind it. David crawled downhill to a small tree, where he found Roberto sprawled on his back, his head resting in a pool of blood. A slug had caught him behind the ear and blown part of his skull away. Seizing Roberto's packstrap, David began dragging the body uphill. Enzo kept shooting at the wall while David dragged Roberto's body and rifle up behind a boulder and placed them at the base of a bush on its uphill side. After taking Roberto's remaining ammunition and emptying his pockets, David covered the body with leaves and dirt as well as he could.

"We'll be back for you," he whispered, crossing himself.

On David's signal, both shot a few rounds at the wall and then began racing uphill again, and were just able to reach a higher clump of trees before the Germans resumed fire. A hail of bullets ripped bark from the trees and sent chips flying from the rocks nearby. David looked up toward the woods. *Still about one hundred meters to go.* The gunfire grew sporadic and stopped altogether as David and Enzo wounded two more of the Germans when they came from behind the wall and tried to run up the field. Then some of the Germans ran along the wall and started up the hill out of range. They were trying to cut off the Alpini.

"Let's go!" David cried.

They started a last, headlong dash to the woods. The Germans yelled to one another and began running up the hill after them, firing wildly. Just as David entered the safety of the woods, he was spun halfway around, as if he had been kicked in the leg. He fell to his knees, then rose and continued running, gritting his teeth against the pain. After several minutes, he realized that his right trouser was warm with blood and he stopped. Enzo, who had run ahead, came back to see what was wrong.

"Can't make it," David said as he began twisting his belt around his thigh to stop the flow of blood.

Enzo saw immediately that he had to get David into shelter. Ignoring David's protests, he lifted him onto his back. "I saw a barn up ahead. I'll take you there," he said. He walked and half-ran, and after about two hundred yards, on the far side of the woods, they came to a small pasture bordered by a stone fence and stretching uphill to a stone barn. Beyond the barn and on three sides of the field were more woods. Enzo followed the wall until he came to the barn. It was beginning to snow. Opening the large wooden door, he went inside. Freshly dried hay, stacked from floor to ceiling along the wall to his left, filled more than half of the barn. A waist-high fence that ran the length of the barn held back the hay and formed a narrow aisle between the hay and the south, or downhill, wall, where there were two large shuttered windows. Enzo lifted David over the fence and laid him gently on a mound of hay near the fence. Working rapidly, he placed David's left hand over the wound and tightened David's belt around his thigh and over the hand to put pressure against the bleeding area. Then he covered David with a thick layer of hay for warmth. David was barely conscious at this point.

"Keep your hand there," Enzo told him, "but don't cut off all circulation. I'll be back later." He had to draw the German patrol away from the barn.

David mumbled a reply. In a few minutes he heard an exchange of gunfire in the distance, and then silence. He closed his eyes.

Shortly before dark he was wakened by the sound of the barn door opening and closing. Thinking it was Enzo, he raised his head to look. A young girl was leaning with her back against the door, her eyes closed and her chest heaving as she caught her breath. Her face was smudged and her jacket torn. Soon she relaxed, took a deep breath and brushed wisps of blonde hair from her forehead. Reaching under a shelf nearby, she took out a wooden bucket and put it upside down by the wall to stand on while she looked outside through a large crack in one of the shutters.

Seeing no one, she stepped down, and as she turned to replace the bucket she noticed David looking at her. Surprised, she stepped back against the door, prepared to run. She wanted to scream, but fought the impulse and said nothing.

"It's all right," David whispered quickly, trying to reassure her. "I'm not going to hurt you."

She noticed his uniform, saw that it was not German, and relaxed somewhat, but remained with her back pressed against the door, still mistrustful.

David smiled at her. "There's nothing to be afraid of. I promise." He asked what had happened.

David's voice calmed her, and she released her grip on the door handle. She said that one of the Germans from the patrol had seen her walking through the pasture near the road and stopped her for questioning. When she saw that he was looking at her strangely, she became frightened and backed away. He grabbed her wrist, but she broke loose and started running up the hill toward the woods. The soldier followed but she easily outdistanced him and reached the woods, where she ran for a while and then hid among some bushes. As soon as she was certain that no one could see her, she made her way to the barn.

"This barn," David asked, motioning with his head, "is it yours?"

She shook her head. "It's my uncle's. We keep hay here for our cattle."

David shifted his weight and the pain made him groan slightly.

"You're hurt!" she said, coming closer. "Let me help you." When she noticed blood oozing slowly from between David's fingers, she stiffened and drew in her breath. "Oooh ... I'll have to get some water and take care of that."

In minutes she returned with a bucket of ice cold spring water. David could see that she had also washed her face, and her skin gleamed. When she sat beside him, he lifted her chin with his free hand. Her skin was soft and warm to his touch. "Hmmm," he said, "Much better. Now I can see how pretty you are."

She turned away to hide the flush that came to her cheeks. The touch of his fingers had made the hair on the back of her neck rise.

David began to feel faint and he lay back again, and she turned to look down at him. She had deep blue eyes, delicate and regular features and full, red lips. Her chin had a slight cleft, almost a dimple. The cornsilk-blonde hair that framed her face with soft curls was loosely braided in back. *What a beauty she'll be*, he thought as he began to lose consciousness.

The girl quickly tore open David's trouser leg up to his thigh. As she moved his hand away from the wound, blood began oozing out again, and she tore strips of cloth from her slip and used them to hold down a compress that she made from a rag that she filled with hay. She kept her hand on the bandage to maintain pressure. Raised on a farm, the girl was used to caring for cuts and injuries, and she worked quickly and surely. It was not until several minutes later that she realized that her hand was resting on the inside of David's thigh. She was no stranger to sexual behavior; sex was just another natural process, and a normal part of farm life. After all, she had seen a bull mount their cows and had watched other animals copulate. But as she sat there looking at her hand on David's thigh, she felt a strange stirring deep inside. She had never been this close to a man before.

For more than an hour she sat by David, keeping her hand on his wound, looking at him, wondering what sort of person he was. *Educated, certainly - and gentle*, she thought. His voice had been soft, and his eyes warm. Finally, she too fell asleep.

When David came to, it was morning. He could see shafts of sunlight streaming in through the gaps in the wooden shutters. His leg throbbed. Looking down, he saw his torn trouser and the heavy bandage around his thigh. The girl was sitting cross-legged on the hay, looking over at him. When she spoke, there was laughter and music in her voice. He recognized immediately the Tyrolean accent. When she smiled, her eyes sparkled and her nose wrinkled slightly.

"You slept well, soldier."

"Thanks for taking such good care of me," he said, returning her smile. He was struck by how soft and melodic she made the words sound, with none of the usual Germanic raspiness. Her name was Elena. She and her brother were living with their aunt and uncle.

"You were still bleeding," she said. "I put on a tight compress, but that leg looks bad. I'll have to go down to fetch our doctor."

David was too weak to object. Elena handed him some bread and cheese from her rucksack and turned to leave. At the door she turned. "Oh, a man came to see you last night. He said his name was Enzo and he told me to tell you that the men are safe and that Roberto sleeps well. They're waiting for you."

Later that morning Elena returned, along with a little old man clutching a brown leather medical kit. She introduced the family doctor, who was from the nearby town of Vilpiano. The doctor wasted no time talking. He checked David's wound, took out his instruments, and put David to sleep. As soon as the anesthetic took effect, he cut into the inside of David's right thigh and sutured the femoral artery. David was coming to as the doctor finished the dressing and bandage.

The doctor straightened up, removed his metal-rimmed glasses and looked closely at David. "You're damned lucky, my friend," he said, and explained that the bullet had missed David's femur by a fraction of an inch, and just grazed the artery. His running had caused the artery to rupture. "Without pressure on that wound, you'd have bled to death. This girl saved your life."

David nodded and smiled at Elena. He was eager to catch up with his men and wondered how soon he could walk. The doctor said that the earliest would be after a week, maybe ten days. It was best not to risk re-opening the wound. He would leave some fresh bandages and blankets.

As he prepared to go, he wished David good luck and added: "I guess I don't have to tell you to be careful around here. The place is crawling with *Fascisti*."

"I hope this isn't going to get you into trouble," David said.

"I'm an old man," the doctor replied, shrugging his narrow shoulders. "I've just done what I could to help another human being. If the Germans find out and want to shoot me for it, I could care less. I've already made my peace with God."

After the doctor left, David asked Elena to take a message to his unit. He wanted Enzo to bring his pack and skis to the barn that night, and he tried to give her directions.

"I know every bush around here," she said, proudly, standing up straight. "I'll find them." She bounded out of the door. In less than an hour, she was back. Enzo would come after dark, she announced. Then she left, because her aunt and uncle were expecting her.

When Enzo arrived, he opened the door quietly, turned on his flashlight and went over to David and looked closely at him. "You look like hell, sir. How d'you feel?"

"Better," David said, wincing as he shifted his body. But he wouldn't be able to walk for at least a week, and Enzo and the men couldn't wait that long. They had to keep going. Enzo nodded in agreement. He knew as well as David did that they had to leave right away. Before long, the Stelvio Pass would be completely snowed in.

"If you can spare me a mule," David said, "it'd help a lot. I'll try to catch up with you."

"I'll bring you Clara."

David knew how difficult it was for Enzo to part with Clara, a strong, sure-footed and affectionate animal that had become like a pet for him. David promised to take care of her. "And thanks for taking care of Roberto," he said, handing him the identification and other papers he had removed from Roberto's pockets. "When you see his family, tell them how sorry I am. He and I grew up together." He paused. "If I don't catch up with you, tell my family I'm on my way."

Enzo's grunt meant 'yes.' He saluted and left.

Elena watched over David during the next days, changing his bandage, bringing him food and generally fussing over him. She was obviously infatuated, and too inexperienced to mask her feelings. She came to sit by him and talk as often as she could. Knowing that he would be leaving soon, she treasured every minute they were together. She would find excuses to touch him, and then turn away, blushing, when he saw her looking at him. A shy girl, Elena would have been deeply shocked and hurt if anyone had suggested that she was flirting.

David tried not to encourage Elena's interest, but he was flattered by it and frankly enjoyed her company more and more. He looked forward to her visits, and felt strongly attracted to her in spite of himself. Disarmingly unaware of her unspoiled beauty, Elena was like no other woman he had ever known, and certainly not like Mariana DeLuca, the girl that everyone in San Nicola assumed he would marry. Mariana was well aware of her aristocratic beauty; she knew that the designer clothes made specially for her in Milano were stunning; and she was coolly conscious of how to use her looks to get what she wanted. David looked at Elena: sitting there in the barn, wearing a blouse that she had made for herself, an old skirt and a heavy worn jacket; with absolutely no makeup; and a shaft of sunlight playing on her loosely braided hair. She was more than a match for Mariana.

But David had no intention of trying to make a conquest of this vulnerable young creature. He looked closely at Elena as she busied herself with their food. *How old can she be?* He wondered. *Not much more than seventeen, probably.* She was tall, but her skin was as smooth and clear as a child's. He already knew that she was well on the way to being a generously endowed woman. On the second day, when he was still very weak and she helped him shift places, his head was resting on her chest, and when he turned to say something, his cheek had pressed against a full breast, and he could feel its sweet warmth. She had started a bit, but had not moved away.

The two spent hours talking together; Elena wanted to know everything about him, and bombarded him with questions. When he told her about his family and their yearly trips to England to visit his father's law clients, she insisted that he mention every place they had stopped on each trip, what they had eaten, what they had done and what the people looked like. Where his memory failed to come up with details, David invented.

"And where did you go with the Army?" she asked.

"Army?" he said in mock anger. "Did you say army? That's a dirty word with us. We're the Alpini, and we think we're special. You've seen the Alpini, haven't you? They wear caps like this, with an eagle feather," he said, looking around in the hay until he found his battered cap. He held it lovingly, and tried to straighten the feather that was attached on the left side, just in front of the wide upturned rear brim, but it sagged weakly to one side. "I'll have to find a new feather somewhere," he sighed. "This one's from a crow instead of an eagle, but I'll even dye a chicken feather if I have to."

"I saw some Alpini marching once in a parade," she said, wanting to show interest so he would continue talking. "The officers were all in black. They had colored sashes and all."

"That's us," he said proudly. "And the Montenegro were special."

He explained how his battalion had been recruited from the small towns in Valle d'Aosta, where the Alpini had their training school for mountain warfare. "You know how you yell 'track!' when you're skiing downhill and you want someone to get out of your way? Well, that's our motto: *Make way for the Montenegro!*"

They both laughed.

Elena asked about Russia, and David told her about how his unit almost got trapped on the Eastern Front.

"It must've been awfully cold," she volunteered.

He groaned. "Cold? You wouldn't believe how cold it was. Winter here's like spring compared to what we had. Machine guns wouldn't work unless we built fires under them. It was the same thing with our trucks. The grease and oil froze solid. Nothing moved." His voice dropped almost to a whisper. "The ones who didn't make it either froze to death or were killed. The ones with the worst luck were captured by the Russians." He fell silent, holding his cap and slowly folding the brim up and down. He was thinking of all the friends he would never see again.

After four more days of Elena's care and plenty of rest and food, David felt his strength returning. His leg was still stiff, but at least it no longer throbbed. He was in good spirits. Elena came in with warm food for breakfast and sat down next to him in the hay to watch him as he ate. She had loosened her braids and her hair spilled down over her shoulders. He reached over, brushed a stray lock away from her forehead and let his fingers linger on her cheek, looking at her with frank admiration. Elena felt her skin tingle at his touch. Finishing his food, he put the tray aside and moved so he was sitting next to her. He put his arm around her shoulder and drew her close.

"Elena," he said, looking at her as she averted her eyes slightly, "you've been so good to me. I can't tell you how much I've enjoyed being with you. I have to leave soon, and I'm going to miss you."

With his other hand he touched her cheek and turned her head so they were facing one another. Her eyes were still downcast. She was too shy to look directly at him. He kissed her cheek lightly, then her ear. Finally, pulling her gently with him onto the hay, he cradling her face in his hands and kissed her full on the mouth—a long, lingering kiss—and felt the soft pressure of her strong young body. More kisses followed.

Exercising more self-control than he thought he possessed, David slowly drew away from her. He realized that if he did not stop now he might not be able to, and he would never forgive himself if he took advantage of Elena like this.

"No, Elena," he whispered. "We can't."

Her cheeks were flushed and her eyes looked frantic and confused. Pulling herself free, she dashed out of the barn sobbing. David waited. Evening came, and when Elena still had not returned he grew apprehensive. Struggling to his feet, he limped to the wooden door and peered through the cracks to see whether she was coming. *She's never been this late before*. His mule pressed her muzzle against his thigh, and David turned.

"Well, Clara," he murmured as he stroked the mule's neck,

"at least you're here to keep me company. Maybe I can find some scraps of food, too." He took a few steps, then began to feel dizzy, and lay down again. Within minutes, he was sound asleep.

The creaking of the door wakened him. It was morning, and Elena was standing in the doorway, hesitating.

"Come over here," he said. "I've been worried about you."

She brought his breakfast to him, but moved away as soon as she put it down and kept her eyes down or turned her head to one side so as not to look at him. David called her back. She came reluctantly, still looking down. When he lifted her chin gently, she kept her eyes closed, unable to look into his eyes.

Acting on a sudden impulse, David hugged her. "Elena, Elena! What a sweet and absolutely wonderful person you are! Don't even think about yesterday. It never happened."

She rested her head on his shoulder, but said nothing. After a while, he asked, softly, "Everything all right now? Smiling again?"

He felt her head nod slowly.

"Then let's eat!"

Soon, Elena was her usual bubbly self. But she did not sit near him on the hay again.

Several days later, David began making preparations to leave. He was already almost two weeks behind his unit. Although his leg still twinged when he put his weight on it, he thought it was strong enough to walk on. He asked Elena to bring him some extra food for the trail. When she returned, she was wearing heavy trousers and hiking boots, with her braids tucked under a large knitted cap. She carried a small rucksack.

"And just where do you think you're going?" he asked, taking off her cap.

"With you," she said, as if that resolved everything.

"Impossible," he sputtered. "Much too dangerous. You know what'd happen if we were caught."

"Let me come," she pleaded. "I can help—you know I can help. I know the whole countryside around here, all the way to the Alps. Please, let me come along."

David thought about it. *She's right, of course. I do need a guide. My maps are not detailed enough.* After reflecting a while, he tried to look stern as he said, "All right. But if we run into any problem, you do exactly what I tell you. No questions. Understand?"

She nodded vigorously, her curls bouncing.

He tossed her cap back and tried to keep his voice stern. "And for God's sake, get that hair of yours tucked away and keep it there, and keep that jacket buttoned, too! If we meet any partisans, I don't want them to get any ideas. We've got enough problems as it is."

She laughed and kissed him on the cheek. He shook his head in resignation.

They moved out that afternoon, with Elena leading. At her suggestion, they moved into the hills, following the course of the Adige upstream, and then headed toward the Stelvio Pass. Elena, toughened by farm work and an active outdoor life, forced the pace, striding smoothly along wooded paths, leaping nimbly among the rocks. Several times while David rested she went down into little hamlets to buy food or ask about German troops. David hobbled behind at first, but his leg improved rapidly. By the third day, they walked side by side, with Elena holding Clara's reins. When they neared Trafoi, close to the Pass, David stopped. From that point, the trail would go into the high country and above the timberline.

"I'm sorry, Elena, but this is as far as you can go. Clara can't make it in the deep snow, and I don't dare take you along. You'll have to turn back now."

Her face clouded and her lip trembled slightly. She was on

the verge of tears. David took her hands in his and looked at her, groping for words. They did not come to him easily. By nature David was not demonstrative, and not comfortable talking about his feelings. But he had to tell Elena how much she meant to him. He wanted to be with her, even though his rational self told him that he must return to his family.

He was surprised at how difficult it was to leave her, and even more surprised to hear himself say, "I have to tell you something, Elena, and I wish I could say it better." He paused. "During these days we've been together, you've become so much a part of me that I can't imagine being without you. Now wherever I go, you'll be there with me. I'll see your smile and hear your laughter, and I'll be happy. And you'll be with me in my dreams, too." After a pause, he continued. "I love you. Very much."

Surprised and overwhelmed by what David had said, she threw her arms around his neck and leaned against him. For several moments she stood in silent disbelief. She had been hopelessly in love with him almost from the first time she looked at him, but he had never given her any indication that he regarded her as anything but a friendly companion. Sensitive to the many differences between them, she had regarded David as a kind of distant and unattainable goal—a mountain that she could look at but never climb. She could hardly believe this was happening.

Drawing her head back to look at him, she held his cheeks with her hands and laughed out loud. "You make me so happy!" Then she kissed him fiercely.

It was time for David to leave, and he reluctantly took her hands in his and withdrew slightly.

"I'll be thinking of you always," she said, tears welling in her eyes. "You'll come back, won't you?"

"I promise." He removed his gold signet ring bearing the Della Croce coat of arms and placed it in her hand, closing her fingers over it. "This was my grandfather's. I want you to keep it for me. I'll come back for it."

She clutched it to her bosom and watched silently as he put on his pack and started toward the distant peaks. They waved once to one another. Through her tears Elena caught glimpses of him between the trees as he climbed up the slope, and then he was gone.

# CHAPTER SIX

*Near Trafoi,*
*Heading south to the Stelvio Pass*

The next time David looked back, Elena was already lost to view among the trees. He climbed slowly and steadily at first, conserving energy and stopping every few minutes to rest his leg. Soon he came to the trail that Enzo had taken, and started following it, keeping his head down, concentrating on the trail signs. Stopping at the edge of a barren stretch, he watched the late afternoon sun play on the mountain peaks of the Ortles range. He took off his pack and waited for the sun to set further, so that he would be in shadow as he crossed the open area. Unstrapping his skis from the pack, he waxed them, tested the bindings and then reattached them to his pack, keeping the poles to use for support.

He gritted his teeth as he swung the pack onto his back again, and cursed his sore leg. *Now don't get lazy*, he chided himself as he resumed the climb, detouring around places where rock slides had carried away the trees. From the ashes of a group of small fires built behind some rocks, he could see that Enzo and his unit had come this way. When he finally reached an area covered with snow, he stopped again and took off his pack, breathing heavily, partly from the exertion and partly from the altitude. His shoulders were grateful for the respite. He took out his white windbreaker outfit and put it on quickly, then slipped his boots into the ski bindings, setting the cables for cross-country skiing by lifting them out from under the hooks on the sides of the skis, and prepared for the hardest part of his climb.

*It's great to be back on skis*, he thought as he started off along the trail, which was still faintly visible. He moved smoothly, traversing the snowy slope but climbing steadily. The skis made a soft swishing sound as they glided on the slightly crusted surface, which was covered with a shallow layer of powder snow. David's long strides were helped by powerful arms that kept steady pressure on the poles. The sun was setting rapidly now, and the air was turning cold, but drops of perspiration gathered on his brow from the exertion, and he unbuttoned his jacket to avoid getting overheated. When he stopped to rest his leg, his muscles tingled and he could feel his heart pounding. He looked around; in all directions the view was awe-inspiring. Ahead of him, to the west, the sun was a red-orange ball sinking behind the mountains that stretched out to the horizon. The upper slopes of the peaks behind him were bathed in sunset colors, and the rest were dark and brooding. Below, in the valleys, darkness had already fallen and he could see tiny lights in houses here and there. He inhaled deeply of the crisp, fresh air, feeling a rush of strength. The silence was complete; the only sound he heard was the rustle of his own clothing. He felt like an ancient monarch, surveying a deserted mountain kingdom.

The moment passed, and David resumed his climb. As the sun dipped lower, the wind began to rise, and after another hour he was forced to stop. In the gathering darkness, he could no longer follow the trail. Looking around, he found a large boulder and took shelter on its lee side, where he made the framework of a small lean-to, using his skis and poles, and attached his light tarpaulin on the outside. Settled in the snow, he wrapped himself in his two blankets and prodded his pack until he had a soft indentation for his head. Sleep came almost immediately.

When David peered out from under his covers the next morning, he saw only snow and gray sky. The wind was howling, and had formed a snow cave around him. Still snug and well insulated, he rummaged in his pack for a piece of the rich fruitcake that Elena had packed. The movement dislodged a handful of snow from the edge of the opening above him. It rested on the edge of his blanket and fell on his face just as he looked up.

*Time to get started*, he decided reluctantly. He shook the snow away, and in a matter of minutes was ready to leave. He swung his pack onto his shoulders, stretched a few times to relieve the aches from his lumpy 'bed', then put on his skis and set off. His eyes kept blinking as the wind whipped the snow in his face. After a few minutes he paused to take a hasty bearing, then fell into a steady pace. His skis began sinking deeply into the powder snow, forcing him almost to a walk. Each step became an effort.

As he neared the summit, the wind increased in intensity, still blowing directly into his face, and he had to lean forward to maintain balance. He could see nothing but snow in the air around him, but he was relieved, in a way, because he knew that he did not have to worry about being sighted. From this point, he began skirting the summit, and eventually reached a large level expanse. Another hasty bearing, and he set off again, making better progress now that there was no place for deep drifts and he could ski on packed snow. Heavy flakes continued to swirl around him. Off to the right, he noticed what appeared to be a tall stake and went over to see what it was. Someone had thrust a broken ski into the snow at an angle. Saying a silent thanks to Enzo, David sighted along the ski, took a bearing and headed off.

Before long, he felt the downward slope beginning, so he stopped, set his bindings for downhill and started his descent. The thick snow flurries made it difficult to see, and he had to stop frequently to check his compass and make certain that he was still following the trail taken left by his men. Even so, he moved rapidly. Soon he was below the storm, where the track was easier to follow. Looking down the slope, he was able to see clearly where his unit had gone: the trail was obvious for hundreds of meters ahead.

The temptation was too great to resist. He pushed off and bent over, crouching so that his stomach rested against his knees, tucking his poles under his arms, and aiming his skis straight down the track. Soon he was schussing at full speed. The wind clawed at his face and whipped his hood back off his head. Suddenly he felt an urge to yell. He felt like he was fifteen again, skiing in the first important downhill race he had won, when his every turn was clean and he felt as if he owned the slope. He had skied at the very limits of his control then, yet never felt out of control, even though he had been inches from falling. He felt the same way now—nothing could stop him.

He was sorry when the slope began leveling out and patches of bare ground appeared ahead, forcing him to slow down. After a few hundred meters, he removed his skis. It was unlikely that he would need them any longer, and he needed to lighten his load so he could catch up with his unit. Reluctantly, he took the skis off the trail and left them leaning against a tree where they might be seen and used by someone else. He kept his poles, however, because they were still useful, and continued on foot. By now he was well below the timberline. Looking back, he said farewell to Gran Zebrul, then headed down toward Bormio and the valley of the Adda River.

Halfway down the hill, he noticed a small ribbon tied around a tree limb, just above head height. Searching alongside the trail, he quickly spotted a sack that had been suspended from a nearby limb, and thanked Enzo again. His mouth watered as he slowly cut a thick slice of sausage, an equally thick slice of cheese, and heaped them on a fist-sized bun that he managed to slice in two. Putting the rest of the food in his pack, he pressed on.

Except for a detour to avoid the Germans at Tirano, near the Swiss border, David's trip through the valley of the Adda went smoothly. German troops seemed to be everywhere, so he walked mostly during the early morning and twilight, and ventured out during midday only if he had good cover. Each day seemed colder than the one before, and he was thankful for being on the north slope of the Valtellina, where the hillside was bathed in warm sunshine on clear days. In less than two weeks, he had reached the base of Spluga Peak, near the upper end of Lake Como, and was passing above Caspano.

It was mid-afternoon, and David was walking on a level, narrow path, just above a pasture to his left and skirting a wooded hillside to his right. An overcast sky obscured the Spluga, and he could see the first tentative flakes of a gathering snowstorm filtering through the trees onto the path. Suddenly, he stopped. Out of the corner of his eye he had caught what he thought was movement. *What was that?* Taking out his binoculars, he scanned the bushes on the hillside. Just as he was about to put them away he saw the movement again, halfway up the hill, in front of a clump of trees. Focusing closely on the bush, he saw it quiver slightly again, and he noticed a dark shape behind it. He retraced his steps on the path, back and out of sight of the hillside, then climbed up another slope in order to approach the bush from above. With his pistol drawn, he started down, creeping slowly to a point where he could see the bush. He took out his binoculars again. There was a man lying by the bush, just as he had suspected, but the man was lying on his side and had his head down, as if he were sleeping or unconscious. David approached cautiously.

The man was barely conscious, his scalp bloody and his face bruised and matted with blood. He was shivering and moaning softly. When he noticed David, he tried to speak, but his voice was a raspy whisper.

"Help me," he said in English.

David removed his pack, knelt down beside the man and spoke in English. He had not used the language in almost five years, not since his last trip to England with his family, and he groped for the correct words.

"I am . . . a friend," he said. "I will try to help. Is possible to move?"

"No," the man said, shaking his head and pointing to his right foot, "my ankle's hurt."

David removed the man's boot gingerly and inspected the ankle, which was already beginning to swell. He moved the foot gently back and forth, feeling the bones. From the man's reactions, David decided that the ankle was not broken, only badly sprained. He looked over the other wounds and decided they could wait as well.

"Must remove you," he explained. "This place is pericolous . . . I mean dangerous."

He rummaged quickly through his pack for something to bind the man's ankle. Finding nothing suitable, he took out his blanket and was about to tear off a strip when the man interrupted and spoke in Italian.

"Not that," he said with an effort. "Get my parachute. It's on the other side of the trail, over by the pasture."

David wrapped his blanket around the man and left to get the parachute, which he found tangled in the limbs of a tree, with the empty harness hanging far above his head. He climbed the tree, taking one of his ski poles with him. By standing on one limb and hanging onto a limb above, he was able to reach out with the pole and snag a fold of the parachute. He pushed the rest away from the branches and managed to free most of it by cutting the cords. Then he returned to the fallen man and bound his ankle, using strips cut from the parachute. Finally, satisfied with his binding, he spoke to the man in Italian.

"We can't stay here, not with the rest of that parachute in the tree. We'll have to get you somewhere safe."

Using a ski pole and leaning against David for support, the man—who called himself Tony—was able to hobble slowly uphill. David looked around for a campsite, and after several minutes they came to a small clearing that satisfied him. David gave him a blanket and Tony sat with the blanket wrapped around himself while David began to set up camp. First, David broke off several lower branches of spruce trees nearly, then kicked away the snow from in front of a huge granite outcropping and spread the branches on the ground for Tony to lie on while David started a fire among some nearby rocks.

Dry down wood was plentiful, and David soon had a small fire burning. Tony held out his hands gratefully toward the flames. David heated some soup and handed him a cupful. It was almost too hot to hold, but Tony wrapped his hands around the cup and sipped the soup eagerly.

"Now get some rest," David said as he crouched by the fire, warming himself.

Gradually, as the warmth of the fire and the soup penetrated, Tony stopped shivering and he became talkative. "Thanks, buddy," he said in English as he lay down again with the blanket wrapped around him. "I'd have frozen my balls off down there."

Their conversations were a mixture of Italian and English. David tried to use what English he knew, and switched to Italian whenever a word or phrase escaped him, while Tony relied mostly on English. David recognized Tony's American accent, and wondered what he was doing so far north, behind the German lines.

"I sure didn't expect to find an American up here," he said.

"Ever hear of O.S.S.?" Tony asked.

When David shook his head, Tony continued: "It's an American outfit. We're tryin' to help the partisans, flyin' in weapons, ammo, food, whatever."

"Is that what you were doing here?"

"Yeah. They gave me some money and stuff for one of the groups here. I was supposed to set up a radio, too. Shee-it! Everything got fucked up. First, we got off course. Then I landed in a fuckin' tree and when I tried to get down I fell on some rocks. That's where I banged up my damned ankle. The last straw, though, was them commies that found me. Beat me up, that's what they did. Then took damn near everything I had and dragged me up the hill and took off."

"Where'd you learn Italian?" David asked, curious. "Were you born here?"

"Nah. I'm from Detroit. But my old man was from around these parts. I learned it at home."

Tony had been drafted, and as soon as the Army discovered that he was bilingual in Italian he was recruited by the O.S.S., or Office of Strategic Services. He chattered on about the special training he had been given and the friends who had parachuted into other areas. He lay back and looked over at David. When he noticed David's cap, he chuckled.

"Say, what's with the feather? What part of the army you with, anyway? I ain't ever seen a hat like that."

A sharp glance from David told him that he had gone too far. David was a man accustomed to command and not one to trifle with.

"I'm in the Alpini," David said simply. "Special mountain battalion."

"So what're *you* doing here by yourself?" Tony asked, more carefully this time.

David was in no mood to talk about himself, but Tony insisted.

"It's a long story," David said, reluctantly. "I got separated from my men. They're up ahead somewhere."

A sudden thought occurred to Tony and he interrupted. "Hey, you see any boxes by the pasture?"

"I didn't look. Why?"

"Some of them supply boxes probably fell short. Maybe the commies missed 'em."

David went back to look and about an hour later returned with a large pack on his back that he had fashioned by tying the ends of a blanket together. He dumped out the contents: two more blankets and several boxes of K-rations. "Found two," he said, handing Tony one of the blankets. "I took what I could carry and hid the rest."

When David sat down by the fire again, they discussed plans. Tony wanted to get back to the Swiss border as quickly as possible, but his sprained ankle made that impossible. David suggested that they walk to Bellinzona, but Tony objected that that would take too long. Tony wanted to catch a train to Como, where he said he could sneak over the Swiss border, and he tried to persuade David to help him. David was shaking his head.

"Hey, it'd work," Tony insisted. "I got some gold coins hid on me and identity papers ..."

David interrupted. "No way. The simplest peasant here would spot you as a foreigner right away."

"Hey, c'mon," Tony said. "I'm a real *paisano*. I speaka da lingua."

"Sure you do," David said, patiently, "but that's not enough. You're in Italy now, not in America. We're curious about people here. You ought to know that. We look at them; we notice how they move, how they act, how they talk. And look at you. I could spot you as a foreigner right away. Even the way you're looking at me now tells me you're not Italian. You've got that wide-eyed innocent look that's just different."

Tony started to object, but David cut him off, waving his hand as if to dismiss the entire subject. "No," he said flatly. "You'd be spotted in no time. Some Fascisti would report you to the SS. They'd get you. I don't care how good your identity papers are, the SS would find out they were false, and...." He drew his finger across his throat.

David rigged a shelter against the wind, using his poles, a few long branches and the remains of the parachute. After he fixed his own bed and laid out his bedroll, he opened one of the K-ration boxes and looked inside. Slowly and with great ceremony he took items out one by one, calling out their names and arranging them in a neat line on his blanket: cigarettes, candy, canned stew, coffee. One packet puzzled him. "And what do we have here?" he said, unwrapping it. Then it dawned on him. "Not toilet paper! My good God, this is what you Americans 'survive' on? There's food enough for a week. What I would've given for some of this in Russia."

A light blanket of snow greeted them the next morning. It was cold and clear. After breakfast, Tony was in a talkative mood again and tried to persuade David to come with him. "It really wouldn't take you that far out of your way. And my ankle feels a lot better already. I'd only have to lean on you for a day or so. You could get back over the border easy."

David had already been weighing that possibility in his own mind. Now that he had committed himself to helping Tony to safety, he was reluctant to let him go on alone. "I'll think about it. But right now you're not ready to leave, with or without me."

The following day, David told Tony he had made his decision: he would go with him, but only if Tony promised to help him get back over the border. They would start as soon as Tony could move about, heading first for Bellinzona, where Tony could catch a train down to Lugano. David would continue west from there toward Piemonte by way of Locarno.

Using packs of cloth soaked in an icy mountain stream, David was able to reduce the swelling on Tony's ankle. In three days, with additional wrapping and splints for support, Tony felt ready to start. Using David's ski poles, Tony was able to walk without placing his full weight on the injured leg. They headed down to the trail and started west. Heavy clouds hung in the sky. Looking up, David could see the dark green spruces gradually become dim shapes against the gray and finally disappear into the overhanging mist. The temperature had dropped. All was cold, and there was no sound as they walked, except their own movements and the crunch of their boots in the snow.

David pressed the pace, but stopped frequently so that Tony could rest, partly because of the sore ankle and partly because Tony was out of condition. "Jeez!" he said, gasping for breath. "Let's slow down to a fuckin' gallop. You look like you could go on like this all day."

"A month ago, maybe," David said with a soft laugh, "but not now." He told Tony about being ambushed by the German patrol.

"So how far ahead d'you think your guys are by now?" Tony asked.

"A week or more, I'd guess."

David had been gaining ground on his unit, since he was traveling by himself, with less need for supplies and better able to stay undetected. On the day he found Tony, he had calculated from trail signs that he was only two, maybe three, days behind. A heavy rain had fallen just three days before, but the last campfire he had passed had been completely dry.

"You'll have a helluva time catchin' up."

David shrugged. "Doesn't make much difference. Not now, anyway."

While they walked, Tony chattered incessantly about the new organization that Donovan and Dulles had put together, and how they were planning to help the partisans in Italy fight against the Germans. David listened with growing interest. After setting up camp inside the Swiss border, beyond the San Iorio Pass, Tony broached the subject again. They were wrapped in blankets, stretched out by a warm fire. They had just eaten a hot evening meal and were content. Tony was finishing a cigarette. Lying on his back, he blew a series of small smoke rings, watching them float lazily upward against the inky shapes of the surrounding trees.

"So how about it?" he asked. "Why not come along with me to Lugano like I said? Our people are looking for guys like you, and you could really help. And your unit's long gone by now, that's for damned sure."

David stared into the fire, thinking. *Tony's probably right. I'm too far behind now. Maybe I ought to go with him.* After a while he said, "All right. Let's talk to your people."

In less than a week, David was basking in the sun at the Allied base near Brindisi, on the heel of Italy, the main staging area for secret air missions into the Balkans. After being debriefed, he was transferred to a British SOE Parachute and Instructor school near Algiers, where he was trained in hand-to-hand combat, sabotage techniques and use of radio and explosives. Four months later, he was detailed to the nerve center for U.S. Special Operations, located at Caserta, near Naples. There, he met hundreds of Italian-Americans like Tony, who had come from the Italian sections of Boston, Hartford, New York, Detroit and Chicago. All of them had been recruited to parachute behind the German lines for the same basic mission: to aid the partisans' harassment of German troops as well as gather and transmit reliable information to Allied headquarters on German troop and materiel movements.

The O.S.S., predecessor to the powerful Central Intelligence Agency, sent more than 1,600 operatives on such missions into northern Italy. Many were never heard from again. Some were captured and tortured to death; others, like Tony, had the misfortune to land among fanatic communists. It was estimated that the average useful life of an agent was six months. The British were also active. Between 1942 and the end of the war, their SOE (Special Operations Executive) sent more than 500 liaison officers behind the German lines in northern Italy.

As one would expect with large organizations, there were numerous cases of bungling. Americans who spoke only Sicilian or some other southern Italian dialect found themselves in the Piedmont or Lombardy. The local dialects in these northern regions were like foreign languages to them, and their own southern dialects proved almost gibberish to the local partisans. Many shipments, amounting to hundreds of thousands of dollars in gold and currency, and food and supplies in the millions, either ended in the wrong hands, were diverted to unintended uses or were lost completely through carelessness. It was a massive effort, however, and generally aided the partisan campaign.

The war in Italy was moving northward slowly, and the battle for Florence was just beginning. General Kesselring and his troops were battering the Allies along the Gothic Line, and the Allied advance had ground to a halt. Partisans became bolder and increasingly active, despite the fact that they were being pursued relentlessly by the Germans. *Rastrellamenti*, or 'combings' of areas for suspected partisans, were frequent, and reprisals took grisly forms.

Frustrated by his inability to curb the partisans, Kesselring imposed harsh punitive measures. He issued a general order in August, 1944, instructing his troops how to deal with partisans. In cases where German troops were killed or wounded, the local Fascist militia or a PNF officer was to select an appropriate number of hostages of military age for hanging, generally ten for each German casualty. The entire populace of the town was to assemble in the town square to witness the executions. Bodies were to hang for twelve hours and then the townspeople were to bury them without ceremony. At Marzabotta, a small village near Bologna, 1500 civilians and 300 partisans were shot in September, 1944. The entire town of Sant'Anna - men, women and children - was herded into the main square and machine-gunned. The route of one SS battalion was regularly marked by dozens of corpses hanging from posts or trees.

## Caserta, August 8, 1944

For months now, David had been in training, speaking and reading English several hours a day, and this had done wonders for his command of the language. His vocabulary was extensive, and he had improved his pronunciation to the point where his accent was barely noticeable. In fact, because he had learned English from a British tutor as a youngster, he was often mistaken for British. He was anxious to leave, and was relieved when his orders finally came. Anything to get closer to home. The partisan radio operator outside of Torino had reported that Enzo and the entire unit had arrived safely, but David had not heard anything from his own family or from Elena. He was not even sure that his messages had gotten through to them.

He was called into operations headquarters, where an American colonel met him in the outer office and escorted him to the briefing room. "Della Croce," he said as they walked, "we've got a tough assignment for you. They tell me you're just the man for it."

Looking over the colonel's shoulder, David could see someone waiting for them in the briefing room. It was Dario, grinning broadly. They exchanged nods.

"General Alfieri here just came from Resistance headquarters," the colonel explained. "Special Adviser." Then he asked David: "Know much about eastern Lombardy?"

"A bit. That's where I found Tony."

"Mmm," the colonel grunted. "Romanelli, wasn't it? Heard about that. Damned lucky for him you came along." He puffed on his pipe as he approached a large wall map. "Up here is where one of our operators was just captured," he said, pointing with his pipe stem to a spot between Lecco and Bergamo, northeast of Milan. "We've got to replace him."

The colonel explained what David already knew: the area was a major hub for German communications lines and troop concentrations. Information about troop and materiel movements there would be invaluable for the Allies. Enso Boeri, who had established a radio transmitter network in the north, needed another agent to replace the one who had been captured, and David was a natural choice.

There would be two others in David's team: an American with code name Jeff, who spoke Italian and would be mission chief; and an Italian with code name Raymond, who had been a cryptographer aboard a submarine at the Naples naval base. David was to be the guide, and his code name was Green. He was to pick up his new identity papers at Operations.

"Remember," the colonel said, "the other two guys in your party don't know any more about you than what I've just told you about them. Keep it that way."

"Understood," David said.

"Good luck, Green," the colonel said under his breath as David left.

One week before David was flown north, General Cadorno had parachuted into an area east of Milan, together with Ferruccio Parri of the Action Party and Luigi Longo of the Communists. Their assignment was to centralize and coordinate the Italian resistance in northern Italy. David would be stationed at a key post in the chain of radio transmitters that stretched in an arc from Venezia Giulia, in the west above Trieste, all the way to Piemonte in the northwest corner of Italy. This network, Servizio Informazione Militare-Controspionaggio (military counterintelligence, or SIM-CS for short), provided the link between the Allied High Command at Caserta and Cadorno's organization, supplying vital information on German movements.

David and Dario rode in silence toward the airstrip where a mud-colored DC-3 was waiting to fly David and his team behind the German lines. A sergeant stood in the cargo door, holding a clipboard and checking off boxes as they were loaded into the plane. He looked down at David as their jeep pulled alongside the plane and motioned with his thumb. "Get the lead out, Green! Wheels up in five minutes."

David turned to Dario and they shook hands. Dario gripped David's shoulder. *"Coraggi, amis."*

*"Adiu.* Remember to tell my family I'm all right." David threw his pack and equipment up into the side of the plane and climbed aboard. Before the door closed, he waved good-bye to Dario, then joined the other members of his drop team. He had just sat down when the floor shuddered under him as the plane's engines roared into life.

The co-pilot sauntered back from the cockpit. "May's well make yourselves comfortable. This is gonna take a while."

Hours later, the plane finally began its descent over the Po Valley, and the co-pilot opened the cockpit door and yelled. "Hey, you guys! Get ready! Won't be long now! Jump on signal, one right after the other, just like in training. And don't take too long. We got a shitload of stuff to shove out right after you."

Ahead of the plane, the blackness was suddenly broken by a circle of flares on the ground. They were right on course. One of the crew members opened the side cargo door, and cold air rushed in. David, Jeff and Raymond hooked their ripcords to a metal rod above the door and prepared to jump. Before he realized what had happened, David heard the command "Go!" and dove out into the night. The three team members were followed by cartons on parachutes. As David floated down toward the field, he saw the DC-3 roar away. The ground rose swiftly to meet him, and he flexed his knees slightly, readying himself for impact. He and his team had to act quickly after landing, to clear the area for the plane's second run.

David felt the shock of the ground in his hips and tumbled forward, rolling into the shrouds of his parachute. Almost immediately, dark shapes surrounded him and took him outside the lighted area. Others gathered cartons and removed them, as the plane made a slow, wide circle and came in low for its next approach, barely clearing the treetops. It slowed almost to stall speed over the clearing, and David watched as cartons of 'indestructibles', kicked or shoved out the side door of the DC-3, hurtled directly to the ground.

As soon as the flares were doused, the three began working with the partisans to gather the supplies and equipment and move everything to their campsite. The next morning, Jeff and Raymond set up their radio and established contact with Allied headquarters, while David helped to store the explosives and ammunition and distribute food and other supplies.

The detachment they had joined began an intensified sabotage program, disabling railway switches, blowing up bridges and culverts and harassing German patrols. Sometimes, finding a sealed truck convoy but not wishing to risk an explosion, they would simply open the wire grilles on the sides of the trucks and rearrange the destination labels, creating total confusion at the receiving end. They sent out patrols regularly to watch the railway lines and main roads, and reported traffic and troop movements to Raymond, who relayed the information to Caserta.

There were fifty men in David's detachment, led by a hulking peasant with the code name Wolf. He appeared to be in his forties, with dark, bushy eyebrows and small, piercing eyes that peered out from under a heavy forehead. A grizzled beard emphasized his large, slightly undershot jaw. Every place on the human body where hair could conceivably grow was covered by a dense hirsute jungle, covering the backs of Wolf's arms and hands, and literally sprouting above his collar.

Wolf's detachment was one of the few non-political units operating in the area. On paper, it was part of the 2d battalion of a leftist Garibaldi brigade, but Wolf refused to permit any other group to control him. He had nothing but contempt for the attempts by the communists to organize and exploit partisan activity.

David asked him about this once, and Wolf's reply was vehement. "Civilian representatives? he said contemptuously, putting a finger alongside his nose and blowing it vigorously, then wiping his sleeve under it. "That's all the Commies are interested in. Those bleeding commissars just get in the way. And they want red stars on our berets - that's stupid; about as useful as tits on a boar."

As far as Wolf was concerned, there was only one good thing about being with the Garibaldini: they got most of the supplies.

*Somewhere in Lombardy, October 3, 1944*

Wolf's detachment received orders to move westward, toward Val d'Ossola. One night shortly after they had started, David was leading an advance party through a wooded area when they heard a plane approaching in the distance, and activity among the trees ahead of them. As the plane came nearer, they saw flares lit in a large clearing, where a group of men in partisan uniforms stood looking up. David and his men were about to join them when he realized that something was wrong. *This isn't a regular drop site!* He held up his hand. "Wait!" he whispered. "Something's wrong."

Motioning to four men, he said, "You fellows spread out and come to the edge of the clearing from that other side. The rest of you stay with me. We'll spread out on this side. Everyone stay hidden, and wait for my signal."

"What's up?" one asked.

"Could be a trap," David replied and gathered the men around him. "Now remember," he said softly, "Nobody starts shooting until I do. Then pick your targets carefully. Try to rescue anyone who parachutes in. You ..." He pointed to one man. "Go back to the others and tell Wolf to stay put. The rest of you—move it out."

David and his men crept quietly toward the edge of the clearing. As the plane passed over the drop zone, three men bailed out. Two of them landed in the clearing and were seized immediately; the third was shot as he entered the clearing carrying his parachute. A man holding one of the parachutists began dragging him out of the clearing, directly toward David. When the two were about fifteen feet away, David yelled out in English: "Hit the dirt!"

The man wrenched himself loose and dove forward. In the same instant, David fired. One slug spun the 'partisan' around, just missing his captive. The other two flattened him against a tree, where he twitched a few times and lay still.

David's shots set off total chaos, as his entire advance party began firing at the group in the clearing. David crawled over to the parachutist, who was trying to stand, and pushed him roughly to the ground. "Down!" he hissed.

For the next five minutes there were intermittent bursts of gunfire, and then silence.

"What the hell's going on?" the man whispered.

David motioned to him to keep quiet, then looked around carefully, waiting. Finally, satisfied, he whistled sharply three times, signaling his men to move out."Let's go! Stay with me!"

The two headed away from the clearing on a dead run, with David leading the way, and reached the main body of the detachment about two hundred yards up the hill. David counted quickly. One missing. He turned to one of the advance party." Where's the other man who was captured?"

One of the others spoke up. "Shot. I saw one of the Germans get him as soon as the firing started."

"We'll have to go back," David said, reluctantly. Then he turned to the man he had saved, and asked, in English: "What's your name?"

"Lucky," the man said, and started to explain.

David cut him off. "What was in that shipment?"

"Mostly food," Lucky said. "but we had some crates of automatic weapons and ammo, too."

David thought a moment, then suggested to Wolf that they return to salvage what they could. With enough men, they could take most of it before the Germans got there. Wolf agreed. They could use the food during the winter. David led the men back to the clearing. Two of them carried the corpses of their comrades and the two parachutists up the hill and concealed them, while David and the others brought the cases of weapons and ammunition to Wolf. As they began dividing the food, they heard trucks approaching through the valley: German troops were coming. Taking as much as they could carry, David and his men hurried back to rejoin the main group of the detachment and then set off immediately for their campsite, about six kilometers away. David had no chance to speak to Lucky, who was trying gamely to keep up with the others over the steep and rocky terrain.

Almost an hour later, when they finally stopped, Lucky collapsed, completely exhausted, his breath coming in quick gasps. "My good Christ," he wheezed in English. "I thought you bastards would never stop. I'm beat." He lay back and closed his eyes, his chest still heaving. After a few minutes he looked over at David who was standing nearby. "What do they call you, friend?"

David was not anxious to chat. He said, simply, "Green."

But Lucky wanted to talk. "Well, anyway, thanks for saving me back there, Green ole buddy," he said in English.

Lucky stayed with Wolf's detachment for three weeks, and he and David became friends. When Lucky received orders for reassignment, David took him to the secret airstrip where a plane would come to evacuate him back to Switzerland. Just before boarding the plane, Lucky held out his hand.

Look, Green," he said, "I owe you. Take this." He gave David a card on which he had written his name and home address. "You ever need any help in the States, you get in touch, y'hear? My old man's got connections." He winked at David.

It was because of that card that David came to the attention of the New England Mafia chief, Don Oreste Marini. 'Lucky' was Carlo Marini, the Don's eldest son.

# CHAPTER SEVEN

The winter of 1944-45 was difficult for partisans throughout northern Italy. The weather was unusually severe, and many were short of food, clothing and supplies. The Allies were concentrating their efforts in France, and practically suspended activities along the front in Italy for the winter. That freed more and more German troops to combat sabotage and hunt down partisans. Wolf's detachment was forced to retreat further into the hills, and essentially remained in winter bivouac during January and February except for occasional reconnaissance patrols. As spring arrived in March, they resumed full operations.

At the same time, the Allied armies began pressing north. In April, they launched their final attack, the 8th Army against the German 10th Army on the east coast and the 5th Army against the German 14th Army west of Bologna. Partisan groups throughout the north began operating more and more boldly, and succeeded in thwarting key German plans. They blocked the German flight to the north, capturing more than 150,000 troops. On orders from central resistance headquarters, urban partisans attacked and overwhelmed German troops in the key industrial cities of Genoa, Torino and Milano. Since the war was obviously drawing to a close in Italy, David said good-bye to Wolf and headed straight for Torino.

*Torino May 2, 1945*

Three days later, when all of the remaining German forces of Army Group C surrendered, David arrived at Torino. He tried to call home but got only a line disconnect signal. Then he called a good friend and neighbor.

"I can't get through to my folks, Mario. Is there something wrong with the phones?"

Mario did not answer, but said only that he would come right away, and ended the conversation before David could ask any more questions. David had a strong sense of foreboding. *Something terrible has happened.* He could tell from Mario's voice. When they met, Mario could barely look David in the eye, and David feared the worst.

"Where's my family?"

Mario said nothing. He just placed his hand on David's shoulder and shook his head slowly. They drove in silence toward San Nicola.

Finally, David spoke. "You can tell me now. What happened?"

Mario explained. A Fascist informer had told the SS that David's parents were helping the resistance. When the Germans came to investigate, they found two wounded partisans in the barn and arrested David's entire family. His parents were executed shortly after, and his younger brother and sister died in prison. The land was confiscated, and a German staff officer used the home as his headquarters.

As they passed Carema and neared the town of San Nicola, David looked around. He scarcely noticed the familiar surroundings: the expanse of vineyards sloping up the hills to the dark-green forests; the clusters of stone buildings with red-tiled roofs; the white-washed church and shops in the village. There were no shell holes in the road, no buildings reduced to rubble, no rusting tanks in the field. It was as though the war had passed by San Nicola.

David's home had not been so fortunate. One of the ornate wrought iron gates at the entrance to the Della Croce estate hung tentatively from one hinge. The other lay on the ground by a heap of stones that had served as its post. David picked up two pieces of the slab of Carrara marble that had been the nameplate and fitted them together to form:

*Chate*
*Della Cr*

Then he threw them aside. All he could see of their home was part of a chimney pointing darkly at the sky, surrounded by fallen walls and broken beams. Two weeks before the German forces retreated to the north, the officer living there had fled for Switzerland, leaving orders for his troops to demolish the building. Neighbors had managed to save many of the family's precious possessions before the house was commandeered, and these had been kept safely hidden.

David and Mario walked back to the car, and David turned to look back at the ruins. "The man who told the SS—did they find him?"

Mario nodded. "Enzo and some of the others from your Alpini unit caught him hiding in the woods. He died the SS way: hanging from a meathook through his chin."

During the next days, David visited old friends. The story was the same everywhere: no family had been spared. One third of his law school class—and several of his professors—had perished, executed in reprisals or killed in combat. Some small villages had lost nearly all their young men when Alpini units were destroyed on the Russian front.

A month later, David's older brother Sergio returned, just released from a German prison camp. The two set about rebuilding their home, using the original plans.

During the next weeks, even while David was working, memories of Elena kept coming back to him, and he longed to see her again. He had sent her a message that he would be coming to Vilpiano as soon as possible. But it was his decision to leave Italy that made him realize how much she meant to him.

At dinners and other social occasions, David had been introduced to most of the eligible young ladies from the region. He had also greeted Mariana when she returned, tanned and trim, from her two-year stay at Montreux, far from the 'boring' war. He looked at all of these women, even Mariana, with different eyes now, and they all seemed somehow—the only word he could think of was—irrelevant. David was thinking about the challenge of building a new life. *How would they cope? They were at home in the drawing room or on the bridle path, but could they build a new life with me?* He did not think so. But he knew Elena could.

Sergio did not even bother to object when David announced that he was going back to Vilpiano to marry Elena. He did not dare tell his younger brother what he was thinking: *Elena's a nobody. Beautiful, apparently, but still a nobody. Worse yet, a nobody with no money. As a mistress, fine, but definitely not for marriage.* He saw that David had already made up his mind, however, and wisely kept silent. Just before David left, Sergio handed him a small box. "Elena ought to have something from the family. This is *Nonna* Maria's ruby. The setting's a bit old-fashioned, but I think she'll like it."

Elena was milking when David arrived. She had her back to the open barn door, her kerchiefed head resting against the cow's warm flank. She gripped the cow's tail firmly behind her left knee to prevent it from swishing back and forth, and her strong hands propelled thick jets of milk into the bucket in an even rhythm that sounded like one continuous stream. A cat came by to beg, and Elena greeted it with a short burst of milk that drenched its head and sent it dashing out of the barn. David stood watching her for a few moments, then couldn't contain himself any longer.

"I've come for my ring, Elena."

At the sound of his voice, Elena whirled about, almost upsetting her bucket. *"Oh, mio caro!"* she cried and rushed into his arms.

Elena was no longer a girl, though her cheeks still had a blush of pink from the clean country air. Her body was strong and trim, with a woman's soft curves. When they embraced, she pressed herself hard against him in a frank expression of pent-up love and desire.

After getting the blessings of Elena's aunt and uncle, the two lovers went immediately to the parish priest and arranged for a simple wedding, then left for their honeymoon in Venice. That night, with the muffled sounds of water traffic on the Grand Canal filtering through the shutters of their room, they made love with all the passion of youth, heightened by so many months of separation. David kissed and caressed Elena in places she had never dreamed of, arousing her desire to such a pitch that she rocked back and forth on the bed slowly, moaning incoherently, hungry for his touch, for the warm and electrifying contact between their two bodies. He could feel her tremble as his hands touched her gently and he was starved for her; the softness and sweet scent of her skin were intoxicating.

Elena tingled all over, and her desire mounted. By now her inhibitions were utterly swept away, and she gave in to complete abandon. Reality disappeared, and she felt herself immersed in feelings and longings she had never experienced.

"Do it, do it! Now!" she moaned.

Afterward, for several minutes, she lay as if in a trance, breathing heavily and drained of everything except a warmth that seemed to envelop her.

David had kindled in Elena a hunger for sex that seemed insatiable during these honeymoon days. Sex in any position, at any time of the day or night. She could hardly understand it herself. As they were walking along, desire would suddenly well up inside her and she would press against him invitingly. They would dash back to their hotel room, laughing, and begin tearing off each other's clothes as soon as the door was closed. Sometimes she awoke in the middle of the night; David's warmth next to her would draw her to him, and she would fondle him until he was awake and aroused.

The young lovers savored the romance of Venice, and David enjoyed introducing Elena to its myriad delights. They walked for hours hand in hand along the narrow, twisting lanes; relaxed in the evenings with a cup of espresso on the piazza San Marco; watched the bustling water traffic from their room at the Gritti Palace, overlooking the Grand Canal; and reveled in the treasures of art and architecture for which the city is famous. Each day greeted them with new pleasures and wonders.

After returning to San Nicola, David and Elena helped Sergio rebuild the estate. In six months, the house was almost finished, and the vineyard was ready for winter. When David told his brother that it was time to leave, Sergio tried again to dissuade him. There was so much work to be done, he said, and so many important decisions about the estate.

But David's mind was set; he was eager to leave. The war, with the loss of his family and the senseless slaughter of so many friends, had touched him more deeply than anyone imagined. He felt the presence of ghosts everywhere. Little things stirred memories of what he had lost: the scent of lavender, his mother's favorite; his father's leather-bound *Codice Civile;* the worn walnut seats in the small church where his family had worshipped; wildflowers on a hillside where he and his brothers and sister had played as children. High above the valley, beyond the vineyard in a remote corner of the estate, a rugged outcropping of granite jutted from the side of the mountain. From there one could see for miles up and down the valley. His father had gone there often with him and his brothers after working in the vineyards. They would look out over the valley and talk of their plans and ambitions. David could not bring himself to look in that direction.

Most painful of all for him was the evening hour, when memories would engulf him. Dinner in their family had been an unchanging ritual since as early as he could remember. His father would arrive from his office on the stroke of seven, and the family would gather around the massive dining table, his father seating his mother and he or Sergio seating their sister. The maids would peer from the kitchen, waiting for his mother's signal to begin serving. After pronouncing a brief blessing, his father would ceremoniously withdraw his napkin from its monogrammed silver ring, unfold it slowly and place it on his lap. That was the signal for all to begin eating. But dinner was never just for food; eating was secondary. Dinner for the Della Croces was a time for conversation, and each member of the family was expected to participate. After dinner, they would move onto the verandah overlooking the valley and have coffee (with a touch of brandy for his father) or tea and fruit.

David had decided that he needed to put distance between himself and his home, and studying law in England or the United States made sense. Sergio agreed. Italy would need exports to thrive, and Italian companies would need men like David, who could deal easily with Americans. Their father had studied law at Cambridge, he pointed out, so why shouldn't David study at, say, Harvard or Yale? Afterwards, he could return to Torino and open his own *studio legale*.

The idea appealed to David, but even more to Elena, who was excited about the prospect of living in another country.

Early in January, 1946, David went to the US consulate in Milano. There were long lines.

"How do I get a visa for the United States?" he asked when he finally reached the information desk.

The young Italian clerk who was sorting papers did not look up. "Business or tourist?" she snapped. "What'll you be doing?"

"My wife and I want to live there. I'll be studying law."

"Immigrant visa," she said mechanically, picking up a sheaf of papers and tossing them on the counter without looking at him. "Fill out these forms and don't come back unless you've got all the documents on the list."

David was repelled by this inconsiderate behavior. His parents had taught him from childhood that one should never abuse power, never exploit it at the expense of those who depended on you. It annoyed him that poor people who needed help so desperately, and who found it difficult to be supplicants, had to submit to this indignity.

"What sort of waiting period is there?" he said evenly, a slight edge to his voice.

The clerk was prepared to cut David off as she had so many others that day, but something in his voice made her hesitate. She looked up, and saw immediately from his dress and bearing that he was an *uomo istruito*, a cultured person, well-educated. Above all, however, she responded instinctively to the leadership quality that made others want to work for him.

"*Scusi, dottore,* she apologized, flustered. "Do you have relatives in the United States?"

David had made his point, so he spoke easily: "No. Only some distant cousins."

"Then it could take one, two years or more."

"Mmm." He had not reckoned on such a long wait. "Isn't there a shorter way?"

"No, I'm afraid not. Everyone has to wait in turn unless he has some sort of preference. The quotas are all filled." She paused. "Of course, if you know someone important...." Her gesture said, in effect: *"If you've got friends in the right places, there's always a way."*

"Do I have to come all the way back here to Milano?"

"For now, yes. But you can go to the Embassy at Rome, too. The office at Torino won't open until sometime this summer."

On his way home, as he pondered the bad news, he remembered Lucky's card, and as soon as he arrived, he went straight to his army papers and took it out. "I got this from an American solder," he said, showing it to Elena. "Saved his life. He told me to write to him if I ever needed help."

"Do you think he meant it, or was he just saying that?"

"I don't know, but I have a feeling Lucky might be different. Anyway, I'll write to him. Can't hurt to try."

Three weeks later, a telegram arrived.

> GO TO CONSULAR SECTION AMERICAN EMBASSY ROME. VICE CONSUL WILL HELP WITH VISA DOCUMENTS. LET ME KNOW WHEN YOU WILL ARRIVE. BENVENUTO A BOSTON.   *LUCKY*

David was given VIP treatment at the Embassy, and within a month he and Elena had their visas. Carlo had agreed to be their sponsor, and the State Department had taken a special interest in their case. Letters had been received from the chairmen of both the House and Senate Appropriations Committees, as well as from Senator Saltonstall and Congressman Curley. They cited David's distinguished war record and contribution to the Allied war effort and urged that 'all possible consideration' be given to immediate issuance of their visas. The process of granting an immigrant visa was long and complicated, even in the most straightforward of cases. Identities had to be verified, references had to be checked, and backgrounds had to be investigated, in order to screen out criminals and other 'undesirables.' Consulates in Europe and the Far East were swamped with visa applications. Without the intervention of Congressional leaders, David and Elena could have waited years for their visas.

When they finally arrived at Boston, they were met at the airport by Carlo and one of his father's assistants and taken to a midtown hotel, where a suite had been reserved for them. Carlo himself arranged to have a real estate broker come by the following day to show them apartments that were available for rent. On the third day, Carlo called to say that his father would like to meet David.

David was waiting in front of the Harding Hotel when a long black limousine drove up and stopped in front of him. Carlo bounded out, pulled David inside and the two reminisced on the way up to the North Shore.

Carlo wanted to know about David's plans. He lit a cigarette and leaned back.

"Any idea what you'll be doin'? What kind of work you like?"

He told Carlo about his plan to attend law school in the fall, and said that he would like to find a job until then. He did not really need to work, however; his share of his parents' estate and the vineyard would easily cover their expenses. He simply wanted to be active, and do something related to the law. He had seen an article in the newspaper about men needed for the police department, and mentioned that to Carlo as a possibility.

Carlo almost gagged on his cigarette, then quickly apologized. "Sorry. Something just struck me funny. You oughta tell my dad about the police job. He'd be interested."

David did not know quite what to make of Carlo's reaction. "What kind of business are you in?"

Carlo hesitated briefly. "Ah, I work for my father. He's got a few business deals I take care of."

David sensed that Carlo was being deliberately vague, so he changed the subject.

The Don's assistant met them at the front door and started to move toward David to frisk him, but a glance from Carlo stopped him.

"He's O.K.," Carlo said quietly.

The movement and Carlo's comment piqued David's interest. *What sort of man is Carlo's father?* he wondered. *"And what influence does he have?*

Don Marini was seated at his desk as David and Carlo entered the room, and he looked up from the papers he had been studying. The Don had a full head of steel-gray hair, razor cut every week, a dark mustache and heavy, jet-black eyebrows. What David noticed immediately were his dark, heavy-lidded eyes. They radiated a compelling power. In his early fifties and at the height of his career, the Don was an imposing figure; he moved smoothly and carried his bulk with grace. Speaking in a low and deliberate voice, he chose his words in English very carefully, with a slight accent that lent flavor to his somewhat formal phrasing.

"So you are David," he said, coming around the desk to greet them. "My son Carlo has told me about you. We owe you a great debt of gratitude for what you did for him."

He extended his hand, and David gripped it, unconsciously inclining his head slightly in respect.

David was acutely aware of the contrast between himself and the Don, and knew that the Don felt it as well. The Don was essentially a peasant. His father had been an uneducated stonemason, and his family had eked out a bare existence on a few arid acres in southern Sicily, rented from absentee landlords. The Don's past was obvious to David in the Don's gestures, his bearing and his speech. The Don's whole being projected what he was. David, who was sensitive as all Italians are to such stimuli, and more keenly observant than most, responded intuitively. He knew without thinking that the Don had placed him as a *padrone*, and that the Don had chosen to speak English rather than Italian because his dialect would have marked him as a peasant.

In Italian society, gaps between classes and regions are still visible everywhere. Until recently, the local dialects had flourished, even in the cities. Television and rising literacy have begun to exert a homogenizing influence, but even so, striking differences in vocabulary and pronunciation still divide peoples from different regions.

The Don's roots were fixed in the baked clay hills of Sicily, where peasants lived in seemingly endless poverty. David, on the other hand, came from the industrialized north, the home of the House of Savoy. The *Piemontesi* regarded themselves as the aristocrats of Italy.

The Don also felt these differences between them, but did not analyze his feelings or consciously alter his behavior. But the fact is that he would have been more direct in these first minutes had David been a peasant from southern Italy, or from anywhere, rather than the well-educated son of a *padrone* from Piemonte.

David felt the Don's raw power and drive, a power born of a gift for controlling men: the gift of command, and David respected it. While he sensed the Don's reticence, he did not try to penetrate it. From childhood, David had been taught to ignore class differences. His father had been equally at home with an unskilled laborer as with a prime minister.

"Speak to the man, David," his father had said, "and not to his clothes, his money or his position. Everyone you meet has a self that he considers precious. Speak to that self."

The Don began warming toward his son's friend as their conversation wore on. He realized that David had not come with arrogance; he was open and friendly, and respectful. Most of all, the Don responded to David's calm, level gaze and self-assurance.

Vibrations had passed back and forth between them. The Don could see that, while David was respectful of the Don's power, he was not submitting to it.

Motioning David and Carlo to the leather chairs in front of his desk, the Don walked slowly to the window and stood for a few seconds looking out. "Carlo has told me the sad news about your family," he said after a pause. "We grieve with you." He came back and placed a hand on David's shoulder. "May you find the strength to endure this great loss."

From another person, spoken differently, the words would have sounded stilted and melodramatic, but the Don's sincerity made them fitting.

"You are fortunate that your brother came back from the war," he continued, "and even more fortunate that you married a strong woman."

David started inwardly. *How did Carlo's father know about Sergio?* he wondered. *I haven't written or said anything to Carlo about him. Someone must have done some checking in Italy.*

The Don returned to his desk. Gesturing to the credenza, he asked Carlo to bring some wine for their guest. They raised their glasses, and the Don looked at David. There was warmth in his gaze. "*Salute*, David."

"I can't thank you enough for what you've done for us," David said. "I'll repay you as soon as I can."

Don Oreste closed his eyes and held up his hand. "There is no question of repayment. You saved my son's life. What else can I say?"

The three sipped their wine. After a moment, the Don set his glass down and held out his hands toward David, palms up. "Now, my young friend, tell me about your plans."

"I'd like to start law school this fall. Harvard if I can get in. But for now I'd like to get a job. Something close to the law."

"And what kind of work would you do?"

David hesitated. He sensed that the Don placed importance on his choice, so he spoke slowly. "Well, I don't really have any experience—except the army. But I saw an article in the paper this morning. The Police Department's looking for men. That might be interesting."

He showed the clipping to the Don, who barely glanced at it, but looked closely at David before he replied. Then he nodded. "Very good...very good. A policeman, he works with lawyers. So you'll be a better lawyer that way. Here in this country, even the son of a *senatore* can be a *carabiniere*. Don't make any difference. You support your wife. Become a fine lawyer. *Certo.*" He took David's hand and held it. "Remember now, my son. When you decide what you want to do, you give Carlo here a call, and we'll try to help if we can."

He motioned to Carlo and asked him to show David around, then shook David's hand. "Come back to see us soon."

As they were leaving the house, Carlo put his arms around David's shoulder. "Hey, the old man really likes you!"

David never really intended to stay in the United States. He had planned to get his degree, return to Torino and join a small firm that two of his friends had started. But things did not work out as he had planned, partly because Elena found so many friends and wanted to stay just a little longer and partly because he was so successful. He was certain, although he could never prove it, that the Don's influence had helped him greatly. That was the only way he could explain how quickly and how easily important matters were resolved for him. More than chance had to be at work. He was admitted to law school even without an official transcript from Bologna. Though he was not yet a citizen, he was accepted immediately as a provisional patrolman, and had no problem getting assigned to evening and night duty so that he could continue his law studies. On the force, he was always paired with the most experienced officers.

When he graduated from law school near the head of his class, he was offered a position as an assistant district attorney, a clear indication that he had 'clout' somewhere. From there, his career bloomed. The deep friendship between David and the Don developed without a feeling of obligation. The Don recognized David's need for independence and respected his position, and David did his best—but it was difficult—to avoid situations that would place him in conflict between his friendship and his public duties.

David learned the true extent of the Don's power soon after he became a patrolman. In 1946, the Don had iron control over organized crime in the six-state area from Maine to the New York border. No gambling, loan-sharking, prostitution or protection racket could be started without his personal approval and his usual percentage of the 'take'. Hundreds of people sent him information: hotel clerks, bartenders, pawnshop owners, government employees, and even policemen. Some were actually on his payroll—though not part of his organization—but most simply were eager to help him. Whenever men from other syndicate families came into New England, even on vacation; whenever police raids were scheduled; whenever a burglary, robbery or crime of any consequence took place; in fact, whenever anything out of the ordinary occurred that someone thought might interest the Don, his web of informants responded.

The Don's empire dated from 1929, when his *capo*, 'Joe the Boss' Masseria, gave him permission to move to Boston and set up his own organization. He took over the area quickly, and within six months all of those who had opposed him in the beginning were either working for him or dead.

Oreste Marini, known to the other mobsters as 'Wrist' before he became Don, was a man with no expansionist ambitions. He posed no threat to the Five Families. Content to remain where he was, he managed to avoid becoming involved in the internecine feuds that ravaged the families in New York and Chicago during the thirties. At the same time, however, he defended his own territory viciously. No one from any other family moved into New England unless and until they had Don Oreste's personal blessing.

§ § §

David was brought back to the present as he stopped his car in front of the main building. The huge oak door swung open, and one of the Don's broad-shouldered bodyguards stood framed in the opening, dressed in a dark suit with a slight bulge under the left arm that only a trained eye could detect. The man's eyes held David in a steady gaze, showing respect, yet with a trace of insolence. "Mr. Della Croce?" he asked, mispronouncing the name.

"That's right. You're new here, aren't you?"

"I'm Mr. Marini's assistant," the man said, avoiding David's question. "Please come in." He reminded David of some haughty salespeople he had dealt with in fashionable Fifth Avenue shops.

Closing the outside door behind them, the bodyguard said, not quite apologetically, "Have to frisk you first. You know the routine."

David held his suitcoat open. "By heart."

After a quick but thorough search, the bodyguard nodded. "Mr. Marini's waiting for you in his office" He turned to escort David, but David waved him aside. "Not necessary. I know the way."

The bodyguard followed close behind.

David crossed the foyer to the door leading to the Don's office, where the Don was seated at his desk. The bodyguard followed David inside and stood off to one side. When the Don rose to greet him, David was shocked to see how much the older man had aged just in the last year. He looked much frailer. His collar, which used to fit perfectly, was loose; his cheeks were hollow; and his hair completely white and wispy.

He walked slowly and with some uncertainty. His eyes were still alert, however, and his voice, though somewhat weaker than David remembered, was steady.

They shook hands. The Don's felt bony and cold, the skin parchment-thin. David could see gray stubble on the Don's chin in places that the Don had overlooked or not seen in shaving.

"Good afternoon, Don Marini." David still used the title, even though the Don's son Carlo had been in charge of family matters for several years.

"David, it's so good to see you again. Tell me, my son, how is your lovely Elena, and your son Marco?" The Don had never grasped the fact that Elena had died, and always asked about her.

"They're both fine, sir. They send their regards."

The Don smiled, and put his arm around David's shoulder. The arm was so light that David could scarcely feel its weight. "You've always been like a son to me, David. You've visited me here regularly, even after my retirement. I appreciate that."

Fifteen years ago, just before the Don turned seventy, his two *caporegimes*, together with Carlo, who was then *consigliere*, had taken over the family. Don Oreste and his men had survived—but just barely—a bloody four-year struggle against the Irish-dominated waterfront gangs. Hardly a month went by without a revenge killing. Some of the New York families were said to be thinking seriously about moving in. It became clear to everyone—even to the Don—that he was losing his grip and could not continue. His memory, once so prodigious, had started to slip. Worse still, he seemed unable to understand what motivated the younger men in his organization, and that had led to lapses in judgment. He used to know instinctively how far to trust his men, but their new loyalties were different, and he could not rely upon his men to follow the simplistic code that he had been taught in the old days.

Don Marini had noticed the signs of unrest. He was certain that Carlo would never agree to force him out, and that if his two *caporegimes* decided to move on their own, they would have to kill Carlo as well as him. So, the Don bowed to the inevitable—unlike other dons before him—and he summoned a formal meeting of the entire family to announce his retirement. He vowed never to interfere in family matters, but offered to be available for advice and counsel at any time.

"I told them I was too tired to be their Don any more," he had explained. "After all the problems we had, it was time for someone else to take over. Of course, I wanted to make Carlo the Don, but that wouldn't have been good for him. The family had to choose. It hurt like hell to walk out of that meeting, but they chose Carlo anyway, and they were right. He was the best of the three, even if he was my own flesh and blood."

The transition was peaceful. The Don was permitted to remain in the 'Rock,' with most of his perquisites intact. Though Carlo was now the true head of the family, his father was still highly valued because of his close connections with the other families in the East and Midwest. The respect he was shown now was because of his age, and not his power. And the Don knew it.

"There's a carafe of red wine on the credenza, David. Would you please pour some for us? The glasses are behind the door on your left."

David carried the glasses to the Don, who held his up to the light from the window.

"Ah...important business deserves a fine wine. For me there's nothing like a lusty Barolo. *Salute*, David."

David raised his glass. "*Salute.*"

Don Oreste was enthusiastic about his wine, David recalled, partly because it was custom-bottled for him at his vineyard near La Morra. As he sipped the wine, the Don began reminiscing. His triumphs were in the distant past now, and he dwelt there increasingly. A born storyteller, he had a seemingly endless repertory of stories, many of which were laced with macabre humor. The Don told a few of his favorites. By now David had heard them many times and knew them by heart, but he laughed and exclaimed in the right places as always, knowing how important these stories were to the Don. They were his life. As the Don told them, he began slipping back into the 'tough guy' talk of his youth.

"Y'know, the young punks today, they don't know what it was like in the old days. All they think about now is corporations, profits and losses, launderin' money and things like that. They don't know what we hadda go through." He shook his head slowly. "They take it all for granted. They got no respect for what we did for 'em."

David could see a faraway look in the Don's eyes.

"When we come here from the old country, my mom and dad, they didn't have two *lire* to rub together. All they had was us three kids and two big suitcases, and my old man's masonry tools. We came over like cattle on that ship. I was nine. I still remember. What a mess! All those people jammed together; puke all over; bedbugs and cockroaches somethin' fierce. I had to sneak on deck to get me some fresh air. My mom, she cried most of the time. She wanted to go back, 'cause she missed her goats, for Chrissake. Then when we got here they herded us through Ellis Island. Just like animals they treated us. "

The Don sipped his wine and stared at the glass. "You shoulda seen where we lived in East Harlem." He chuckled and looked off in the distance. "What's the address? 226, or was it 216? Whatever. All us five was in two rooms. My little brother, that's Salvatore, he cried so none of us could get any sleep. You wanted to take a leak, you ran down the hall. There was two other families sharin' the bath. What a place. Tough? You better believe it. You had to be smart just so's to stay alive. Nowadays kids don't know what it's like down at the bottom with nothin'"

His eyes brightened as he warmed to the subject. "You oughta see my great grandchildren, David. They got wide eyes, clean faces, new clothes ... Me? I was makin' a buck a week when I was ten. Ran errands for this madam down the street. She had three-four girls workin' in her place. Old Lupo, he was the big boss. Remember him? Me and the guys used to spend time coppin' fruit from peddlers, knockin' over vending machines for a few pennies: real big-time stuff." He chuckled. "Well, one time me and Big Al we roll this guy, y'see, an' we find a hundred fifty bucks on him! Couldn't believe our eyes. Turns out the guy was a runner for Lupo, for Chrissake. Boy, we damn near got our balls chopped off! No kiddin' But that's an old story.

"You made your bones early in those days. If you wasn't tough, boy, you didn't last long, that's for sure. We had some real mean ones: Johnny Torrio, Al Capone — those two, they moved out to Chicago — then there was Lucky Luciano, Anastasia — that was Big Al — and Joe Adonis, Frank Costello ...All the big shots, the *pezzonovanti*, they come from where we lived. Joe Masseria was later. They called him Joe the Boss. Good *Siciliano*. He set me up here in '29, y'know."

The Don sat silent for a time, looking at his wine. His index finger at the base of the glass pushed it around in small circles. When he looked up at David his eyes were clear again. "A boss, he has to know what his *capos* are thinking all the time. How else you think I lasted so long? But ... there's a time when ideas get old, and it's old ideas that can kill you. I was smart enough to see that, y'know. That's why I'm going to die in bed."

The Don finished his wine, set the glass down, leaned back

in his chair with his hands clasped over his stomach. "All these years, David, you never asked me for help, and I want you to know I understand."

"You helped us when we really needed it. I still owe you."

The Don waved his hand as if to dismiss the thought. "Please. Your help—when you could give it—was greatly valued." Then, the Don's voice took on a more businesslike tone. "But now there's something you need. I can tell. How can I help you?"

"Marco's over in Italy, and I think he's in danger. I need some information so I can help him." He explained what he was doing for Alfieri and what he had learned about Bertaccini's death. "I need to know who sent the killer after Bertaccini. He came from Italy."

"So you would like some discreet inquiries made?"

"Yes."

The Don nodded. "We'll take care of it."

With that, the meeting came to a close. David rose and shook the Don's hand. "Thank you, Don Marini. *Grazie mille.*"

"Goodbye, my son. Don't worry. One of Carlo's men will contact you as soon as we have something."

## X minus 11 Days

*Boston, Monday, November 17*

Five days later, David received an anonymous call. As soon as David identified himself, the man said, "I got some information for you. Be at the Commons today between 11:00 and 12:00. Just wander around near the Frog Pond. I'll find you."

Then the line went dead.

David arrived early, and parked his car in the underground garage on Charles. Taking along a small bag he had filled with bread at home, he strolled about, stopping now and then to toss crumbs to the greedy sparrows and pigeons. The bare trees on the Commons stood out like black skeletons against a light gray sky. A few dry leaves were being whipped about by the wind. Here and there, people were hurrying along the walks that criss-cross the Commons, bundling themselves against the chill of the wind. All of them appeared to have a purpose. David felt conspicuous, because his only reason for being there was to be seen. He walked slowly along the shore of the Pond, then stopped in front of the Army-Navy Monument to watch a brace of mallards.

Just as he was about to resume walking, he heard footsteps behind him, and before he could turn around, a gravelly voice said: "Just keep looking straight ahead. I know you, but you don't want to know me."

"Fair enough. You have anything?"

"Could be. The hit man came through one of the Chicago families."

"Any idea know who he is? Anyone see him?"

"Nah. Just the driver who picked him up. But he ain't around to talk. They found him in the trunk of his car."

"What about the people who sent him?"

"Don't know, but I lay odds on top muscle. The word is the Pinellis are involved."

A shiver ran through David. Even as a child he had heard stories of the small and secret clan that, for almost a century, had been Italy's masters of sudden death, primarily by poison. No one knew their real name, but long ago they had been called the Pinellis and the name stayed with them. The name alone inspired terror in some circles. As toxicology grew more sophisticated, the family had adapted, developing a wide variety of exotic and synthetic poisons that were generally undetectable except by a highly skilled toxicologist. The Pinellis were methodical and careful: they studied a victim's habits and weaknesses thoroughly, and when they struck, death almost always appeared accidental or natural.

David thanked him for the information, then said he needed one more favor: an introduction to one of the family's friends in Milano. "With the Pinellis in this, I need to know who put out the contract."

"Check. Now... move along to your right — slowly — and keep walking. Don't turn around for a minute or so."

The sound of footsteps receded into the distance.

David waited awhile and then walked back through the Commons to his car.

# CHAPTER EIGHT

Mark was not your typical first-generation American, caught between two worlds. He never felt embarrassed by his parents' accent, for example. His father spoke English better than most Americans, and his mother had learned to speak it almost without an accent. Yet the Della Croce family did not ignore its roots. Far from it. Until he was thirteen, Mark spent every summer at the family estate at San Nicola, nestled among the hills of Valle d'Aosta, in the shadow of the Alps. He helped his uncle Sergio in the vineyards, fixing support posts and wires, pulling weeds and repairing equipment. This was a lazy, care-free time for Mark, when he spent days with his cousins and their friends, hiking in the nearby hills. Immersed in the language, he spoke Italian, as well as the local dialect, without a trace of an accent.

His parents had tried to raise him in the European way, but without notable success. He was their first-born and, in typically Italian fashion, they pampered him. They also lectured him constantly on proper decorum: table manners, dressing properly, showing respect for elders, etc. Their eldest was too much of a free spirit, however, and the lessons were listened to but not really followed. David, for example, would never have dreamed of interrupting when his father was expounding on a subject at dinner, but Mark felt no such restraint. Not even a glare from David would stop him from arguing if he thought his father had misspoken. In those situations, David would raise his eyes to the ceiling in silent frustration, wondering what sort of creature he and his wife had spawned.

But some rules were strictly enforced. David insisted on certain formalities. Regardless of how eager Mark might be to gulp down his dinner and dash outside to his friends, no one began eating until David had given the blessing—or left the table until David had folded his napkin and nodded his assent. And the children never called him Dad or Pops—it was always Father.

The subject of proper attire was also a bone of contention between David and his son. David's own clothes were custom made; he insisted that his collars have just the right amount of starch; his shoes were always shined, but not shiny; his trousers were always sharply creased. He held himself erect, as he had been taught by his own father. It was a mystery to him why Mark could not do the same, and why Mark slouched around, wore tattered Levis and sneakers full of holes, and rarely combed his hair. Whenever the subject came up, David could tell from the look in his son's eyes and the set of his jaw that words were having no effect. Mark was going to do what Mark wanted to do.

Even as an adult, Mark acted the rebel, or so it seemed to his father. Oh, Mark's clothes were well tailored, but they were not quite lawyerly. He owned only one suit, and rarely wore it. His sole concession to the firm's dress code was a rep tie. He had three of them, and wore them in unvarying succession, regardless of the jacket and slacks he was wearing. Generally, the match was good, but not always. Mark did not especially care.

Mark's parents were pleasantly surprised at how well he did in school. He never seemed to take particular pains to study, but managed top grades all through high school, even with year-round sports activities and dates almost every weekend. They were pleased to see that he became serious about studies when he went to Cornell, and were delighted when he went on to Yale Law School.

Until Mark's mother was killed in an automobile accident five years ago, life had been pretty much an unbroken series of successes for him: a steady, smooth ride. Whatever he wanted to do, he did well; wherever he went, people liked him. And he also married well: Gillian Page was gorgeous as well as rich; her father was managing partner of a large Wall Street law firm.

Then Gillian left him. She had been unable to make the transition to being the wife of an FBI agent, after a sheltered and pampered existence that included private schools, trips to Europe and the Caribbean, shopping on Fifth Avenue, Junior League, etc. She assumed that Mark eventually would join her father's firm, and she looked upon the FBI as a temporary adventure. She could not understand why he devoted so much time to his work. He could not tell her what he was doing, where he was going or when he would return, and she could not cope with that. She was bored: she wanted him home; she wanted to talk.

Money had been a problem, too. Gillian was accustomed to having furs, expensive clothes, vacations—and other things that Mark could not afford as a rookie agent. When he was assigned to Miami, for example, she desperately wanted to live at Palm Beach, near friends of her family, and tried to convince Mark that they should rent a condo there. *After all, he could commute to Miami, couldn't he?* She was crushed by his insistence that they live closer to his office, and she felt stifled in the small home they rented near Miami Beach. The same thing happened at Denver, his next rotational assignment. Stress gradually built up. There were long silences between them, and they began living separate lives. She went home to New York frequently on short visits, 'to revive herself', as she put it. Those visits gradually grew longer, and finally, after a two-week stay had stretched to a month, she called Mark and asked him to send her things to New York. She began divorce proceedings two months later.

The breakup of their marriage was traumatic for Mark. He felt betrayed. After thinking deeply about what had happened, however, he had to admit that part of the blame was his. What Gillian said was true, of course: he hadn't given her much of his time. He had been too absorbed in his work. But even so, she should have been able to cope with that, he thought. It struck him then how much his notions of marriage had been shaped by his family's traditions. He had assumed that Gillian would simply re-order her life to help him succeed, as his mother had done, and his grandmother before her, and that she would find fulfillment and satisfaction in that success. As an assistant District Attorney, Mark's father had faced the same pressures as Mark had, but Mark's mother had understood. Elena had realized that there was a part of David's world that she could not share, where his work took absolute precedence. So, she had built other bridges of communication. Of course, Elena had had children to help her in this, while Gillian had wanted to 'wait a few more years' before starting a family.

The day after Mark left the Bureau and joined his father's firm, Gillian called. She was in Boston visiting friends, she said, and really wanted to see him. They had a quiet lunch, and she gradually brought the conversation around to the subject of reconciliation. Their divorce decree was not yet final, she said with a significant look, and now he was with a fine law firm ... "I miss you."

Mark studied her face. *It's not that easy.* During their many months of separation, he had reflected often on why their marriage had not worked. Finally he decided that the real problem was that Gillian had to have constant support; she needed someone around to care for her, entertain her; she needed social interaction much more than he did. He knew that he would never be able to respond to all those needs.

After a pause he said, "I don't think it'll work, Gillian." His voice was soft but the tone of finality in it was unmistakable, and she averted her eyes.

After Gillian, Mark built an emotional wall around himself, and avoided any relationship that could lead to a romantic commitment. When he dated, it was only with women whom he found interesting, but who also had their own careers and were not looking for a husband. Most women found him attractive; they followed him with their eyes—the secretaries in the office called him their 'Robert Redford'—but Mark ignored their attention and in fact went out of his way to discourage it.

A perfectionist, he buried himself in his work. On mergers and acquisitions, for example, his "due diligence" was relentless. He would spend hours poring over the other side's financial reports, contracts and other corporate documents, searching out all their 'warts and pimples': the under-funded pension plan; the potential environmental problems; the overvalued or missing inventory; the unprofitable but iron-clad requirements contract; etc. Time meant nothing to him. Often, he would stand up to stretch his legs and find to his surprise that he was the only one left in the office. The people from the cleaning service who came at 1:00 AM grew accustomed to finding him still at his desk with his shirtsleeves rolled up, surrounded by piles of folders and loose papers.

After his father left for Italy to meet with Alfieri, Mark began preparing background files for his own trip, referring now and then to documents in the firm's 'bible' on the joint venture: a thick volume bound in black buckram containing the key documents that had led to its formation. Scanning those documents brought back memories of the long months of discussions that had resulted in the creation of AB Industries, the joint venture. Barnett, Daly & Della Croce had represented Alfindustria in the negotiations, and this was the first time Mark had seen Alfieri in action.

As a senior associate, Mark had been assigned to help in the drafting of the joint venture agreement, and was seated with the Alfindustria negotiating team at the conference table. The latest round of talks had dragged on for days and finally reached an impasse. Ten negotiators, five from each company, were seated on opposite sides of a long conference table. The Burlingame team was led by beefy Stan Tillson, its Senior Vice President for Finance. Opposite Tillson, heading the Italian team, sat Dr. Enrico Gallieri. Tall and distinguished, Gallieri had handled countless acquisitions for the giant company during a career that spanned more than thirty years. The ten men had spent more than eight hours in the stuffy conference room, breaking only for coffee and a lunch of open-faced sandwiches, soft drinks and wine. Cigarette smoke hovered in a light-blue haze over the table.

The Americans, their coats off, were obviously impatient with the slow pace of the negotiations. The Italians, on the other hand, were annoyed because the Americans doggedly refused to defer to them on issues dealing with operation of the joint venture. Since Alfindustria would own seventy percent of the stock, they assumed that they should be able to run it their own way, so long as Burlingame was protected as a minority shareholder.

Tempers were frayed. Tillson, brash as always, tried to force the issue. He hit the table with his open hand, causing the gray-haired Gallieri to start. "Look, Rico," Tillson said hoarsely. "We've been sitting here for ages and made absolutely no progress. I've just about had it. Either we get some fair method for valuing our assets or we'd better call it quits!"

Mark glanced over at Dr. Gallieri, who had barely managed to avoid wincing. *Tillson's done it again,* Mark thought with dismay. *He's going to blow this deal yet.* Mark knew that if Tillson pushed Gallieri too far, Gallieri would cut Tillson to ribbons, but do it so politely that Tillson would never know what happened until Gallieri gathered up his papers and ended the negotiations.

Tillson, bright but insensitive, had traveled extensively, but had learned little about other cultures. He ignored, or was incapable of dealing with, cultural differences, and he persisted in behaving everywhere as if he were still back in Cleveland. The matter of first names was typical. He seemed unwilling to accept the fact that in some countries the use of first names, particularly among professional people, was still largely reserved for family and close friends. Mark had tried without success to get the message across to Tillson through Burlingame's general counsel. Tillson regularly referred to Dr. Gallieri as 'Enrico', and now he had shortened it to 'Rico'.

Mark saw the courtly Gallieri smile sweetly at Tillson. *Too sweetly*, he thought.

Dr. Gallieri's jaw muscles moved slightly as he clenched his teeth, and the members of the Alfindustria team braced themselves for the storm. Gallieri took off his metal-rimmed glasses slowly and with his right hand gently smoothed the silver hair on his temple. The tension in the room rose. "Mr. Tillson," Gallieri began in a low voice, "We would..."

Into this highly charged atmosphere strode the legendary Dario Alfieri. No aide announced him; it was not necessary. As soon as he entered, he owned the room.

The Italians scrambled to their feet. Utterly gracious, moving quietly from person to person, Alfieri first greeted Dr. Gallieri and then introduced himself, in flawless Oxford English, to each of the members of the Burlingame team. He greeted the Alfindustria negotiators one by one, with a brief personal observation that made each of them feel—for that moment—that he was the most important person in the room.

Mark watched, fascinated. *This is star quality*.

Alfieri exuded presence. His entire bearing, and particularly his easy self-confidence, announced clearly: *the king has arrived*. He took a seat at the head of the table. After listening intently to a summary in Italian from Gallieri concerning the status of discussions and the impasse that had been reached,

Alfieri put his elbows on the table, steepled his fingers together and closed his eyes for a few moments. The room was absolutely silent. He looked around slowly, fixing his gaze briefly on the lead negotiators for each side. Then he spoke in English, choosing his words carefully. "We are indeed grateful to our good friends from Burlingame who have spent so many days here laboring with us on the agreement. Please be assured that we all share the same objective. Both of us want a joint venture that will grow and prosper—like a good marriage. I know that I speak for each of my colleagues when I say that we are ready to explore all ideas in order to arrive at a solution that is equitable."

Mark could feel the tension ease, as both Tillson and Gallieri sat back in their chairs, nodding agreement.

Alfieri then reviewed the thirteen points of contention one by one—never referring to notes. "Mr. Tillson has raised a valid point about the exchange rate for converting Lire to Dollars under the agreement," he said to Dr. Gallieri. "I am sure that we could agree to use, say, a six-month average exchange rate prior to the closing date instead of the rate at the closing." Turning to Tillson, he said: "You understand why we have difficulty with your company's long-term amortization rate. We write off our plant and equipment much more rapidly than you do, so their book value is much lower than it would be under your system. Couldn't we agree on a compromise system—just for valuing contributed assets?"

In less than ten minutes, Alfieri had obtained agreement on every point, extracting a concession first from one side and then from the other, with realistic compromise proposals for other points. After exchanging a few words of polite small talk with Dr. Gallieri, he left.

It was only then that Mark realized how perfectly Alfieri had orchestrated everything. He had delayed his appearance until the negotiations had reached a stalemate, and with the force of his personality he had convinced both sides to moderate their positions. But he had done it in a way that made each side feel that the other had conceded on the substantive issues and that the procedural ones had been settled fairly. As one of the Alfindustria negotiators confided to Mark afterward, "Dario can borrow your overcoat in a snowstorm and make you sorry you hadn't lent him your boots, too."

Mark's work during the negotiations had impressed Alfieri. He had taken an instant liking to Mark, who was about the same age as his own oldest son would have been. One evening he invited Mark to a reception at his villa in the exclusive Crocetta section of Torino. Two uniformed valets waited outside the large gates bearing the coat of arms that marked the entrance to the Alfieri compound. High, stucco-covered stone walls stretched far on either side. One of the valets checked Mark's invitation and escorted him along a walkway lined with perennials and trimmed shrubs, then opened the front door to let Mark in. The butler took Mark's coat and directed him to the foyer, where Dario and his wife were receiving their guests.

Mark had heard people at Alfindustria speak with envy about Alfieri's villa, and now he understood why. The high-ceilinged rooms were light and inviting, with furniture that once had graced the salons and rooms of French chateaux. In every room he saw paintings and art objects that any museum would have been proud to possess. Most of them had been purchased by Dario and his wife, and Dario's father before him, through an agent in Rome who had represented the Alfieri family for almost forty years, and who had an unerring instinct for an artist's best works. The Alfieris demanded no less. Over a legendary career, the agent had negotiated for them with major collectors and museum directors throughout the world. His reputation was such that, whenever a major work was about to come onto the market, he would invariably be among the first contacted. The pride and joy of Dario's library were the leather-bound folio-sized catalogs of their art collection, compiled by their curators, describing each of the works and giving its provenance.

Beneath the Alfieri villa was a huge vault blasted out of solid rock, in which the most precious pieces of their collection were stored. But Dario insisted on enjoying his art, so whenever he and his wife, Adriana, were in residence they had a selection brought out and replaced every month. At the rate the Alfieris were buying, years would pass before the art objects that Mark was looking at would be seen again after they were returned to the vault. There were two paintings, however, that invariably hung while the Alfieris were at home. These were their favorites; by no means the finest of their collection, but the ones they most enjoyed living with: a quiet view of Torino by Canaletto, which hung in Dario's study; and a Madonna by Andrea del Sarto in their private chapel.

Dario and his wife were receiving their guests in the foyer. Before Mark had a chance to introduce himself, Dario greeted him with a smile and introduced him to his wife. "So you are David's son," she said in perfect English. "We are delighted that you could come. Dario tells me that you have been a great help to him these last weeks."

They chatted briefly about family matters, and then Dario introduced Mark to the guest of honor and excused himself to receive other guests.

Suitably equipped with a drink, Mark made his way into the main salon, where he chatted briefly with several of the Alfindustria senior executives. Four smaller rooms opened onto the long salon, two on either side. The sliding doors to one of them were open and the light was on. Mark noticed several raised display cases and, curious, excused himself and went in. An elaborately carved ivory chess set caught his eye, and he leaned over to look at it more closely.

"Do you play chess?"

He turned around and saw Alfieri, who was smiling.

"A bit," Mark said, modestly. "But I haven't had a real match in more than a month."

"Let me show you around."

Mark detected a hint of excitement in Dario's voice. Mark's father had told him once that chess was one of Dario's passions, and that he was an inveterate collector of classic chess sets. The set Mark was looking at was French, Dario explained, made in Dieppe about 1760, a classic for the period and considered unsurpassed for workmanship, beautiful carving, proportion and balance. In another case, he pointed out an ivory set from England that was one of his favorites, a fine example of Charles Handilow's work.

"This one," Dario said as he moved on to the next case, "is another favorite. It's medieval. If you look closely, you'll notice that the pieces are not all alike."

He explained that there were no complete single sets from the period. He himself had been collecting pieces for several years, buying them whenever they appeared at sales or auctions. He still needed three more white pawns, a black rook and a white queen for his set. He motioned to the other cases, which contained sets made of amber, agate, hardwood - even one made of china by Meissen. "I still like ivory best. Beautiful pieces are as important to me as a good, close match."

Mark remembered that Dario was an enthusiastic amateur player, and had reached high tournament ranking during his student days in England. He sensed that Dario was testing him, curious about how strong a player he was. "You could probably spot me a rook and still smother me."

Dario's eyes lit up. "Unless I am mistaken, I detect a—how do you say it—hustler? Come over this way, please." He put his arm around Mark's shoulders and led him to a cocktail table with an inlaid chessboard top. Then he went to a cabinet and took out a box of chessmen and began placing pieces on the board. He motioned to Mark to sit opposite him. "I have a little problem for you," he said, taking five pieces—two rooks, a bishop and the king and queen—from each side and placing them on the board so that Mark would be playing black. Then he arranged four black and five white pawns. When he was finished, he sat back and folded his arms. "This is one of my favorite situations. Very elegant. Black to move and mate. Would you like to try?"

"I'll probably make a mess of it," Mark said with a grin as he leaned forward and studied the board. He had not played competitively in over a year, but he had made a practice of studying annotated games. There was something vaguely familiar about the positioning, particularly the doubled white pawn with the black pawn facing them with its bishop behind, and the white queen deep in black territory at QB7. *White is threatening*, Mark thought. *How can I put the white king in check and keep him there until I can bring my rooks into action?* As soon as he looked at his rook at Kkn1 the answer came to him: *Morphy. Of course! This was one of his masterpieces*. He started to reach for the rook and stopped. Something told him not to move just yet, because that would make the puzzle seem too easy. He pretended to deliberate several seconds. "I have it," he said as he sacrificed his rook by moving it next to the king to put the king into check. Then, keeping the white king in check with his queen until the king was forced to move in front of its own rook on the KB file, he moved the other black rook in for checkmate.

Alfieri smiled. "You are *molto cortese*, Mark. May I call you Mark? I think perhaps we ought to play even. My 'formidable' puzzle took you less than a minute. I saw the way you started to reach for that rook right away."

Mark flushed slightly and began to demur.

Alfieri waved his hand slightly. "No need to explain," he said with a grin. "In your position I would have done the same. 'Don't embarrass the old warrior', that sort of thing." He paused. "Whenever someone tells me he plays chess, I ask him to try one of my problems. I don't really care whether he solves it or not. What I look at is how he handles it. I always learn something about his character. And character, after all, is everything."

# CHAPTER NINE

## X minus 19 Days

*Boston*
*Sunday, November 9*

Mark arrived at Logan Airport in good time for his flight to Frankfurt. Knowing that he would arrive rumpled and stiff, he had dressed casually, with a long-sleeved navy sport shirt, gray slacks and a well-worn Harris tweed jacket. His Burberry trench coat with a winter lining was draped over his arm.

Waiting to check in, he glanced idly around at the other travelers. Before long, he got the uncanny feeling that he was being watched. That sixth sense had never left him after his years with the Bureau. *Who could it be?* Gazing idly about, he saw nothing unusual, only the daily bustle of a major international terminal: a few passengers following porters pushing piles of suitcases; others struggling with more luggage than they should have taken; parents trying futilely to keep their children from skittering beyond their control; homogenized executives with mile-weary looks. Everyone bent on getting someplace in a hurry. Everyone seemingly intent on his own affairs. *But someone out there is interested in me.*

Nonchalantly, Mark scanned the people waiting in line as well as those who were standing about, and wondered how many of them would show up on his flight.

Eight of them did. A mixed bag: two talkative couples; a tall slim man in his late twenties with a beard and faded jeans; two middle-aged men, short and heavyset, in business suits; a rangy brunette who flowed herself into the seat ahead of him; a young man with a crewcut who looked like a serviceman returning from leave; and a gray-haired dowager, rearranged by corset and posture so that she resembled one of the figureheads he remembered from the museum at Old Mystic Seaport.

When Mark's plane finally arrived at Frankfurt, he was exhausted. He had spent hours in a futile effort to sleep. The mindless chatter of the couple in the row behind him had been a constant irritant, and he had drifted in and out of a semi-conscious state, finally dozing off near the end of the flight. At the terminal, Mark walked slowly from the plane as other passengers streamed by, heading for the exit or the transit lounge. He lost one of the couples, the dowager, the returning G.I. and one of the businessmen. Passing through the transit lounge on his way to the washroom, he noticed that the brunette was already in the lounge. She was sitting alone at one of the tables, engrossed in a paperback. Dressed in a classic black wool suit, she had thrown her camels hair coat carelessly on the seat next to her. She had a matching handbag in her lap. The only jewelry she wore was a gold embossed comb that held her soft curls back. Her long, shapely legs were crossed, and one camel-colored pump dangled indolently from her toes.

Sylvia looked up after Mark passed by. *Tall and broad-shouldered: exactly how they described him.* She was amused by the loose-limbed way he walked, and pictured him more as a young liberal arts professor than a junior partner in a prominent law firm. *A three-piece suit somehow would not be right for him.* Mentally, she ran over the other facts about him that they had given her: parents born in Italy; father from a prominent Piemonte family, and a close friend of Dario Alfieri, also with links to New England Mafia chief, Oreste Marini; Cornell undergrad; Yale Law; four years with F.B.I.; junior corporate partner with father's law firm.

She tried to look casual as she waited for him to return to the cafeteria, but she was nervous and tense. *I'm supposed to make contact with him and gain his confidence. Why on earth did I tell them I would do this? And what if he finds out?* The thought of her lover caused a tremor of panic.

What had started as a glamorous escapade—a romance with a dashing, immensely wealthy man—had turned into a nightmare. He had been so thoughtful and considerate when they first met three months ago, showering her with attention, inviting her to lavish parties on his yacht, giving her expensive presents, that she had been completely won over. She knew that he was married, but shut her eyes to it.

Their relationship had started out innocently enough. The bank where she worked was financing a small acquisition for his company, and she had come to the closing to help with documents. During the brief ceremonies in the bank's main conference room, as she organized the signing and notarizing of agreements and attachments, she had felt his eyes on her. Later, as they were leaving the cavernous room, he came up behind her, and spoke in perfect English.

"Miss D'Angelo, let me thank you for your help this morning. I've rarely had a closing that smooth—and I'm sure you were responsible."

"Thank you, *dottore*."

He complimented her on her Italian and then, taking her hand and kissing it, he said good-bye. He called the next day and asked her for lunch. That was followed by a whirlwind of dinners, evenings at the opera, trips to Cannes, London, Rio by his company's private jet.

The first indication of trouble came the day after she went to spend a weekend at his lodge, a sprawling log structure perched on a cliff north of the town of Courmayeur, near the Swiss border. He was on the veranda, leaning on the railing and looking out at the mountains, while she was in the living room by the fireplace. As she happened to look out toward the glass doors leading to the veranda, she noticed that the cook's cat was walking back and forth on the railing, its tail held high so it would touch him as it passed. Suddenly, he reached out and brushed the cat off the railing, watching without expression as it tumbled in the air and smashed against the rocks far below. The cook found the cat's body, and later she overheard the cook talking in the kitchen about it. The conversation was unclear, but she caught the words *pervertito* (pervert) and *sadico* (sadist). She also noticed that her lover was becoming more temperamental and withdrawn, and given to violent mood swings. Even the most trivial contradiction could change his expression to ice or send him into a rage. And he was plotting something, she was sure of it—something that was extremely important to him—and it consumed all of his energies and attention. She had caught snatches of arguments with a strange man, and muffled telephone conversations at strange hours.

After several days of agonizing, Sylvia finally decided to break off the affair and return to the States. She had felt drawn into a web and unable to escape, but once she reached her decision, it was as if a weight had been lifted from her. In a few days she would be on her way home and she would start getting ready for the spring semester at Wharton.

The day before she was planning to tell him she was leaving, she received a call at the bank that changed everything. The man on the other end introduced himself, and said that he was a political attache at the American Embassy. He wanted to speak with her—in private. Sylvia was puzzled. *What on earth would the State Department want from me?* Aloud, she said, "I don't understand. Why can't we talk about it on the phone?

He was insistent. "I'm sorry, Miss D'Angelo, but I can't really discuss it now. All I can say is that it's a matter of national security."

Sylvia reluctantly agreed to meet. The attache, who called himself Zimmerman, drove her to a *trattoria* far enough away from the bank so that she would not be recognized. They sat in a quiet corner where they could talk freely. Zimmerman attempted to make small talk to put her at ease.

Sylvia cut him off. "Hey, look, Mr. Zimmerman—if that's

your real name—I don't mean to be rude, but I want to know what this is all about. Just why do you have to talk with me?"

The attache was taken aback, and stammered, "It's pretty complicated, and has to do with espionage. We're not sure yet, but we think that your friend—let's just call him Mr. X—may be a Russian agent."

Sylvia feigned ignorance. "What makes you think I know this Mr. X?"

"Oh, come now. You think we don't know you're having an affair with him?" He whispered the name.

She sat silent for a moment, then said, "Well, suppose I do know him. What business is that of yours?"

"As a matter of fact, it is very much our business." He went on to explain how the political section of the Embassy followed developments in foreign countries, gathering information about government plans and policies, about important people and organizations, and working with local intelligence services to follow activities—overt as well as clandestine—of other governments, particularly the Soviets and their East Bloc allies.

Sylvia shook her head. "I hear what you're saying, but I don't see how I can help you. I'm leaving for good in a week or so."

Zimmerman was not discouraged. He used his most persuasive manner, and appealed to Sylvia's patriotism. "You have to help us. If Mr. X is the one we're after, he could be a serious threat to Italy as well as the United States. Right now, we don't know if he is, but we have to find out, and you're in a perfect position to help. We need to know everything possible about him: who he sees, where he goes, what he does. Everything. You never know what might be important. I can't tell you much more than that."

"You're trying to tell me he's a communist? You must be joking."

"I'm not saying he is. We're not sure, but he's one of the men we're checking."

She pondered a moment. "How long do I have to do this?"

"A month or so. Max. We should know for sure by then."

"What are you going to do? Arrest him or something?"

"Nah. We just want to *know*. The Soviets are planning something big, and we need to know if he's part of it." Then Zimmerman backed off slightly. "Of course, we can't force you to do this. And it could be dangerous." He paused. "Will you help?"

"Let me think about it."

When he called the next day, she said yes, but she had no idea why—maybe it was the excitement of foreign intrigue that attracted her. Years of competing with three older brothers had given her a spirit of adventure and made her something of a rebel. Whatever her brothers did, she wanted to do. When they played work-up softball, she chased foul balls for them. As soon as she was strong enough to hold a bat, she was a regular in right field, catching flies easily even if she could hardly get her hands around the ball well enough to throw it. When her brothers climbed trees, she was right behind them, trying to reach a higher limb. Two of her brothers swam with a local AAU team, and did quite well, but eventually she outswam both of them, qualifying twice for Junior Olympics and becoming a star on the Brown swim team. One of her brothers had backpacked on the Appalachian Trail from Hanover, NH through the White Mountains, so she did it too—by herself— and almost froze to death when she was caught in a sudden Autumn snowstorm on Mt. Washington. Sylvia bridled at rules or conventions that prevented her from doing something that boys were permitted to do. As far as she was concerned, she could take care of herself very well, thank you.

So, Sylvia agreed to stay on in Torino and spy on her lover. She was given a contact, a woman who called herself Bianca, and she and Bianca talked regularly about what Sylvia's lover was doing. Sylvia never saw her contact; she would be given a number to call—a different one each time—and she would tell Bianca where he was going, who he was planning to see, and anything unusual that she saw or heard. Bianca was particularly interested in telephone calls that her lover made, and she asked Sylvia to try to remember exact words that were said and any names that she heard mentioned.

Ten days ago, on the spur of the moment, Sylvia had decided to fly to Connecticut and spend some time with her parents. She wanted to get away, if only for a few days. One sunny afternoon she drove into the countryside and stopped at Cornwall Bridge. She took our her camera and began walking here and there, trying to find the best place to catch the contrast between the picturesque town buildings and the dark green of some blue spruces.

A man came up to her and stopped.

"Miss D'Angelo?"

She was immediately suspicious. "Yes. What is it?"

He showed her an ID card with an official emblem. "I'm from the State Department. "I'd like to talk to you about Bianca."

Her eyes widened in surprise. "I can't believe you people! How did you know where I was?"

He gave her a small smile. "We have our ways. But we've got another assignment for you."

She held up her hand in protest. "Stop right there! I'm done with this cloak and dagger stuff. One more week and I'm leaving Italy—I'm out of there for good."

He was insistent. "But this is part of the same thing. There's an attorney flying over to Torino on Sunday. He's going to check on a company there. The problem is that he could interfere with our whole plan. And it could be dangerous for him."

"What am I supposed to do, break his legs?"

The man smiled. "Nothing that drastic. For now, all you have to do is make contact with him on the way over and maybe get to know him." He handed her a folder with a small photograph of Mark attached with a paper clip. "This is what he looks like and here's some background on him."

As soon as Sylvia saw Mark return to the lounge area and head for the cafeteria line, she put down her paperback and went to stand behind him. He had just shaved, and she caught a faint musky scent of aftershave lotion. Sylvia was tall for a woman—in her heels she was not much shorter than Mark—and she found herself looking at the back of his head. She noticed that he had not had a haircut in several weeks, and when she saw the leather patches on his elbows, she smiled to herself. *Those didn't come with the jacket. I'll bet he had them sewn on later. Probably so attached to the jacket that he refused to retire it.* She was sure he would love puppies.

Now was the time for her to speak to him, but the words refused to come. *How am I supposed to 'make contact'? And what sophisticated line do I use?* She had rehearsed this scene several times, but nothing she practiced seemed right. Finally, she just said the first thing that came into her mind. "I see you survived the flight." As soon as she said it, she cringed inside. *How incredibly banal!*

But he turned and gave her a wan smile. "Afraid the jury's still out on that. I'll tell you after my coffee. I'm still half asleep."

Sylvia liked his easy, lopsided grin, but she was taken aback by his gray eyes and steady gaze. For just an instant, she saw a hardness in them, and then they turned friendly and warm. Even as he spoke, she felt as if he were analyzing her and deliberately keeping her at a distance. She knew that men considered her attractive; she was accustomed to having them flirt with her, and amused by their sexual preening and exhibition when they thought she might be watching. But she did not sense this in Mark. He was not trying to impress her; on the contrary, she sensed a reserve in him, a holding back, even though his words sounded friendly and open. There was a quiet strength about him, and she was reminded of a leopard, lean and graceful, always observant. At the cash register, she mentioned that she had a table and asked Mark to join her.

As Sylvia led the way, Mark admired how smoothly she walked, with a long, even stride, holding her head high and her back straight, as if she were balancing something on her head. She looked as if she had just stepped out of a showcase: makeup perfect, eyes bright, not a hair out of place and not a wrinkle in her clothes. He, on the other hand, felt as if he had slept in the same clothes for three days. *How did she do it?*

They sat and talked quietly, and as Mark drank his coffee he looked at her more closely. What impressed him most was her skin, which was pale and smooth, almost like ivory against her dark hair and her full, red lips, and it reminded him of the Odalisque by Ingres. *A real natural beauty.*

Sylvia would have been surprised if Mark had said that aloud. She never thought of herself as particularly attractive. Growing up, she had been a quintessential tomboy, skinny and seemingly all legs. The year she turned 14 was the year of the butterfly for her: her braces came off; her freckles disappeared; and her figure began filling out. The boys she had competed with began hovering around her, like bees and honey. She was a little nonplussed by it all. Gradually she came to understand what her mother had been telling her all along about how ladies should look and act. The end product was dazzling.

Sylvia felt Mark's eyes on her and she looked back with a small smile. "Caught you staring."

"Sorry about that. You reminded me of a painting. I swear."

Her cheeks glowed slightly.

During their conversation, they discovered that they were both traveling to Torino, and introduced themselves. Mark was curious about her. Torino was an unlikely place for a career girl, and an American at that, so he asked her how she happened to come to Italy to work.

Sylvia seemed anxious to talk. She said that she had planned to get her MBA after she graduated from Brown, but decided that she needed more business experience first. She had worked summers for her father, who ran a small manufacturing company in New Britain, and he had suggested banking. Through one of his friends, she had interviewed and gotten a position with City National Bank. Because she was fluent in Italian, they sent her to their Rome office. After about a year, when she was preparing to go back to the States, Banca Commerciale offered her a position in Torino, in its foreign exchange department. She came to Torino thinking that she would stay perhaps six months, but that was almost a year ago. She did not mention why she had stayed.

Sylvia looked at Mark over her cup of coffee. "And how about you? What takes you to Torino?"

"Me? I'm just a lawyer, visiting a client. Nothing exciting." He parried her questions about what he was going to be doing, and they talked mostly about life in Italy, things they had seen and done.

There was something about Sylvia that puzzled Mark, and he couldn't put a finger on it. It seemed illogical. She appeared so self-assured, so in control, yet when he looked in her eyes he thought he also saw vulnerability, and now and then caught a hint of fear. He had noticed it first when she avoided his questions about people she knew in Torino.

Soon the call came for them to board the Alitalia flight bound for Milan and Rome. Seated together on the plane, they continued a lively conversation. In spite of himself, Mark was strongly attracted to her, and the flight to Milan went quickly.

Before leaving the baggage area, Mark looked around. Sylvia was the only one of his special passengers who had gotten off. *Ah, well, another theory shot. Maybe no one was following.* He offered her a ride to Torino, but she demurred, saying that she was being met.

Mark wanted to see more of her. "Y'know, I'll probably be here a week or so. How about getting together one evening?"

She smiled. "I'd like that. Give me a call at the bank." As soon as her bags arrived, she waved to him. *"Ciao."*

Mark passed through customs and went over to meet Guido, who was waiting for him in the lobby, and they walked to the company car. They had not gone far when Mark heard a car approaching behind them, and recognized its deep-throated rumble. "That Ferrari coming up behind us needs a tune-up, Guido."

Guido turned to look at the car, then looked over at Mark, surprised. "Hey. How'd you know it was a Ferrari?"

"The way it sounds. Like the Jag 6 and the Maserati V8 Quattroporte. I could pick one out anywhere." He turned to look as a silver classic 1970 365 GT 2x2 went by. He could not see the driver, but he thought the passenger looked like Sylvia.

Mark sat in the back seat of the Fiat so that he could stretch out better and perhaps sleep on the way to Torino. Soon they were out of the parking area and on the A-4 Autostrada, and the Fiat kilometer signs and plane trees lining the shoulder flashed past as the 130 purred its rapid way through the flat rice country. Mark leaned back.

Guido stayed in the passing lane, his headlights flashing to warn drivers ahead to give way and let him by. Just as he was about to pass two trucks, the rear truck pulled out into the passing lane, forcing him to brake and swerve to his right, into the outside lane. Blocked now by a truck in both lanes, Guido cursed under his breath. The truck that had moved out began slowing down, keeping their car in the outside lane. Just then a silver Mercedes roared up behind, boxing them in completely, and the truck on their left began edging over into their lane. Guido honked and shook his fist up at the cab.

The sudden movement had thrown Mark forward. "What the hell's the matter with that guy?"

Guido was concentrating, and only grunted.

The truck on their left kept moving over, forcing Guido toward the edge of the road. The line of trees, whizzing by, came closer and closer. Mark could see that there was not enough room on the narrow shoulder for the car.

"Hold on!" Guido yelled.

Mark was thrown against the back of the front seat as Guido downshifted and jammed on the brakes. Their car lurched and shuddered under the combined effect. As brakes squealed, Mark felt the Mercedes ram into their rear. At that instant Guido found his opening. He swerved to his left, pushing the accelerator to the floor. Mark was pressed back against his seat as they catapulted forward. They shot through the opening between the median barrier and the passing truck and sped ahead before its driver could react and close the gap. Looking back, Mark saw the Mercedes go out of control and careen crazily along the shoulder, ending up on its side against a plane tree. He half-whistled in admiration. *"Magnifico!"*

Guido looked at Mark in the rear view mirror and allowed a slight smile to crease his lean, lined face. He wig-wagged his right hand as if to say: "Eh...not bad."

The rest of the trip sped by, and soon they were pulling into the small parking area in front of the Principi. Mark had enjoyed the tired elegance of the hotel during the many weeks he had spent there on the joint venture negotiations. He checked in and went into the lounge area near the hotel's bar. As he sat there, thinking about what lay ahead, he could already feel a growing sense of excitement, the same feeling he had had when he was in the Bureau.

Mark's friends at law school had been surprised when he decided to join the FBI after getting his degree. Of all the top students in his class, he was the one everyone assumed was headed for a Supreme Court clerkship or a career in corporate law. After all, he had landed a summer clerk's job with a prestigious Wall Street firm after his first year, and they had invited him back for a second summer, meaning that they were thinking seriously of him as a possible associate. In his third year he was selected as one of the editors of the Law Journal, a signal honor.

He spent four years as an FBI agent. Though he enjoyed the work immensely, he rebelled at the Bureau's petty regimentation. His father's firm was growing rapidly and prospering, so when David asked Mark to join them, Mark accepted, starting as an associate in the corporate and securities department. He loved his work there as well, but now and then he still felt a twinge of nostalgia when he thought about the Bureau. He had experienced a special thrill on assignments—an exhilaration that came from an all-encompassing involvement in battle—and it *was* a battle of sorts that the Bureau was waging against crime. It was partly that thrill that sustained agents during the weeks and months they were forced to spend on major investigations, when they had to devote practically every waking hour to their 'case' or other Bureau activity.

Mark was sitting at a table near the hotel bar, nursing a martini. He reached over to the next table to pick up a copy of *Corriera della Sera* that someone had left and was browsing through it when he saw Sylvia enter. She came toward him, and he half rose, smiled in greeting, and offered her a seat. As she walked by, she signaled that she could not stop, and continued walking into the alcove between the bar and the reading room and sat next to a man whose back was turned to Mark. The two began a whispered conversation.

After a few minutes, Mark picked up his key and went up to his room.

Sylvia's contact had called her not more than ten minutes after she reached her apartment and started unpacking.

"Bianca here. How did it go on the plane?"

"OK, I guess. He says he wants to take me to dinner."

"Good." Then, after a pause, "He's staying at the Principi, room 357. We'd like you to see him again tonight and give him a message. Can you do that?"

"I guess so." "You don't have to worry about your friend. He's out of town on business and won't be back for a couple days."

"What am I supposed to do?"

"Go up to his room and ..."

Sylvia interrupted, "To his room? I can't do that!"

Bianca's voice was calm. "Just listen. All you have to do is give him a message. Tell him he's in danger, and that he could get hurt if he gets mixed up with AB Industries. That's it. If he asks you why, say you don't know. But arrange to see him - soon. And call me first thing tomorrow. Got that?"

"I guess so." Sylvia sat by the telephone, stunned. *What kind of mess am I getting myself into? Mark's nice, all right, but go to his room? What will he think?*

Mark had just finished drying off after a hot shower when he heard a soft knock at the door. It was not quite eleven. He wrapped a large bath towel around his waist like a sarong, grabbed a kimono and went to the door.

"Yes? What is it?"

He opened the door slightly and saw Sylvia standing in the hall. She looked up and down the hall, a frightened expression on her face, then moved toward the door.

"I've got to talk with you," she whispered.

Mark opened the door and let her in. A hint of Chanel wafted after her as she moved by him.

"You're in danger, Mark! If you get mixed up with AB Industries, you could get hurt. Believe me."

Mark took her in his arms and held her gently. "Now just calm down. Nobody's going to do any hurting." He could feel her body shuddering slightly. When she raised her head to speak, he kissed her on the forehead. "Shhh. Don't talk." Then, in a stern voice, he said, "Now, what's all this about me getting hurt? And who told you about AB Industries?"

"I can't say, but they told me to give you the message."

Mark was about to ask her again when she put her index finger lightly on his lips. He could feel the tenseness leave her body as she gradually relaxed. She leaned almost limply against him, and they stood together silently, bodies lightly touching, enjoying the warmth and softness of the contact.

Sylvia felt surrounded by a deep sense of contentment and peace in Mark's arms, as if she had been a boat in a storm, battered by waves, and had finally reached a sheltered harbor. He made her feel as if nothing could touch her while she was with him. After a while, completely relaxed and composed once more, she drew away slightly, put her hands on his chest, running her fingers slowly through the thick curly hairs. Reaching under his kimono, she ran her hands over his biceps and shoulders, feeling his taut skin and the whipcord-like muscles reacting to her touch. Then she raised herself on tiptoe and kissed him lightly on the cheek. Her voice was husky.

"You're very sweet, Mark, you know that? I only wish..." Then she stopped and pulled away to leave.

He looked at her questioningly.

"Nothing. Just, I wish…"

He released her reluctantly. She opened the door far enough so that she could look up and down the corridor. Seeing it empty, she hurried down to the elevator. Mark watched her walk away. At the end of the corridor, she waved back to him and was gone.

# CHAPTER TEN

## X minus 18 Days

*Torino*
*Monday, November 10*

As usual during the first days after arriving in Italy, Mark was half-awake about 3:00 a.m. He struggled to sleep again, but was only partially rested when he answered his wake-up call. He groaned as he slumped out of bed and onto the floor, where he lay motionless for almost a minute. Then he began a series of slow stretching exercises, and finally forced himself to do some sit-ups and pushups. He had started this routine in high school, long before fitness became a fad, and rarely began or ended a day without some type of exercise. Generally, he found it refreshing, but this morning it was a chore.

When he finally made his way to the lobby, Guido was waiting, and they stepped out into a cold November day. The sky was completely overcast, and a light drizzle was falling. Guido was chipper, despite the weather, and asked brightly what was on the day's schedule.

"A couple errands, first. Can you get me a revolver?"

Guido looked at him, surprised. "It all depends. What kind?"

"How about a Smith & Wesson? .38 Chief Special, three-inch barrel, if you can."

Guido rubbed his chin. "That might not be so easy, but I'll give it a try. A Beretta, that'd be no problem. German, Swiss or British aren't so hard to find, either. And you want a revolver instead of an automatic. Hmmm." He explained that Mark would need a special firearms permit, which normally took about six months. "We can handle that, though. I'll ask Dr. Alfieri's office to make a couple calls."

"Second thing. I need a place where I can work out while I'm here. Can you find me a karate master?"

Guido looked sharply at Mark, wanting to be sure he was serious. "I think I know just the guy for you if he's still teaching. I trained with him myself a few years ago."

"He's pretty good, is he?"

Guido nodded."Santucci's one of the best. Has had his own dojo here for years. If he's still teaching and agrees to work with you, you couldn't do any better."

In less than ten minutes, Guido was steering the Fiat 130 past the gatekeeper at Alfindustria corporate headquarters and into the underground garage. He parked the car in an enclosed space, which he locked, and then escorted Mark to Dr. Alfieri's office. After the usual pleasantries, Dario reviewed briefly what he had told David. Mark reported that his father was already out in Illinois investigating Bertaccini's death, and he expected to hear from him very soon.

Then he asked whether he could have his friend Jim help. He explained that they had gone to college and served in the FBI together, and said that Jim would be a great help. "Father also thought it would be a good idea. Jim might be a little 'rough around the edges,' but he's a computer genius, and a bulldog when it comes to investigation. If there's anything fishy going on at AB Industries, he'll find it."

"If you think he can help, by all means bring him over."

"I wanted him to work with me on the bids and the financials. He knows someone high up in SISMI, too."

At the mention of the Italian secret intelligence agency, Dario registered mild surprise, but he said nothing. As he escorted Mark to the door, he said, half apologetically, "I won't be able to help much with your investigation, I'm afraid. But that shouldn't surprise you. I would be the last person to ask people questions here, because they would either be too nervous or too busy trying to figure out what I want to hear."

Dario said that he wanted the three to do exactly what Mark had just done: explain what he was doing and why, and mention any new theories or ideas. He wanted to stay abreast of their investigation but doubted that he himself would be able to contribute much.

After the meeting, Mark gave Dario's secretary a sheet of paper listing files that he would need. After looking over the list, she explained that some of the items were confidential and would require an official requisition. She would have the others delivered to him immediately.

Within minutes after Mark had settled into his office, the files that he had requested began arriving in large manila folders, all neatly tied and sealed. He spent more than three hours poring over the bid files of the marketing department and the detailed reports that had been written about the fire at the Modena plant and the fiasco with the financials. He went back to Dario's secretary just before noon and asked her for a computer run of the Alfindustria stockholder register, listing any organizations or individuals holding more than 100,000 shares. She protested that that would take days, but Mark persuaded her to speed up the process.

Mark had barely gathered his papers when Guido appeared at the door. He announced that the karate teacher still had his dojo. He was semi-retired, but he still had a few students and he agreed to work with Mark.

As one of the largest employers in northern Italy, Alfindustria maintained sports facilities near all of its larger factories; no office was so small that its employees did not at least have access to a soccer field and a place to play *bocce*. Santucci's dojo was attached to the sports building by one of Alfindustria's factories on the outskirts of town. The drive to the factory took fifteen minutes, as they had to negotiate their way through the noon traffic. They arrived a little early, so Guido showed Mark around before leaving. The dojo was a large hall, completely functional and devoid of decoration except for an Alpini banner hung on one wall. The floor, immaculate, had a rich sheen. The only equipment visible was a heavy bag suspended from one of the large overhead beams, a speed bag and a neat pile of mats in one corner. The locker room was like some Mark had seen in health clubs, but without any commercial frills: no announcements of coming events, no clippings, no ads, no distractions. The clear message was that this place was meant for serious work. Open wooden lockers with name tags lined two walls. Mark chose an empty one and changed quickly into his well-worn *gi* and started for the hall.

Holding a towel in his right hand, he pulled open the door of the dojo with his left and stepped inside. As he took the next step, he noticed a shape hurtling toward him. Instinctively, he ducked his head and dove to his left, just as a foot came to within inches of his ear. He rolled to his feet in the cat position.

Facing him was a man about his own height, wearing a black gi that had been re-sewn and patched several times. He had a red kerchief tied around his neck, and his grizzled hair was clipped short. A craggy face betrayed his age, which Mark estimated at sixty or so, but he moved with the ease of a much younger man. With heavy muscles through the shoulders and upper arms, he reminded Mark of an ox.

Since this was his teacher, or *senpai*, Mark bowed in greeting. "Good afternoon, Santucci *senpai*," Mark said, using the Japanese title that was universal in the world of karate.

The older man returned the bow. "Welcome to our dojo."

Mark thanked him and added, "It's an honor to be here."

Mark and Enzo did not recognize one another. They had met before, of course, but the last time was several years ago, at an Alpini reunion, when Mark was much younger. Guido had not told Enzo Mark's name, only that he was a visitor and a friend of Alfieri. The name Santucci did not register with Mark, either. His father had told Mark many stories about

Enzo, but had always referred to him by his nickname, Toro, and Mark had never known him by any other name.

Standing at rigid attention with his thick arms crossed, Enzo studied Mark. He had little use for most so-called black belts, feeling that they did not deserve the rank. Mark, for example, had come into the gym unprepared, which was dangerous. On the other hand, his reflexes were sharp and he moved quickly, which was good. And he seemed to be in reasonably good shape.

Enzo rubbed his hands together. "So what're you looking for?"

"My timing's way off, and I need to work on it. I haven't done any real sparring in over a year, only some *kata*."

Enzo said that he had little use for the ritual karate moves. His classes were mostly for self-defense. "No flashy tournament stuff here. Nothing fancy. Just your basic moves—with power. My students can handle themselves anywhere—street fights, whatever. That all right?"

Mark nodded.

Enzo strode into the center of the gym. "First we stretch, then warm up." He led Mark through a series of calisthenics to limber up, gradually picking up the cadence until beads of sweat appeared on Mark's forehead and drops began trickling from the end of his nose. Enzo threw Mark a towel. "Dry off and walk around. Soon we start working."

When he felt that Mark was ready, Enzo tossed him a pair of bag gloves. In his dojo, he said, he stressed arm technique, and he believed that boxing moves were important because they developed fast movement and power. He started Mark with the speed bag. Mark began slowly: straight right, sideways right, straight left, sideways left. Gradually, he felt himself moving smoothly through his old routine, building up speed. The room resounded with the rapid tattoo of the bag.

Enzo watched with approval, and then he moved Mark to

the heavy bag. At first, he let Mark work out on the bag alone, watching critically as Mark snapped out left jabs, moving in with hard rights and hook combinations, meeting the bag yet keeping it moving, now and then feinting at the bag to let it swing past and meeting it again on the downswing with a flurry of short punches.

"Feet closer together! Shoulder-width apart. Balance! Balance! More shoulder with the right!" Enzo got behind the bag and supported it, directing Mark's movements. "In with a jab and back out... Jab, straight right and hook, then a left and back. Finish up with the left—get yourself back into position. Watch the left—you're dropping it! Keep it up! Elbows in. Don't drop your shoulder after the jab. Hit! Hit!"

Focusing now on one spot, Mark watched as his punches deepened the dent in the bag, forcing Enzo back slightly, and he felt each impact all the way to his calves. He paused to stretch and rest while Enzo left to get target mitts. He was a little short of breath and had a slight stitch in his side, but he felt loose. In any case, he was not about to let Enzo suspect that he was getting tired.

Enzo returned with two mitts, and placed one on each hand. "Ready? Straight punches and right hooks here." He held up his right mitt. "Left hooks into the other. Watch your feet."

Mark followed him around the gym, keeping his balance, concentrating on the targets that moved in front of him.

"Jab...jab...1-2...left hook...1-2 and left hook...Now work in some kicks."

Not having sparred recently, Mark felt awkward and off balance in his first attempts, which were off target or short. Enzo asked for a mixture of kicks, slowly at first, then faster and faster. Front kicks, side kicks, roundhouse kicks, wheel kicks. Mark felt his whole body flow into the motion, and his feet exploded at the targets.

Enzo ended the session with ten minutes of light contact

sparring. When they finished the sparring, he put his hand on Mark's shoulder. "I was wrong about you."

"Oh? How so?"

"When you came in here, I thought you were just another easy black belt. But you're pretty damn good."

Mark was pleased. He could tell that compliments did not come easily from Enzo.

After a long hot shower, Mark dressed and went to Enzo's office to thank him for the session. He mentioned that he had seen the Alpini banner in the dojo and told Enzo that his father had been with the Alpini, too, and had been on the Russian front.

"The Russian front?" Enzo asked, his voice full of curiosity. "Then we might know one another. What was his unit?"

"The Montenegro."

Now Mark had Enzo's complete attention. Everyone from the Montenegro kept in touch. He had to know who this young fellow's father was. "I know your father for sure, but don't tell me his name. Let me try to figure it out. Did your father make it back after the Russian front, or was he captured?"

"He got back OK, and then he was sent to Yugoslavia."

"I was there, too."

Immediately they were certain that there was a bond between them, but they wanted to savor the moment of recognition. They gave clues to one another. As soon as Mark told Enzo that his father had been a captain, Enzo knew it was David, and as he looked at Mark he could see a real resemblance between father and son. It took Mark a little longer to figure out who Enzo was.

"After the armistice, he helped his unit to get back to Italy."

"I know. I was with him," said Enzo.

Mark was frustrated. "Were you one of his officers?"

"No. I was his sergeant."

Suddenly, everything came into focus, and Mark remembered all the stories his father had told him about Enzo. "Then you must be Toro, right? My Dad's top sergeant? He's always talking about the wild bull that dragged him across a field after he was shot."

Enzo roared with laughter and clapped Mark on the shoulder, almost knocking him over. Mark was delighted when Enzo invited him to his home for dinner. He wanted to learn more about this man who had shared so many experiences with his father. He was only sorry that he could not tell Enzo that David would be coming to Torino very soon.

Back at the office that afternoon, Mark hurriedly put together a package of documents for Jim. He was certain that his friend would agree to help, and he wanted Jim to be able to review basic documents dealing with the joint venture and familiarize himself with some of the problems that had been plaguing the company. He requisitioned the personnel files of all employees at the *dirigente* (bottom management) level and above, selected thirty of them for photocopying, and asked for copies of the corporate organization charts for the past two years and a list of all positions that had access to computer records and data storage. Then he added a file of press clippings dealing with most of the incidents they would be investigating. He put everything into neat piles, secured them with heavy rubber bands and put everything into a large manila folder, which he taped shut. He scribbled a hasty note, placed it in an envelope, and taped the envelope to the outside of the folder. Then he arranged for an Alfindustria driver to take the package to the airport for express delivery to Jim's office.

During a break, while his secretary was photocopying documents, Mark called Sylvia and invited her for dinner. She was delighted to hear from him, and would have wanted to see him again even if Bianca had not told her to do so. Her lover was on a business trip and was not expected back until Friday, so she felt carefree and a little reckless. They went to her favorite restaurant, the wickedly expensive Villa Sassi, perched on a hillside outside of town.

Mark would have preferred a more intimate setting for dinner, and knew of several small family-operated restaurants in and around Torino that served excellent food. But he did not press the point, because he saw how excited Sylvia was about dining in the old world splendor of Villa Sassi. It had been months since she been there, and she was in a party mood. Her outfit was new—a silver fox stole, classic black dinner dress that displayed her trim figure, with a double strand necklace of Mikimoto pearls and pearl and diamond ring and earrings—and she looked stunning. Mark was proud to be seen with her. As they walked through the dining room he was amused at the way men turned instantly to look at her, and women followed her with their eyes slightly narrowed, openly envious. If he had been walking with Sylvia down Via Roma, he would have heard open expressions of admiration from passersby *(Bellissima! Che bella! Squisita!)*.

The evening passed quickly, with much frivolous talk and laughter. Mark tried several times to question her about their strange meeting the night before, but she would have none of it. Each time, she would wrinkle her nose and chide him, saying something like: "Now don't be a party-pooper, Mark. We can talk about that tomorrow. This night's for fun."

After dinner they strolled slowly through the gardens. A cold front had passed through, the skies were clear and the air was crisp and wintry. Sylvia held her stole tightly around her shoulders to stay warm in the chill air, and Mark held her close to his side. In the distance, spread out below them, Torino was like a blanket of twinkling lights. Now and then they stopped and talked quietly, but they felt no need for constant conversation, and often there were long periods of silence when they simply enjoyed being together.

At first, Mark tried to analyze his feelings toward Sylvia, wondering why he was unable to keep her at a distance as he had with other women, but he quickly gave up the struggle. All he knew was that he wanted to be with her, to protect her. She was singularly beautiful, of course, but so were other women he had known. She was fun to be with, but that did not make her different. He felt a need to look at her. In fact, he found it impossible to keep himself from staring. Several times during dinner he forced himself to look away as he spoke with her, but after a few moments he would find himself looking fixedly at some feature that happened to catch his attention: her hairline, her earlobe, her forehead, her lips, whatever. Everything about her interested and excited him.

For her part, Sylvia was acutely aware of his attention, and her cheeks tingled when she felt his gaze. She saw—and it made her happy—that his eyes had lost most of the hardness she had noticed at their first meeting. As she remembered the feel of his muscles under her hands the night before and the warm smell of his body when he held her, she felt a great desire to be touched by him again.

What happened later in Sylvia's apartment was inevitable. The entire evening had been foreplay of a sort, a hovering around one another, a dance without touching. The sheer animal attraction between them became almost palpable by the time they arrived. As soon as the door shut behind them, Mark reached out for Sylvia and brought her close to him. The darkness of the apartment was broken only by moonlight streaming through large picture windows. He held her face in his hands. In the dimness of the moonlight he could just see her, and he looked into her eyes.

"A perfect evening, Sylvia. I can't remember a better one."

She tossed away her stole and hugged him as she purred, "Same for me. I had a wonderful time."

Mark kissed her lightly on the forehead, put his arms around her waist and drew her closer.

"It's so good when I'm with you, Mark. You make my problems melt away."

As they stood talking softly, Mark became increasingly conscious of Sylvia's warmth and every curve in her body. He rested his cheek on her head, and caught the fragrance from her hair. Sylvia, content to rid herself of anxieties, leaned against him, her arms wrapped around his neck. When Mark lifted her chin slowly and kissed her cheek, she turned her head so their lips were just touching, and when he kissed her she pressed tightly against him, and they kissed again, long and deep. He moved his hands slowly across and down her back until they cradled her buttocks, and he pulled her toward him. Another long kiss, and waves of desire began sweeping over her. His hands, moving across her body and caressing her, set off erotic signals. She clutched Mark almost frantically.

The next minutes were in a half-dream for both of them, propelled as they were by drives that, once set in motion, could not be suppressed. They began taking clothes off feverishly, their lips still together as if unable to separate. Desperately hungry for one another, they groped their way to her bedroom and fell onto the bed.

Several minutes passed as they lay entwined. Then both drifted off into a kind of reverie, not quite sleeping, but not fully awake, breathing deeply. Sylvia's head rested on Mark's outstretched arm. Mark became conscious of her silky smooth body beside him and he turned his head to look at her. He could see that her eyes were closed and her mouth was just slightly open. *What a classic profile! Just like Nefertiti.* He let his eyes wander along the outline of her body, silhouetted against the dim light from the window, sweeping down from the fullness of her breast to a narrow waist and rising again to the roundness of her hips that were resting against him.

Feeling his eyes on her, Sylvia glanced over at Mark.

"My God, but you're beautiful," he whispered.

She rolled over against him, resting her face on his chest, purring with contentment. She felt the curly hairs against her cheeks and nose, and was filled with a sense of peace. *He's so gentle, yet so strong.* She ran her fingers idly over his chest, tracing the edge of his rib-cage and then onto his stomach, feeling his muscles tighten at the contact.

"Mmmmm," she murmured softly, the warmth and strength of his body re-awakening her desire. "I can't get enough of you," she whispered, laughing.

Sylvia was almost asleep when Mark kissed her cheek and moved away. She tried feebly to hold him back.

"It's getting late," he said. "I have to go. Meet me tomorrow morning at 7:00. The piazza at the end of Re Umberto Bridge."

## X minus 17 Days

*Tuesday, November 11*

Mark made certain that no one followed him when he set out from the hotel into the cold morning air. He turned up the collar of his raincoat, closed the lapels and walked briskly for several blocks. Gradually, he began to feel comfortably warm and slowed down slightly. The sidewalks were empty, and only the morning movement of trucks in and out of the city broke the quiet. He crossed the bridge and checked his watch. *Only 6:45. Still lots of time.*

He strolled slowly along the sidewalk on Corso Moncalieri, looking at the traffic and the shop windows, and then crossed the road and returned. *Still no one around. No one interested in me.* Passing the piazza at the foot of the bridge, he stopped and waited, again looking in both directions to make sure he was not being followed. Sylvia was just rounding the corner of the piazza when he saw her. She wore a fitted burgundy wool coat, with matching leather purse and pumps by Celeste. He admired her trim figure and smooth, confident stride. Then he looked away from her and down the river. As she came near, he said, still looking away, "Don't stop. Just keep walking. I'll catch up."

Mark could hear the sound of her heels on the sidewalk as she continued. After waiting to see if anyone followed her, he sauntered to the other side of the road and began walking in the same direction. They were still the only persons out. Mark gradually increased his pace so that he was abreast of Sylvia, who had stopped to shake a tiny pebble out of her shoe. He looked both ways, saw no one, and crossed over to her.

She looked up at him, puzzled. "What was that all about?"

"Had to make sure you weren't being followed," he said as he kissed her on the cheek. He motioned toward the corner ahead. "Let's go that way. There's a path down to the river."

Soon they were walking side by side on the footpath. On their left was the Po, wide and sluggish, gray-brown in the early morning light. It was low, and moved slowly between its banks, where algae-covered rocks at the edges had turned brown. The flow over the spillway by Ponte Emmanuele was gentle. Across the river, the city was just beginning its daily bustle. The hillside to their right was covered with undergrowth leading up to the road. After a few hundred yards, he turned to her. "You started to tell me something last night. We can talk here."

"Something's happening," she said. "I don't know what it is, and I'm worried."

"Let's stop."

Mark felt drawn to her and wanted to protect her, but at the same time he knew she was holding something back. He held her by the shoulders, at arms-length. His steady gaze bore into her. "Now, who told you to warn me?" he asked in a low voice. "What's going on? You've got to trust me."

She avoided his eyes, and looked toward the river. Her voice sounded uncertain. "I'm not sure who I can trust." Then she sighed. "A few weeks ago, a man came to the bank to see me. He said he was from the State Department, and that the government needed me to help them. When I asked what it was about, he said he couldn't talk about it, and he took me to lunch. What he wanted was for me to report on someone I know."

"Like what?"

"They wanted me to tell them what my friend was doing, who he was seeing, everything. They promised me no one would know I was helping them."

"Sounds like CIA," Mark said. "Why did they want you to do this? Did he say?"

"Not at first, but I got worried and told them I wouldn't do anything more unless they told me what it was all about. So, they did. But it wasn't much help; just something about the Russians and terrorism. They think my friend might have something to do with it, but they didn't want to go after him unless they had proof that he was the one they were looking for."

For years, CIA had wondered who "Giant" was. He had first come to their attention back in 1959. A British intelligence analyst who was screening intercepted Soviet reports noticed a reference to a 'top-level source' that had been recruited by the KGB in England and was working with an agent in northern Italy. After that, U.S. and British intelligence began picking up scattered references to this source. For a brief period ten years ago, the comments became more frequent. The KGB agent, claiming that his source was 'invaluable', repeatedly cautioned that it was essential to bring him along slowly. The agent stated flatly that his source could be crucial to the success of Soviet efforts in Italy. Then there was no mention of the source for several years. Because the source had been inactive for so long, the analyst at CIA headquarters at Langley who had been following his reports dubbed him 'Sleeping Giant'. From time to time routine information was attributed to 'Giant': nothing really sensitive, mainly disclosures of Italian government economic plans, new foreign investments and the like. Giant hovered near the surface for years, never doing anything noteworthy.

CIA classified Giant as a low-level watch item until six months ago, when a newly assigned KGB agent stationed in Torino was reported to be working with him. In the agent's first report, he boasted of the possibility of a new method of financing terrorist activities, not only in Italy but in other countries as well. Somehow Giant was involved. CIA decided that Giant had 'awakened' and assigned top priority to identifying him. Their station chief at Rome was directed to follow the case personally. Five weeks ago, a British agent had intercepted a series of messages to Moscow; one of them was from the KGB agent in Torino. He was putting into action a plan for Giant that, according to the dispatch, would have 'incalculable significance for the worldwide struggle of Communism'. It was then that CIA began working with a small, top-secret liaison group at their Italian counterpart, SISMI.

Several business executives had been identified as possible candidates for Giant, and Sylvia's friend was one of them, but CIA needed more information. Mark's investigation was complicating matters.

Mark frowned slightly. "I guess I'm missing something. Why did your contact want you to tell me all this?" He paused. "They want something from me, right?"

Sylvia took a deep breath and nodded. "They said to tell you to be careful about AB Industries. They're not sure my friend's the one they're looking for and they're worried that if he sees Americans over here investigating, he might think you're after him and ..." She hesitated. "What was it they said? He could 'go under', whatever that means."

Mark was silent, thinking. *So it is CIA. And the Russians are in it somehow. How to fit that in?* Then he explained to Sylvia. "This is what I think's happening. The Agency's probably after someone who's supposed to be a key source, or contact, for the Soviets. When a contact stops activities for awhile, they say he's 'gone under'." He paused, then continued: "And they think your friend might be a contact? Hmmm. Has he ever mentioned AB Industries?"

"No. All he ever talks about is 'the company'. No names. But there's something else. He's got some really big plan. I heard him mention two dates: November 28 and December 1."

November 28. That's just a little more than two weeks away. Mark asked whether her friend had said why those dates were important.

Sylvia shook her head. "No, and that's what's frustrating the people from CIA."

It was getting late and Sylvia had to get to the office, so they turned and walked back along the river. Sylvia took Mark's hand, and they walked in silence for a while. They turned onto the first path leading back to the road and walked up together. When they reached the sidewalk, he told her to walk on ahead. She squeezed his hand and left.

Mark had a busy day at the office, and his desk was piled high with folders as he reviewed all the material that he had sent to Jim. Late that afternoon, he was called up to Dario's office; his father was on the telephone. David told him briefly about his trip to Illinois. "I can't tell you any more right now, son, except that what happened to Bertaccini wasn't any accident, though someone tried to make it look that way."

Mark whistled softly. "When you coming over?"

"Can't say, but I'll be there. Just be careful, and don't take any chances."

After hanging up, Mark sent a telex to Jim.

# CHAPTER ELEVEN

## X minus 17 Days

*Chicago*
*Tuesday, November 11*

Jim DiStefano's secretary looked puzzled as she handed him a telex from Torino. It was marked URGENT and had arrived before the office opened.

He read:

> BIG JIM. NEED YOU URGENTLY ON SPECIAL INVESTIGATION. GOOD FEE: SOME NIGHT WORK. SENDING YOU PACKAGE OF DOCUMENTS — WILL BE DELIVERED THIS AFTERNOON.     MARK

Jim burst into a grin when he saw 'Big Jim.' As long as he could remember, that was what people had called him. Not that he was especially tall—he was not more than six feet two, about the same as Mark—but he projected BIG. His face was crowned by a curly mass of dark hair, his shoulders and arms were thickly muscled, and his thighs were so large that his trousers always seemed too tight.

Jim had always been big: after he was born his mother vowed never to have another child. She said that his ten pounds had almost torn her apart. He matured early, and all through the lower grades he was taller and bigger by far than any of his classmates, but his size quickly became a burden for him. Though he was really very bright, he was also more active and boisterous than teachers liked, and other children often were overwhelmed by him. Not that he was a bully, but his size and energy were difficult to oppose. Teachers became more interested in controlling him than educating him. Most of them were insensitive to the effect this was having on him, and some of them were outright cruel, implying that we was just big and dumb. Eventually he had the reputation of being just that. After a while, even he began to believe what the teachers were saying and he played the role that they had created for him, managing to pass his courses but devoting more attention than he should to sports and 'cruising around.' He did well in math, though, and worked part time in a computer store, where he spent free time playing games and sampling different software.

Jim's body practically demanded physical activity, and he loved contact sports. His mother was kept in a constant state of anxiety, worrying about her son's safety, never knowing what cuts and bruises he would bring home, particularly during the winter when he spent every spare minute playing hockey. He was so strong and so full of enthusiasm that he often lifted his opponent into the air with his body. He would rather skate through a defenseman than around him. A high pain threshold helped. For example, when he dislocated his shoulder in a pickup hockey game he skated off the ice and asked a friend to pull on his arm while he eased the bone back into the socket. Then Jim raised the arm, moved it around a bit and dashed back onto the ice without a second thought.

On the football field he was in his element. Agile and powerful, he became a fearsome linebacker. His high school coach loved to have Jim on defense, because when Jim tackled he stopped runners cold. No arm-tackling for Jim. He would throw himself into legs and knees with abandon, doing what the coach had told him: 'hit 'em low and hit 'em hard'.

For Jim, being drafted into the army during the Vietnam War was a blessing in disguise. For the first time in his life he found himself with people who knew nothing about him, and he was able to be what he wanted to be instead of what others expected him to be. To his surprise, he discovered that he was a lot smarter than he thought, as he scored near the top percentile in every test he took. When he got to Vietnam he was promoted rapidly, and soon was assigned to a cryptographic unit because of his experience with computers. At some point, and he couldn't tell when, he realized that he wanted to better himself, and that to do this he needed to go to college. Maybe it was his contact with officers and his realization that he had wasted his time in high school. He mentioned his interest in college to his commanding officer, who encouraged him to try for Officer's Candidate School. At first that idea had attracted him and he even filled out an application, but the more he thought it over the more he realized that he had just been looking at externals: the uniform, the command role. What he really needed and wanted was an education.

Once Jim set his mind on going to college, he began a serious and wide-ranging reading and study program, trying to make up for the years he had wasted. He spent hours in the base library devouring texts and literature classics. Months before his discharge, he began preparing for SAT and AP tests, which he had not bothered to take before. Choosing a college was not easy. He could have been accepted readily at second and third-rate schools, but he followed his CO's advice: *Go to the best school you can get into.* He also wanted to play hockey, so he narrowed his choices to Michigan and Cornell. His friends suggested that he apply to at least one "safe" school, but he decided against that. "Let's just see what happens," he said.

Jim's high school grades were marginal, and Cornell would never have considered accepting him, even on probation, except for his CO's strong letter of recommendation, and his high SAT and AP scores.

It was at Cornell that he met Mark. He had arrived at Ithaca early, right after his discharge, and received special permission to move into their dorm room in McFadden Hall, so he was already well ensconced by the time Mark arrived with his suitcases and boxes of books and other things. To Jim, Mark looked like a typical Grosse Point type, four or five years younger than himself, and Jim wondered how they had come to be assigned to room together.

The two said a guarded hello to one another.

Jim sat on his bed, leaning against the wall, watching as Mark began hanging his clothes in the closet: several pairs of neatly pressed trousers, three sport jackets (a Harris tweed, a cashmere and a summer weight dark blue blazer), a dark suit, at least fifteen sport shirts and five dress shirts, innumerable ties, a full assortment of footwear (sneakers, dress shoes, boots, running shoes, etc.), and several pairs of worn and faded jeans. Jim was astounded. He had come with only his old Army clothes, plus a few T-shirts. He had never had a suit except for graduation, and had never had more than one dress shirt. *This guy must have tons of dough*, he thought with a twinge of envy and a bit of scorn. Then he started singing softly to himself in Italian, in mock opera fashion. He made up his own lyrics, which went something like:

*Here we have the rich kid, set to have his empty head filled.*
*He should study with his ass—it has more brains than his head.*

Before Jim could start on the second verse, Mark finished what he was doing and turned to Jim. "Hey," he said in Italian, "What say we cut out the Italian tenor shit and go get us a pizza at Johnny's Big Red Grill?"

That broke the ice. The two roommates were curious about each other, and soon they started asking personal questions. Mark could tell from Jim's faded Army shirt and the clothes hanging in Jim's closet that he had been in the service, and wanted to know about Vietnam: how long Jim had been there, what he had done, what he had seen, etc. Jim wasn't particularly anxious to talk about the war, but he agreed that it was "pretty rough."

"I was lucky. Only had to spend six months getting shot at. Someone found out I'd been working at a computer company and they yanked me into a cryptographic unit." Jim explained what he did there and how he decided to come to Cornell. Then he asked Mark, "How about you? What've you been doing?

"Nothing much to tell," Mark said with a shrug. "The usual: high school, dull summer jobs, that's about it." When Mark had spoken to Jim in Italian, Jim noticed that Mark's accent in Italian was different from his, and asked what kind of dialect it was.

"A mixture, I guess, but mostly Piemontese, though." He explained that his parents had come from two different areas in northern Italy and since they didn't really speak one another's dialect, they had to use mostly standard Italian when they talked with one another. Mark had learned his dialect in Italy, where he had spent at least part of every summer, working with his uncle and his family up in the mountains of Valle d'Aosta, not far from France. "And how about you?" he asked. "Your folks make you learn it?"

Jim burst into laughter. "You got it! They hadda beat it into me, though. I thought Italian was some kinda disease. Used to be embarrassed 'cause the folks couldn't speak English so good, but you know how dumb kids can be."

Mark nodded as he continued unpacking his things, and tossed his kickboard and goggles in his closet.

"What're those for, swimming?" Jim asked.

"Yeah. I thought I'd try out for the team."

"You pretty good?"

Mark gave a so-so gesture. "Swam at summer camp the last three years, but we didn't have any good pools or competition around home. All they do in Boston is play hockey."

"Hockey! Hey, now that's my kinda game. We used to spend all winter whacking the puck around on rinks, ponds —

anywhere we could find a patch of ice. That's why I came here. I'm going to try out for the team."

"Hockey gets rough, though. I like swimming: water doesn't hit you back if you slap it."

"Boy, you talk about rough!" Jim said with a laugh. He went over to Mark and pushed his own nose back and forth with his forefinger so Mark could hear it click. "Hear that? This ole schnoz must've been broken four times. Once when I was thirteen I caught a stick right across the face. Guess I just like to bang heads together."

The two roommates made an unlikely pair. Jim was almost five years older than Mark, and had come from a working class family and from Salina, an area of Dearborn, Michigan, on the outskirts of Detroit where fighting ability was more important than I.Q. His parents had come to America from southern Italy with nothing, and their marriage had been arranged by their families. His father worked as a tool and die maker at the Ford plant at River Rouge. His mother still had not learned enough English to be comfortable in public. She bought everything she could at shops run by fellow countrymen, where she could speak Italian without being embarrassed. Otherwise, she went with one of her children and they translated for her.

Mark, on the other hand, came from one of the leading families in Valle d'Aosta. His grandfather, an attorney, had been a *senatore*, owned a prosperous winery, and had served in the Italian parliament. Mark's father was senior partner of a prosperous Boston law firm, and for years had been *consigliere* o the wealthy Alfieri family.

These differences were irrelevant to the two friends. They visited one another's homes and worked together during summer vacations. On weekends during the winter, Mark took Jim to his family's cabin near Mt. Snow for cross-country and downhill skiing.

With Jim's computer background and talent with numbers,

he gravitated naturally toward math, and majored in computer science, where he took honors courses. He was also active in sports. He played football, but hockey was his favorite. After one year on the freshman team, he was called up to the varsity, where he was a starting defenseman the next three years, adding to his collection of scars and injuries. A thin two-inch white line—his "dueling scar"—crossed his left cheek. In a pileup during the final minutes of the NCAA championship game, when Cornell edged North Dakota 1-0, a skate had caught him in the cheek and laid it open to the bone.

After graduation, Jim joined a small but highly respected consulting firm that specialized in computer security. He did very well, partly because he was competent and reliable but also because he worked so well with clients. He went out of his way to explain clearly what he was doing and why he felt that changes were necessary, and did it in a way that made his clients feel they were part of the solution and not the problem. After a year or so, the firm was called by the CFO of the multinational holding company, American Intercontinental Corp. The client needed help with a fraud audit at one of its subsidiaries, based in Naples. Because Jim knew the local dialect, he was part of the three-man team that was flown to Italy. His job was to work closely with the Italian national police there and serve as liaison between his team and the police and the official State auditors. It was because of his work in Italy that Jim came to the attention of the FBI's legal attaché at Rome. When Jim returned to Chicago, the Bureau recruited him.

Jim's first long-term assignment in the FBI was the Miami field office, an exciting place for an investigator. The Miami area was just beginning to be flooded with money linked with drugs; it also abounded with Mafia and a variety of unsavory characters who were under surveillance. Jim was assigned to the office's organized crime squad. After six months he was given a top-level assignment involving stolen securities. The Bureau had received reports that the New York families were transshipping securities through a connection in Miami, and Jim's office was told to look into it. There were also rumors of a large shipment of stolen and counterfeit securities about to be sent down to Florida. His partner in the investigation turned out to be Mark, who had just finished his training at the FBI Academy and was assigned to Miami on rotation. The two worked together most of the next two months, spending their days tracing registration numbers of stolen stocks and bonds, checking with banks and working with informers.

Stolen securities were difficult to trace, because they were generally not sold. Instead, most of them were used by the mob's front men and pledged as collateral for loans or letters of credit. In those days, banks were notoriously lax in checking whether pledged securities were even genuine, let alone whether they were really owned by the person who was taking out the loan or letter of credit. Many of the securities would turn up in Europe as deposits for loans or letters of credit. They could sit in a bank's vault for months, even years, before detection, and then only because of a default, when the bank tried to realize on its collateral. It was only then that the bank would discover that the stocks or bonds had been stolen.

Gradually, Jim and Mark managed to identify most of the people in the chain between the bank and brokerage house thefts in New York, Chicago and Los Angeles and the flow of funds through Miami. Jim followed closely all of the reports of missing or stolen securities carried by the computerized National Crime Information System. One day, he noticed that stocks worth over $50 million had just been reported missing from a large New York City brokerage house. Acting on a hunch that they might be sent to Miami, he gave the major Miami area banks his telephone number and a list of the securities and their CUSIP numbers, asking their loan officers to be on the lookout for the securities on the list and to contact him right away if any of them were presented as collateral for a loan or letter of credit.

He and Mark were in the office when the manager called from the Surfside branch of Citrus Belt Bank. Jim answered the phone.

The manager almost whispered. "There's a fellow here applying for a loan, and he's using ten thousand shares of Condata for collateral. That company's on the list you gave us, and the numbers match. What d'you want me to do?"

"Stall him. Keep him there as long as you can. Tell him anything; just don't let the guy get away. It'll take us fifteen-twenty minutes to get there."

Jim and Mark ran out to their car and started up Collins Avenue. Mark dropped Jim at the bank entrance and drove around the block to wait next to the bank, on 93d Street. As Jim entered, he caught the loan officer's eye and met with him in the back office. Jim told him to complete the transaction on paper, but not to transfer funds. The man who had brought the stolen stock certificates was allowed to leave. Jim was right behind him.

"That's him! he said to Mark. "Stay on his tail."

"D'you know him?"

Jim shook his head. "Nah, just some stooge. Probably doesn't even know the paper's hot. But maybe he'll lead us to the family."

This turned out to be the first major breakthrough in the case, and led eventually to indictments against three of the top lieutenants in the Bugliosi family, which at that time was handling more than $700 million in stolen securities every year.

Jim enjoyed investigative work but, like Mark, he found himself chafing at the Bureau's rigid and puritanical standards. He was too much of a free spirit to tolerate rules that he considered petty but had to be obeyed without question and to the letter. He stayed with the Bureau for six years, though, before returning to his old consulting firm, where he was made a partner. His specialty was designing and helping his clients implement policies and procedures to prevent security breaches and interception of confidential data. In short, to keep out hackers and other intruders and to protect against viruses.

Jim worked late that afternoon, waiting for Mark's package to arrive. The KLM flight from Amsterdam had been delayed an hour in departure and spent another forty-five minutes in a holding pattern north of O'Hare together with other incoming European flights, waiting for clearance to land. At 6:30 PM he received a call from the night porter that his package had just arrived. He picked it up on his way down to the basement garage, where he tossed his briefcase and the package in the back seat of his car and hurried into the evening traffic on Adams. Before long, he was heading north in the swarming congestion on the Edens Expressway. It took him almost an hour before he left Route 41 and slowed down, turning onto Westleigh, heading for home. He passed the campus of Lake Forest College and turned into his driveway, where he was besieged by his two older boys, five and eleven. Each wanted to be the first to tell him what he had done that day. Jim swooped them up in his massive arms and marched into the house.

The sibling rivalry continued through dinner, and Jim refereed a running argument between the two boys about who had or had not washed his hands before coming to the table, who had really broken the big wheeler, who had stuffed the baby's diaper in the toilet, etc. The youngest, gurgling in his high chair, ate and spat out or dribbled almost equal amounts of food.

Jim retreated from the chaos, taking Mark's package into a large room that served as a library and office. He spread out

Mark's papers on a long desk that faced a picture window overlooking a wooded ravine, and spent the better part of the night poring over them. By the time he finished taking notes, birds were already chirping beneath the window, and as he looked out over the ravine, he could see the first light of dawn through the trees.

## CHAPTER TWELVE

## X minus 15 Days

*Torino*
*Thursday, November 13*

If the beginning of Jim's visit was any indication, his assignment was going to be long on paperwork and short on excitement. But appearances can be deceiving.

It all started quietly enough. Jim was already exhausted when he boarded his plane, and he slept most of the way to Frankfurt and then dozed until his plane touched down at Milano, where Guido was waiting for him. Soon they were on A-4 heading west toward Torino and Jim sat back and let the countryside roll by. He and Guido kept up a steady conversation about the scenery (this was Jim's first time in northern Italy), Italian driving (Jim said he wished he had doubled his life insurance), soccer (Jim merely listened; he knew nothing about the game) and the current US political situation (they agreed that the US should force Iran to release the American hostages, but they didn't know how). By the time they reached the outskirts of Torino, the industrial haze that nestled on the city blocked any view of the mountains. Jim checked in at the hotel and called Mark at his office at Alfindustria. They agreed to meet that evening at a downtown restaurant, The *Cambio*, where they ate a leisurely dinner, seated at a secluded table where they could talk freely.

Mark explained the situation, listing the various things that had gone wrong at AB Industries. "At first, I thought maybe Alfieri was only having some organizational problems, but it's more than that."

He told Jim about the truck that tried to run his car off the road.

"And that's not all," he said, leaning forward. "That same night I had a visitor." He told Jim about Sylvia. "She warned me against nosing around AB Industries . . . said I could get hurt. I got the impression that what we're doing here could be inconvenient—or worse—for someone."

As they walked back to the hotel, Jim asked, "Just what the hell is it we're supposed to do over here, anyway?"

"Find out what's been going on, and who's behind it."

"And what kind of cover story do we use?"

"Mine's simple, 'cause I've worked on the company before. I'm just here looking over corporate records. As for you, I told people you're a consultant, and that you were brought in to work on systems. You're supposed to be looking into data processing and see how best to use the company's main computer facility."

"Do we use any police contacts? We might need help."

"I'm going to check with the Legat at Rome. He might be able to suggest someone. How about your friend at SISMI? Could you get him to help?"

"Ferrero? Yeah, he's got the right political connections, too. If he can't help us himself, I bet he can find someone we can work with. He owes me one."

## X minus 14 Days

*Torino*
*Friday, November 14*

After breakfast, Mark took Jim to see Dr. Alfieri. After introductions, they sat down and Mark explained how he had been checking on share transfers and was planning to investigate the fire at the Modena plant.

Dario turned to Jim. "And you, Mr. DiStefano. What are your plans?"

Mark could tell that Jim was a bit uneasy in Dario's presence. Normally, Jim was completely unaffected by the status of people he dealt with. Deliveryman or tycoon, it made no difference to him. He was always the same: open and direct. But Dario could have an unsettling effect on people, and Mark was only half surprised to see it happen to Jim.

Jim coughed slightly. "Well, sir, I thought I'd start looking into data processing. See how it's organized, try to find out what went wrong with the financials and those bids."

Everyone at Alfindustria had been very helpful so far, Mark said, but the investigation might well go outside the company, particularly since some sort of plot was involved. Two Americans couldn't be very effective on their own, and he wondered whether they could go to the police for assistance.

Dario did not answer immediately. He rubbed his chin, thinking. "I expect it was unrealistic to think we could avoid involving them. What did you have in mind?"

"Jim has a contact at SISMI who might be able to help. His name is Ferrero."

Jim told Dario how he and Ferrero had worked together in Naples. "Paolo's well connected and I thought he could give us a hand."

"Ferrero, Paolo . . . ." Dario said slowly, trying to place the name. Then it came to him. "But of course. Ferrero. I know his father well. Paolo's a good man." Then his voice turned serious. "If you have to deal with the authorities, do so, of course. But remember: we have to keep this investigation confidential. That means we can't have too many people involved. I'll have a chat with Paolo myself, so that he understands."

Mark and Jim rose to leave.

"If you need to get in touch with us," Mark said, "Jim'll be over at Orbassano. I'll be in my office, downstairs."

Mark stopped in the outer office to ask Dario's secretary for the daily stock transfer sheets for Alfindustria for the last three months. He wanted to see whether there had been any large stock movements.

After he returned to his desk, she called him. Her voice was plaintive. "There are more than 300,000 Alfindustria shareholders. Our transfer agent won't want to release a list of all transfers. How about just the large ones?"

They finally agreed on a list of all persons who had had more than 10,000 shares of stock transferred into their names during that period. She promised to have it ready for Mark by noon the next day, which was Saturday, and the bank would keep it current, as Mark requested.

Guido drove Jim into the countryside west of Torino to the small town of Orbassano, site of the Italian headquarters of AB Industries. The general manager had received strict instructions from Alfieri's office to cooperate with Jim in every way, and he was most eager to help. He set aside an office for Jim in the data processing department, and within an hour Jim was surrounded by stacks of file folders and computer printouts. He also asked for a list of all personnel who had been assigned to the purchasing and data processing departments during the preceding two years, together with the names of the officers who had authorized the personnel actions. Working with the director in charge of data processing, Jim was able to develop a flow chart for the handling of computer data: who was responsible for raw data input; who had access to the data retrieval system; who had access to the master codes to create or modify instructions or erase critical material; and who was in charge of security. What he discovered was discouraging but not overly surprising: there was little, if any, security, so that virtually anyone with the title of *dirigente* who possessed reasonable experience with computers could penetrate the system if he had access to the master codes.

Next, Jim worked with the controller to develop a similar flow chart for the people who prepared financial statements. By talking to some of the people involved, he was able to identify all of the persons who participated in this group effort. He did the same for the processing of bids on foreign tenders.

The afternoon passed quickly, and before he realized it the office staff was starting to leave for the day. He worked on for an hour and drove back to the hotel in a company car, taking along all his notes and workpapers in a large briefcase so he could work on them over the weekend. At Mark's suggestion, they ate dinner at one of Mark's favorite restaurants: a small *trattoria* a few blocks from the hotel. It was only 7:30, and a bit early for dinner, but they were both hungry and they decided to walk there. The proprietor was seated at a table near the cash register and the bar eating his own dinner with his family when Jim and Mark came in. He recognized Mark and came to greet him.

When Mark saw that he had interrupted their dinner, he held up his hands in apology and offered to come back later. The proprietor would have none of it. "No no no! Come right on in. We're almost ready."

He showed them to a table in the corner of the side room, which was empty at that hour. Mark ordered the pasta specialty of the house for both of them — *agnolotti alla bolognese* — with a carafe of house wine. While they waited for the food to arrive, they munched on the delicate *grissini*, or breadsticks, that were stuck in a tall glass jar that stood in the middle of their table.

Jim explained briefly to Mark what he had been doing. "I'm up to my eyeballs in paper. Deadly dull stuff. And I don't know if I'm even going to find anything. I'm trying to get the names of everyone who could've fooled around with the bids and the financials. My hunch is we're talking about one person, probably someone brought into the data processing department within the past year. That oughta narrow the list of suspects." He reached for another breadstick.

As they walked briskly back to their hotel in the cold mist, Jim told Mark that he was going to fly down to Rome to see his friend Ferrero—"to check out some information." "My guess is that Alfieri's already talked with him. And while I'm there I'm gonna see that attorney, too. You know, the one who handles the trusts."

"Ambruzzo?"

"Yeah, that's the one. I need to know who the trustees are for the trusts that hold a lot of Alfindustria stock."

Mark could tell that Jim was enjoying himself, now that he was back in Italy and working on a real investigation again.

Jim's voice was buoyant, "It's really been a lot easier working here than I thought it'd be. You know how people usually clam up just as soon as you start asking questions? Here in Italy, especially? Well, I haven't had any trouble at all so far. Alfieri must've put the fear of the Lord in the general manager, and he passed it along to his staff. They're all working with me like old buddies and I even get invited to eat with them in the company cafeteria. They can't help snickering at my accent, though."

Mark was pleased, but not surprised. His ability to put people at ease was one of Jim's real assets as an investigator. He could make people want to confide in him. Language did not create any barrier, since his Italian was fluent. Mark had even taught him a few choice Piemontese phrases, which Jim never really learned to say without betraying the fact that he was a *Napolitano*.

## X minus 12 Days

*Saturday/Sunday, November 15-16*

On Saturday Mark asked Jim to come with him for a workout with Enzo. He had deliberately not told Jim anything about Enzo except that he was an older man. Remembering Jim's fearsome reputation, Mark was curious to see what would happen when the two met. He wasn't disappointed.

Jim had never bothered to develop precise karate technique. His great strengths were speed and power, and these helped him in full contact tournaments. He generally won, but sometimes would be outpointed by opponents who used spectacular kicks and rapid combinations. The judges failed to notice, or perhaps did not care, that the blows that landed on Jim had no effect on him. In fact, Jim hardly felt most of them, and was surprised whenever he lost. His usual tactic was to bide his time, blocking or parrying kicks and punches, waiting for the right moment to deliver one telling combination. Several times in tournaments, when Jim appeared to be hopelessly behind on points, he would suddenly lash out with his massive leg, and his foot would batter the opponent's ribs or catch him behind the ear. Generally, that decided the match. Not very elegant, but effective. He had difficulty finding sparring partners.

Mark introduced Jim to Enzo. He could see Enzo appraising Jim as they went through stretching routines. When they were warmed up, Enzo asked Jim casually whether he wanted some *kumite*, or light contact sparring practice.

Jim rose to the bait. "Sure, if it's O.K. with you. I haven't had the gloves on in months."

Mark sat back to watch the two bull elephants stalk one another.

At first, Jim held back because he was concerned about Enzo's age, but he soon changed his mind. His first kick bounced harmlessly off Enzo's sinewy shoulder, and Enzo countered with one of his own that rocked Jim back on his heels. For three rounds, every move that Jim made was calmly blocked, parried or slipped by Enzo. Several times, Jim was caught in exposed positions, but the older man stopped his blows short of contact.

At the end of the session, Jim was wringing wet. "Whew! That's enough for me! My legs are like rubber."

Mark saw from the twinkle in Enzo's eyes how much he had enjoyed the sparring.

"Your timing'll come back soon," Enzo said to Jim. "Then you couldn't *pay* me to spar with you. Your kicks would break an old man like me in two."

They agreed to meet for another session during the coming week.

As Jim and Mark walked back to their cars, Jim groaned, "You should've warned me about that old mother! A public menace, that's what he is. I feel like he took me apart and put me together again without all the pieces. I've never seen a guy his size move so damned fast. You saw him out there - the old fart was just playing with me. If he hadn't pulled his punches I wouldn't have lasted a minute."

That afternoon, Mark and Jim were buried in paper again. Mark plowed through transfer sheets and Jim pored over his flow charts.

On Sunday Jim achieved a breakthrough. He told Mark about it that evening. He reviewed the three bid files for a third time, just to eliminate the possibility that the incorrect bids were caused by an innocent mistake in communication.

"I think I've finally got a lead. I've got the worksheets for the financials and I've already tested the programs, so I'm dead certain that erasing the computer data for the financials was no accident."

"How about the people involved?"

"That's what I was coming to. I think I've pinpointed the guy who could've crashed the main disk. I checked and rechecked the flow charts. Whoever screwed up the bids and the financials had to have access to the computer room and he also had to be involved in preparing both the bids and the financials. There's only one guy who fits. His name's Riolfo. He's deputy controller out there. And get this: he was transferred in just about a year ago, from the parent company, Industrial Products Group."

Mark looked over his own organization chart. "Giambetta's the head of that group. He's chief financial officer."

"Yeah, I got his name here, too. He's the one who approved Riolfo's transfer."

Mark was excited. He knew that Jim would solve the puzzle. *Finally we've got something to work with!*

*X minus 11 Days*
*Monday, November 17*

As soon as Mark arrived at the office, he asked Alfieri's secretary to arrange an appointment with Francesco Giambetta. He had met Giambetta only once, at a meeting of the company's executive committee during the joint venture negotiations. Before his appointment he took time to review Giambetta's record. It was impressive. Handsome and wealthy, the executive came from one of the more prominent families in northern Italy and had been bred for success. His father had persuaded Francesco to join Alfindustria in 1955, shortly after he had finished three years in England, one at the London School of Economics and two at the London branch of one of the leading Italian commercial banks. He had risen fast in Alfindustria; the fact that his father had been an early investor in Alfindustria and his family owned about 10% of the company's shares could have accelerated his progress, but his abilities would have earned him a rapid promotion in any case. He had become a vice president in only ten years, and a member of the *consiglio di amministrazione*, or board of directors, five years later. Three years ago, he had been elected to the five-man *comitato esecutivo*, or executive committee, which held the real power in Alfindustria.

No one, not even senior executives, knew Giambetta very well. He was an ultimate perfectionist and staff members dreaded working for him. Even though he rewarded good performance handsomely, he made unreasonable demands and seemed totally impervious to pleas for time extensions or excuses for less than one hundred percent results. Once he decided on a course of action he was unremitting. In everything he had his own agenda, and he shared that with no one, not even his senior staff, until the project was completed. Only then would it become clear how well he had orchestrated everything - and everyone. Even Dario was in awe of him.

As soon as Mark arrived, Giambetta came out to meet him. He stood fully an inch taller than Mark and moved fluidly, like a dancer. A world-class fencer (saber) in his youth, he still fenced regularly. His thick black hair was combed straight back. He had a long, narrow face, with an easy smile that revealed even rows of perfect teeth. Mark caught the faint scent of an expensive cologne. Even in a country where good tailoring was taken for granted, Giambetta's elegance and style were remarkable. The effect that he created was not one of sartorial splendor, however, but rather a subtle harmony. In an interview for a men's fashion magazine, he had been quoted as saying, "One should never wear clothing that calls attention to itself, or attempt to make a statement with one's attire. I insist on good tailoring, of course, but it is more important that clothing reflect the person and the situation. The right clothes aren't just appropriate; they are inevitable."

Giambetta greeted Mark in flawless English. "Good morning, Mr. Della Croce. Won't you please come in?"

They shook hands and Mark followed Giambetta into his spacious office. After making themselves comfortable in two leather-covered chairs, Giambetta lit his pipe and began the ritual small talk preparatory to their business discussion. He continued in English, which he spoke easily and rapidly. His secretary brought in a silver tray with demitasse cups of espresso and a plate of cookies.

Leaning back in his chair with his cup and saucer, Giambetta looked over at Mark. It was time for business. "Dr. Alfieri's office said you had a few questions you would like me to answer."

He gave Mark—perhaps unintentionally—the impression of being mildly amused at the idea of being interrogated.

Mark decided to ignore the signal, and spoke in a matter-of-fact voice, "I wanted to ask about two problems that AB Industries had recently."

Since Dario had not given him authority to tell others—not even members of the Executive Committee—about their mission, Mark mentioned only the lost bids and the computer erasure. "Dr. Alfieri asked me to look into them," he continued. "It seems there was a breakdown in computer records. There was also a mix-up in handling overseas bids and financial statements. We need to speak with everyone who may have been involved."

Giambetta carefully placed his cup and saucer on the cocktail table. "And you think someone may have caused these problems deliberately?"

"We're not sure, but we believe so, yes."

Giambetta studied Mark. "I see. That sounds quite serious. How can I help you?" he said in his most engaging manner.

"We've made a list of people to check, and there's one you might be able to help with." Mark took out the transfer requisition. "Alfredo Riolfo... he was transferred to AB Industries from the Industrial Vehicles Division. Ordinarily, I'd go to the division vice president, but you signed the transfer order personally, so I came to you instead. Sorry to trouble you."

"No trouble at all, I assure you," Giambetta said with a smile as he took the paper and glanced at it. Then he paused to reflect, repeating slowly to himself as if trying to recollect, "Riolfo ..." Finally, he said, "Yes, I remember approving his transfer. The division vice president was out at the time, I believe, and the order came to me. Normally I don't get involved in those matters."

Mark had already confirmed that the division vice president had in fact been out, as Giambetta had said. "Do you know anything about Riolfo, or his work?" he asked.

"I'm afraid not. In fact, I don't believe I've ever met the man. But I must have had a favorable recommendation from his supervisor or else I wouldn't have signed the order."

Mark was mildly curious why he said that. It was a standing joke at AB Industries that both parent companies were trying to use the joint venture as a dumping ground for executive deadwood. No supervisor would recommend a good employee for transfer to AB Industries except under pressure. "I'd like to find out more about Riolfo. Is it all right if I speak with someone in his old division?"

"But of course. Let me see... Riolfo reported to the division controller. I'm sure he can answer all your questions. If you like, I'll arrange for you to speak with him this morning."

Mark was certain that he would get little or nothing from the man's supervisor, but he smiled. "Fine. Then I'll have a chat with Riolfo himself."

As Mark expected, Riolfo's supervisor was no help at all. He gave Mark only the most noncommittal replies and Mark did not press the matter. Instead, he called Riolfo directly and arranged to meet him at Riolfo's hotel that evening. He brought along Pasquale Biasi, a senior *agente* (detective) from the national police organization *(Guardie di Pubblica Sicurezza)* who had been recommended by Paolo Ferrero. The detective, squarely built, was about Mark's age. He had an intimidating appearance, with black, bushy eyebrows and piercing eyes.

Riolfo was not in the lobby when Mark and Pasquale arrived, so they sat in the lobby. While they waited, Mark explained how Jim had determined that Riolfo probably was responsible for some of the problems that AB Industries had been having. Fifteen minutes went by, without a sign of Riolfo. Pasquale asked the hotel operator to ring Riolfo's room, but there was no answer.

"Are you sure?" Pasquale asked. "He was expecting us."

When the desk clerk said that Riolfo had arrived just thirty minutes earlier and no one had seen him leave, Pasquale had him instruct the floor maid to check Riolfo's room. The floor maid called right back, and as soon as Mark saw the expression on the desk clerk's face he knew that they would never have an opportunity to question Riolfo. He and Pasquale went to Riolfo's room, where the maid was still standing, so terrified she could not speak. Riolfo was lying dead on the bed, his face contorted in agony.

# CHAPTER THIRTEEN

## X minus 11 Days

*Rome*
*Monday, November 17*

Before the weekend, Jim had arranged two appointments in Rome: one with Paolo Ferrero, branch director of SISMI, Italy's intelligence service responsible for national security matters; the other with avv. Ottavio Ambruzzo. He landed early at Fiumicino and took a taxi directly to Ambruzzo's law office. A red Volvo with three men inside left the terminal at the same time, and it stayed close behind the taxi all the way into the city.

Overlooking the Tiber, the offices of Ambruzzo's firm were part of a complex of apartments and offices abutting the ruins of a Roman temple that dated from 210 AD. Corinthian columns lined one side of the building. The wall between the columns was made of brick, interspersed with pieces of marble rubble scavenged from the surrounding ruins. Graffiti and political advertisements vied for space here as on all walls in the major cities. A spray paint war of sorts raged: no sooner were the offending slogans painted over than others appeared in their places. A soccer fan from Torino had sprayed *Viva Juve!* for his team, Juventus, one of the country's perennial soccer powers. Beneath, an unbeliever had countered with *Juve Merde*. Women's liberation was fully represented: *Violenza Femminista* and *aborto Libero* were sprayed at angles across the wall. The columns themselves were covered at eye level with layer upon layer of posters announcing concerts, exhibitions, political rallies and elections. Archaeologists from the Department of Antiquities worked in the area when funds were available. Pieces of marble—parts of friezes, steps and other parts of the temple and surrounding buildings from the time of Imperial Rome — were scattered about like pieces of some giant puzzle that no one seemed to be trying to put together.

Ambruzzo's offices were impressive. Some choice pieces of the temple itself graced an atrium that contained a small white marble fountain. Antique maps, prints and paintings hung in the waiting room and Ambruzzo's own office. With fifteen lawyers, Studio Legale Ambruzzo was one of the largest firms in the city and one of the most influential. Besides being counsel to the Alfieri family and its various corporate holdings, the firm represented many leading U.S. corporations in their dealings in Italy.

A doorman escorted Jim to Ambruzzo's office. Jim introduced himself, and explained that Dr. Alfieri had asked him and Mark to help on a matter involving AB Industries.

A slight man in his sixties, Ambruzzo looked even smaller next to Jim's bulk. He escorted Jim to a chair by a cocktail table and spoke in English. He knew that Jim spoke Italian fluently, but he welcomed the opportunity to use English, which he spoke slowly and with a precision that was heightened by a Cambridge-acquired accent. "Ah yes, the joint venture. Dario told me that he thought something was wrong there, but that was all he said. Have you been able to unravel the mystery?"

"Not yet. We're just starting." Jim told Ambruzzo generally what he was working on, but did not discuss what he hoped to glean from his materials.

Sensing Jim's reticence, the attorney smiled. "As counsel to Alfindustria I am of course deeply interested in your project. And Dr. Alfieri is a dear personal friend. But I can see that what you are doing is highly sensitive. Is there any way I can help?"

"Yes," said Jim, handing the lawyer a list. "Do you know if there are any large holdings of Alfindustria stock outside of the Alfieri family and these trusts?"

Ambruzzo studied the list for a few seconds, then handed it back. "No. These are the only ones."

"How soon could you get me the names of the trustees?"

"I can give you the trustees for five of them right away. Dr. Alfieri is trustee for three of them, and Francesco Giambetta for the other two. The names for the other two trusts will take a day or so. How can I send them to you?"

"I'll be at the AB Industries office at Orbassano," Jim said. "Just send me a telex there."

After thanking Ambruzzo for his help, Jim said good-bye and left for SISMI headquarters, where he had a noon meeting with Paolo Ferrero. He noticed the red Volvo waiting in the piazza. Two men were standing by it, one in a black leather jacket and the other in a long blue overcoat. They got in as soon as Jim's taxi started, and the Volvo shadowed the taxi all the way to Via Goito. Jim left the taxi at the head of the road and walked toward the address that Paolo had given him. He stopped after two blocks in front of a nondescript apartment building, squinting in the sun to see the number so he could compare it with what he had written. They were the same, but Jim wondered whether he might have made a mistake.

A woman's voice greeted him when he pressed the button for the fourth floor and announced himself. "Someone will be right down."

In a few minutes the door to the lobby opened and Ferrero came out to greet Jim. The two had not seen one another since they had worked together in Naples, some twelve years ago. Paolo had risen rapidly in the intelligence service, and two years ago he had been assigned to organize a special counter-terrorist task force within SISMI. His family was very wealthy, which explained his Gucci loafers and hand-tailored gray flannel suit. His long, black hair looked newly trimmed, and he had an even tan. Though his slight build hardly sugggested it, Paolo was generally 250 yards off the tee, and carried a 2 handicap.

They greeted one another as old friends. At the end of the

hall, Paolo inserted a plastic card in a slot and spoke his name into a small microphone. The door clicked open.

"You're keeping a mighty low profile here," Jim said. "You ought to know there are two guys outside following me."

"Nothing to worry about. All the flats here are genuine except this one, and we never come in the front way. We have two secure entrances on another street."

"I see you've got a voiceprint ID system. Why the tight security?"

"I couldn't explain much on the telephone. We try not to advertise who we are. It's hard enough to catch terrorists as it is."

After SIFAR, the former Italian intelligence service, was disbanded in the early seventies, Paolo explained, the country in effect had no intelligence service at all for almost four years. Many of the political terrorist groups got their start during that period. They became increasingly difficult to identify, partly because they managed to stay inconspicuous. Many came from respected middle-class families, and were dedicated and intelligent. They lived in different parts of a city, paid their rent on time, kept regular hours and blended in. In most cases, the people in their neighborhoods thought they were just young workers.

"We're sure that some of the groups are getting help from the Soviets, and we know that some of them are even being supported by people in our own bureaucracy."

Jim raised his eyebrows. "How's that?"

"After the government dissolved SIFAR, it became obvious that information was leaking. These left-wing groups would know exactly what the police were doing, and what their next moves would be. It was frustrating, believe me. My unit's been around for a little over two years now, and we're only just beginning to infiltrate the groups. It takes time."

He explained that while the terrorist groups were generally

difficult to infiltrate, they became vulnerable when they tried to raise money. At that point they were often forced to work with ordinary criminals, who were not dedicated to any political cause. The police were able to get information about the groups from these criminals, and that made identification and infiltration easier.

"What we're worried about now," Paolo said in a serious tone, "is how these groups are being financed. When they steal money, they leave tracks, but we think some of them might be getting funds through dummy corporations. That's a lot harder to trace."

The operations of Paolo's unit were top secret, and its records were open only to the deputy ministers of defense and internal affairs, subject, however, to Paolo's clearance. The men in the unit were hand-picked by Paolo, and then subjected to an intensive and thorough security check. Their names were not listed in any government personnel file. Even their salary was handled separately. Breaches of security were dealt with summarily.

"If we have even the slightest suspicion about one of our men," Paolo explained, "he gets called before our own board of inquiry. If he doesn't give us satisfactory answers, there won't be any resignation. He'll just disappear—literally. As far as our own records are concerned, there won't be any trace of him. Everyone who comes here knows that. Maybe that's why we've never had a problem."

He paused and grinned. "But that's enough about me. What're you doing here in Italy? When you called last week, you didn't say. Then I got a call from Dr. Alfieri. He told me a little about what was going on with AB Industries and said you were helping him. He said he wanted us to help you." Paolo imitated Dario's British accent, "'I trust you will do what you can to assist Mr. DiStefano.' So what else could I do? Sure. We'll help you ... if we can. But everything confidential, though." He paused. "What have you got so far?"

"Not much. No real leads yet, so we're casting in all directions. I thought maybe one of the company's suppliers or competitors might be involved, so I had these lists run off."

Jim handed Ferrero two folders of computer printout. "The supplier list here is consolidated with the one for Alfindustria. That's why it's so long. Could you check whether you have anything on any of those companies?

Paolo pursed his lips. "This'll take time."

"Yeah, I know, but I thought maybe you could get some of your people to work overtime. It'd be worth a few hundred bucks apiece."

Given the low salaries of civil servants, such payments were standard, and expected. They were more in the nature of incentive awards than bribes, and neither side felt the slightest bit of guilt.

"We should have something for you by tomorrow or Wednesday. Where can I reach you?"

"Let me call you instead. That'd be safer. Five o'clock all right?"

"Sure," Paolo said, and gave Jim a slip of paper. "Here's a secure number. Just give your name when you call. It'll come directly to me."

Since Jim's plane did not leave for Torino until late that evening, he had more than three hours to wander around Rome. The afternoon air was warm for November, almost balmy. He looked forward to walking, and he headed directly for the shopping area on Via Condotti. His wife had warned him that she might not let him back in the house if he returned without a present from his trip. At the end of Via Condotti he could see, several blocks away, the twin spires of *Trinita dei Monti*. He was acutely conscious of the two men who were still following him, and he felt the old Bureau challenge again.

Each time Jim stopped at a window, the two men stopped as well. *Either they're rookies at this or they're arrogant as hell. Almost looks as if they want me to see them.* He pretended not to notice. In the window of the Gucci shop, he saw a small leather purse that he knew Sally would like and went in to price it. After a few minutes he came out again. *Too expensive. Maybe I'll see something else.*

Jim hated shopping. His wife's periodic shopping forays into the Loop were agony for him. He would range back and forth restlessly while she tried on things, compared prices, chatted with the salesgirls. His own shopping was quick and direct. He fixed a target price and decided what he wanted and tried to finish the task as quickly as possible. He did not savor the process.

Seeing nothing in any of the other shops around the *Piazza di Spagna*, he turned back toward Gucci's. *What the hell. I'll get the bag. She'll like it, and I can pay for it out of the money I make on this job.*

As he headed back down Via Condotti, he wondered what his two tails would do. When they saw Jim heading back toward them, they simply stopped and stood looking at a show window until after he had passed. He bought the purse and left. When he opened the door to the shop, he could see the two men at the corner, waiting.

He checked the time. Two more hours before I have to start for the airport. *Great. I can make it, easy. Mom'll be happy.*

Before leaving for Italy, Jim had called his parents to say good-bye, and his mother had begged him to visit the Holy Stairs. "If you gotta the time, you climba La Scala Santa. Thatsa good for you soul. You go up ona you knees, and you think about Jesus ona the Cross. You do that, my son, I be very happy."

So Jim had agreed to try. He went to one of the cabs waiting in the piazza, and as he got in, he noticed the red Volvo parked by one of the two horsecarts at the base of the Spanish Steps. The two men started toward it.

Jim's taxi dropped him off in front of the Basilica of St. John Lateran, and he crossed over to the small gray building that shared the esplanade and climbed the steps toward the entrance. His followers in the Volvo parked nearby. Inside, he looked up at the three staircases and consulted his guidebook. *The one in the center must be the one they brought from Jerusalem.*

The treads of the center staircase were covered with wood to protect the stone from being worn by the knees of countless pilgrims and penitents. The other two staircases, one on either side, were barely lit, and were used for descending. Jim saw figures huddled here and there on the twenty-eight steps, making their slow way to the top.

Against the front wall of the lobby, a souvenir booth faced the bottom of the staircase; inside the booth, a white-haired monk sat absentmindedly chomping his toothless gums together. His chin bobbed up and down. A family coming down a side staircase passed the two statue groups in the lobby on either side of the Holy Stairs. The father and mother ran a hand over the feet of the two statues, then touched the hand to their lips. The mother lifted her son so he could touch the feet also. The contact was important to them. Jim read the inscription under the first group: *Osculo Filium Hominis Tradis* (You betray the Son of Man with a kiss). He was mildly amused by the fact that the touches of the faithful had worn down the foot of Judas almost as much as that of Jesus.

The signs on the walls leading to the steps explained that, by an autograph rescript of February 26, 1908, Pope Pius X had decreed

> *plenary indulgence in perpetuum applicable to souls in Purgatory and to be gained toties quoties by anyone who, meditating on the Passion of our Blessed Lord, ascends on their knees the Holy Stairs.*

Bowing his head, Jim recited the prefatory prayer:

> *My Jesus, I ask you through the merits of your Passion to grant me pardon for my sins and to inspire me with sentiments of faith, hope and charity. Before I ascend these Stairs, which I venerate as a memorial of your Sacrifice and which I regard as an encouragement to trust in your mercy in this life and as a hope for eternal salvation in the next, I promise to amend my life. Amen.*

Holding his briefcase in front of him, Jim took his position on the bottom step, following the cue of those ahead of him. The wooden surface of the step covering, worn down by the knees of countless pilgrims, was smooth but uneven, and Jim found it impossible to avoid high spots that ground into the bone just below his knees.

> *My Jesus, through the sorrow you suffered in being separated from your dear Mother and your beloved disciples, have mercy on me*
>
> > *Holy Mother, pierce me through*
> > *In my heart each Wound renew*
> > *Of my Saviour Crucified.*

Jim could see no system in the movement of the pilgrims on the steps. His heart sank when he realized that he was right behind an especially devout woman who remained on each step for two minutes or more, and his knees started aching. His thoughts began to stray to wondering how soon she would move, so he could shift position. A man passed him on his right, hardly stopping longer than thirty seconds on each step. Some people recited only the ritual prayer, while others remained bowed in silent meditation. The woman ahead of him was a meditator. Jim moved over to his right and eased himself ahead a stop, next to the devout woman.

*My Jesus, through the meekness you showed when charged*
*before an unjust tribunal, have mercy on me.*
*Holy Mother, pierce me through,*
*In my heart each Wound renew*
*of my Savior Crucified.*

*Now I'm on the fast track*, Jim said to himself, ignoring the irreverence. *Only twenty-three more.* He struggled to keep his mind on the Passion but the unyielding surface of the wood ground into his knees, and he kept shifting position to find the best place in the undulating surface to rest them.

Struggling to his feet after the last step, Jim went to the Byzantine altar facing the top of the steps and slipped an offering through the slot 'for the poor.' Then he rubbed his knees, sighing inwardly with relief. He noticed out of the corner of his eye that the man in the leather jacket had followed him on the Holy Stairs, and was right behind him. As Jim turned toward the descending staircase on his right, he saw the man in the overcoat nearing the top of it. *One in front of me and one behind. Wonder what they're up to? They wouldn't dare do anything here...* He readied himself.

Suddenly the man behind Jim reached out and grabbed him around the neck, and the man in the overcoat lunged for the briefcase. The struggle was brief and quiet, but violent. Jim held onto his briefcase and swung his heel backward, crashing it against the shin of the man in the jacket, forcing him to relax his hold. A quick backward blow to the scrotum with his left arm disabled the man and left Jim free to protect his briefcase. He yanked the briefcase back, pulling the man in the overcoat toward him, then he slammed the edge of his left hand under the man's nose, forcing him to release the briefcase. Almost as if continuing the same motion, Jim drew his left arm back again and, whirling to his left, brought his left elbow in a devastating horizontal arc, right into the face of the man behind him. He felt bone and tissue give under the impact. Then he hurried down the staircase, leaving one man writhing on the floor and the other leaning dazed against the wall, nursing his nose. No one had said a word.

Jim was sorry that the struggle had defiled the church, and he genuflected automatically when he passed in front of the altar. As he was walking out, he heard loud conversation at the head of the staircase and saw the old monk shuffling over to find out what was happening.

That evening, Jim told Mark about his trip. He did not go into details about the two men who had attacked him. He only said that he'd been followed and had to fight two men off. Mark laughed to himself. He could tell from Jim's terse comment that Jim had demolished them.

Jim never talked much about himself, particularly about fights he had, partly out of modesty and partly because he was sensitive on the subject. He could not seem to avoid fights, and his friends loved to tease him about it. Not that Jim went out of his way to look for trouble; trouble somehow seemed to find him. He had been in and out of minor scrapes with the law as a youngster, and tried his parents' patience. Finally, the Army took him in hand. The military discipline suited him; it was predictable and he could live with it. He matured. But trouble did not really leave him. Most of his friends said it was because Jim looked so tough, and was too tempting a target for barroom swaggerers. None of his friends could understand why any person in his right mind would go out of his way to antagonize 220 pounds of raw muscle, but loudmouths seemed to gravitate to Jim like moths to a candle, and most of them got their courage from a drink or two. Tales of Jim's challenges were legion.

Mark's favorite involved Clancy McKay, one of Jim's clients. Mark had heard the full story from Clancy himself; it was almost impossible to get Jim to talk about his 'incidents'. One evening while he and Clancy were waiting for Clancy's flight to New York, the two went to a restaurant in a suburb near O'Hare Airport. Jim parked the car while Clancy went into the restaurant. Coming in out of the bright sunlight, Clancy lost his way in the dimly-lit bar area and tripped and half-stumbled against a man standing at the bar with two others. The man wheeled around. Well over six feet tall, he towered over the slightly-built Clancy.

"Watch your Goddamn feet, Mac!"

"Sorry," Clancy stammered, "Couldn't see in the dark."

"Couldn't see in the dark," the man repeated in a falsetto and advanced on Clancy. "I oughta push your face in."

Just then, Jim came in. He went over to his friend, who was thoroughly terrified by this time.

"What's up?" Jim asked quietly.

"What's up?" the man repeated in a falsetto. Then he growled, "Who's this idiot, your mother?"

Jim ignored him, and listened as Clancy explained what had happened. "Is that all?"

Clancy nodded.

Jim turned to the man. "Look, my friend said he was sorry. Let's leave it there, O.K.?" He looked over to the bartender as if to ask whether the bartender could help.

"Come on, Bruce," the bartender said. "Lay off. Leave the guys alone."

By then, Bruce saw that he was attracting some attention

from others. He winked to his friends and laughed at Jim. "Hey! You some kinda asshole babysitter, or what?"

Jim ignored him and started toward the dining room.

Bruce caught up with Jim and poked his shoulder. "I'm talkin' to you, creep!"

Jim stopped and turned slowly to face Bruce. He spoke so low that only the people close by could hear. "Let it go, friend. We just came in for a quiet dinner. I don't want any trouble with you."

Jim's calm remarks only seemed to inflame Bruce's desire to show off. He turned to his companions again. "Guess I'm gonna have to straighten this sucker out. He thinks he's some kinda he-man."

His friends encouraged him.

"Show 'im, Bruce, baby!"

"You're dead meat, buddy!"

Bruce reached out to grab Jim's lapel. With a *shuto* knife fist, Jim slashed at Bruce's forearm, about four inches above the wrist.

Bruce felt his arm go numb. "What the fu . . . !"

The rest of Bruce's sentence was lost in a grunt as Jim ducked and drove his right fist into Bruce's midsection. Bruce doubled over, and Jim caught him under the arms and eased him into a nearby chair. It was all over in a matter of seconds. Bruce sat gasping for breath. Jim walked over to the bartender. "Sorry I had to do that. He'll be all right in a few minutes."

"He had it comin'."

Clancy was impressed. "Boy, you really took that guy out! Where'd you learn that?"

Jim dismissed it with a shrug and they went to their table.

They left right after dinner so Jim could take Clancy to the airport, and walked together to the parking lot. As they passed the first car, someone stepped out in front of them. It was Bruce.

"You ain't goin' nowhere, you sonovabitch. You gave me a cheap shot in there."

Jim moved in front of Clancy. "Stay behind me."

Bruce waved his arm. "I'm not after the little guy. I want you."

Jim held up his hand. "Look, I'm sorry about what happened in there," he said calmly. "I've got no quarrel with you." He shifted gradually into a defensive position, though, with his left side facing Bruce.

"Well, I got one with you, motherfucker!" Bruce said as he built up his anger.

It was at this point that Jim's karate spirit broke down. He tried mightily to stay calm and avoid fights like this, but succeeded only up to a point. Now he lost patience. "Look, Mac," he growled, "I don't know what the fuck you're tryin' to prove, but if it's a fight you want, come on. Let's do it!"

Bruce flailed away, missing widely as Jim moved easily out of range. He circled away from Bruce's right hand, biding his time. Bruce tried some awkward kicks, which Jim was able to jam easily. Finally, Bruce became frustrated, and Jim could see that he was ready to charge, so he moved in closer, raking a side kick down Bruce's shin. As Bruce yelled, he also dropped his guard, and Jim was able to thrust the heel of his left hand upwards against Bruce's nose, not breaking it but causing exquisite pain. Then he cuffed Bruce on the cheek with an open right hand, and spun him around with a backhand against the other cheek. He seized Bruce's right wrist and twisted the arm behind Bruce's back in a comalong, and shoved Bruce's face hard against the hood of a nearby car.

"It's over!" Jim rasped. "Got that? Over! Understand?"

Bruce nodded weakly.

"We gonna have any more trouble from you?"

Bruce shook his head.

Jim released him and straightened his own jacket. "O.K. Let's just take it easy now."

On the way to the airport, Jim apologized to Clancy. "I'm sorry, Clance, but it always happens like that! I try like hell to be nice, y'know, but some loudmouths just won't quit. Have to show off their genes or something. Bugs the hell outa me." Even as he was saying this, however, Jim had to admit to himself that he had enjoyed the fight, and that he probably could have tried harder to avoid it.

# CHAPTER FOURTEEN

## X minus 10 Days

*Torino*
*Tuesday, November 18*

After breakfast with Jim, Mark made his daily visit to Alfieri to report on developments.

"We came this close to getting an answer yesterday," he said, holding up his hand with his thumb and forefinger barely apart. "Jim found out who messed up the computer and the financials. The problem is, the man was killed before we had a chance to find out who he was working for. I'm going to his autopsy this afternoon." He paused. "Jim was working on some leads in Rome yesterday, and two men tried to take his briefcase away. Looks like someone thinks we're getting close."

Dario expressed concern about Jim, but Mark shook his head. "No need to worry about old Jim. I just pity the other two fellows. He plays rough."

"What happened?"

"He never gives me the whole story about his fights, but he thinks they were after his briefcase. They didn't get it, though." Then he changed the subject. "We've got another lead, but I don't know what it means or whether it even applies to AB Industries. We heard that two dates could be important: November 28 and December 1. Do they mean anything at all to you?"

Dario thought a moment and then went through his calendar. The only event that coincided was the annual shareholders meeting on December 1, but it was a formality, since the Alfieri family controlled a majority of the shares. Dario did have a dinner scheduled for November 28, but that was all. He promised to let Mark know if anything special or unusual turned up for those days. Then he picked up an envelope from his desk and handed it to Mark. It had just come from Detective Biasi.

Mark read the note on the outside:

*We found these under the seat in Bassino's car.*

Inside the envelope were copies of computer printouts. Mark took them out and held them up for Dario to see. "Any idea why Vittorio had these?"

Dario shook his head. "No. All he said was that he had something important to tell me, and he needed to do it in private. He wouldn't even discuss it on the telephone."

"Remember Bassino, the Alfindustria exec who shot?" Mark asked.

"Yes. He called me that morning."

"Can you remember his exact words? That might give us a clue."

"Let me see . . . ," said Dario, concentrating. "What he said was 'I need to show you something. I can hardly believe it.' Then he asked me how soon I would be back in Torino. When I asked what he wanted to see me about, he said he couldn't talk right then. We agreed to meet in my office as soon as I arrived."

"He must've been onto something, and probably had all his working papers with him. I'll give these to Jim. Maybe he can make something out of them."

"And what are you working on now?"

"I've got Riolfo's autopsy this afternoon. Then tomorrow I'll call about the Modena fire. Detective Biasi said he'd send two of his men down there. They'll be posing as insurance investigators."

Dario put his hand on Mark's arm. "If you don't mind, I'd like you to go down there yourself instead of just phoning. If you're there in person you'll be able to put the manager at ease so he won't be too curious, but what I really want is your own assessment of what happened there."

Mark did not think that a trip was really necessary, but

agreed immediately to drive down to Modena the next morning. *Alfieri knows his people, and he's calling the shots, so I get a trip to Modena.*

When Mark left, he went to the medical examiner's office for the autopsy and introduced himself to the chief examiner.

Doctor Fabiano rarely had foreign visitors, and he greeted Mark effusively. As they walked together toward the autopsy room, he seemed eager to impress Mark. Several inches shorter than Mark, he raised himself on his toes with each step, so that his head bobbed up and down. "Have you ever seen an autopsy?"

"Yes, a few, but that was years ago. Is the procedure different here?"

"Not really."

As a matter of fact, the doctor pointed out, the overall technique has been about the same for almost ninety years. He was quite proud of Italy's role in the history of forensic medicine and lectured to Mark as they walked. When he led Mark into the autopsy room, he pointed with pride to the new equipment he had had installed recently and provided a running commentary on what each one cost and what it was used for.

By the time they reached the theater, Riolfo's body had already been moved from the cold room, placed onto one of the four marble slabs used for autopsies, and covered with a white sheet. Fabiano moved methodically and precisely through the examination of the body surfaces for lesions or other evidences of injury, carefully noting the condition of the superficial membranes of the eyes, nose and mouth. He worked down the body, dictating his findings into a microphone suspended from the ceiling over the body. When he reached Riolfo's feet, he had a puzzled look on his face.

"Something's missing," he said, more to himself than to Mark. He inspected the skin surfaces again very carefully, found nothing on one side, and turned the body over onto its stomach. "Aha!" he said as he came to Riolfo's shoulder. "Look at this." He was pointing to a small area of discoloration barely noticeable to Mark. He said it might be a needle puncture, so he was going to examine the area microscopically and check the subcutaneous tissues to analyze the needle track. "We'll send tissue blocks to Toxicology."

"So you think he was poisoned?"

"Yes, definitely. But we'll do the internal examination anyway."

Without waiting for a response from Mark, Fabiano made incisions swiftly and surely and in less than a minute was probing the victim's chest cavity. Finally, he switched off his recorder and turned to Mark. "Just as I suspected. Nothing unusual or abnormal inside. This man was poisoned."

Mark wrote down his telephone number on a business card and gave it to the doctor, asking him to call as soon as he had the laboratory results.

That evening, he called Sylvia's apartment but got no answer.

## X minus 9 Days

*Wednesday, November 19*

Early the next morning Mark had a quick breakfast and left the hotel. The sky was covered with low, gray clouds, and a cold drizzle was falling. He raised the collar of his raincoat and sprinted to the company car, which Guido had parked by the newsstand. "We're off to Modena. The components plant. Know where it is?"

Guido nodded. "I grew up there. It's not far from the Maserati factory."

Mark settled back in the leather seat and took a paperback from his briefcase.

Guido sped through town toward the *Tangenziale*, or circumferential highway. Whenever he saw no traffic on cross streets, he simply ran through red lights or stop signs. Soon they were on A-21, racing through the mist-bound landscape. Mark began reading. Before long, they reached Piacenza and turned south on A-1 toward Bologna. It was only a few minutes after ten when he was ushered into the general manager's office.

The manager appeared somewhat mystified by Mark's visit, and annoyance showed in his voice. "I did what you asked, and those insurance investigators have spent two whole days here now, picking over the machine and going through all the stuff we haven't cleaned up yet. And they've been asking lots of questions. Really wasted our time."

Mark did not want to upset the manager any further, so he said that Dr. Alfieri has asked him personally to come down to meet the manager — putting just a little emphasis on 'personally'—and that the Chairman wanted to be sure that the company's insurance rating wouldn't be affected by the fire. "That's why we have to let these fellows do a complete investigation," he said. "I also came down here so I could speak with them before they turned in their report. Sorry if we've messed up your work schedule, but you know how we have to keep the insurance boys happy."

The manager was mollified. At the same time, he was intimidated by Mark's reference to Alfieri. He decided quickly that he ought to cooperate with Mark and changed his tone. His people were helping the investigators as much as they could, he noted ingratiatingly. They should be just about finished. He showed Mark to an empty office that he could use.

After a few minutes, a young man knocked and entered. He and his partner had been sent by Detective Biasi to investigate the fire. They were almost finished. As expected, the official report had been useless. He and his partner had pieced together the machine that had exploded and had questioned some of the employees. Most of what we did was really to make the employees think that they really were from the insurance company. Their own investigation hadn't taken that long.

"Did you turn up anything?"

"Yeah, but it wasn't easy. The guy who did this was a pro. He shorted the circuit so it would look like an accident."

"Any way you can find out who might've done it?"

The man made a slight face. "We're not here officially, so our hands are kinda tied. But maybe we can pick up something on the street. One thing helps, though. There aren't too many burn men who work the way this guy did."

"Well, if you get any leads at all, have Biasi give me a call, O.K.?"

The man nodded and left, and Mark went to chat with the plant manager. After lunch and a quick tour of the plant, Mark returned to Torino.

## X minus 8 Days

*Thursday, November 20*

Mark's phone rang just as he arrived at the office.

The pedantic voice on the line was unmistakable; it was Dr. Fabiano, and he had just received the lab report on Riolfo. Before Mark could ask a question, the doctor started lecturing in his sing-song voice. The puncture wound in the discolored area on Riolfo's shoulder was made by an unusual kind of needle. He found a tiny glass tip deep in the wound. Whatever was injected was forced out into the surrounding tissues.

When Fabiano paused briefly, Mark tried to insert his question, but he got only as far as "have you iden..." and the doctor overrode him, raising his own voice.

"I believe," Fabiano said significantly, "that the tip was on the end of the needle when it entered, and then was forced off under great pressure. That would explain the tiny puncture on the skin surface. Highly unusual...."

Mark found his opening. "What was the injection?"

The doctor's voice became less confident. His toxicologists hadn't identified the poison yet, but they had determined that it was synthesized. They also knew something about its effects: it attacked the nervous system and interfered with normal regulatory functions, so that everything in the body stopped working: heart, kidneys, liver, breathing, etc. And it was very quick-acting.

"What do you make of it?"

Fabiano paused before replying. "It's obvious the man was murdered, of course. And I'd say it was done by a professional killer."

Mark thanked the doctor, reminding him that Alfieri wanted everything kept confidential. Then he arranged a meeting with Detective Biasi to get his reaction to Fabiano's autopsy report.

Mark sensed that Pasquale was uneasy when he raised the subject and asked why.

The detective lowered his voice. "You ever hear the name Pinelli?"

"Pinelli? No. Doesn't ring a bell. Why?"

Pasquale kept his voice low, so Mark had to lean forward to hear. "I'm no expert, but let me tell you what I heard. The name Pinelli crops up whenever a murder can't be solved.

No one knows who they are. They're supposed to be a family of hired assassins, and poison's their specialty. Silent killers. You know, like the ninjas, but without the costume. Supposed to be beastly clever. Make a killing look like a natural death. That's why most of what they do goes undetected. No one from the family's ever been caught. Witnesses have a way of disappearing."

"You think they killed Riolfo?"

"Fits the pattern."

"Well, I'm only interested in one thing, and that's who paid for the killing. He's the guy we're after."

That evening, Mark took Sylvia to dinner at Da Alfredo. Without realizing it, he was falling in love with her. During the week, they had been together often. Her lover was out of town again, and she was enjoying her freedom. He called her at work every day and they ate lunch together whenever possible, and when she was free in the evening they went out. In the last three days they had gone to the opera, to a recital of a promising cellist from Milano, and to dinner again at Villa Sassi. They often walked hand in hand or sat close together, talking about their families, their experiences, their interests.

In less than two weeks, Mark felt closer to Sylvia, and knew more important things about her, than any woman he had ever known—including Gillian. When they were together, it was as if their minds were working in tandem. The same things would catch their attention—a play of sunlight on the water, an unusually shaped tree, a humorous slogan on a wall, a happy child—and when one of them pointed it out, the other would say something like "Isn't that funny? I was just going to ask you the same thing." After a while, it almost got to be a joke between them.

They shared many of the same values from their traditional European upbringing, and both had rebelled against some of the same things, such as *la bella figura*. But they both had the same love of family, the same sensitivity, the same joy of living, and their parents had given them both an intense pride in their Italian heritage. And many of the same things interested them, such as art, literature, and music.

The first time Sylvia really surprised Mark was at Torino Nuoto. He had arranged to work out at the private pool, and he took Sylvia along.

"I'm just going to warm up a bit first," Mark said as he prepared to dive in.

Sylvia adjusted her goggles. "Me, too."

They dove in adjoining lanes of the twenty-five meter pool, gliding underwater for a distance. The water was crystal clear, and the temperature just low enough to be invigorating. Mark eased into a slow breaststroke, to allow Sylvia to catch up, but she was already alongside. After 500 meters of kicking and easy free-style and backstroke drills, Mark suggested that they do some free-style interval work. He had watched her as they swam side by side and could tell that she had good stroke mechanics.

"You've got a super stroke," he said. "Swam AAU, right?"

"A couple years."

On each hundred-meter interval, Mark tried to swim faster, thinking that Sylvia would begin to drop back. But she didn't. She matched him stroke for stroke, touching almost at the same time as he did, and even a little ahead of him twice.

On the last of the series, he suggested that they go all out. When he came to the fifty-meter mark he turned, but then stopped so that he could watch Sylvia swim the last fifty meters. Then he saw what he had only guessed before: she had textbook perfect technique, her body streamlined and every stroke sending her forward with no wasted effort.

"Why'd you stop?" she asked after she finished.

Laughing, he splashed water in her face. "Couple years of age-group swimming, my eye! Where else?"

"Well, a little at Brown, too."

"Captain of the team, right?"

She laughed, and they continued their workout, competing against one another just as they had been taught to do when they trained as youngsters, pushing one another to faster times. After cooling down, Sylvia took off her goggles and bathing cap, ducked her head backwards in the water and then lifted it so that her hair swept back from her face. Her cheeks glowed from the exercise.

It was that moment when Mark realized that he was in love. On impulse, he reached over the lane line, took her cheeks between his hands and kissed her soundly.

She returned the kiss, then drew away slightly. She saw the look in his eyes and felt a tremor inside herself. They said nothing, but from that moment their relationship changed. They were no longer two people thinking of themselves, but two people thinking only of each other. By unspoken agreement, they avoided discussing what had brought them together in the first place. Mark could not tell her what he was doing, and Sylvia had no idea whether her mystery man's activities had anything to do with Mark.

That evening after dinner Mark drove Sylvia up the winding road to the basilica at Superga, southeast of Torino, and they stood looking at the view. Sylvia was in front of Mark.

He held his arms around her. "Remember when you took off your bathing cap in the pool today? I wanted to tell you something then, but I couldn't." He hesitated a moment, searching for the right words. "I don't know how to say this without sounding like a B movie ... ."

She turned halfway toward him, waiting.

"When I looked at you across the lane line from me, everything else just faded away. It was like your face was the only thing I could see." He laughed slightly. "I told you this was going to sound dumb. But y'know, it came over me all of a sudden that I just wanted you all for myself. I wanted to roar like a lion and tell the world, 'Keep away! This one's MINE.'" Another pause. He kissed her forehead. "I've never felt like that before ... and I'm not sure I know how to cope with it."

She kissed his cheek lightly. "That's the sweetest thing anyone has ever said to me, Mark."

"Well, just as soon as I finish this mess here, let's talk about us. O.K.?"

"Mmm," she purred and rumpled his hair. "I'd like that." Changing the subject, Mark asked her to drive down to Florence with him and spend the weekend to see the David and wander through the Uffizzi and the Bargello galleries.

She desperately wanted to be with him, but her mystery man had arranged for them to go to Courmayeur on Saturday. "That'd be great fun, but I can't. I'm going to be out of town." Seeing the look of mild disapproval in Mark's eyes, she added, "This is the last time, Mark. I promise. I'm through with the CIA stuff and this whole mess. I'll tell them Monday."

Mark was relieved. "Well, be sure to call me as soon as you get back."

## X minus 7 Days

*Friday, November 21*

Mark and Jim met at breakfast in the sitting room of the Principi, away from the early-morning traffic, and talked about what they were doing.

Mark told Jim about his visit to Modena, then switched to Riolfo's autopsy. "I got a report yesterday from the medical examiner. They found a puncture wound on Riolfo's shoulder.

The doc says Riolfo was poisoned, but they don't know what kind of poison it was. They're still working on it. The detective, Biasi, says he thinks it was a professional job. Something about a family that does that sort of thing for hire.

"Sounds jolly."

"He's checking now to see whether there's any information on the street about these two jobs. Didn't exactly run over with hope, though." Mark reached for his briefcase and gave Jim the envelope with the papers that the *carabinieri* had found under the seat in Vittorio Bassino's car after he was ambushed. "Remember Bassino, the Alfindustria exec. who was shot? Well, this is the stuff they found in his car. Not much, but I thought they might give you some clue about what he was working on." He paused. "How about Ferrero? Thought he was supposed to give you a call."

"That's tomorrow," Jim said.

Mark stopped by Dario's office to report on the latest developments, and Dario listened attentively as Mark repeated Pasquale's comment about the Pinellis. It was difficult for Dario to stand aside while others conducted the investigation, and it was even more difficult to have to deal with second or third hand observations. But he had no other choice. At least he was getting solid information from Mark and Jim. *Eventually, maybe we will make sense of it...*

After work, Sylvia called Bianca from her apartment to notify her that she was going to be in Courmayeur over the weekend. She wanted to know how to contact Mark. "You don't want me to call him if I get something, do you?"

"No. That wouldn't be a good idea. Better call us, and we'll get the message to Mark."

"And what if I need help? What do I do then?"

"Call me. If you can't get through, then call Griswold. We'll take care of you, don't worry." She gave Sylvia a 24-hour number for Griswold.

## CHAPTER FIFTEEN

## X minus 10 Days

*Boston*
*Tuesday, November 18*

David had just pulled into the parking lot at his club for lunch when a black Lincoln Continental pulled close alongside. He looked over but could see only shapes through the heavily tinted windows.

The rear window rolled down. It was Carlo. "Hold up a sec," he called out. "I'll ride with you."

David had not seen Carlo for some time, and he watched as Carlo got out and walked around to the passenger side. Over the years, and particularly after he took over as Don, Carlo had gotten heavier, but he carried the extra weight well. In his three-piece Brooks Brothers charcoal gray suit and small-patterned red silk tie, he could have been taken for a successful banker or businessman. Carlo was genuinely happy to see David, and greeted him warmly as he slid into the seat. He waved to his own driver and then turned to David.

"How about we drive around? I'd rather talk here, in the car."

David backed out and drove into traffic. He saw the Continental fall in behind. They chatted briefly, then Carlo came to the point. "I hear you wanna know who hired a hit man for a job in Illinois, right?"

David nodded. "It's important as hell. Mark and his friend are over there now, and they could get hurt. All I need is a contact—someone who can get me some information on the quiet. I can't go over there and do it myself."

Carlo laughed low, but his face was serious. "That's for damn sure." He put a slip of paper on the seat between them. "When you get to Milano, you call this number. Tell 'em who you are and say, 'Carlo said to ask for Domenico.' The guy you wanna see is Lombroso. If he agrees to see you—and I ain't saying he will—they'll give you directions. Follow them, and don't ask questions."

"Who's Lombroso?"

Carlo shook his head slowly. "It's best you don't know too much. But lemme tell you, there ain't nothing goes on in or around Milano that Lombroso don't know about or have his fingers in. He's got people everywhere reporting to 'im, feeding 'im info. Just like my old man used to, remember? Lombroso's got some ties with the States, too, and they go 'way back. One of his uncles used to work for my old man, and he's got two cousins in Chicago." Carlo looked around uneasily and continued. "This is gonna be up to you. All we can do is ask Lombroso for an accommodation."

"I understand," said David, nodding.

Carlo was still hesitant. "Remember now, I told the Lombroso family they could trust you just like one of us, so we got our necks way out on this. They're gonna be edgy as hell, 'cause we're talking family matters, and the Pinellis to boot. One thing: nothing gets to the police about who you see or whatever Lombroso tells you. Otherwise, I don't even want to think about what'd happen."

David put his hand on Carlo's arm. "Depend on me."

Carlo relaxed. "O.K., you can pull up anywhere along here. I'm gonna get out. Can't stay for lunch. Sorry."

The Continental stopped behind them. Before Carlo closed the door, he stuck his head back in David's car. "You take care, *paisano*."

## X minus 7 Days

*Milano*
*Friday, November 21*

As soon as David cleared customs at the airport he called the number that Carlo had given him. A woman's voice answered. David introduced himself and asked to speak with Domenico.

"Just a second." There was a click and then silence for almost a minute. Another click and a man's voice was on the line.

"Be outside your hotel Monday morning. Where you staying?"

"Principessa."

Another pause. Then, "Wait outside. A car'll come for you at ten. Carry your coat on your arm and a newspaper rolled up in your hand."

"How will I recognize the car?"

"We'll find you." A click and the line was dead.

After calling Mark to let him know that he had arrived, David rented a car and drove to Torino. He and Mark met with Dario to report on the progress they had made.

Mark mentioned that Jim was close to a breakthrough. "He's waiting for a report from Ferrero that might help, but time's getting short. Our man's supposed to make his move in less than a week."

David looked concerned, and turned to Dario. "Don't you think it's time we got Ferrero and his people more involved?"

"Not yet," Dario said wearily. "Not yet."

Immediately after the meeting with Dario, David headed out of town toward the A-5 *autostrada* that would take him toward Ivrea. At the Quincinetto exit, he left the *autostrada* and turned north on highway 26, headed for Carema. He looked up at the rows of vines that covered the hillsides. *Now we're getting into real wine country!* In this small area north of Ivrea, the grapes from the Nebbiolo vine produced one of the premier vintages of Italian red wine. San Nicola du val was in the heart of the region. While not so well known as the wines from Carema, the reds of Chateau Della Croce were highly prized by those who knew Italian wines. Somewhat delicate, it did not travel well, however, so it was seldom seen outside of Italy.

The little village of San Nicola, perched on a gentle slope just north of Carema, was a welcome sight to David. Modern technology had not conquered or transformed it. The village had developed during the last thirty years, but had not really changed. A few new buildings had been built on the outskirts, but those in the center were just as he remembered them from his youth. He cherished the old familiar landmarks and the stability they represented. Mario the butcher ran the same shop that his great-grandfather had built. the grocery next to it had been operated by the Domigliano family for four generations. Modern goods were available, of course, but the shops themselves were the same ones David had known as a boy. He thought of the apartment building in Boston where he and Elena had spent their first years. It did not exist anymore. In its place was a ten-story office building.

There had always been migration to the cities from this area, but the broad current of life in San Nicola remained unaltered. David's heart warmed as he drove slowly through the town.

Sergio and his entire family ran out as David drove up to the family home. There was much kissing, hugging, waving of arms and happy greetings. David was ushered inside. The two brothers greeted one another. David gripped his brother's shoulder. "It's great to be back home again. Y'know, I miss San Nicola more and more these days. Maybe I'm getting old. Just looking for a place to stop, away from all the change ... ." He leaned back and sighed.

Sergio returned David's grip. He was always glad to see his younger brother.

Later that evening, just before dinner, Sergio escorted David toward the front door, where their overcoats were hanging. "Let's go. Giovanni's expecting us."

The sign over Giovanni's restaurant entrance was not lit. One could barely make out *RISTORANTE*. As the two brothers entered, the proprietor rushed over to greet them. Many of the tables in the front room were already filled, and other guests were arriving. Giovanni called his wife and daughter over. A handsome woman with brunette hair in a long, thick braid came from the kitchen, and a slim, but blossoming teenager with the same strong features came to take their coats. Giovanni introduced them. "Sergio you know, of course. This is his brother, David."

Everyone shook hands, and Giovanni's mother, wiping her hands on her apron, came from the kitchen to meet them, too. More hugs all around.

Giovanni motioned to Sergio. "We reserved a table in the back room just for you."

Waiting for them were fifteen members of David's old Alpini unit. They started with a rousing chorus of *Sul Cappello che noi portiamo* (On the Cap We All Wear). Everyone was wearing a battered Alpini cap. Sergio brought out his, too, and put it on at a rakish angle. He had an extra one for David. Enzo was there, too, and bellowed greetings to David, enveloping him with his powerful arms.

More loud greetings all around. Old war stories flew back and forth. The other diners watched, amused and interested, as the group talked all at the same time. Whenever there was a lull in the conversation, one of the Alpini would start a song and the rest would join in. Soon everyone in the room was singing along with them. Toward the end of the evening, as the wine took hold, they sang some of the melodies that brought back painful memories of old friends lost in the war. The restaurant was awash in sentiment.

## X minus 4 Days

*Milano*
*Monday, November 24*

David spent most of the weekend with Sergio and his family, and drove to Milano late on Sunday, arriving at his hotel well after midnight. Even so, he rose early and was able to take a brisk walk in the cold morning fog before breakfast. Precisely at ten o'clock, he walked out of the hotel and stood in the cold breeze that swept by the entrance, watching a steady stream of cars and taxis that entered the wide driveway that curved from the piazza to pass under the canopied entrance. Within a minute, a black Citroen stopped beyond David and a man in a dark overcoat and hat got out and came up to David.

"Follow me." The man walked to the Citroen and motioned to David to sit in the rear seat beside a tall man. David got in, and the man in the overcoat followed, wedging David between them. The driver started and they drove in silence. After twenty minutes, the driver stopped in front of a high metal gate at the entrance to a walled compound and blinked the headlights twice. The gate opened, and the Citroen entered the compound, stopping alongside a two-story gray stucco building. All four went into the lobby, and the driver pressed a button alongside the front door.

A well-dressed man in his forties opened the door and motioned to David to follow. The driver and the man in the dark overcoat stayed in the lobby. David was escorted into a large room with a desk in the middle, on a slight dais. Opposite the desk was a single chair. David's escort turned to him, frisked him quickly and motioned for him to sit in the chair.

David sat down. The escort sat in a chair by the wall behind the desk, facing David, and the tall man from the car remained standing, by the door. They waited for several minutes. Finally, the door in the far side of the room opened and a thickset man with a gleaming bald pate strode in, followed by two retainers who closed the door and remained nearby at attention. The man appeared to be a few years younger than David. It was Lombroso. He did not look in David's direction until after he sat down at his desk.

When Lombroso turned his way, David felt himself skewered by a cold, steady stare. He could see that Lombroso was appraising him, and he returned the gaze calmly, waiting for Lombroso to begin the conversation. After several moments, Lombroso spoke. His voice was rich and deep and he paused frequently for dramatic effect.

"Welcome to Milano, Mr. Della Croce. We have heard about you from America. I know you have many friends here in Italy. My father — bless his memory — knew your father well, although they were at opposite ends of the Socialist Party. They both died fighting the *Fascisti* scum." He spat out the last two words. "Our American friends have asked me to help you — as an accommodation."

Never taking his eyes off David, Lombroso opened a silver case, took out a cigarette slowly and tapped it on the desk. One of his bodyguards was ready with a lighter the moment the cigarette touched Lombroso's lips. David watched the tip glow red. Lombroso inhaled deeply and exhaled slowly through his nose, then continued. "Tell me, what is it you would like us to do?"

David explained slowly and simply. "An Italian engineer with AB Industries, Renato Bertaccini, died recently in the

United States. I found out he'd been poisoned. Later I was told that the Pinellis were responsible."

David saw Lombroso glance sharply at one of his bodyguards.

"If this is true," David continued, "then my son and his friend are in grave danger. They're here in Italy and may be a target, and I have to help them. I'm not interested at all in the Pinellis or the man who killed Bertaccini. I only want to find out who arranged it. My life if that's not true."

Lombroso shrugged his shoulders imperceptibly. "It better be," he said slowly, with a hint of a curl to his lip. "But we'll always know how to reach you ... or your family."

David said nothing. There was absolute quiet in the room except for the sound of Lombroso's thick right index finger slowly tapping the top of the desk. Lombroso looked at him, lips drawn tightly together. The seconds ticked by. Finally, as if having made a decision, Lombroso barely lifted his right hand. One of the men standing at the door behind him came to his side immediately and leaned forward. Lombroso, still looking fixedly at David, turned his head slightly and whispered to the man.

Then he spoke to David. "We will help you, but only because your friend is a man of great respect *(un uomo di gran rispetto)*. In this, I am acting against my better judgment. And against the advice of my *consigliere*. We have never had any trouble with the Pinellis and I don't intend to begin now. If we can get your information without complications, we'll do it. But I promise nothing. Pietro here..." He indicated with his head the man to whom he had just spoken... will let you know if we find anything." He rose and prepared to leave.

David half rose, intending to thank him, but before he could say a word Lombroso strode out of the room, followed by his two bodyguards.

Pietro caught up with David after they left the building and arranged to meet him inside the Duomo on Thursday, between one and two. He added, "Don't look around for me. I'll find you."

## CHAPTER SIXTEEN

## X minus 8 Days

*Orbassano*
*Thursday, November 20*

It was almost closing time at the office when Jim heard a knock on the door. His secretary brought in a telex from Rome. Jim admired the ungirdled working of her hips as she swished out, then he glanced down at the telex.

```
34802 STUDAMB  ROMA 20/11/80
ABIND ORBASSANO 1358329

ATTENTION J. DISTEFANO

BOTH TRUSTEES DIED RECENTLY. NO
SUBSTITUTES NAMED AS YET. WILL KEEP
YOU ADVISED.
                         AVV. O. AMBRUZZO
```

The telex puzzled him. *That's not a whole helluva lot of help. Most of the non-public shares are held by the two families. So what if there's a change in trustees for two small trusts? What difference would that make?*

He called Paolo Ferrero in Rome and asked whether Paolo had gotten any information about the companies on the list Jim had given him.

"I was just going to call you," Paolo said. "Remember what I was telling you about terrorists getting money through dummy corporations?"

"Yes."

"Well, three of the companies we've been following were on your list. They're too small for any big payments. At least right now. But some of the left-wing groups have been bragging that they're coming into real money soon."

Jim drew in his breath with a slight whistle. "You'd have one bitch of a problem if they started getting that kind of help."

"That's just what we're afraid of."

"Any info yet on directors and officers?"

"Not yet, but we're working on it. Give me a call Saturday morning."

## X minus 6 Days

*Torino*
*Saturday, November 22*

A cold morning drizzle met Jim as he left the hotel. He leaned into the wind and sprinted across the street and down the short block to reach the shelter of the arcade along Via Roma. Then he walked briskly to one of the private telephone booths at the Porta Nuova railway station to call Ferrero. Paolo came on the line immediately.

"Paolo? Jim here. "You get anything on those names?"

Ferrero laughed. "I didn't promise, Jim. I only said I'd try."

"But you do have something for me, don't you?"

"Yes. If you've got a pen or pencil handy, I'll read them to you."

Jim scribbled furiously as Paolo read the names. "Thanks, Paolo. I owe you one."

After hanging up, Jim remained in the booth and looked over the lists. One name he remembered from the AB Industries organization chart appeared on all three lists: Riolfo. *But he's dead. Must've been a front for someone higher up. But who?* He half-whistled to himself. He recalled what Mark had said earlier:

"I feel we're shadow-boxing. Maybe our real target is somewhere else."

*But what other target is there except Alfindustria itself?*

He took a cab to his office at Orbassano, south of Torino. As he sat at his desk, he opened the envelope Mark had given him and took out the two sheets of computer printout from Vittorio Bassino's car. They listed names, addresses and shareholdings. He studied them briefly and set them aside.

Just then, a secretary came in with a thick folder. "Here are the stock transfer sheets Mr. Della Croce asked for."

Jim took the folder. "Thanks. I'll make sure he gets them."

He sat down and began leafing idly through the sheets. Suddenly, he leaned forward, took out his pen and started jotting down numbers. The three corporations on his list had bought blocks of Alfindustria shares Monday and Tuesday. On Tuesday, each of Giambetta's two trusts had also made purchases. The number of shares held by brokers increased steadily, to a level much higher than normal. *Something's happening, all right. This buying's got to be connected in some way. But with all the shares that Alfieri and Giambetta control, who could ever have any hope of taking over Alfindustria?*

He reached over and spread out the two sheets from Bassino's car. Something clicked. *Where'd I see those names?* He began flipping rapidly through the transfer sheets in Mark's folder, starting with August. Midway through the sheets for September, he stopped and reached for the two pages from Bassino's car. They matched part of the runs for September 13 and 14. *I'll bet Vittorio figured something out—and he did it with these.* Jim was excited, and sat looking at the list of major shareholdings. The more he studied the numbers the more intrigued he became with a thought that he had dismissed at first. If Giambetta combined the shares owned by his family, plus the votes of the two trusts and the shares held by the dummy three corporations, he would control almost 40% of Alfindustria's shares. But that would still leave Dario with

32%. And Dario's always been completely supported by the public shareholders. So long as he's alive, then...

Jim slammed his hand down on the desk so hard some of the papers scattered on the floor. *That's it! That sonovabitch Giambetta's making a play for Alfindustria, and he's gonna knock off Alfieri to do it!*

The notion that a trusted senior executive like Giambetta would be involved in such a scheme seemed so far-fetched that Jim hesitated before calling Mark. As soon as Mark answered, however, the line was filled with static so Jim could not hear what Mark was saying.

In desperation, he yelled into the receiver, "I'm leaving right now! See you in thirty-forty minutes!"

He hung up and dialed again to call for a cab.

At the same time, a man seated in a small office in the basement of the same building removed his headset, turned two dials on the electronic equipment he was using, then picked up a telephone.

Jim gathered up his work papers, put them carefully into his briefcase and went to the lobby of the office to wait. The sky was clearing, and gave promise of sunny weather. In a few minutes, a cab pulled up in front of the office. There were two men in the front seat, and the driver apparently was instructing the other man on the routes and use of the dispatcher radio. Jim saw nothing unusual in this. Drivers often took friends along in their cabs.

He got in. "Principi, and hurry."

Soon the cab was rounding the castle at Stupinigi, heading into town. As they passed the warehouses lining the road, the driver suddenly turned off into a driveway, between two of the warehouses. Jim began to object, and the passenger turned around and pointed a gun at him. The driver stopped the car behind one of the warehouses.

"Get out," the passenger rasped. "Hands up, where I can see 'em."

They all got out, Jim and the passenger on one side and the driver on the other. The passenger kept Jim covered. Jim watched carefully, and was relieved when he noticed that the driver was unarmed. *All I've got to do is take the one with the gun. He won't be expecting me to do anything.*

The man with the gun waved it at Jim. "Around by the trunk!"

Jim turned around and stepped toward the rear of the car. Just before he reached the rear bumper, he turned to face the car, so that his right side was facing the gunman. As soon as the gunman took his next step, Jim roared his tournament *kiiai*: 'Haa-eee!" and launched a vicious side kick. Completely disconcerted by the yell, the gunman took the full force of Jim's kick on the hip. His gun went off harmlessly as he sprawled backwards to the ground, and Jim kicked it out of his hand. The driver ran to help his colleague, carrying a heavy metal rod. As Jim bent over to retrieve the gun, he caught a glimpse of movement behind him and raised his right arm instinctively. In that same instant, the rod crashed into his arm and glanced off his temple. He was badly dazed, and unable to protect himself from the blows that followed as part of a disjointed dream.

Jim awoke in the dark, with a dull, throbbing pain in his head, his face pressed against the dirty floor mat of a car trunk. He was lying on his side, his arms trussed tightly behind his back. His ribs ached with every breath. He explored his teeth and his lips with his tongue, taking inventory: two teeth slightly loosened, but not broken, and upper lip split. The rusty taste and smell of blood surrounded him. *Aside from a banged-up face and some bruises, I guess I'm still in one piece. Wonder where they're taking me?* He tried to concentrate, recording his impressions, trying to visualize where the car was going. *Damned floor: it's got lumps in the wrong places.* He moved to adjust his position, knowing that he would have to shift position again shortly. He could hear that they were passing other cars. *Feels like we're on the Autostrada. Going high speed. No curves.*

Finally, the car slowed to a stop, moved forward a few feet and stopped again. He heard a voice.

"Two thousand lire."

The car started again, before Jim could shift to kick the side of the trunk. He cursed to himself.

Jim's body hurt all over. The cords around his wrists were cutting into the flesh, his shoulder felt raw from lying on part of the jack, and the pain in his head made it difficult to concentrate. He could tell that they had left the Autostrada. Soon he was being thrown from side to side as the car swung around sharp curves, and the engine strained as the car climbed, almost stopping on a hairpin curve. At one of the stops, he heard conversation, and people walking by in front of the car. *Must be a stop light.* The car continued upward, and his ears popped. The air turned colder, and he shivered slightly.

Eventually, he felt the road level off, and the car passed through two more villages. Jim could tell by the way the car slowed down. Suddenly, the car made a sharp left turn and as the driver shifted into low gear Jim could feel the engine straining again on a steep hill, and his body pressed against the rear of the trunk. He could not hear any other traffic.

Finally they stopped and one of the doors opened.

"The old man must be asleep. I'll get him."

Then, from a distance, "Hey! Open up, for Chrissake!"

Jim could not make out what the answer was. Soon he heard the sound of a chain clanking against metal and a creaking sound like that of a heavy gate moving. The car started upward again, then leveled off and finally stopped. Both doors were opened. Two men were talking. The first voice was high-pitched.

"We oughta get rid of this pig right away! Why wait?"

"Aldo said we had to. He wants to keep him here a while."

"I'm getting pretty damn fed up with 'Aldo this' and 'Aldo that'. He didn't start this group, I did. I'll take his money and help, but it bugs the shit out of me the way he orders us around."

"Watch it. Here he comes."

A third voice came closer. It sounded older. Jim noticed an accent.

"Everything all right?"

The high-pitched voice answered. "Yeah. He's in the trunk. Why you want to keep him, anyway?"

"We've got an important plan, and..."

The high-pitched voice interrupted. "Well what about that plan? What the hell is it? We oughta know what you're doin'. We're the ones taking all the risks."

The older voice was calm and patient. "As I said before, Rodolfo, I can't tell you anything right now. But that fellow in the trunk's part of it. Put him in storage room 3 on the lower level. There's a cot there. Keep a close eye on him."

The trunk was opened, and Jim had to blink his eyes against the bright sunlight.

"Here he is."

Two young men reached in the trunk and turned Jim onto his back so they could lift him out.

"C'mon," one of them said. "Get your ass up outa there."

Jim was lifted up roughly and brought to his feet on large black basalt cobblestones. He leaned against the car to keep his balance. When he stretched, pain shot through his back; every muscle in his body complained. Gradually, his eyes adjusted to the light and he was able to look around. The sky was clearing, and the early afternoon sun felt warm on his face. He was in an open courtyard, and he noticed a tall, gaunt man in a dark suit standing off to one side. The two men holding him appeared to be much younger. One of them pushed him toward a door.

"That way."

He recognized the high-pitched voice and looked at him, automatically studying and classifying his features. *Medium build, messy hair, mousy face, bad case of acne. So you're Rodolfo.*

They walked across the outer courtyard, where Jim could see that the joints between the cobblestones were still damp from the morning rain. As he looked up, he was surprised to see that they were headed for the stone wall of a building that looked like an old castle. Servants' quarters and various other outbuildings lined the courtyard to his right. The wall to his left and the wall behind formed the other sides of the courtyard. The two men led Jim toward a door next to a tower at the left corner of the courtyard. He could see battlements and a series of embrasures in the tower. To the right of the door, in the center of the castle wall, an archway led into an inner courtyard, and beyond the archway there was another tower. Looking over the low wall that stretched from the far tower to the servants' quarters, he could see, in the distance, the far slope of the valley.

Jim had little time to study the scene, as the two men shoved him roughly toward the door. The older man opened it, walked down four steps to switch on a light, and Jim followed. Ahead, Jim could see a long, low corridor, lit by a single dusty bulb hanging from the center of the ceiling. A series of doors, made of heavy oak planks and reinforced with wrought iron rivets, stretched along both sides of the corridor. One of the guards slid a heavy beam aside, placed his foot against the jamb and tugged on the handle. The door swung out heavily, but without squeaking, and the man pushed Jim inside.

"Get in there."

Jim almost fell over the end of a metal cot when he was shoved. The door thudded shut behind him and he heard the bolt closed. He walked slowly to the far end of the small room and stood under a mud-spattered window that was covered with bars. On tiptoe, he could just barely see outside through a clear spot in the glass. He was looking across the inner courtyard, toward the second story of the main building. A slate roof, decorated on its ridge with a wrought iron crest, ended in a tower to the left. From this angle, Jim could see only the second floor, which was lined with leaded bulls-eye windows.

A high-pitched voice interrupted Jim's thoughts. "Don't even think about yelling. Nobody here but us, anyway."

Turning, Jim saw two eyes peering through the grille. It was Rodolfo. Before Jim could answer, Rodolfo laughed and walked away.

Jim looked around the room. Except for a cot, it was bare. The walls were plain gray plaster, with blocks of granite rubble showing in places where large chunks of the plaster had peeled away. Evidently used as a storeroom, its floor was strewn with bits of straw and short pieces of twine and shreds of aged burlap. The moist, heavy smell of a root cellar hung in the air. Jim went to the cot and lay down to rest; with his hands tied behind him, he could only stretch out on his stomach. Despite the discomfort and the damp cold of the room, he was asleep in a few minutes.

A loud banging on the door wakened him. It was Rodolfo again. "Hey, you in there! Wake up!"

The door was unbolted and the man in the dark suit entered, carrying a small medical kit. "I'm going to put something on those cuts. Stand up and turn around." He cut the cords binding Jim's wrists and as Jim turned to face him, he took a step backwards and raised one hand in warning. "Now don't try anything. I don't have a gun, but the fellow behind me does. He'd love to use it, too."

Jim glanced at the hulk who almost filled the door opening. He was holding a sawed-off shotgun with an air of purpose that Jim found disquieting. The man in the suit wiped the dried blood from Jim's cheek with a small wet cloth.

"Where am I?" Jim asked.

"No questions," the man said as he applied antiseptic. "Hold still; this'll sting some."

The antiseptic made Jim suck in his breath through clenched teeth.

The man placed a bandage over the cut. "You can call me Aldo."

Jim studied Aldo's face. Jim had always been a 'face' man, paying close attention to facial features and expressions. This was in contrast to Mark, who remembered more about how people were built and how they moved and walked. Even after only a casual meeting, Jim would be able to describe a person's face in exhaustive detail, almost as if working from a photograph, but he sometimes overlooked a person's height or weight. Looking at Aldo, he was struck by the man's long, narrow face, with deep-set eyes and a thin, prominent nose.

"Just in case you're wondering," Aldo said in a modulated, cultured voice, "you're a long way from any town here, and this place is empty except for those who are with me. There's no way out of your... room. Those walls are more than forty centimeters thick. Stones in the floor go down almost a meter. The bars in that window up there haven't rusted much in four hundred years, so don't bother trying to budge them."

"I get the picture. What do you people want?"

Aldo crossed his arms and leaned back against the wall.

"We're a political action group. Terrorists, if you will. We're holding you for ransom and in a day or so we'll send Dr. Alfieri a message about you."

"What makes you think he'll pay anything?"

Aldo smiled slightly. "Oh, I think he will." He started to leave, and turned at the door. "You'll get food three times a day. The guard will take you to the bathroom at the end of the hall twice a day, once in the morning and once in the evening. Otherwise, use the container under your cot."

That evening, Jim heard a car stop and begin backing through the archway into the inner courtyard. He pulled his cot to the window and stood on it to see better. A black Fiat

130 passed by slowly and stopped. He could just make out the side of a large archway to his left, where the driver got out. Because of the tinted windows of the car, he could not identify who was inside. After a few moments, a door opened down the hall.

A new voice called out angrily, "Are you bastards out of your mind, bringing that guy here? The boss'll be furious when he finds out! What the hell's the idea?" The two guards made no effort to lower their voices.

"Don't ask me," one of them protested. "It wasn't my idea. Aldo told us to. You wanna bitch, do it to him, not me."

The new voice came closer. "Look, you guys can't be crawling around the countryside here. Don't you know any better? Someone from the village'll see you. And for God's sake, don't make such a mess. Don't you know how to use the garbage can?"

As the door was slamming shut, Jim heard the man's parting shot: "Damned slobs!"

Looking into the corridor, Jim saw the litter that had been so upsetting. The young guard walked back through the mess, kicked an empty bottle out of his way, and sat down. He turned on his cassette player and peeled another orange, tossing the peels idly over his shoulder.

Jim wondered about the man who had just left. *That last one didn't sound like he was from the same bunch. He's older, too ... and he sure doesn't want me here.*

Before long, Jim's guard was joined by Rodolfo and a third man. All of them appeared to be in their twenties. They were speaking softly, so Jim could not hear what they were saying. He watched Rodolfo. *Real nervous Nellie, always fidgeting and ranging back and forth while he's talkin'. Bites his fingernails, too.*

As the three men talked, Rodolfo became more and more agitated, and he began to talk more loudly, punctuating his remarks with short choppy gestures. "I'm getting pretty damn fed up with this commissar shit. Aldo's stalling on the ransom note, sure as I'm sitting here. I don't know what he's tryin' to pull, but I don't fuckin' like it! We need the dough. If Aldo don't move pretty soon, we're going ahead without him."

"But we need his help, don't we?" one of the others asked.

"All we've gotten from him so far's advice," Rodolfo said. "What we need is money." He started raising his voice so that he was almost shouting. "We don't need some fuckin' russki to tell us what to do, y'know. We did O.K. without him before!"

Jim puzzled about those remarks. *Now that's a new twist. What the hell do the Russians have to do with this?*

## X minus 3 Days

*North of Ivrea*
*Tuesday, November 25*

A numbing monotony had settled on Jim's days. Nondescript food and one-half liter of red wine were shoved through his door three times a day. His only other contact with the world outside his room was the trek to and from the foul-smelling toilet. His cuts and bruises had begun to mend, but the penetrating chill of the basement made him miserable. He thought often about his wife and children, wondering what they were doing. Often, he would sit on the edge of his cot, take their pictures from his wallet and look at them, and he felt almost as if he were with them. Then he would put the pictures away with a sigh and begin pacing back and forth in his cell, trying to stay warm. Standing at the barred window in his door, his blanket draped over his shoulders, he would watch with envy as the guards sat in the corridor, warming their hands over a small electric heater. Three days and nights in the same clothes, and no chance to wash or clean up, had left him with strange itchings and a foul-tasting mouth.

Jim assessed his situation, and was discouraged. *Too bad you don't know more about this area. Otherwise, you'd know where you were. This place has to be impressive. The guys who brought you here didn't seem to care whether you could identify it, and that's no good. But if they were gonna kill you, why didn't they do it right away? What're they up to? And that guy Aldo. Why did they call him a russki? He's some kinda pro, all right, and he's trying to direct these punks, but Rodolfo acts like he's a leader, too. The others are just a bunch of trigger-happy kids. Then that other guy, the one who said the boss wouldn't want you here. Bet he works for Giambetta.*

At first, Jim hoped that he had been kidnapped for ransom and would be released when it was paid. It was not long before he discovered that his guards had something else in mind. He heard Rodolfo arguing with someone at the end of the corridor. The high-pitched voice was unmistakable.

"Just how long does Aldo expect us to hold that guy here?"

"How the hell should I know?" the other voice answered.

"I say we dump the sonovabitch right now," Rodolfo said. "No sense waiting. Anyway, we can't be hanging around here very long. Some of the locals'll spot us."

"Go tell that to Aldo, not me!"

Rodolfo was getting angry. "I've already done that. Twice. The bastard says he's got some plan, but he won't even tell me. As far as I'm concerned, that guy down the hall's gotta go!"

Jim decided he had no options. He had to try to escape. *These crazies aren't about to release me. No way. They're just waiting for an excuse to put me away.*

There were few alternatives. The window was out of the question. He could not even wiggle the bars. With the heavy bolt on the outside of the door, there was no way he could get through it without overpowering the guard. That left only the evening visit to the w.c.

His guard that evening was a good-natured type who spent

most of his time listening to music on his tape player, humming and whistling along. He rarely let one song end before he skipped around on the tape and started another one or switched cassettes. He was the only guard who had really spoken to Jim, probably because he recognized Jim's Neapolitan accent. "I from Benevento," he had said proudly in English. *Vicino Napoli.* Spick English too. Good morning. 'Ow are you?"

He had smirked with delight when Jim answered him in English. "Very good!" Jim said slowly. His plan was to disarm the guard and try to escape out the basement door, through the courtyard and into the valley. He called out, "Hey! I gotta go to the w.c."

The guard looked up, his eyes squinting. He turned off the player and checked his watch. "O.K., guess it's about time." He picked up a shotgun that was leaning against the wall and came toward Jim's cell.

When the guard opened the door, Jim spoke to him in English, slowly. "How are you?"

The guard's eyes became alert. He smiled and nodded, "Ver-ry good... Tank you...," he said in English, pleased with himself. "One, two, tree, four, fife."

While they walked down the hall, Jim said other phrases in English that the guard tried to repeat. They came to the door just as the guard was trying to say 'seven o'clock.' He did not finish. Jim grabbed the door and slammed it against him. The guard raised the shotgun across his chest to protect himself, and in that instant Jim grabbed the gun and tried to wrench it away, but the guard's finger slipped over the trigger guard and caught on the trigger. The gun went off, and chunks of plaster and fragments of wood showered down on them from where the shot had ripped into the ceiling. The explosion deafened them temporarily as it reverberated in the closed hallway. Jim knocked the guard out with the butt of the gun and fumbled in the man's pockets for shells. Just then, a shot from the other end of the corridor slammed into the wall above Jim, and he froze.

"One move and you're dead!"

Jim looked up and saw Rodolfo and another guard at the far end of the hall, their guns aimed at him. The two men came toward him, guns ready. They checked the guard on the floor, who was moaning and starting to sit up.

"He's coming around," one of them said. "He'll be all right."

Rodolfo poked his gun at Jim. "Stand up!" He handed his gun to the other guard. "Keep him covered." There was fury in Rodolfo's eyes. Before Jim could move, Rodolfo doubled him over with a vicious right to the stomach.

If Jim had not been in excellent shape, that blow would have knocked him down. He twisted and turned to block or parry the other blows that rained on him, but was knocked senseless by a gun butt to the side of his head. His first thought when he came to was that they ought to clean the floor. He was lying on his stomach, his cheek resting on the cold stones. He could hear people arguing, and recognized the high-pitched voice.

Rodolfo was furious. "Aldo, that's it. If you don't do something soon we're gonna take care of this guy whether you like it or not."

"Patience, Rodolfo," Aldo said, trying to calm him. "Just a few more..."

Rodolfo cut him off. "No more patience bullshit! No more lectures. What about the ransom?"

Aldo continued, his voice unchanged. "Please, just a few more days, and then we'll have all the money you'll ever need. But this has to be handled carefully. Don't worry about the ransom. That's nothing compared to what we're going to have. For right now, we need this fellow. Just don't do anything rash. You and I — we've got to work together." He paused. "Now, let's get him back to the cell."

A foot lifted Jim's shoulder and turned him over. As he lay there, he opened his eyes and saw dim shapes over him, Then he was inundated by a bucket of dirty water. He choked and gasped for breath.

Rodolfo was standing over him. "See what you get for trying to be a smartass hero? Try that again and you're *dead*. Now back to your room," he said, grabbing Jim by the coat collar and yanking him up.

As Jim stumbled down the corridor, he heard Rodolfo cursing the guard who had let Jim surprise him.

# CHAPTER SEVENTEEN

## X minus 6 Days

*Torino*
*Saturday, November 22*

When Jim called from Orbassano, Mark recognized his voice through the static but could not understand anything except that Jim was coming. Mark waited in his room for a half hour, then he went down to the lobby and sat reading an old copy of La Stampa that he found on a table by the bar area. Another half hour passed and he began to get restless, so he checked with the front desk. No messages. More time passed. Finally, he decided to call the Orbassano office. Everyone had left for the day already, so he spoke with the security guard at the entrance to the office grounds, who told him that Jim had left in a cab almost two hours earlier.

Concerned, Mark called Detective Biasi.

Within seconds, Pasquale was on the line. "Anything wrong?" he asked.

"I sure hope not. Jim called me from Orbassano a couple hours ago and said he'd be here in a half hour, but he hasn't shown up."

"Let me check on it. I'll call you back."

When Pasquale called fifteen minutes later, Mark could tell from his voice that something was wrong. A radio taxi had been stolen a few hours ago and was just found abandoned on the outskirts of town. It could have been coming from Orbassano. Pasquale was on his way to inspect it and offered to come by the hotel to pick up Mark.

As they drove, Pasquale explained that they had checked the dispatcher's log, and this taxi was the one that had answered Jim's call. Technicians from Ferrero's unit were already going over the vehicle when Mark and Pasquale arrived.

One of the technicians came over to meet them. "Someone drove that cab all over the countryside. There's mud under the fenders and dust all over."

"Anything else?" Pasquale asked, taking notes.

The man opened the trunk. "Well, it looks like there was a body in here, and we found some blood on the mat. Not a whole lot, though. Probably a superficial wound. We're running tests on the blood now."

"Get the results as fast as you can," Pasquale said, writing down Jim's name, "then check 'em against this guy's medical file at the FBI."

Mark called his father at San Nicola immediately. "Afraid I've got bad news, Father. Jim's been taken." He explained what had happened, and what Pasquale and his men had found out about the taxi. "Well, the other side's made its move. What now?"

David thought a moment. He trusted his son's judgment, but since Mark's best friend was in danger, he urged caution and suggested that they let Ferrero's people try to locate .

"If he's been kidnapped, we'll be notified. As for us, let's just keep on with what we're doing, and wait."

Mark reluctantly agreed. Later that evening, Pasquale called to tell Mark that the FBI had confirmed that the blood sample matched with Jim's record, but they could not be positive. Mark called Ferrero at his home the next morning. Paolo also suggested waiting. He was sure that Jim had been taken by one of the terrorist groups. His staff would be working on it full time and he promised to stay in touch.

# X minus 4 Days

*Monday, November 24*

Two days after Jim was seized a boy ran into the reception area at Alfindustria headquarters, handed a plain white envelope to one of the receptionists and dashed out. It was addressed to Dario Alfieri and labeled: STRICTLY CONFIDENTIAL.

Mark was at his desk, talking with David, when Dario called and asked them to come right away. When they arrived, Dario was standing by his desk, his face grim. He pointed to the letter spread out on his desk. "This just came."

David and Mark were not surprised by what they read:

> *We have your american capitalist pig. You will receive instructions soon. If you go to police he dies.*
> *friends of the revolution*

"We'll get this to Ferrero as soon as possible," Mark said. "Maybe their lab can find something in the writing, the ink or the paper."

"What about your own investigation?" Dario asked.

"We both think we should just continue what we're doing," David said. "We don't want to endanger Jim, and there's not much we can do to help."

Dario nodded.

David and Mark returned slowly to Mark's office. David called his Milano number to see whether he could make contact with Lombroso's lieutenant, Pietro, earlier than Thursday. Within five minutes, Pietro called back and David explained that an emergency had come up and he needed his information before Thursday, if possible. Pietro said that they would try, and hung up without waiting for a reply.

After his father left, Mark sat in his office, trying to collect his thoughts, wondering what to do. He had his eyes shut and was pinching the bridge of his nose. *Should I call Jim's wife and tell her what's happened to him? No, that wouldn't help find Jim. She'd only be frantic, and might even do something that would let the press get wind of it.* He was certain in his own mind that Jim had been taken because of their investigation, and he was worried that the terrorists might kill Jim without even bothering to ask for ransom. He also blamed himself for having gotten Jim involved.

Mark went to the bank where Sylvia worked and asked to speak with her, but the receptionist told him that she was on vacation and was not due to return for a week. When he introduced himself as her friend and tried to find out where he could reach her, he ran into stony silence. He was told in no uncertain terms that that information was personal and could not be released.

Mark drove to the apartment complex where Sylvia lived. He knocked on her door several times but got no answer. A door down the hall opened and a maid walked by on her way to the elevator. He decided to ask her where Sylvia might be.

"Do you know where I might find Miss D'Angelo?" he asked.

She gave him a suspicious look. "The *americana?* She's out."

"Do you know when she'll be back?"

She shrugged her shoulders. Her face went blank.

Mark tried again. "Do you know where she went?"

Another shrug as she entered the elevator.

Mark cursed to himself and got in with her. They rode down in silence. As the woman plodded out, Mark went to the superintendent's basement apartment and knocked. The door opened and Mark's heart sank as the superintendent opened the door, still chewing. *Damn! I've interrupted the man's lunch.* The smell of garlic and pasta rolled over Mark.

"Excuse me, sir," he said in broken Italian. "I'm a friend of Miss D'Angelo. I'd like to see her. Do you know where she is?" Mark played the role of tourist, mispronouncing words and making errors in basic grammar.

The superintendent's eyes narrowed as soon as Mark opened his mouth. "Sorry. Don't know anything about her." He started to close the door.

"Just a second," Mark said, pulling out a 10,000 Lire note. "I've got to see her! I'm only here for a couple days."

The superintendent opened the door and reached out for the bill. He gave Mark an almost toothless smile. "Ah, yes. The *americana*. She left Saturday. All of a sudden she comes to me and asks me to pick up her mail. Nice girl. No noise. No parties. Speaks with respect; not like some today."

"Did she say how long she'd be away, or where she was going?"

He rubbed his stomach and squinted upward. "No," he said slowly, "just that she'd be away for a while."

"Did she take a bag with her?"

"Not when I saw her," the man said, then turned around to yell to his wife. "Hey, Mamma! The *americana*. When she left, did you see her? She take a suitcase or anything?"

From the next room, a disheveled head appeared. "Yeah, a little overnight bag, I think. Why?"

"Nothing!" he shouted. "Don't worry about it." Then, turning to Mark, "That's about it, I guess." He was anxious to get back to his meal.

Mark thanked him and turned to leave. Just before the door closed, Mark held up his hand, holding ten 1,000 Lire bills. "Wait a second. One more thing. Did she leave in her own car?"

The superintendent took them with two hands. As he counted them, he shook his head. "No. The car came for her. The 130."

"You've seen it before?"

"Oh, yeah. Same black job always picks her up."

"You wouldn't happen to remember the license number, would you?"

From the way the superintendent shook his head, Mark could tell he did not know, and was sorry because otherwise he could have squeezed Mark for another ten thousand.

# X minus 1 Day

*Torino*
*Thursday, November 27*

Mark was working in the office early when a second letter arrived at Alfindustria headquarters. A man on a moped tossed it to the gatekeeper at the entrance to the parking area at the rear of the building. Mark went down to fetch it.

The attendant was so nervous that he stuttered as he handed the envelope to Mark. "H-here it is."

Mark took the envelope carefully by the edges and examined it briefly, then turned to the gatekeeper. "How did you get this?"

"S-s-someone th-threw it here."

When Dario arrived, Mark took the directors' elevator up to the sixth floor and walked quickly to the chairman's office. Dario was seated at his desk.

Mark showed him the letter. "Another one. Let me open it." He slit the edge with a letter opener, shook the letter out and spread it open, using the opener and a ruler. They read:

*Have 250 million lire ready in 100,000 lire notes. Used, no number sequences. Put in plain cardboard box. We will call tomorrow, and tell you where to deliver.*

*friends of the revolution*

Dario studied the note. "This is just like the first one. Did anyone see who delivered it?"

"No," said Mark, shaking his head. "I'm sorry. We alerted everyone in the lobby to report any messages, but this one wasn't delivered there. Someone tossed it to the gatekeeper."

Neither man spoke for several seconds. Then Mark asked Dario what he planned to do about the ransom.

"I'm prepared to pay it, of course, but I want to be sure Jim is safe."

"If they're really holding him for ransom, then chances are he's still alive. But we don't have much time. I'm on my way down to Rome now to check out a lead. My contact's out of town, but I'm going to try to locate her through some friends there. While I'm down, I could call on Ferrero, too."

"Yes, it's time we started working closely with Paolo. Tell him everything."

Guido drove Mark to the Torino airport as fast as traffic would permit, and Mark just managed to catch the 11:00 a.m. flight to Rome. He arrived at the American Embassy just before two o'clock and walked under the portico. Looking through the glass door, he waved at the receptionist seated behind a protective Lexan barrier. She released the door with a buzzer.

He introduced himself, handed her his passport and asked to see the Legal Attache. She looked at his face and at the passport. "Do you have an appointment?"

"No, but just give him my name and tell him I'm passing

through and want to say hello. I used to be with the Bureau."

She dialed a number and chatted briefly, then turned to him with a smile. "Mr. Fingal's secretary'll be right down."

Mark sat on the short couch in the lobby, waiting. Through the glass window in the opposite wall, he could see the Marine guard at his desk in the adjoining corridor. After a few minutes a secretary came and led him through the security check to the elevator. On the third floor, she took him into an outer office and motioned toward an open door.

"Mr. Fingal's through there."

Lester Fingal was one of the FBI agents stationed abroad as legal attaches ('Legats' in Bureau parlance) to maintain liaison with law enforcement agencies in the major capitals. He had been posted at Rome for almost six years. Both he and his wife spoke fluent Italian. Because he had developed such a close working relationship with the Italian police authorities, he could probably stay there as long as he wanted, even though usual policy was to reassign an agent after three or four years of Legat duty.

A lanky and slightly rumpled six feet three inches, Fingal ambled over to greet Mark. Mark's hand was almost lost in Fingal's paw. He motioned Mark to a seat and they reminisced briefly about life in the Bureau and chatted about common friends and the standard gripes.

"Ever wish you were back in the Bureau?" Fingal asked. "Maybe SAC (Special Agent in Charge) in Boston?"

"Yeah, at times. Particularly when I'm slogging through trust indentures. We're talking dull, dull. Come payday, though, and I'm not so eager."

"I can imagine."

"Seriously, though, I do miss the Bureau," Mark said. "That's where I wanted to be ever since I was a kid. I grew up with police work. My Dad was on the force in Boston before he went with the D.A.'s office."

"Kinda had it in your blood, right?"

Mark gave a little sigh. "That's about it. Y'know, even with all the chickenshit regulations and the lousy pay, at least you felt you were doing a job that mattered ... That you mattered."

Fingal nodded. "Yeah. Know how you feel. That's what keeps me in."

Sensing that the right moment had arrived, Mark asked Fingal to arrange a meeting with the CIA station chief. He said to mention the name Sylvia D'Angelo.

Fingal dialed. "Is he in? This is Fingal ... What say, Big Chief? I've got a fellow here ... used to be with the Bureau. He'd like to talk with you about a girl. Her name is Sylvia D'Angelo. He said you knew her ... His name?" Fingal looked at Mark's card. "It's Mark Della Croce."

Fingal told Mark that the station chief, Griswold, would meet him down in the lobby. They shook hands and Mark went down to wait for Griswold. After a few minutes, Griswold rushed in. He appeared to be in a hurry and almost grabbed Mark by the elbow to take him outside. Everything about him seemed hurried: his words tumbled over one another, and he walked with short, rapid steps.

"Let's walk," he said.

They started up Via Veneto toward Porta Pinciana, and Mark had to lengthen his own stride to keep up.

"How did you meet Sylvia?" Griswold asked, casually.

"Why're you asking me? Don't *you* know? She said you arranged for her to be on my flight here, and you told her to make contact."

Griswold's head bobbed up and down. "Yes, yes, quite right. Just checking. But we didn't handle Sylvia at first. That was done out of Washington. Go on."

"You already know why I came to Torino, and you know that my friend and I are working for Dr. Alfieri. We're checking out some problems at AB Industries. She said that the fellow you're interested in might 'go under' because of what I'm doing. Is that so?"

Griswold did not answer directly. "How much did Sylvia tell you about what she was doing?"

Mark became cautious. *The guy's fishing.* "Not very much, actually. She said basically that you guys wanted me to stay clear of the company."

"Did she tell you her friend's name?"

"That's what I'm here to find out."

"I'm sorry, but I can't tell you that." They crossed Via Torto and started into the Borghese Gardens. Mark noticed a tall man follow them across.

"One of yours?" he asked, indicating with his head.

Griswold nodded.

They walked into the park, where Mark stopped and turned to face Griswold. "Let's talk here. This is the situation we've got: a friend of mine, Jim DiStefano, has been working with me. He's been missing since Saturday. And now I don't know where Sylvia is. She went out of town for the weekend and was supposed to be back in town Monday, but she's not there. I checked her apartment and the bank. No one will tell me where she is."

Mark saw Griswold's eyes widen.

"What I need is information, Griswold, and I need it fast. The fellow you were interested in might have something to do with Jim's disappearance, so I need to know his name and where I can find Sylvia. She might be with him."

"What about the police? Have you reported it yet?"

"No. That might just make it worse for Jim."

Griswold knitted his eyebrows, thinking. "Hmmm. Yes, I see."

From the tone of his voice, Mark got the uneasy feeling that Griswold was holding back. He decided to press. "I've already told you what I know. And now I need something from you. Who's the fellow Sylvia's been seeing?"

Griswold put on his most 'hush-hush' pose, and lowered his voice almost to a whisper. "We think the Soviets are helping left-wing terrorists. We're onto something really big now, and Sylvia's friend is a prime suspect. We think there's a connection between him and money for those groups, but we don't know what it is."

Mark persisted. "O.K., I get the picture. But what's his name? I need to know."

Griswold shook his head. "I can't tell you yet."

Mark fought to conceal his growing anger.

"And why not?" he asked evenly.

Griswold looked around to make sure that no one else could hear. The tall man had stopped at the edge of the park and was watching them from a distance. Griswold kept his voice low. "If we're right, we're talking about something a lot more important than AB Industries." His voice dripped with significance, and he sounded as if he were reading one of his own dispatches. "We're onto a plot that involves the very stability of the Italian economy and political system. It could have grave consequences for NATO and western security."

Griswold had not intended to sound patronizing, but he had that effect on Mark.

"You just won't listen, will you?" Mark said, fighting to keep his voice under control. "I'm talking about my best friend! Right now, he's strung up God knows where, not knowing when someone might blow his brains out. Can't you get that through your skull?"

Mark moved toward Griswold, who recoiled slightly.

"And save the 'stability' and 'grave consequences' shit for your people in Washington! This country's been here for centuries, and doesn't need your damned meddling to survive." He grabbed Griswold by the coat lapels and brought him close, so that Griswold's feet were just touching the ground and their faces were only six inches apart. Mark's eyes bored into him. "Now get this!" he growled. "I'm going after that bastard any way I can. You can take your global concerns and ram them up your sphincter!"

Griswold, ashen-faced, started to stammer a reply, but Mark had already left.

The tall man rushed up to Griswold. "What the hell was that all about?"

Griswold straightened his trenchcoat. He was still upset. "Let's get back to the office. That guy's going to blow our whole plan. He's going after Giant!"

Mark took a cab to Paolo Ferrero's office and reported that Dario had received a second ransom note.

Paolo looked thoughtful. "Yes," he said calmly, "He called me about the first one. Our people in Torino analyzed it."

"Dario said the analysis didn't turn up anything."

"That's true, as far as it goes." Paolo explained that his analysts had checked the first note against all the other ransom and kidnapping notes that had been received in the last several years, comparing handwriting, syntax and vocabulary. Sometimes they were able to find helpful similarities between notes, and they were intrigued by the first note because it resembled the ones that AB Industries had received from a group called 'Workers Arise' when two executives were kidnapped. "We're pretty sure the note about Jim came from the same group."

Mark handed him a photocopy of the second note. "It came early this morning."

Paolo took the note and gave it to his secretary. "The lab'll work on it while we talk. They won't take long. I know you're in a hurry." He went on to explain to Mark what he and Jim had been working on. Paolo's men had been trying to find out where terrorist groups were getting money, and thought that some of it might be coming from small corporations. "Jim gave us a list of Alfindustria suppliers to check out, and three of them were ones we were following, too. He called me Saturday morning, and we talked about it."

"I bet that was just before he called me. I couldn't hear what he said, though. The phone wasn't working. What was it you told him?"

"Nothing much, really. I just gave him the names of shareholders and directors of the three companies."

"Could I see them?"

Paolo reached over to a pile of folders, opened one and gave a sheet to Mark, who studied it briefly. Riolfo's name leaped out.

"The only name I recognize here is Riolfo," said Mark, "but he's dead. Someone got to him before we had a chance to question him." He handed back the list, discouraged. "I wonder what Jim saw in it. There must've been something else."

At that moment, the secretary brought Paolo a note.

"Aha!" he said, turning to Mark. "This is from the lab. The chances are 95% that the second note was prepared by the same group that sent the notes from 'Workers Arise.' That means we don't have any time to lose. This isn't any ransom kidnapping."

Before leaving, Mark told Paolo about Sylvia and what she had told him and what little he knew about the man Sylvia had been seeing. "The guy's got money, lots of it." Then he remembered the day he had arrived at the airport. "And check on silver 1970 Ferraris in Torino. I think he owns one." He thought a moment. "There could be some connection between this guy and AB Industries, too, and maybe that's why CIA was worried about what I was doing. See what you can find out, O.K.?"

Paolo promised to do his best.

Mark caught the next flight for Torino. Guido was waiting at the airport, and they drove straight to Sylvia's apartment house.

The superintendent greeted Mark like a long-lost relative. "Come in, come in! What can I do for you?"

As Mark stepped inside, he caught dinner smells again. "Just for a minute. I don't want to disturb you."

"No problem," the superintendent said, waving his hands. "Your girl friend... you found her?"

Mark shook his head. "No, not yet. I was hoping you could help me." He reached for his wallet. "I need to know where she goes when she's out of town. You have any idea?"

The superintendent's eyes followed Mark's hand. "Just a second. Let me ask my wife. She knows everything that goes on around here." He winked and hurried out of the room.

Mark could hear rapid conversation but could not make out what the two were saying. When the superintendent returned, Mark knew he had something.

The superintendent scratched his stomach. "I *think* maybe I can help you..." His voice trailed off as he waited to see what Mark would do. Mark took out a ten thousand lire note. *The sly bastard.*

The superintendent looked at it and rolled his eyes with uncertainty. "Hmmm."

Mark added a five thousand lire note.

The superintendent smiled as he took them. "The time before this, she went to Courmayeur. She's been there a lot, my old lady says."

"Do you know where she stays up there?"

The superintendent shook his head. Mark thanked him and left. At the hotel, he asked Guido to come by early the next morning. As Guido left, a blue Renault pulled into the hotel parking area.

Mark went to his favorite *trattoria* for dinner and walked around town afterward. He needed the exercise—needed to work off some of the tension that had been building inside him. He strolled along the esplanade by Via Roma through Piazza San Carlo, all the way to the castle and through the narrow archway leading into the royal gardens. The night air was cool and refreshing. As he walked, he could feel the tension falling away. It was after ten when he finally returned to the hotel.

He unlocked the door to his room, switched on the light in the small anteroom and hung up his coat. When he opened the door to his bedroom and reached for the light switch, his senses became instantly alert. *Someone's here!* He heard a slight rustle to his left and, without thinking, he dove forward to the floor. The room exploded as two shotgun blasts tore open the wall behind the spot where he had been standing. Even as he fell, he was reaching for his revolver. The sounds of the shotgun were still echoing in his ears when he squeezed off three rapid shots in the general direction of the gun flash. He heard the sound of breaking glass and a thud as something hit the floor. Then silence. The only sound Mark was conscious of was his own breathing.

Mark waited until he thought it was safe to move, then he got up and switched on the room lights. He could hear doors of other rooms being opened, and people in the hall talking, asking questions. He called the portiere.

"Hello? This is room 357. There's been an accident. You'd better come up right away. Alone."

Mark hung up and called Pasquale.

"Pasquale? This is Mark. I'm at the Principi. Room 357. Get over here as soon as you can. Someone just tried to kill me."

"You all right?"

"Yeah, but the room's a mess and I've got a dead man on my hands.""Be right there."

Mark went out into the hall, where several guests were milling about, asking one another what had happened. When they saw him they rushed forward, bombarding him with questions.

He raised his arm for quiet. "Please. Everything's all right," he said in English and Italian and began herding them away from his door. "Just an accident. Water pipe exploded. Sorry about the disturbance."

The guests were already dispersing when the portiere arrived. Before anyone could speak with him, Mark went up to him.

"Ah, portiere!" he said in a loud voice as they walked back to Mark's room. "There's been an accident. A problem with the pipes. Fortunately, no one was hurt."

The other guests, apparently reassured by the calm discussion between these two, returned to their own rooms.

Mark could not understand what the portiere gasped when he looked at the room, but his meaning was obvious. He sucked in his breath and almost broke into tears when he looked at the wall. The fully-choked blasts of buckshot had torn gaping holes through the plaster and chewed away the lathwork beneath. Stray pellets, tracing separate paths of destruction, made their marks in the plaster around the edges of the two holes.

"My God! What happened?"

Mark pointed to where the gunman lay sprawled. "That man over there tried to kill me."

The portiere took one look at the man on the floor and ran to the bathroom to throw up. The gunman was slumped beneath the window, still holding his shotgun with one hand. His left eye was a blood-filled hole, and fragments of brain tissue and a spray of blood on the drapes behind him covered a spot where one slug had buried itself. Five inches away was a hole made by one that missed. The third had hit somewhere in the man's chest, or so Mark guessed from the bloodstain in that area. The body partly covered a sign saying,

DEATH TO CAPITALIST PIGS!

When the portiere re-emerged from the bathroom he appeared to have recovered.

Mark cautioned him. "The police are going to be here any

second. Be sure Detective Biasi comes up first — alone. You don't want a lot of police storming up here, waking everyone again. Neither do I."

The portiere stood silently, apparently unable to function.

Mark had to get his attention. "See that?" he asked in a loud voice, pointing to the sign by the gunman's body. "You know what the press would do with something like that? How'd you like a headline in *La Stampa*: 'Terrorist attack at Principi'? Be great for business, wouldn't it?"

The portiere began to regain his composure. "Obviously not," he sniffed.

"Then you make damn sure that when Detective Biasi comes up, he's alone. No one will be disturbed while the police investigate. It's your job to take care of the guests. Just say there was an accident. No big deal; strictly routine. Stick to one story: a pipe burst, lots of noise, some damage to the room, but that's all. Got that?"

"I understand."

Mark escorted him to the door. You'd better get on downstairs."

Pasquale arrived five minutes later. He gave a surprised whistle when he saw the room, and looked at Mark with new admiration. "I don't see how you're still in one piece. You should've been cut in two." He went to look at the corpse, then turned back to Mark. "I've asked one of our men to take pictures and collect other evidence."

"Can you make sure this is all handled quietly? No press?"

"Do what I can."

"One more thing," Mark said. "I have to go to Courmayeur tomorrow. I'm trying to locate a girl. Her name is Sylvia D'Angelo. She works at Banca Commerciale. The fellow she's been seeing may be involved in this mess. I'd like to find out who he is, but I need a picture of her. Could you go to the bank and get one from their personnel files?" Pasquale nodded.

Mark continued. "... and I'll need someone to work with

me in Courmayeur while I canvass the hotels and inns there."

"I'll take care of it. When you leaving?"

"Just as soon as you can get me that photograph."

The special investigator arrived after fifteen minutes, together with two other men and a stretcher. After taking several photographs of the corpse and marking its position on the floor, he had the body and weapon removed. When he took Mark's statement, he shook his head in disbelief. "I'll need your gun and permit," he said, holding open a large manila envelope. "Put the gun in here."

"When can I have it back? I'm going to need it again."

The investigator took out a pad and jotted down some notes from Mark's permit and handed it back to him. "We should be finished with it tomorrow morning. You can pick it up anytime after eleven."

Pasquale came over to talk with the investigator. "He's leaving town early tomorrow. I'll pick up the gun for him first thing. You should be done by then."

Mark thought that the investigator would object, but instead he nodded. "As you wish." The investigator relaxed visibly when Pasquale explained that Mark had been with the FBI and that he and Mark were working together.

## Day X

*Torino*
*Friday, November 28*

Pasquale joined Mark for breakfast. As he sat down, he handed Mark a heavy manila envelope. He was smiling. "Here's your gun back. My boss gave me a hard time about it. He didn't like the idea of you shooting up Torino."

"Oh? What was his problem?"

"He was afraid you might use it in the wrong place and wipe out some innocent people. You're lucky you're working for Alfieri. Otherwise..."

"And what the hell was I supposed to do last night? Let myself get perforated?"

Pasquale raised his hands in peace. "Hey, you don't have to convince me. My boss just gets nervous when foreigners have guns — and use them."

"He's been seeing too many movies. Last night was the first time I ever even shot at anyone."

They ate in silence. After a few minutes, Pasquale pushed his plate away and got ready to leave. "I'll have that picture for you pretty soon. The office manager of the bank promised to come in early to pull the girl's file. And I'll call ahead and get someone to help you at Courmayeur."

Within a half hour, Guido was back with an envelope containing Sylvia's photograph. He and Mark started off immediately, heading toward the Tangenziale and the Autostrada that would take them north to Valle d'Aosta. Near Ivrea, they broke out of the fog into crisp clear air, and could see the full splendor of the Alps spanning the horizon to the west and north. Lulled by the smooth ride, Mark dozed off, and did not awaken until they neared Courmayeur. He recognized the houses along the road with the curious roofs made of wide, irregular pieces of slate.

"This is where Lieutenant Cerone works," Guido said as drew up to the local police station. "He's the one that *agente* Biasi called."

The lieutenant was eager to help. Shorter than Mark, thin and wiry, he spoke rapidly, using jerky gestures for emphasis. Mark even had difficulty understanding him at first. They sat together in the rear seat of the car.

The Lieutenant smiled. "Pasquale tells me you're trying to find someone here."

"That's right. This is what she looks like." Mark handed the lieutenant the photograph. "She was visiting someone up here a few days ago, and I need to know who it was."

The lieutenant kissed the tips of his fingers in appreciation. "What a beauty!"

Mark was in no mood for jokes. "This girl is an American, Lieutenant," he said evenly. "She's a friend of mine. I have to get the name of the man she was staying with. Lives depend on it."

The lieutenant had been on the verge of a joke, but stopped. "We'll do what we can. Let's start out with the main hotels. I'll ask the questions there, 'cause I know the people. We work together, and they won't give me any problems."

"What about the smaller places?"

"I'd be glad to help, but you'll do better on your own there. People don't trust the police. Who does, these days? They won't talk at all if I'm with you." He paused. "Look, just pretend this woman's your girl friend. What good Italian can resist helping a lover?"

They made the rounds of the main hotels and restaurants, but with no results. Then they took the lieutenant back to his office. He gave Mark a list of other inns and restaurants in the area. Starting out by himself, Mark had no success at all until he came to the Bellevista.

The headwaiter there nodded as he looked at Sylvia's picture. "Sure. I know her. But she never comes in here. She eats sometimes at a small restaurant up the hill from here. Il Rifugio. My cousin used to work there. Maybe they can help."

Mark thanked him and hurried to the car and got in. "Let's check this one, Guido. Il Rifugio."

Guido looked at the address list and the map. "Here it is. Just three blocks away."

As Mark entered the restaurant, he was greeted by a buxom woman in her thirties who was busily cleaning the counter, getting ready for the dinner trade. Her generous breasts danced about in her loose, low-cut peasant blouse as she wiped back and forth. Aware that Mark was looking at her, she looked up with a smile. She relished the fact that she was worth watching.

"Sorry, *signore*. We're closed until dinner."

"I was hoping you could help me," he said with a wide smile, speaking Italian with a broad American accent. "I'm looking for a friend of mine. She was up here about ten days ago. They say she eats here sometimes. Here's a picture of her."

She straightened up, throwing her chest out so that her nipples stood out clearly in her blouse, then she wiped her hands on her apron, took the photograph and walked to the front window to look at it in the light.

"*Certo. L'americana.* She comes here with..." She stopped abruptly.

Sensing her reluctance, Mark turned on all his charm. He went to retrieve the photograph, holding her hand just a little longer than necessary. Her eyes sparkled.

"I know she was here with her lover," he said. "She's only a good friend from home. I came here for a few days and I'd like to see her before I leave for Rome, but no one where she works can help me. They only say she's on vacation. I thought she might be up here."

"Yes, I know. Let me ask my husband." Turning toward the kitchen, she called out, "Julio!"

A yell erupted from the kitchen. "What?"

"Come here a second," she trilled.

The kitchen door swung open and her husband burst through and stood in the opening, one hand on the door. "I'm busy, Anna," he said impatiently. Then, seeing a stranger, he stopped.

His wife explained. "Julio, this *signore* is a friend of the *americana*. He's visiting here and wants to know where her friend lives."

Her husband, a hefty man with a neatly trimmed jet black beard, wiped his flour-covered hands on his dirty apron as he approached.

Mark held out his own hand and introduced himself as George Richards. "I'm traveling through and promised to look her up. The trouble is, I can't find her. They tell me she's on vacation up here." He handed the cook the photograph. "This is her picture. I thought she might be here with her big-shot friend."

The cook looked at the photograph and then at Mark without speaking. Mark held his gaze, trying to look his most innocent.

"Yeah, the *signorina* comes here," he said curtly. We don't know anything about any friends." He handed the photograph back to Mark and started to return to the kitchen.

On a hunch, Mark asked, "Say, did she ever come here in a 1970 silver Ferrari?"

The cook did not stop. "Sure." He tossed the word over his shoulder and then said to his wife, "Get busy, Anna! We open in two hours."

Mark could barely contain his excitement. *So the Ferrari might be the key to this! There can't be too many of those around.* He thanked the woman for their help and left quickly and rushed out to the waiting car.

"I've got something! The fellow I'm looking for owns that Ferrari we saw at the airport. Let's get to a phone right away."

Guido turned around in the front seat to face Mark, and Mark found himself looking at the muzzle of a 9 mm. automatic.

"No telephone calls now. Just wait here quietly."

Mark was aghast. "Guido! You've got to be kidding."

"I like you, but you're too close to dangerous information. I can't let you call Dr. Alfieri."

"What're you going to do?"

Guido merely shrugged.
"What's happened to Jim?"
No answer.
"Why you, Guido?"
"It's a family matter — a long story. You wouldn't understand.

# CHAPTER EIGHTEEN

## Day X

*Courmayeur*
*November 28*

While Mark was checking restaurants in Courmayeur, Sylvia was sitting on the verandah of Giambetta's lodge, which was perched on a rocky outcropping on the far north outskirts of the little town. The picture window and verandah gave a panoramic view of the Aosta Valley. Behind the lodge, to the north, the massive peaks of the Alps soared into the sky.

The air was crisp and cool here near the base of Mt. Blanc, and she was glad of the warmth of the high-necked knitted wool *Setesdals-kofte* that Giambetta had bought her in Oslo. She warmed her hands on the mug of hot coffee the maid had just brought, trying to look calm, even though she was growing more and more desperate. She had been at the lodge for almost a week now, and still had not been able to contact Mark to warn him. Several times, she had tried to go into town by herself, but someone always went with her. *Time's running out. It's the 28th already, and I still haven't called Mark.* She felt her hands begin to tremble.

Just then, the telephone rang. Someone downstairs answered it. Sylvia went inside and picked up the extension, holding her hand over the speaker. It was Aldo. She could not recognize the other man's voice.

"What's he doing now?" Aldo asked.

"Going around to all the hotels and restaurants," the man answered. "Asking questions about the *americana*. He'll be stopping at Il Rifugio next."

"We can't let him get to Alfieri, Guido. You'd better take him."

Sylvia gasped inwardly, *Oh, no! Not Mark!*

"What'll I do with him?" Guido asked.

"I'll send Rico down. You two take him to the Castello."

Sylvia's mind was in a turmoil. *I've got to tell someone about Mark, but how can I get into town? Francesco was furious yesterday when I tried to go shopping.* She decided to risk a call from the lodge, and rationalized the dangers. She told herself that she had to help Mark and there was no other way; she had to call from there. She hesitated briefly, then picked up the receiver and dialed Griswold's private number in Rome. Griswold's secretary said that he was out of the office, and would be gone all day.

"If you'd like to leave your name and number, I'll give him your message when he calls in."

Sylvia was frustrated. She had to think things out again. "No, thanks," she said and hung up.

Aldo hung up at the same time.

Sylvia was on the verandah when Giambetta's car arrived some minutes later. Sylvia could hear him talking downstairs with Aldo. When he came up, she tried to make small talk with him but he barely answered. He changed into chino trousers and a windbreaker, then started putting on hiking boots.

"Come my dear. Get your boots on and let's take a walk. The weather's perfect."

The last thing in the world she wanted at that particular moment was to go hiking. She feigned fatigue.

"I really don't feel much like hiking right now, darling."

His voice was firm. "Nonsense. It'll do wonders for you. I insist. We'll take hot coffee and sandwiches."

Bowing to the force of his will, she put on her heavy Limmer boots, hooded down jacket, and a small day pack.

Giambetta led the way. He hardly spoke, however, only saying 'hmmm' in response to her comments on the scenery. At first, the pace was easy, but gradually Sylvia realized that this was more than a leisurely stroll. An hour passed, and the trail went steadily upward, around and over huge boulders. She had to struggle to keep up. They were in a desolate area—a thin blanket of fresh snow covered the trail. A strong wind was blowing in their faces, and she could feel its edge of chill, so she pulled up her hood and put on her lined mittens. They were headed north, into the wind, and she blinked as the wind whipped snowflakes into her face.

"Don't you think we ought to turn back?" she asked, her voice concerned.

He turned to look at her and she shrank from his eyes.

"We'll be there in just a minute," he said slowly as he turned off the main trail and headed away from the crest.

"What's this trail called?"

"Goat Ledge. Not many people know about it."

The trail turned from the crest and began skirting the north side of the mountain. In the shadow, the wind was even colder. Below and to their right, Sylvia could see the slope drop off sharply. The trail was getting narrower.

At a small opening in the trail, Giambetta stopped. Sylvia took off her day pack and poured each of them a cup of coffee from her Stanley thermos.

"There it is," Giambetta said, pointing ahead with his cup.

The trail widened briefly in the place they had stopped. Up ahead, the trail narrowed again to a smooth ledge not more than eighteen inches wide that skirted a sheer rock face. The trail was like a break in the face of the wall, as if some godlike force had simply pushed the top part of the wall to the left, leaving the ledge exposed. To the right of the ledge, the drop-off was steep, with a series of narrow ledges about twenty feet down and then a 200 foot vertical drop to a massive bowl-like depression that was filled with snow. During the summer, the noonday sun melted some of the snow at the far edge of the bowl, forming a tiny waterfall that trickled down into a clear blue lake. Beyond and to the north, the rugged peaks of the Alps were bathed in sunlight.

Giambetta was reflective, lost in memories. "I used to come here often when I was young..."

Sylvia wondered why he had decided to bring her here. She tried to sound casual. "It's really an incredible view."

"It's not the view. It's something else."

"Oh?"

He looked down and pointed to the snow-filled bowl. "See that snow?" he asked in a monotone, not really speaking to her. "It hardly ever melts, even in the summer. The sun never touches it except for a couple weeks in July. Isn't that fascinating? If you went deep enough in that snow, you'd find flakes that fell when Hannibal was crossing these mountains."

"This place meant a lot to you?"

He turned to look at her. She thought his eyes looked sad. "In a way, yes. Things are unchanged here... constant. For thousands of years."

Sylvia was not cold, but she shivered slightly. "It's kind of desolate, though."

"But that's one reason why I liked it," he said as he looked closely at her. "People cause clutter... and they change, too, don't they?"

"Yes, I guess so." *Why did he say that?*

He changed the subject abruptly. "I haven't told you about my project, have I, Sylvia?" He said her name automatically, without a trace of affection.

"What project?"

He continued as if he had not heard her. "No, I've kept it secret. It was very important to me. I didn't want anyone else to know. Otherwise, it might have been ruined. You can see that, can't you, my dear?"

She nodded weakly. *What did I do wrong? Did Aldo hear me calling?* Her knees trembled. *He knows!* She wanted to run, do anything to get away, but she could not move.

Giambetta finished his coffee. "All right, let's put on our packs and cross the ledge." He started out.

Sylvia was as much at home in the mountains as he, and she walked onto the narrow walkway without hesitating. When he reached the halfway point, he stopped and turned, blocking her path.

Fear surged through her. "What are you doing? I don't understand!"

"Why did you do it, Sylvia," he said in a sad voice. "I trusted you... I trusted you."

"I don't know what you're talking about!"

He stepped toward her. "Yes, you do." He came to her and held her face in his hands. They were cold as ice. She looked down, unable to meet his gaze.

His voice was stern. "Don't look away, Sylvia. Do you know why I'm telling you this?"

"No," she said, shaking her head.

"I think you do."

With that, Giambetta seized her arms. She struggled free, but when she turned to go back she saw Aldo standing at the end of the ledge and hesitated a split second. Giambetta reached out and grabbed her pack, throwing her off balance so that one foot slipped off the ledge. Instinctively, she reached out for the wall, but she could not keep herself from falling. Giambetta watched without expression as she slid, then rolled, down to the first ledge, where she landed hard and then fell several more feet to a second ledge. She lay there motionless, just inches from the edge. Giambetta stood looking down at her body for almost a minute, watching for signs of movement. Seeing none, he walked over to where Aldo was standing, looking down at the body sprawled on the ledge.

As if in answer to the Russian's unspoken question, Giambetta said, "Don't worry about her. She won't be able to climb up, and if she doesn't fall from there, she'll freeze to death. With this snow, you won't even be able to see her in an hour or so."

Seated in the car in Courmayeur, Mark thought about the events of the last weeks. *So that's how they knew what we were doing all the time! Then the trucks on the Autostrada. But why? Not to scare us away, 'cause they should've known it wouldn't work.* It suddenly became clear to him that everything at AB Industries had been used to divert their attention from some other objective. *But what was that?*

After five minutes, a black car pulled alongside with two men inside. The passenger came over to Guido's car, opened the door and covered Mark with a gun. "Out of there."

Guido took Mark's revolver, then blindfolded him and put him back in the car. Both cars headed south. They passed Aosta and turned off the Autostrada, toward Val di Gressoney. Mark could feel the road switching back and forth as they climbed steadily into the valley. They crossed a bridge and followed the course of the River Lys upstream for what seemed like ten minutes to Mark, then turned into a lane marked *INGRESSO VIETATO* (Keep Out). The lane wound up a steep hill and then leveled off. The driver stopped while an old man came from a small building behind a gatepost and opened a large pair of iron gates. The outline of a castle was just visible over the treetops in the distance.

The four brooding towers of Castello Giambetta dominated the rise, looking out over a wide expanse of lawn, hundreds of hectares of woodland and the entire valley. Originally built in the 14th century, it had been heavily damaged by the Spanish in the 16th century and abandoned. Only the foundation, one tower and portions of two walls were standing when Giambetta's grandfather decided to rebuild it. Using rubble from the original walls and following the original plans, he created what experts hailed as a miracle of authentic medieval reconstruction. Some modern conveniences were a concession to comfort.

The car continued around the building, under an arch, and stopped in the outer courtyard. The passenger from the lodge got out first and opened Mark's door. "Keep your hands up and get out slowly."

Guido came around the car. "What now, Rico?"

Rico started for the inner courtyard. "Keep him here. I've got to check with the boss and find out what to do with him."

After a short while, Rico returned. He had not been able to reach Giambetta.

"Why not stick him in the same room with the other one?" Guido suggested.

"O.K." Rico said. "When the boss gets here, I'll tell him what happened. You better get on back to Torino."

Guido drove off.

A young man came out into the courtyard through a door next to the near tower. He was annoyed. "Hey, what's goin' on? Who's this?"

"Another one for you guys to baby-sit," Rico said.

"Aldo know about this?"

"No, but so what? We gotta put him someplace."

The young man, stubborn, tried to stop Rico. "Keep him out of here until Aldo gets back, or Rodolfo."

Rico, not bothering to answer, simply brushed by him. "Out of my way, kid." He pushed Mark toward the door. "In through there. Watch the steps."

Mark groped his way down the short flight of steps into the corridor. Two young men stood in the middle. One of them was holding a revolver. "What the hell's going on?" he asked. "Who the fuck brought this guy?"

"Don't ask dumb questions," Rico said simply. "Just take care of him, O.K.?"

Rico shut the door, leaving Mark alone with the other two. The guard with the revolver took off Mark's blindfold and beckoned with his arm. "Straight ahead, over here," he said, pointing to the door of Jim's room.

"Welcome to Fun City!" It was Jim, looking out through the bars in a small window of the door. One of the guards grabbed a stick by the wall and hit the bars. Jim withdrew his fingers just in time.

"Away from the door!"

The guard slid the thick bolt back and tugged the door open. Rico shoved Mark inside and closed the door.

Mark was shocked at Jim's appearance: hunched over, he was clutching an old gray blanket around his shoulders. There were dark circles under his eyes, and one eye was puffed up and discolored. Dried blood had stained the bandage on his temple. Red bruises showed through a heavy growth of beard, and his clothes were dirty and disheveled.

He grabbed Jim by the shoulders. "Boy, am I ever glad to see you, you old bastard! You had us worried as hell."

They spoke rapidly, knowing they had little time together.

"Any idea where we are?" Jim asked.

"No. They blindfolded me. How'd they get you?"

Jim started telling Mark what had happened to him. When he mentioned Giambetta's name, Mark interrupted.

"Of course! Giambetta!" Inwardly, Mark cursed himself for not pressing Sylvia to tell him the name of the man she was seeing. Then he remembered CIA and felt somewhat relieved. *They'll take care of her.* To Jim, he said, "It all fits. This is Castello Giambetta. And he must be the guy who owns the silver Ferrari."

"What's a silver Ferrari got to do with this?"

Mark explained how he had searched for Sylvia and how he found out about the car. "I told Guido we were going to check on the Ferrari, and that's when he pulled a gun on me."

Jim was shocked. "Guido?"

"Yeah, trusty old Guido." Mark studied Jim, and was concerned. He put a hand on Jim's shoulder. "You O.K., old buddy?"

Jim's voice was tired, and he sat down heavily. "Sure. Just a little ragged around the edges. But O.K., yeah."

"Well, buck up, *paisano!*" Mark said, trying to encourage him. "We're gonna get out of this all right."

A slight smile appeared on Jim's face. "I sure hope so. Anyway, kid, it's great to have you here."

"All right," Mark said, rubbing his hands together, "Let's figure out how we're going to get out of this mess."

Jim looked uncertain. "That's a helluva lot easier said than done. Those guys all have weapons. They only let me out twice a day to go to the can."

"We don't have much choice now, though. Time's running out. It's already the 28th, and that means Giambetta won't need us much longer. We were only good for a diversion anyway. They already tried to get rid of me."

He told Jim about the gunman in the hotel room, then went to the door to look out. When he came back and sat down next to Jim he motioned toward the door with his head. "What do you know about these guys?"

"I figure we've got two groups: five or six here and a couple like Rico, who seem to be part of Giambetta's staff. These young guys are part of some terrorist gang. Their leader's a little older, maybe thirty-five or forty. Tall, thin fellow called Aldo. Looks like John Carradine. I haven't seen him around today. Then there's Rodolfo. He's wild. Real bad news. It wouldn't take much to set him off. I'm just lucky Aldo's kept a lid on him this long. Otherwise, he'd have wasted me."

They heard two men arguing at the end of the corridor.

Jim nudged Mark. "Hear the high voice? That's Rodolfo. The guy he's talking to is Aldo. You can tell they hate one another's guts. They've been like this ever since I got here."

"Think we can take two or three of them?"

Jim straightened up. "Hell, yes. We can handle any four of those guys. All we gotta do is get them away from the others."

"Look," said Mark. "I've got an idea. If we can just get 'em to take both of us to the can, or if we can get out into the corridor somehow, we'll make a move. If we're together, I'll make an excuse so I can drop back. As soon as you hear me make my move, you do the same."

"What if we're separated?"

"Then we go ahead on our own."

Mark took a piece of paper from his pocket and wrote. "This is Dario's number if you can get to a phone to warn him."

The voices approached. "Your men should've known better. Why'd they put them in the same cell?"

"Oh, get the fuck off my back!"

The door to the cell was opened and Rodolfo motioned to Mark with a revolver. "You! Out here."

Aldo took Mark to a room farther down the corridor. "You'll stay here...for now."

It was almost sunset when Mark heard a car backing into the inner courtyard and recognized a familiar sound. *It's the Ferrari! Timing's still off, too.*

He called out to Jim. "Giambetta's here, good buddy!"

Jim stood on his cot and watched as a figure walked around the car and opened the rear door. Lights went on in the hallway and then on the second floor. Through the bulls-eye windows lining the inner courtyard, Jim could see the top of a door being opened and a light turned on in a room. Then the door closed. *I'll bet that's his office.* He called out, "I see him!"

"Shut up in there!" Rodolfo yelled.

Jim stepped back as a stick shattered against the door opening.

# CHAPTER NINETEEN

## X minus 1 Day

*Milano*
*Thursday, November 27*

David had been waiting impatiently to meet with Pietro for two days now. Twice before, a meeting had been arranged and then canceled at the last minute. He was getting anxious; time was running out. He hailed a taxi outside his hotel and asked to be dropped off a few blocks from the Duomo so that he could approach it on foot. A car pulled out and followed David's taxi as it left the hotel

As he neared the magnificent cathedral from the side, he was overwhelmed once again by the incredible richness of its decoration: a veritable upward eruption of 2,000 statues and delicate spires. Even the black layer of grime from decades of air pollution could not completely mask the beauty of the white marble. The Duomo always affected him like this; as if he were seeing it for the first time. Since he was early for his meeting, he took time to walk slowly around the entire structure, admiring the play of the sunlight on it from different angles. Before going inside, he went to the far end of the piazza to look at the facade from a distance. The day was clear, and he welcomed the warmth of the sun on his face. After he went inside, a man followed him and stationed himself near the entrance.

The chill of the stark interior of the church was hardly affected by the mid-morning sunlight that struggled through the tall, narrow stained glass windows. Looking upward as he stood at the base of one of the massive supporting pillars, David could see a slight mist from his breath. He moved slowly around the inside perimeter, stopping briefly at each of the shrines. As he stood by the iron fence in front of the *capello del crocifisso* (Chapel of the Crucifixion), he noticed Pietro to his right, approaching alongside the nearby confessional together with a young woman and a small boy. They appeared to be making a family visit to the cathedral. David looked away toward the chapel. When Pietro and the young woman drew next to him, they touched the medallion in the top center of the iron railing, then brought their fingers to their lips and made the sign of the Cross as they genuflected.

Pietro held his son up to touch the medallion and spoke softly to David. "We don't have any name but we know there's a big contract out on Alfieri for November 28. It's from the same guy."

David moved slowly away, heading toward the entrance.

The man standing by the chapel closest to the door watched closely and followed David when he left the Duomo. As David walked away, the man brought out a walkie-talkie and spoke into it.

David threaded his way through the pedestrian traffic toward the taxi stand, where he saw a taxi waiting. Just as he opened the door to get in, he sensed that someone was coming up behind him and he turned to look. Stars exploded in his head and everything went black for a moment. Half-conscious, he could tell that someone was holding him under the arms, and he struggled feebly when he felt a sharp sting in his shoulder. Two men pushed him into the taxi and held him securely. He quickly became drowsy and felt his arms and legs grow too heavy to move. The next injection did not rouse him at all. The last thing he remembered before blacking out completely was that his chest hurt.

Even before he opened his eyes, David knew that he was in a hospital; he recognized the smell of the institution, which was unmistakable, and he felt crisp sheets against his skin. When he tried to move, he realized that both of his arms were in restraints. His head pulsed with pain. *What's going on? How did I get here? What time is it?*

He had difficulty focusing his eyes. At first, he saw only blurred and fuzzy outlines, but gradually he was able to pick out details in the room. Looking up to his left he saw an I.V. bag suspended above him. When he heard someone at the door, he closed his eyes again, leaving them open just far enough to see that was happening. A man in a white surgical smock entered and came beside the bed.

David looked up at him and was about to speak when the man looked down and started to take David's pulse. Danger signals went off. Instinctively. *The left eye. The left eye. Not looking at me. Right eye is. Why is this important?* Then the answer came to him: *Pavone!* He closed his eyes again and said, sleepily, "What happened?"

"Just a mild heart attack. You'll stay here a day or so for observation and then everything will be all right."

David pretended to relax, but he watched carefully to see what Pavone was doing. Pavone took a syringe from his case and moved toward the I.V. bag. Noticing that David was watching him, he said, calmly, "Just adjusting your solution, sir."

Pavone inserted the needle through the soft rubber seal of the I.V. bag and emptied the syringe inside. Then he reached into his case again and brought out another syringe. "This will help you rest."

Before David could object, Pavone leaned over and injected the contents into David's shoulder. Then he left.

David tried not to panic. He knew that time was precious: he had to remove the I.V. needle from his arm before he lost consciousness. He moved his arms, but was unable to free them from the restraining ties. Turning over on his left side, he bent forward as far as he could and tried to grab the I.V. tube with his teeth. He began feeling drowsy, and had difficulty focusing his eyes, but just managed to get the tube between his teeth. Then he pulled backward.

The tape holding the needle would not budge, and the tube slipped out of David's teeth. He fell back, exhausted.

*One more time. Try again.* He could barely see now, but he bent forward again, his stomach muscles beginning to cramp from the effort, and forced his head down, inch by inch. He could see nothing, and went only by feel, and was beginning to have difficulty breathing. Finally, the cold of the tube brushed against his cheek, and he moved his head gradually so that he could get a firm grip on it with his teeth. Then he wrenched backward with all the strength he could muster, just before passing out completely.

"You were a naughty patient to take out the needle."

He looked up. Everything was blurred. Gradually, a figure came into focus. A young nurse was standing by his bed, fixing the I.V. bottle. He could feel the wetness in the sheet by his arm, where the solution had continued to drip.

The nurse was scolding him gently. "Part of this solution drained onto your bed. Now we'll have to change the linen."

As she spoke, David's mind began to clear. He saw the nurse wipe his arm and prepare to re-insert the I.V. needle.

"Don't put that needle in me!" he told her firmly.

The nurse looked shocked. "But your doctor ordered it."

"Who's in charge here? Let me speak with him. This is an emergency!"

"I'm sorry, but that's impossible. All the doctors are busy."

Seeing that he could not reason with her, he tried another tack.

"Nurse," he said in a tone of complete authority, "I am a personal guest of Dario Alfieri." He let the name hang in the air between them for a second. "If you don't take these restraints off and stop treating me like a prisoner, the management of this hospital will be in deep trouble."

He raised himself in the bed as far as he could, riveted her with his eyes and lowered his voice to a hiss, pausing on each word.

"Now...you take these things off!"

Her hands trembled as she loosened the restraints. Then she burst into tears and started for the door.

David stopped her with a sharp command. "No! "Stay here!"

She hesitated at the half-open door and then closed it again. In a softer voice, David asked her to page one of the senior resident physicians and ask him to come to the room.

She was relieved to turn over her problems to someone else, and went to the telephone. "Please page Dr. Torre and ask him to come to Room 325 immediately."

David fell back in the bed and began massaging his wrists. Within seconds, a man entered and stood by the door with his arms folded.

"What's the meaning of this, nurse?" he blustered. "Why did you have me paged?"

She did not answer, but looked pleadingly to David.

The doctor took David's chart from the base of the bed. His voice was stern. "Mr. Della Croce, you've upset your nurse and taken me away from important duties. She..."

David cut him off with a wave of his hand. "Please, doctor, let me explain." Turning to the nurse, he said, "I'm sorry I was abrupt with you, Miss, but I had to stop you from putting that I.V. needle back in."

"But that's the solution your own doctor prescribed," said the doctor.

"Have that solution analyzed. You'll see what I mean."

Dr. Torre called for an orderly and told him to take the bottle to the laboratory and have one of the chemists analyze the contents as soon as possible.

David introduced himself to the doctor and explained. "Someone tried to kill me. I was attacked by two men. They gave me some injections and I started having chest pains just before I blacked out."

"That would explain the angina. According to your chart, though, you were brought here by Dr. Fontana. He said you'd had a severe anginal attack."

"Do you know him?"

"No, not really. He rarely comes here. His office is closer to the municipal hospital."

"Well, whoever brought me here was no doctor. You can check with Fontana."

The doctor called the switchboard and asked to be connected to Dr. Fontana's office. His office assistant said that Dr. Fontana hadn't been at the hospital for two weeks. Seconds later, the phone rang. It was the laboratory. David saw the doctor's eyes narrow as he listened to their report. The doctor drew in his breath sharply and then clamped his lips together in a thin line. "Are you sure? Thank you." He hung up and turned to David. "In twenty minutes, you'd have been a dead man, and no one would've known why." He explained that the solution in the bottle would have caused a general paralysis, leading to cardiac arrest. The nurse on duty, following standard procedure, would have increased the flow of the solution, thereby compounding the problem.

"I'm going to make an unusual request," David said. "You've seen what almost happened?"

The doctor nodded. The nurse was still too shocked to react.

David continued. "At least three people have been murdered already by the people who are after me. Whoever just tried to kill me will try again if he finds out I'm still alive. The only way to stop him is to make him think he's succeeded. That'll give me more time."

"What do you want us to do?"

"Just continue here as if I'd had a cardiac arrest and died."

The doctor shook his head. "But that's out of the question!"

"Please, it's absolutely necessary. In any case, you don't need to actually file the forms. Just make them out and hold them here. In a few days, you can correct them. I'll take care of everything through proper channels when I see Dr. Alfieri. He'll be very grateful."

The doctor and the nurse reluctantly agreed to help. The doctor asked her to fill out the necessary forms and bring them back to the room for signature. "Make sure no one disturbs this room," the doctor said to the nurse. When the nurse closed the door, he turned to David. "The only safe way to get you out of the hospital is by ambulance, I guess."

*Good thinking.* Aloud, David said: "I'll leave that up to you. And don't say anything about this to anyone ... not even your superiors."

The doctor shook his head slowly. "That really isn't possible. At the very least, I have to tell the chief administrator. He can be trusted. I've known him for more than twenty years."

"If you have to tell him, so be it. But just remember: the more people who know about this, the greater the danger. How soon do you think you can get me out of here?"

"I'll do what I can." He left and returned shortly with a gurney. David stretched out on the cold metallic surface and the doctor covered him with a sheet and wheeled the cart out of the room. He lay as still as he could. He felt the cart stop and then enter an elevator and descend. The cart left the elevator and was pushed down a hall and through a door.

The doctor removed the sheet. "All right. You can sit up now. I'll have your clothes brought down here. You can dress when we send the attendant on an errand. I'll borrow a mini-ambulance and pick you up at the rear door of the cold room. Slip inside and lie down on the cot so no one will see you."

"We've got a problem," David said with a sigh. "I won't be able to wear my own clothes. People will see that I'm an American. Could you get me some others?"

"We've got some unclaimed ones in the basement."

"Perfect. Just pick out what you can. I'm a little shorter and a little heavier than you. It doesn't make any difference what the clothes look like."

Everything went as Dr. Torre had planned. They had no trouble. No sooner had David lain down on the cot in the ambulance than the nurse slid a box of clothing inside and slammed the rear doors shut. Dr. Torre returned in a few minutes.

David looked at his watch as they drove away. *Almost five.* "I have to get to a telephone, Doctor. Let's go to the railway station; I can call from there."

At Porta Garibaldi, David thanked the doctor again and said good-bye. Then he phoned Dario's private number and arranged to meet him at Alfredo's the next morning. Finally, he called his brother Sergio and asked him to meet the 2215 *rapido* from Milano.

On the train, David began reviewing everything that had happened and everything that he, Mark and Jim had learned so far about the incidents. Of course, he had no idea of what Jim had learned from Bassino's shareholder list. Closing his eyes, he began classifying the known facts, mentally placing them on a chart. He started from the assumption that people generally intend the obvious consequences of their actions, e.g. a person who shoots someone generally intends to frighten, harm, or kill that person, and a person who drops a vase generally intends to break it. The intention is not necessarily the motive, however, and finding the motive is more difficult. If two or more incidents have been caused by the same person, an investigator might be able to deduce motivation starting from the effects caused by the incidents.

As David went down the list, some of the incidents, such as the metallurgy problems, the fire and the lost bids, were clearly intended to harm AB Industries. Others, however, such as the kidnapping and the murders of Bassino and Bertaccini, were not obviously aimed at hurting AB Industries ... at least that was not their most apparent effect. One thing all of the incidents had in common was that they called attention to themselves; they engaged the attention of management. *But why?* There was nothing subtle about the sabotage of the bids and the financials, and no lasting harm was done, if it was harm that was really their objective.

At this point, David felt that he had reached an impasse, so he deliberately set the subject aside temporarily, opened his eyes and began looking around at the people seated nearby in the coach. He studied their faces, their clothes, their manners, and tried to imagine what they did for a living, why they were traveling this evening, and what kind of people they were. Often when he returned to a puzzle, he found that his facts had rearranged themselves somehow, so he was able to look at them from a different perspective. This time was no exception.

The first thought that struck him was: *Maybe whoever is doing this wants to focus attention on AB Industries. But why? That company is unimportant. But it is good enough as a diversion. What could be the REAL objective?* Suddenly the answer loomed in front of him, so obvious he was shocked that he had not thought of it earlier. *The parent company. Alfindustria itself! How could I have been so blind? But who?* That question answered itself: *Giambetta.* He was the only person who had opportunity and motive. He was the logical one, at least, because choosing him required the fewest additional assumptions. He was already being groomed as Dario's successor, and owned or controlled a sizable block of the company's shares. With Dario out of the way he could move right in.

# CHAPTER TWENTY

## Day X

*Castello Giambetta, Val di Gressoney*
*Friday, November 28*

The hours passed slowly, and shadows began to lengthen as the afternoon wore on. Mark was worried. *Today's the day. Time's running out. If we're going to make a move, it'll have to be soon.*

He called over to Jim. "Looks like we better have D-Day soon, good buddy."

"Roger. Not much time left."

Just after dark, Mark heard Rodolfo's voice at the end of the corridor.

"Look, that does it! Screw Aldo. Let's off those two right now and get the hell out of here. Aldo's not helping us. All he ever does is talk."

Rodolfo came to Mark's door. "You get the big guy," he said to his comrade. "I'll take this one." He opened the door and growled to Mark. "Awright, you. Out of there! Now!"

Mark had taken off his shoes just before Rodolfo arrived, and he began fumbling with them. "Just a second. I've got to get these shoes back on."

"Well, don't take all fuckin' day. And come out with your hands up."

When Jim passed by, Mark was relieved to see that both Rodolfo and the other guard had revolvers instead of shotguns. He tied his shoes and left the room, walking slowly, hoping that Rodolfo would become impatient and prod him in the back with the barrel of the gun.

Finally, Rodolfo did. "Move it! You can go faster than that!"

Now Mark waited for the right moment. *Just put that gun against my back one more time.* He had practiced disarming moves like this many times, and had always been able to knock a gun away long before the man holding it could pull the trigger, but the gun had always been empty. *This is the real thing*, he told himself. *Do it fast.* He readied himself to make his move as soon as he and Rodolfo passed through the door at the far end of the hall, but before they started on the stairs, because then he and Rodolfo would be on different levels.

Rodolfo opened the door and told Mark to go through and wait.

Mark walked inside slowly and stopped. Ten feet ahead of him he saw a winding staircase leading upward along the inside of the tower. To his left, another staircase disappeared downward. He could hear the echo of footsteps from below. *So Jim's down there.* On the wall of the lower staircase, Mark could see the reflection of a small light farther down. He waited, hoping that Rodolfo would switch his gun back into his right hand after closing the door. That was important, because Mark did not want the barrel of the gun passing over his back as he struck.

Rodolfo closed the door and came up behind Mark. "Down the steps!"

Mark stood still, ready to move the instant he felt the gun barrel touch his back.

Rodolfo, irritated by Mark's delay, prodded him. "Get going, you bas . . ."

Those were his last words. As soon as Mark felt the pressure of the barrel against his back, he brought his left arm down swiftly in an arc, whirling to his left at the same time. His arm struck Rodolfo's wrist before Rodolfo could react, and the gun clattered to the stone floor. In the same motion, Mark brought his right hand around and knifed his stiff fingers with all his might into Rodolfo's windpipe. Rodolfo stumbled backward, eyes bulging as he gasped vainly for breath through blood-clogged broken cartilage. A two-handed chop to the side of the neck stretched him out on the floor.

Muted sounds of a struggle echoed up from the staircase below. Mark retrieved Rodolfo's revolver and pressed himself back against the heavy stones on the inside of the stairwell. In a few moments he heard someone starting up the stairs. He could make out the shadow of a figure against the outer wall, moving slowly upward. He raised his gun and aimed.

"That you, Jim?" he asked quietly, and breathed a sigh of relief when Jim answered. "Come on up. You lead the way."

As they started up the stairs, Jim glanced over at Rodolfo, who lay crumpled in a heap against the wall. A smile crossed his face. "Wish I'd had a chance to do that."

Jim stopped at the large door on the ground floor. Giambetta's office was on the second floor, he explained, next to the far front tower. Opening the door, he could see two of the corridors that bordered the inner courtyard. The corridor to the right, lined with leaded glass windows, had a large paneled door in the center that opened onto the lighted courtyard. The front corridor, directly ahead, stretched the entire distance between the towers and was broken only by a large central archway on the left that led into the kitchen. They had to pass in front of the archway to reach the other tower.

Jim held out his hand for caution as they moved toward the archway. From inside the kitchen they could hear the sound of plates being stacked. Jim looked cautiously around the corner of the archway into the kitchen, signaling to Mark to stay close behind him. As soon as the person working in the kitchen turned his back, the two bolted across the opening without being noticed and entered the circular stairwell inside the far tower. When they reached the heavy door leading to the second floor, Jim opened it slightly and peered out. Rico was walking slowly back and forth in front of the door to Giambetta's office.

Inside his office, Francesco Giambetta was seated at his walnut Louis XV desk, writing. The desk was at the far end of the long room, with a delicately carved walnut credenza against the long wall behind him. To the left of the desk were large windows that looked out over the entire valley. The end by the door was dominated by a sculptured fireplace in the style of Rovezzano, with the Giambetta coat-of-arms above the mantle. A log fire smoldered. Two large Persian rugs covered most of the parquet floor. Giambetta was wearing his father's black velvet smoking jacket, with the family crest on the breast pocket. This office had been his father's favorite room, and he, too, felt that it offered a special tranquility. This was where Francesco went when he needed a refuge, a place to ponder important matters.

And today was a special day. Just a few minutes ago, he had received a telephone call from Ivrea: his message had arrived. With that, a small smile crept over his face. *Finally. It's done. Father would have been pleased. Dario's out of the way and the company's ours now.* He was filled with contentment now that so many years of waiting were finally over and he had succeeded.

Back in the tower, Jim closed the door when he noticed that Rico was guarding Giambetta's door. "There's a guard," he whispered. "As soon as he faces the other direction or walks away, I'll get him. You go in for Giambetta."

Just then, shouts came from the far end of the corridor, and Rico ran over to investigate. Jim looked out, saw that the door was unguarded, and both he and Mark were able to cross the hall and enter undetected. Jim locked the door behind them.

Giambetta's eyes registered just a trace of surprise as Mark leveled his gun at him.

"Keep your hands on top of the desk," Mark said quietly, "and don't raise your voice."

Giambetta looked faintly amused. He took the cigarette out of his carved ivory holder and crushed it carefully in a silver ashtray. "My, my, we *are* bold and brave this evening, aren't we?"

Mark ignored the sarcasm and held Giambetta's gaze. His

voice was firm. "We don't have much time. We've got to call Dr. Alfieri. Then you're going to help us get out of here."

Jim went to find something to tie Giambetta to his chair, and returned shortly with an extension cord. Giambetta made no resistance as Jim bound him securely.

Giambetta smiled confidently at Mark. "Sorry to disappoint you, but don't waste your time calling Dario. He's already dead."

Mark was shocked, but he kept his expression unchanged.

"I don't believe you."

"Take my word for it. I received a telephone call just a few minutes ago, and it's 8:20 now. He should've been dead several minutes by now."

# CHAPTER TWENTY ONE

## X minus 12 hours

*Torino*
*Friday morning, November 28*

Sergio drove David to Da Alfredo and stayed in the car while David went to the side entrance and knocked. Alfredo's son, who answered the door, recognized David and escorted him directly to Dario's private room. David sat down beside Dario.

"I think I know who's behind all of your problems," he said "but I'm not sure yet."

When David mentioned Giambetta's name, Dario was thunderstruck. "Francesco!?"

He sat silent for several seconds. "So... That explains many things." Then, almost to himself, he said: "But why?" He could hardly believe what he had heard. The Alfieri and Giambetta families had been close for many years, long before Dario's father started his company. Count Giambetta had been one of the original investors in Alfindustria.

"That would explain what happened to the two trustees," David said. "Remember, they died suddenly, and I'd be willing to bet that Giambetta's been proposed as successor trustee."

Dario looked doubtful. "That wouldn't give him a majority, though. Not with our family holdings and the three trusts I control."

"But what if you were dead?" David asked. "Who'd be in control then?"

"You're right, of course. Francesco would be the natural choice to succeed me."

"Well, right now we've got a bigger problem. Someone's

going to try to kill you today. It's the 28th, and that's when it's supposed to happen. What's your schedule?"

Dario did not flinch. He had been exposed to the dangers of kidnapping and assassination ever since he could remember. "Nothing that I couldn't change; except that we invited some of our close friends for dinner."

David stood up and began pacing back and forth, deep in thought. He was certain that Pavone himself would come to kill Dario; the assignment was too important to leave to others. Now he had to protect Dario as well as capture Pavone. He had Dario cancel all office appointments and all meetings, and stay at home in order to avoid an 'accident' on the way to the office. Since Dario had said that all the dinner guests were close and trusted friends, David assumed that danger would likely come from one of the incoming tradespeople. He recommended against canceling the dinner, however, despite the danger, because it might just put the killer on his guard. It was imperative that Dario act as if he suspected nothing.

"How do you think they'll try to kill me?"

"I wish I knew," David replied with a sigh. "My guess is that it'll be the same guy who killed Bertaccini and tried to kill me. He'll use poison again. What we've got to do is intercept him."

Sergio returned to San Nicola, and David rode with Dario to Torino. Before entering the compound of his villa, Dario instructed his driver to wait outside at least five minutes before escorting David to the security room. Dario went into the house and called a meeting of the household staff to discuss dinner arrangements, giving David an opportunity to slip inside the house without being seen.

The driver unlocked a door next to the kitchen and showed David inside. "This is the security room. If you need anything, just call extension 10. That's for Giordano. He's head of security."

David looked around. The room was soundproofed and had

a large one-way window in one wall. On the adjoining wall was a bank of four TV monitors, connected to closed-circuit cameras in different parts of the house. One covered the delivery area.

David called Giordano and gave him Enzo's telephone number. "Please call Enzo and ask him to come as soon as possible. Just say 'Your captain needs you,' but don't mention my name. He'll come without asking any questions."

Enzo arrived in the early afternoon and was shown to the security room. David explained the situation to him and together they watched the monitors, following activities in and around the house. For a long time, nothing noteworthy happened. Then, shortly before 6:00 p.m., tradesmen began arriving. A bakery van drove up, and two men began carrying trays of *brioche* into the house. David leaned forward. One of them was wearing dark glasses. It was Pavone.

David recognized him immediately. "That's the guy! The one with the glasses. Get outside and make sure no one leaves the compound!"

Enzo left, and David went to the delivery area and waited behind a door that Pavone had to pass. As Pavone walked by with a tray, David moved in behind him and put the muzzle of his revolver behind the man's ear. He kept his voice low. "Stop right there! Don't turn around. Put that tray down carefully, then put your hands behind your back where I can see them, and walk into that room ahead of you, on the right."

Next, David took Pavone into the security room, closed the door and frisked him, emptying his pockets.

"O.K., you can turn around now."

Pavone recognized David immediately, and his eyes widened slightly, but he said nothing at first.

*You're a cool one*, David thought.

"So. It's you again." Pavone's voice was flat. "Back from the dead."

David merely looked at him, then told him to turn around again and face the wall. "I'm calling someone in and I don't want him to see your face."

"This is the man we were after," David said to Giordano when he came in. "But don't look at him. I don't want anyone here to see his face, and that is critical. Just guard him while I check with Dr. Alfieri."

"Understood."

David went to the large salon, caught Dario's eye, and they met in the library. I've got our man. He came with the bakery truck. Giordano's with him in the security room now."

Dario almost embraced David.

Just then, Paolo Ferrero rushed into the room. He had flown up to Torino that morning. He was about to speak, but looked uncertainly at David.

"You can talk freely," Dario said, and introduced them.

"It's Giambetta," Paolo said. "He's trying to take over Alfindustria."

"Yes, I know," said Dario. "David suspected him, too."

After a brief exchange of pleasantries, David excused himself and said that he had to return to the security room. He was certain that the killer had arranged for some sort of signal with Giambetta, and he would have to find out what it was, so that they could make Giambetta think that his plan had succeeded.

Dario was skeptical. "He won't talk, will he? *Omertà*, that sort of thing?"

"I think maybe there's a way," said David. "Can I guarantee that his family'll get paid for the contract?"

"Of course, if you think it'll work."

Pavone was still facing the wall when David came into the security room. David relieved Giordano, warning him on his way out not to breathe a word to anyone about the captured man. After Giordano left, David told Pavone to turn around.

From the belligerent look on Pavone's face, David could see that he was going to have difficulty persuading him to cooperate. He began in a matter-of-fact tone. "You and I both know what you did to Bertaccini, and what you almost did to me." He pointed to the items that he had taken from Pavone's pockets. "With all the equipment you brought here, it wouldn't be hard for us to prove you planned to kill Dr. Alfieri, too."

The man stood impassively looking at David.

"You're in deep trouble," David continued, "but I don't have to tell you that. You know as well as I do that you're almost as good as dead, whatever happens. You exposed your family and blew one of the biggest contracts it's ever had."

David looked at Pavone for several seconds without speaking. Then he said, "Listen to me. You and I don't give a damn about the politics here; all we're really interested in is business, right? So let me make you a proposition. I need your help; I need to know what signal you agreed on. And you've got a problem, too, with your family, and I can get you out of it. I can help you square things—even guarantee they'll get paid for the contract. And as for me . . . I won't remember anything."

David noticed a flicker of interest, and he pressed on, trying to convince Pavone that the only thing he wanted was to make the other side think its plan had succeeded. He could imagine the thoughts that were racing through Pavone's mind: *wonder what this guy's up to? He looks like an American, but he speaks and acts Italian. Maybe he's got connections? Maybe I can show the family I didn't really screw up, if they get paid. I wonder how he can guarantee they'll get paid? Maybe the Don'll believe that this guy's the only one who saw me. Maybe what he's offering makes sense. What have I got to lose?*

Pavone sighed. David knew he had him.

"How can we trust you?" Pavone asked.

From the statesmanlike tone of Pavone's voice, David could tell that he was not speaking only for himself now. He was no longer someone who had been caught attempting murder; he was a representative of a powerful organization.

David responded in the same tone. "We have to trust one another in this. My friends here in Italy—the family that helped me—know and respect your family and its business interests. I gave them my word that I was only interested in one thing, and that was to protect my son. That's why I am going to let you go: to prove that I meant what I said. The family wants no misunderstanding, so when you report to your people, you be sure to tell them this."

"Agreed," said Pavone.

"Then let this be our deal: you tell me the signal and I will arrange for your family to get paid. As soon as I'm sure my son is safe, I'll have you released. No one will see your face."

Pavone nodded. "I'm supposed to call a number in Ivrea at 8:00 this evening and let it ring three times."

David had Pavone turn his chair around, facing the wall, and he put cuffs on Pavone's hands behind his back and tied them securely to the chair. Then he left.

Giordano was waiting outside the security office, and he assured David that all appeared to be under control.

"How about the staff? Everyone here?"

"Yes, all here," Giordano said, looking around. "Except one of my men ..." He called out, "Hey, anyone seen diPalma?"

One of the men spoke up, "Yeah. He just went outside."

David started for the door. "Which direction? Quick!"

The man pointed.

"Follow me!" David cried. "We can't let him get to a telephone!"

As he ran toward the door, David cursed himself for forgetting that there might be a backup man.

One of the guards called out, "Watch it! He's headed for the cars."

David intercepted diPalma before he could reach his car. DiPalma turned, his gun leveled at David.

At that instant, the air was pierced by a yell, and a dark shape hurtled through the air, smashing DiPalma against the side of the car, where he sank to his knees and fell on his face, unconscious.

Enzo got up and wiped himself off. "Sorry I didn't get him earlier. I wasn't sure he was the one until I saw you coming after him."

David grinned from ear to ear. "Not half shabby for an old man, Toro!"

Enzo just shrugged, but he was smiling.

Two of Giordano's men came running up to help. DiPalma was coming to, and they yanked him to his feet and dragged him away.

David and Enzo returned to the security room, where David positioned Enzo as guard. "Stay right here, will you, Enzo? I don't want *anyone* to go in there unless I give the word."

Enzo nodded. "Understood."

David located Dario and Paolo and they all returned to the study, where David gave Dario a slip of paper with the number that Pavone had been instructed to call. "Everything's set. Just call this number at 8:00 sharp and let it ring three times." He explained that the security room was closed and guarded and that no one was to go in without his instruction. Then he and Paolo and some of Paolo's men left for Ivrea.

On the way north, Paolo explained how SISMI had found out about Giambetta. He reviewed the story of the 'Giant' project, and how they had been keeping track of Giambetta for several weeks.

David was incredulous. "And you had no idea this was going on?"

"None at all. This project was assigned to a small team at SISMI, directly under the minister. No one else knew about it. I didn't find out about it myself until this afternoon, when I called Rome to ask for more help. The 'Giant' team has been working with CIA on this for several weeks, and Giambetta's been a suspect all along. And Mark asked me to check on a silver 1970 Ferrari, which belongs to Giambetta. Griswold—he's the CIA station chief at Rome—called SISMI today to say that Mark had been at the Embassy trying to find out how he could locate Jim."

"Have any idea what Griswold told Mark?"

"Not much, I'm afraid. But Griswold's sure that Mark was taken by the same group that got Jim. They've been hiding out at Giambetta's place, near Ivrea. We've got some of our men there now."

"Castello Giambetta," David said.

# CHAPTER TWENTY TWO

## Day X

*Castello Giambetta, Val di Gressoney*
*November 28*

Mark pondered Giambetta's remark. His first reaction was despair. If Alfieri were dead, then his own father had failed, and might be a victim as well. Anger followed, and he felt like killing Giambetta. "You..." He choked off the words he wanted to say and drew Jim aside. His voice was low. "We've got to call Dario."

"That's kinda risky, isn't it?"

Mark looked over toward Giambetta. "But how else are we going to find out if he's telling the truth?"

"Well, the way he looks, I'd say he sure thinks Alfieri's dead or he's one hell of an actor."

Mark went back to the desk and faced Giambetta. "Tell me how to phone out of here, and put the call on the speaker."

"This is futile," Giambetta said with a shrug, "but if you insist..."

The telephone was answered by one of Alfieri's maids. When Mark asked to speak with Dr. Alfieri, she said he was in a meeting and had asked not to be disturbed.

"Please interrupt him. This is an emergency."

After a minute or so, Alfieri's voice came on the speaker. "Hello? Mark?"

Mark picked up the receiver. "Yes. Are you O.K.? We've got Giambetta, and I wanted to warn you he's your man."

"We just found out, too. Everything's fine here. Where are you?"

"With Jim, at the Castello. We're going to need help, though. Can you get hold of Ferrero?"

"He and your father are already on the way."

"Great!" Mark said. "If you can get a message to them, tell my father we're holding Giambetta in his office, but there are five terrorists here, well armed, plus other men on Giambetta's staff. We're trying to figure out something."

Alfieri wished him luck and they hung up. Mark turned to Giambetta.

"It looks like your plan—whatever it was—didn't work."

Giambetta did not answer, and appeared to be reevaluating his position. When he finally spoke, it was much as if he were discussing the day's news, casually and without a trace of nervousness. "You know, you're still in trouble here, no matter what Dario does."

"And just how do you figure that?"

Giambetta reviewed the situation, his voice confident. "Just look at the facts. First of all, you don't have any proof that will link me with any illegal activity. Neither does anyone else. What do you think the police will do if they find you here like this, holding me prisoner in my own home? And with weapons? Do you seriously think they'll believe that I had you kidnapped and brought here? Absurd. And as for those louts in the basement, this castle's large, and it's not my fault if someone breaks into the basement and uses part of it without my knowledge. I only use a few rooms here myself, and everyone around here knows that."

He looked first at Mark and then at Jim. "Second, suppose you try to escape. In that case, you'll be shot outside as trespassers. How should my men know you're not burglars or terrorists yourselves?"

Mark looked silently at Giambetta and then motioned to Jim and they went off to one side where they could talk without being overheard.

Jim looked over at Giambetta. "That sonovabitch is right. All we've really got is motive, opportunity and some dealing in Alfindustria shares. That's pretty thin."

Mark was concentrating, his brow furrowed. "You're right: he knows we won't kill him. But maybe his men don't. I say let's wait a while and then try to use him as a screen to get out of here."

Jim agreed.

They could hear sounds of activity in other parts of the building as the terrorists continued to search for them. Mark went over to sit on the edge of Giambetta's desk.

Giambetta looked up at him. "What do you think those men out there are going to do when they find out you're here in my office? You're as good as dead right now."

"They won't find out until we're good and ready," Mark said, "and you're not going to tell them."

He pointed the gun menacingly at Giambetta, who smiled and said, smugly, "You won't use that, Mark. You know it and so do I."

That was too much for Jim, and he lost his patience. He went to Giambetta, lifted him bodily in his chair and turned the chair around so that the two were facing one another. There was fury in Jim's eyes. He put the edge of his hand against his own throat, "I've had it up to there with you!" Then he grabbed Giambetta's tie and brought Giambetta's face up close to his own. "You're right. We're not gonna shoot you. But those guys out there don't know that. And hear this: one fuckin' sound outa line and you're gonna get hurt. I kid you not!"

When he released Giambetta, Jim stood looking silently down at him. *Didn't I notice a flinch when I grabbed him? Didn't he seem frightened?* An idea formed. *The man's afraid — afraid I might mess up that pretty face he's been nursing all these years.* He came closer to Giambetta, and his unshaven, bruised face formed a stark contrast to Giambetta's.

"In the Army," Jim said, "we learned a lotta ways to make guys cooperate ... " He pretended to inspect Giambetta's face. "Say, you're quite a handsome dude," he said in mock admiration. "Look at that nice straight nose and those shiny white teeth."

He moved closer, within arm's reach. "How'd you like to have that nose rearranged? I guarantee it don't feel good. And I oughta know. See this nose of mine? I've had people walk on it. And those pearly white teeth... D'you know what it feels like to have 'em knocked out? Not half good, and I know, 'cause I lost four of mine that way."

Jim could sense that he was striking a sensitive area, and he bored in. "Yeah, you're right. We're not gonna shoot you. But I promise you: if you don't help us get outa here, you're gonna cry the next time you look in a mirror."

Giambetta was visibly shaken by the time Jim released him, but he regained his composure quickly. "I believe you've made your point," he said, stiffly.

In a few minutes, there was a knock at the door. Mark whispered to Giambetta not to let anyone in.

Another knock.

"Dr. Giambetta?"

"Yes, Rico. What is it?"

"The two prisoners. They've escaped."

"Any idea where they've gone?"

"No, but they haven't gotten out of the castle. We're looking for them now. I'll post someone here to watch your door in case they come this way."

"That won't be necessary. The door's locked."

Rico left.

"We're not leaving just yet," Mark said.

Jim and Mark started involuntarily at the sound of a motor; it seemed to come from the wall behind Giambetta.

"What's that?" Mark asked.

"The dumbwaiter," said Giambetta. "It's behind the large panel over the credenza. The cook's leaving for the night and he sent up my evening coffee and brandy."

Mark slid the panel to the right, revealing a silver tray with a coffee pot, a brandy snifter and an unopened bottle of

Courvoisier. As he took out the tray, he looked inside the shaft and asked, "Why's the shaft here so large?"

Giambetta explained that the dumbwaiter was actually designed for the banquet hall in the next room. All the food and supplies for parties were sent up that way. He had put in the opening for his office a year ago.

The minutes ticked by. Giambetta sat calmly studying Jim and Mark. Mark leafed idly through the papers on Giambetta's desk. Jim paced slowly back and forth.

Finally, Mark sat on the edge of the desk and faced Giambetta. "Y'know, I can't figure you out. Here you've got everything anyone would want: education, position, money, power...How in God's name could you get mixed up with the commies? How could you agree to destroy your own company, and maybe your country? For what?"

Giambetta had no reason to hide things from these two Americans now. With a trace of scorn, he replied, "What do you think you know about my plans? 'Get mixed up with the Commies' you say. Do you seriously believe that I would turn over my company to anyone else or allow it to be used by the kind of rabble you saw in the basement? Never. I waited too long for this."

When he talked about his past, he was on stage and enjoying it. He had indeed been recruited by the KGB, but had never seriously embraced communism. He had been a rebel of sorts as a young man, and derived a kind of smug satisfaction from thinking that he—a member of the nobility—was actually masquerading as a leftwing radical. The idea of an actual takeover came to him when the KGB agent asked whether Alfindustria could be a channel for financing some local terrorist groups, but the takeover plan and strategy were all his. Only he knew how to mastermind it.

"So AB Industries was just a diversion, then? asked Mark.

"Precisely. And it worked exactly as I planned it. The more

problems you uncovered, the more time you and your friends spent searching for answers, and the easier it was for me to complete my plans. Only I didn't expect that you — "indicating Jim — " would figure out the mystery so soon. That was a mistake. I rarely underestimate an opponent."

"Then why didn't you kill us, like Bassino?"

"Ah, Vittorio. That was a shame. Such a brilliant young man. But he got in my way. As for you two, you were never in any danger from me. I would have released you this evening — 'rescued you from terrorists.' " I didn't want SISMI and your CIA investigating me, not that they could have found any evidence that I was involved in what happened to you."

"Then what about the shotgun at the Principi?"

"Terrorists have their own agenda. I said that you were in no danger from *me*. My orders were to let you do your investigating and to bring you here — not kill you — if you came too close to finding answers."

Mark couldn't believe what he was hearing. The man was talking about human lives, families, as if they meant nothing; as if they could be simply eliminated if they stood in his way. His voice reflected his disgust. "You actually sound as if you had some right to take over the company."

Giambetta raised his chin slightly. "There wouldn't have been any Alfindustria without my father. He was just as much a founder of the company as Dario's father was, and maybe even more so. After Tosca took over management of the company, he and my father planned that I would eventually replace Tosca as Chairman. But Dario got rid of him. Otherwise, in a couple more years Tosca would have seen to it that I was named Chairman. Then it would have *been* my company. So don't talk to me about rights."

"Well," Mark said, with just a hint of satisfaction, "You can't say 'my company' — not now. You're ruined, and I can't help being glad about it."

"Not 'ruined', Mark, just momentarily frustrated. So I don't take over Alfindustria. So what? I've committed no crime that anyone can prove. I have other options; I never plan without alternatives."

Mark walked away from the desk and stood with his back to the door, his arms folded. He was amazed at how quickly Giambetta had adjusted to new circumstances; almost as if he had in fact planned for them. But now he was tired of Giambetta's performance. "Look," he said, "I'm not here to play crusader. The only thing we're interested in is getting out of here in one piece, and you're going to by God help us."

Rico was at the door again. "Dr. Giambetta?"

"Yes, what is it, Rico?"

Mark shook his head in warning.

"The prisoners... We haven't found them yet."

"Please keep looking."

Rico's voice sounded suspicious. "You sure you're all right in there?"

"Yes, of course."

Rico continued: "We've looked everywhere except here in your office, sir. Please open the door and let me in."

"No need to be concerned. Everything's all right."

A pause.

"Sorry, sir. If you don't open the door, I'm coming in."

Jim whispered to Mark: "May as well make our move now as ever. What do you think?"

"Let's do it."

Mark went to the door. "Rico? Listen! We've got Giambetta."

Jim prodded Giambetta with his gun. "Tell him to do what Mark says."

"Rico, the two Americans have guns. I've decided to release them. Please follow their directions."

Mark spoke slowly, making certain that Rico understood."Listen carefully. You bring a car around to the front entrance. The 130. Leave the motor running, with the lights on and the doors open. I want everyone outside. No guns. All of you stand in a line, out by the southeast tower. I want to see hands in the air. Honk the horn of the car when everything's set, and then move back into line. I'll have my gun stuck in Giambetta's ear, so no tricks."

"Do as he says, Rico," Giambetta said.

"It's no use. It won't work."

"What do you mean, it won't work?" Mark asked.

"I just came from downstairs. Those young punks are running amok. They're ready to shoot everyone and anyone. No way they'll follow my orders."

"What about Aldo?" Jim asked. "Can't he keep 'em in line?"

"I'll go ask, but I know what he's going to say."

Rico left and returned in less than five minutes. "Aldo's right here with me. Let us in; we've got a proposition."

Mark looked at Jim, who nodded. "All right," Mark said. "I'm going to open the door. Leave your guns outside on the floor and come in with your hands up. We've got two guns here, and both of them are aimed at you."

When they came in, Jim frisked them quickly. As Mark closed the door, he noticed that one of the .45 automatics had an extra-large custom silencer.

"What's going on, Aldo?" Jim asked.

Aldo threw up his hands in frustration. "Those kids are completely out of control. Liable to turn on anyone. You couldn't get out of here even if you used Dr. Giambetta as a shield. They'd just as soon shoot all of us."

Jim weighed what Aldo had said. "Can't say as I'm surprised. But where does that leave us? We don't have much time."

"That's right," Aldo said. "They'll keep looking until they find you, and they'll blast their way in here if necessary. After that, who knows?" He rubbed his chin, and appeared to be weighing alternatives. When he looked up, it was clear that he had made a crucial decision. He said he knew how to get rid of the terrorists, but that he needed five hours to escape and he insisted that Mark agree there would be no pursuit. Aldo's plan was direct and ruthless: he and Rico would tell the terrorists that Mark and Jim were trapped in the loft above one of the towers and when the terrorists went into the loft he and Rico would kill them.

Rico nodded in agreement.

"All right," Mark said to Aldo. "You've got your five hours."

Aldo turned to Giambetta. "It's all over, Francesco. I can't stay. Sorry."

Aldo and Rico left and Mark closed the door behind them. The sound of footsteps receded down the hall. Mark, Jim and Giambetta waited. After several minutes, they heard gunfire.

*Enroute to Castello Giambetta*

Immediately after talking with Mark, Alfieri called SISMI headquarters and arranged telephone contact with Paolo, who was speeding north with David on the Autostrada. He told them that Mark and Jim were safe and were holding Giambetta as a hostage. David breathed a sigh of relief. Paolo called ahead to the leader of the advance unit by the castle and told him to seal off the area and prevent any escape but not to approach the castle.

When David and Paolo neared the castle entrance, they parked on a side road, took all five men from the other car and walked toward the gatehouse. One of Paolo's men was already there, guarding the gatekeeper. Paolo asked the old man how many were left in the castle.

"Let me see..." The old man's brow furrowed. He counted with his eyes closed. "*Dottore*, Rico and three more, Aldo, and four... no, five... of the young ones. And the two *americani*. How many's that?"

"Thirteen?" Paolo asked. "Are you sure that's all?"

"Yessir. I see 'em all come and go here."

"What kind of weapons do they have? Do you know?"

"All kinds. They all look the same to me."

Paolo had the guard draw a rough sketch of the castle and grounds so he and his men would know generally where to look for Mark and Jim. They took seven men and started up the hill toward the castle. After a few minutes, they heard sounds of gunfire from inside the castle, and soon after, a car started out of the courtyard.

Paolo switched on his two-way radio and called the gatehouse. "Car coming down. Don't let it through. Let me know what you find out."

In a few moments, the man reported from the gatehouse that they had stopped three of Giambetta's men who were trying to get away from the terrorists. The three said that the terrorists were running wild and that Rico and Aldo were going to take care of them.

"How many are left up there now?" Paolo asked.

A pause. "Just Giambetta, Rico, Aldo and the two Americans. Rico and Aldo took care of the others."

David and his men continued up the hill. Suddenly, Paolo's radio crackled. "Car on its way up to the castle. It's Guido. Went by before we could close the gate."

They saw Guido's car speed by and into the outer courtyard, where its tires squealed as Guido braked and whipped around toward the inner courtyard. They followed at a dead run.

Meanwhile, in Giambetta's office, several minutes had gone by in silence. When Rico did not return, Mark and Jim decided to see what had delayed him. They told Giambetta to keep still, and opened the door. Jim looked down the two corridors that lined the south and west sides of the courtyard, and saw no one. Mark locked the door behind them, taking the key, and they moved cautiously down the front corridor, guns ready, passing the banquet hall on their right. When they reached the tower where Rico and Aldo had taken the terrorists, Jim swung the studded door open slowly.

Rico was lying on the landing, propped against the outer wall of the tower, clutching his midsection with both arms. He was barely conscious.

Jim looked him over quickly. "He's taken one in the gut."

Mark kneeled beside Rico. "What happened?"

Rico could barely keep his eyes open. "Aldo..." he whispered hoarsely, "He's..." His eyes closed in pain.

Jim hurried into the banquet hall, took a small pillow from a sofa, and returned to the tower with it. "This'll help some. He can use it to keep pressure on that wound."

Mark uncrossed Rico's arms, placed the pillow over the wound, and re-crossed the arms. Rico opened his eyes again.

"Take it easy," Mark said. "Head down and don't try to sit up. Keep pressure on that pillow. As soon as we can, we'll get you to a doctor."

Rico smiled wanly and tried to speak again. He began having difficulty keeping his eyes in focus. His lips moved, but Mark had to lean close to hear what he was saying.

"Aldo... still here... Kill..." Then Rico passed out.

Mark and Jim went back into the corridor, pressing their backs against the wall.

Silence.

They reached the French doors leading into the banquet hall, where Jim stopped. One of the doors was ajar. He had closed it earlier.

"Aldo's in there," he whispered to Mark. "I can feel it."

Mark crawled to the opening and slowly pushed the door wide open. Still no movement.

Suddenly, they heard the sound of a motor.

"The dumbwaiter!" Mark yelled as he somersaulted into the banquet hall. Three muffled reports came from the right side of the hall, shattering the bottom half of one of the French doors. Mark shot once toward the open door of the dumbwaiter and then ran out into the corridor. "He's going down to the kitchen!"

Through the courtyard windows, they saw the headlights of a car speeding toward the castle, skidding as it came to a stop in the inner courtyard. Mark and Jim raced to the tower and down the steps to the ground floor to try to prevent Aldo from getting to the car.

When Mark and Jim reached one of the several doors opening onto the courtyard, they saw Guido and Aldo struggling beside the car. Guido, on his knees, had just grabbed Aldo's leg and stopped him from getting into the car. Aldo swung his gun at Guido, but missed, and Guido seized the arm and twisted it so that Aldo dropped the gun. Then, ignoring the blows that Aldo rained on him, Guido raised himself to his feet unsteadily and wrapped his arms around Aldo's waist and began bending Aldo slowly backward. Aldo screamed in agony as he tried to escape the vise-like pressure of Guido's arms. Finally, Guido gave a supreme effort; Jim and Mark heard a dry snap and saw Aldo's body go limp. The two men fell over in a heap onto the cobblestones.

Guido lay motionless on top of Aldo, whose bulging eyes stared sightless up at the courtyard lights. Blood made dark stains in the back of Guido's jacket, but he was still breathing. As Mark rolled him over gently, Guido gripped Mark's arm with one hand and opened his eyes. "Ah! My two *americani!* I'm gla..." He coughed, and blood ran from the corners of his mouth. Before he could speak again, his eyes glazed over, his grip on Mark's arm tightened with tremendous power for an instant and then relaxed and the hand fell away to his side.

Mark placed his fingers along Guido's windpipe to feel for the carotid artery, but there was no pulse. He straightened up.

David's voice came from the entrance to the courtyard. "Mark? Jim?"

David and Paolo, together with several of Paolo's men, came into the courtyard.

"All of the terrorists are dead," Mark said. " We've got Giambetta tied up in his office."

"We caught some of his men trying to escape," Paolo said. "Are there any left here?"

Jim pointed to the southeast tower. "Just one. He's up there. It's Rico, and he's badly wounded. He was trying to help us."

"We'll take care of him," Paolo said.

He took out his transmitter and gave quick instructions, then went to the car where Aldo and Guido lay.

"The thin guy's Aldo," Jim said. "He was some kind of Russian agent. The other's Guido."

"Yes, I know," Paolo said heavily, "He was working with us."

Mark and Jim were shocked.

"It sure didn't look like it when he brought me here from Courmayeur," Mark said.

"I'm sure he thought you'd be safer here than up there."

"Well, we're really sorry about him," Mark said. "I liked the guy."

Paolo started for the courtyard door. "Now let's get Giambetta, and tell me what happened."

When they came to Giambetta's office, Jim unlocked the office door for Paolo."What the devil!" Paolo exclaimed as he entered.

The others rushed in. Giambetta was slumped over in his chair, his face a pulpy mass resting on the glass desktop. Blood and gore were spattered over the papers on the desk and the Persian carpet.

Jim glanced at the body. "Messy business, those soft-nosed bullets," he said in a professional tone.

Mark noticed that the panel for the dumbwaiter was open. "So that's why Aldo was in the dumbwaiter! He came back to get Giambetta."

"He had to," Paolo said. "Giambetta knew too much. Aldo

couldn't risk leaving him alive once their plan failed. Otherwise, he'd have risked his entire intelligence network."

David picked up the telephone and called Dario, who was immensely relieved to learn that Mark and Jim were all right. David mentioned that Giambetta had been killed by one of the terrorists and said that he would give the complete story when he returned to Torino. In an urgent tone, he said Enzo should release the man tied up in the security room but that no one should look at the man. "Warn Enzo, please — or everyone's safety — that absolutely no one sees the man's face or tries to follow him. Give the guy a sock or something to put over his head. I'll tell you about it later, but it is super important."

Dario assured David that he would take care of everything, and he asked to speak with Paolo about how to handle the press.

David handed the receiver to Paolo, who turned slightly away from the others as he spoke. Paolo said very little, except for an occasional 'yes' or 'I understand,' and ended the conversation with, "Don't worry about a thing, sir. We'll do it." He hung up and turned to David. "You and the others can go back to Torino now. We'll take over from here. Dr. Alfieri's office is going to handle the press. He'd like to see you three in his office tomorrow morning around nine."

"We'll be there," David said and excused himself to make another call.

As Mark was leaving the office with Jim and Paolo, he told Paolo about Sylvia and her involvement with CIA. "I'm really worried about her. She could still be up at Courmayeur, for all I know. The CIA chief at Rome said they would take care of her, but I don't trust him one bit."

Paolo promised to try to locate Sylvia, and said that he would leave a message at Mark's hotel if he had any information.

When the others had left the office, David dialed Lombroso's number and arranged to see Lombroso early the next afternoon, saying that he needed to explain about the Pinelli hit man.

# EPILOGUE

## X plus 1 Day

*Torino*
*Saturday morning, November 29*

The main topic of conversation at breakfast was the lead article in the morning edition of *La Stampa:*

### ALFINDUSTRIA AIDE DIES IN FIERY CRASH
*Giambetta Killed on Autostrada*

Francesco Giambetta, a top executive at Alfindustria, was killed instantly last night when his Ferrari went out of control and crashed into an abutment on A-5, just north of Ivrea. The car burst into flames on impact, and Giambetta was trapped in the wreckage.

Police at the scene said that witnesses saw the car swerve suddenly off the road just before the fatal crash.

Member of the powerful Executive Committee of the multi-billion dollar worldwide concern, Giambetta, 51, was considered by many a logical successor to Dr. Alfieri himself. In a brief statement just issued by Alfindustria headquarters, Alfieri called Dr. Giambetta's death a 'hard blow' for Alfindustria. Francesco's death is a deep personal loss for me as well," he said. "He will be sorely missed. He was a close friend and a key contributor to our company's progress during the last twenty-five years."

Dr. Giambetta's father, Count Alessandro Giambetta, was one of the original investors in Alfindustria at its founding more than 70 years ago.

He is survived by his wife, Renata, and two sons....

Mark noticed a small article on page 6:

### SIX DEAD NEAR IVREA
*Terrorists Suspected*

The bodies of six men were found early this morning in the back of an abandoned truck at Pont St. Martin. They were burned beyond recognition. Police are investigating and attempting to identify the victims. The killings are thought to be the work of professionals.

Paolo Ferrero had left his number with the portiere, with a request that Mark call him. Mark asked the operator to call the number and stopped to take the call at the lobby telephone booth. Paolo did not have much information about Sylvia, but he said that his people had spoken with some of Giambetta's staff, and they said she had left Courmayeur the day before, early in the afternoon.

"She's probably with the CIA people now," suggested Paolo, then added, "but we'll keep looking and let you know if we find anything."

Mark thanked him and went in for breakfast. He felt somewhat less anxious than before, but the feeling that she was in trouble refused to go away. *She needs me. Something's not right.* He found Griswold waiting for him in the salon next to the dining room, pacing rapidly back and forth, hands behind his back, striking one fist in the other open palm. Griswold scurried over as Mark came out, and led him to a far corner of the room. Mark followed slowly. They sat facing one another.

Griswold fairly bubbled with enthusiasm. "You're looking great! Tell me all about it!"

Mark kept his face blank. "All about what?"

Griswold brought out a copy of the morning newspaper. "This, of course. What's the real story? What did Giambetta say when you saw him?"

Mark feigned surprise. "Giambetta? You're kidding. What makes you think I saw him?"

"Come on, I know you were after him."

Mark kept a straight face. "I don't know anything about Giambetta except what's there in the paper."

Griswold dropped his 'let's-everyone-pull-together' pose.

"I've got to know what happened. You did see him, didn't you?"

When Mark did not reply, Griswold slapped his newspaper. "You expect me to believe this bullshit? I can find out what went on—you know that. But I want to hear it from you. We've worked like hell on this case, and we need your cooperation. I could say 'demand', but I don't like to lean on people." He paused for effect. "But I'll do that, too, if necessary."

Mark had no use for Griswold after the way Griswold had refused to help him locate Jim. He decided to counter Griswold's ploy with one of his own. "Get off it, will you?" he said, quietly. "I don't care whether what you said is really true or you're just making it up, but get this straight. Don't push. I've got some friends here and in the States who'd break one of your legs if I asked them to. And both of them if I gave 'em a few bucks." He looked around as if to make certain they were alone. "For a couple big ones, I could have you floating in the Po tonight."

All of this was pure fabrication, but Mark was sure Griswold did not know it.

Griswold blanched visibly. Unable to give an adequate response, he stood up and sputtered, "I hope you realize that your attitude is jeopardizing our mission here."

Mark sat calmly with his arms folded; he knew that Ferrero would brief Griswold on what happened. He smiled. "Up yours with the mission."

Griswold pointed at Mark. "I'm going to report to Washington that you refused to cooperate with us."

Mark rose and started for the lobby. "You do whatever you have to do."

Griswold followed him. "Hey, wait a sec! What's happened to Sylvia? She hasn't answered any of our calls."

A chill ran through Mark, and he turned to face Griswold. "What? You mean to tell me you don't know where she is? Or if she's all right? I thought she was with you. What the hell have you guys been doing?"

"We haven't heard from her in days."

Mark was livid. "You lousy..." He was about to hit Griswold, but restrained himself. His voice was icy. "You miserable sleazebag. You got her into this mess and then just left her on her own, didn't you?"

Even before Griswold said a word, Mark knew that he would get no help from him, so he turned his back on him and went to call Ferrero. He told Paolo what Griswold had said. "I've got to find her, Paolo. Really. She might be hiding somewhere, or hurt. Can you help me?" He was desperate.

Paolo agreed to go with Mark back to Courmayeur.

Mark returned to the dining room, where David and Jim were just finishing breakfast. He told them briefly about Sylvia and what she had been doing. He fought to keep his voice under control. "I can't go with you to see Dario, Father. Sylvia's in trouble, and I've got to get up to Courmayeur right away. Tell Dario I'm sorry." Then he left.

David and Jim went to Alfindustria later that morning, and Dario greeted them. He looked exhausted, and his voice was hoarse. "I wish I could tell you how truly grateful I am for what you three did," he said slowly and with deep feeling. "You not only helped me immensely; you also helped Italy. But I'm so sorry about what you went through. We can never repay you for that." He picked up the morning newspaper. "This is why I wanted to see you. Only a few of us know what really happened. Obviously, none of this must reach the press. It would only cause a scandal. No need to—as you say—air dirty linen."

He paused and went to the window. "The Alfieri and

Giambetta families are very close. The Giambettas have always been, and will be, loyal servants of Italy. What happened concerned only Francesco." He turned to look at them. "You can imagine what people would think if the real story came out. There were many things involved: ambition, pride, lust for power..."

"Well, the press won't get anything from us," David said. "We'll be leaving right away. The sooner the better."

Alfieri gripped David by the shoulders, and said good-bye.

A cable was waiting for David when he and Jim checked out. It was from Karen, who was in Venice. He placed it in his inside pocket without reading it and patted the pocket gently. Then a company chauffeur drove Jim to the airport and continued on to Milano with David.

## Day X

*North of Courmayeur*
*Friday, November 28*

Sylvia came to several minutes after her fall. She was lying on her side, her right arm thrown over her body. Her face was wet and cold from the snow that was still falling, and the back of her head throbbed with pain. When she reached to the side with her right arm she realized that she was less than six inches from the edge. Her whole body ached and complained as she tried to move back toward the face of the cliff. Her left arm was tangled in the straps of her pack.

The ledge was fairly wide where Sylvia had landed, with a rocky overhang that formed a long opening perhaps two feet high and three feet deep. Painfully, inch by inch, she slid herself deeper into the opening, so that finally she was lying on her side, pressed tightly against the rock wall. Then she passed out again. A few minutes later, she came to. She managed to unhook the straps of her pack and maneuver it so she could use it as a kind of pillow. The snow on the ledge continued to rise, as thick flakes swirled down.

*You're in deep merde, Sylvia,* she thought to herself, *but thank God you're alive.* As she struggled to get reasonably comfortable, she thought, *You've been in tough places before...* Then she laughed inwardly. *No, dummy, this is the worst mess you've ever gotten yourself into.*

A twinge of pain shot through her upper left arm when she moved, and she reached over carefully to touch the spot, fearful of what she might find. The whole area was extremely sensitive and painful in a way she had never felt before, so she was sure that the arm was broken. She could not feel anything that suggested a complete break, so she decided that the bone was still aligned. *Have to keep it still,* she told herself, remembering her first aid lessons. *Something's wrong with the left hip, too. Maybe that's where I landed.*

To protect her head and face from the cold, Sylvia pulled the strings on her hood, tightening the opening until just her nose was showing. She knew what she had to do. She would have to survive somehow until she could climb back up the cliff, which might be impossible with her broken arm, or until someone rescued her, which might be never. She remembered what the park ranger had said about cold weather camping and winter survival after bringing her down from Mt. Washington, *"Don't lose body heat!"* She was fortunate to have warm clothing, and she blessed her Gore-Tex lined boots and woolen socks, which would keep her feet warm and dry. On the negative side, she was lying on a stone ledge that would extract heat from her body. She remembered her pack, and said another prayer of thanks for the hot cocoa that was left in the thermos and for the sandwiches they hadn't eaten yet. She always carried a small emergency kit, and now she tried to remember what was in it, mentally listing them: *needle and thread, some line, some first aid stuff, a compass, a candle and matches for starting fires, a pocket flashlight and batteries...Why didn't I test the batteries before we left?... space blanket.* She almost shouted out loud with joy.

She turned the pack as quickly as she could, opened it and finally found the plastic pouch with the tightly folded pocket blanket that she had bought five years ago at an army surplus store, but never used in all her hiking in the Berkshires or on the Appalachian Trail. *Bless you, space blanket!* With her broken arm, she was unable to unfold the blanket properly, but with a great deal of effort she managed to work part of the blanket under herself so that it reflected some of her body heat away from the stone. She flipped the rest of the blanket over herself and rotated her body so that gradually she was almost completely enveloped by it.

She started to feel hunger pangs but fought the temptation to eat or drink immediately. *You don't know how long you're going to be here, so don't go using things up right away. Save the cocoa. It'll stay warm for a long time. And don't eat right away, either.* Curled up in a fetal position, she relaxed and tried to sleep. Meanwhile, the snow kept falling. She awoke now and then during the night and began shivering, so she drank some of the cocoa and tried flexing her muscles and moving her free arm and her legs to increase circulation. She could move her left hand and wrist, but she tried her best to avoid moving the whole arm. As dawn approached, she drank the last of the cocoa and ate part of a sandwich. She was pleased to see that the snow on the ledge was deep enough to cover a part of the opening. *Now I've almost got a little snow cave. It even feels kind of snug.*

Despair is the worst enemy of survival; what probably saved Sylvia was her refusal to accept defeat. She kept thinking of the various ways that people could find out she was missing and come for her, and she blocked out any thought of failure. *You'll get out of this somehow. Somebody's got to come.*

Time crept by. Every movement, no matter how minute, caused pain in various parts of her body, and her head still throbbed. She was growing cold again, so she took the candle from her pack and lit it, standing the candle as close to her as she felt was safe. Cupping her hands around the tiny flame, she tried to absorb as much of the heat as possible. She had many matches, but only the one precious candle, so she only let the candle burn for a few minutes at a time, or until she felt warmed. The candle grew shorter and shorter.

## Day X plus 1

*Courmayeur*
*Saturday, November 29*

The Giambetta lodge was in a state of confusion when Paolo and Mark arrived by helicopter. The news of Giambetta's death had shocked the staff, and they were still milling about, asking questions. Francesco's brother was already there, removing personal effects. When Paolo explained that they were looking for Sylvia, he allowed Paolo to question the staff.

All of the servants agreed that Sylvia had left the lodge the day before. Her things were gone. Still, Paolo was not satisfied. One of the maids had said she saw Sylvia start up the trail with Giambetta, so Paolo called her in again. The woman was nervous, and kept straightening her sleeves and looking at her hands. She admitted that she had not actually seen Sylvia return from the hike.

Paolo tried to reassure her, explaining that they were only trying to locate Sylvia. His voice was gentle. "Now, you said that she left in the car. Are you sure about that?"

"Yes."

"Did you see her get into the car?"

"No, but he told me that ..."

Paolo interrupted, "Who? Who told you?"

"The thin one. I don't know his name."

"Can you remember what he said?"

"He said . . . He said he was driving the *americana* — that's what we called her — down to the railroad station."

"Then you didn't actually see her go, did you?"

The maid looked down and shook her head.

Paolo asked one of the local policemen who was familiar with the trails to accompany them, and all three went to the helicopter. They started out along the Ridge Trail, which passed very close to the lodge. The helicopter lifted off and they flew low over the trail. As they gained altitude and headed north, Mark noticed that the tops of the boulders were covered with a heavy blanket of snow. They had seen nothing by the time they reached the crest, so the pilot swung the craft around, ready to turn back. The policeman went forward and tapped the pilot on the shoulder and pointed down. The pilot nodded, and took the helicopter down again, curving to the right. The policeman came back to Mark and Paolo. They could barely hear him shouting over the noise of the engine and the whirring blades.

"There's a side trail here. Called Goat Ledge. Maybe they went that way."

The helicopter dipped down and went slowly by the face of the mountain. As they passed over the snow bowl below the narrow path that gave the trail its name, the policeman yelled to the pilot, "Down there! Let's take a look."

Paolo signaled to the pilot to take the chopper down for a closer look. Finding nothing, the pilot headed the craft upward.

In the distance, Sylvia heard the throbbing of the rotors as the helicopter first flew over the trail. As the sound came nearer, she started kicking with her good foot at the snow in front of the opening. Hope turned to despair as the helicopter began moving away, then returned when the pilot brought the craft toward Goat Ledge. When the pilot took the helicopter down to the snow bowl and passed by the ledge where she lay, the wash from the rotors created such a swirling of snow in her narrow opening that she was almost blinded. In a desperation move, Sylvia yanked the space blanket from under her body, held onto one corner of it and let the rest fall over the edge. *They could not miss that signal.*

The pilot lowered blankets and emergency supplies to Sylvia, and signaled to her that he would be right back. He called ahead for a medical evacuation team to be ready when they arrived. In less than an hour, the team had reached Sylvia and transferred her carefully onto a metal stretcher so she could be hoisted up and into the helicopter. Mark watched anxiously as the stretcher came slowly upward, swinging to and fro in the wind, and he only relaxed after she was safely on board.

When Sylvia looked up and saw Mark's face, she was filled with a sense of deep peace. *Everything will be all right now that I'm with him.* She smiled weakly.

Mark smiled back, leaned over and kissed her forehead, then whispered in her ear, "I don't know what I would have done if we hadn't found you. Don't ever leave me."

Sylvia reached up with her good arm and held him close.

*Milano*

David asked his driver to take him to the Principessa and return for him in two hours. It was just one o'clock.

In exactly ten minutes, David was picked up and taken to Lombroso's office. Lombroso was already seated at his desk when David was shown in, and continued to study the papers before him, David sat in the chair opposite the desk, watching as Lombroso slowly moved pages from one pile to another. Finally Lombroso looked up. His voice was like ice.

"You had something you wanted to tell me?"

"Yes. I wanted to thank you for helping me rescue my son."

Lombroso shrugged his shoulders and waved his hand imperceptibly as if to suggest that what he had done was not important.

David then described briefly what had happened to him at the hospital and at Alfieri's home. Lombroso listened intently, his heavy eyelids half closed. When David told how he had captured Pavone and let him go, Lombroso's two bodyguards exchanged glances. David could tell that they were interested. Lombroso studied his fingernails.

"We've spoken with the Pinellis," he said after David finished. "Not directly, of course. The man you released told them essentially the same story you just gave me. But they are still nervous. And so are we."

"I'm the only one who can identify that man," David said. "I can vouch for that. I also have Dr. Alfieri's promise that he will pay the contract price to the Pinelli family. I thought you might want to have your family make the payment arrangements. You can send the instructions to me in Venice. I'll be there a week, at the Gritti. I'll relay them directly to Dr. Alfieri."

David saw a hint of a smile on Lombroso's face. "We were hoping you would suggest that. We'll notify the Pinellis."

That ended the interview. David was taken back to the hotel and his driver took him to the railway station, where he caught the next train to Venice. After he settled into his window seat in the compartment, he removed Karen's cable from his coat pocket and looked at it for a few moments, as if reluctant to look inside. Then, with a fatalistic expression, he broke the seal and opened the cable. The message was obviously short, because he no sooner glanced at it than he leaned back in his seat, a mischievous smile spreading across his face.

He thought about his relationship with Karen: what it might be, what it ought to be, etc. but without trying to come to any decisions. He realized that it had to be temporary, in fairness to her. She was young, and needed someone her own age. But he would be with her soon, and the prospect excited him. They would have a marvelous time; he would see to that. And, just as it had been with Elena, he would see the beauties of Venice afresh, through Karen's eyes.

The more he thought about Karen the more he realized that she had truly enriched him. She had helped him bring an end to his grieving process. Because of her, a new future had opened up for him. For the first time, with Karen, he had been able to enjoy an emotional relationship without constantly being reminded of Elena and feeling guilty. Until Karen, the memories of Elena had been ever-present and inescapable for him, as if he in a sense were controlled by them. Now he was beginning to look forward, and not constantly aching for the joys that he had shared with Elena. Now, for the first time, he felt in control: able to place those precious memories in their own special room, away from daily life but accessible by him any time he wished.

A sleek wooden-hulled ChrisCraft from the Gritti was waiting for David at the pier opposite the railroad terminal and took him down the Grand Canal. Evening traffic was heavy, and on the way the young skipper maneuvered the launch deftly around gondolas and *vaporetti*. David stood up after passing under the bridge at the Academy of Arts, watching for the candy-striped mooring poles that marked the hotel. When the Gritti came into view, his eyes went to the second floor, seeking out the window of the suite where he and Elena had always stayed. A woman was standing at the window, which was open. She was watching the boat and as it neared the dock she smiled down at David and waved to him.

*Two Weeks Later*
*Milano*

David and Karen waited in the transit lounge for their flight to London. As it was announced, he glanced at the clock and froze instantly. A man standing beneath the clock was looking directly at them, his hand in his pocket. *It's Pavone!*

When their eyes met, Pavone raised one hand to his chest, gave a quick 'thumbs-up' sign, smiled and left.